"You are beautiful, my Tempest," he murmured huskily as he divested her of her gown, leaving her alabaster flesh naked to his hot searing eyes.

Thor's hands and lips continued their sensual torture, his mouth recapturing her breast, his tongue teasing her flesh as it burned a path down her flat belly, enticingly moving through her silky meadow of curls to the mystical valley below.

No longer able to withhold his passion, Thor's virile body slid between her thighs and plunged into the moist sheath of her womanhood.

His mouth absorbed her startled cry as her body arched away from the sudden pain. Her eyes flew wide.

Stunned by her reaction, Thor lay still as the realization of her virginity assaulted him.

"No!" his mind screamed. "It can't be! She's a convicted prostitute!"

LOVE STORM

Cordia Byers

FAWCETT GOLD MEDAL • NEW YORK

A Fawcett Gold Medal Book
Published by Ballantine Books
Copyright © 1985 by Cordia Byers

Library of Congress Catalog Card Number: 85-91240

ISBN 0-449-12817-2

Manufactured in the United States of America

First Edition: January 1986

To the five-hour lunch group:
Barbara, Nancy and Paula

Chapter 1

The wigmaker wrinkled his thin hooked nose at the odor that assailed his nostrils when the heavyset guard opened the thick oak door to the cell. No matter how often he came to Newgate, Henry Thacker could not accustom himself to the foul smell that seemed embedded even in the granite walls. Each time he entered the prison, the stench made his stomach churn with nausea, but he would not let his squeamish insides detour him from his daily excursion into the hellhole of human misery. The profit from the wigs he fabricated out of the hair of the convicted criminals was too high.

Placing a perfumed handkerchief against his nose, Thacker stepped into the cell. The satchel that contained the tools of his trade rattled as he handed it to the guard. "Hold this so I can get a better look at the merchandise."

Thacker's rodent-like eyes narrowed speculatively as he surveyed the long, waist-length hair he had come to purchase. Thinking not of its owner but of the money that would fill his pockets, he picked up a stygian strand and judged the quality of its silken texture between his fingers.

Nodding his approval, he let it fall back into place. This would do nicely once it was cleaned and free of vermin. Some rich lady would enjoy the extravagant headdress he would concoct from such thick tresses.

Ignoring the pain he saw reflected in the prisoner's wide sapphire eyes, Thacker opened the bag and withdrew a pair of shears and a small basket to hold the precious goods. Clicking the blades together several times, testing their sharpness, Thacker grasped the thick mass of hair with his bony hand, preparing to sever it as close to the scalp as possible to get the most value for his coin.

Pale and tense, Storm Kingsley sat frozen on the rickety stool the guard had earlier brought to her cell to accommodate the wigmaker in his task. At the sound of the scissors, she pressed her eyes tightly closed, determined to show none of the emotion sweeping over her as her treasured hair fell to the sharp blades. She had made a bargain and would not go back on it. Too much depended on the few coins the man would give the guards.

Storm flinched inwardly as the shears snipped, cutting away the last thing of value she possessed. With each lock that found its way into the basket to lie there coiled like a black snake, Storm's spirits sank further into the quagmire of despair.

At that moment she felt little like the tempest for which she had been named. All the vivacious spirit that usually manifested itself in her easy smile and warm laughter had drained from Storm when the judge's heavy gavel had descended onto his high desk, sealing the sentence. That had sapped the essence of her being, mangling her with a gnawing guilt at the fact that she had not been condemned to die as had her mother.

Storm's shoulders bowed under the heavy weight of her thoughts, her head drooping forward as a lump formed in her throat, threatening to choke her. But she was jerked upright once more by the roots of her hair as the wigmaker cursed. "Damn it, wench. I've not got all day."

The muscles in Storm's throat worked convulsively, but she let no sound of her pain escape her tightly closed lips. Her eyes burned, but there were no tears left to weep. Her skin itched from the vermin that infested her body, but her mind was burdened with too much misery to heed the discomfort.

Storm's eyes fluttered open again as she felt the last long lock slither down her back. It was done. Drawing in a deep breath, she looked at the ebony tresses nearly overflowing the basket. There lay the last gift she could give her mother. In that silken pile lay the bribe for the executioner. The greedy guards had informed Storm that in some cases in which the sentence was death by being burned at the stake, the hangman would accept a bribe to strangle the victim before the flames could reach him or her.

One tremulous hand slowly crept up to feel the stubby hair left by the blades of the shears. Storm's once-beautiful mane had been her pride and joy, but she had willingly sold it to get the money to secure the services of the black-hooded man who would end Alisa Kingsley Ashfort's life. It was all Storm could do for Alisa, her mother.

The clink of coins drew Storm's attention to Thacker as he dropped several shiny pieces into the guard's fat hand. The wigmaker was tall and skinny, his hooknosed profile sharp and bony. His thin body, draped in the heavy folds of his black cloak, his skeletal legs, jutting out from beneath the garment, further served to make him look like the vulture he was. Like that great scavenger, the wigmaker lived off the misery of others, growing wealthy from the shearing of the condemned.

Hatred like bile rose in Storm's throat as she watched the transaction. Men could work their evil deeds and go unpunished while women suffered the brunt of condemnation for even the smallest infraction of the rules that had been set also by man.

Storm balled her fists at her sides, her dirt-lined nails biting into the palms of her hands as she watched the wigmaker gather up his basket filled with her hair and wrinkle his nose once more in her direction. She longed to lash out and claw the superior smirk from the man's hollow-cheeked face but knew she could not. She could not jeopardize the guard's cooperation by such a rash act. If she did, her mother would only suffer more for it.

As the wigmaker hurried from the cell, the guard turned to Storm. "Off the stool, wench. Ye ain't allowed such luxuries." Before she could move, he shoved her roughly from the seat and she landed with a jolt upon the cold stone floor.

Picking up the stool, the guard strode through the door and slammed it shut behind him, the key grating loudly in the rusty lock as he left Storm alone once more in her black cell.

A strangled sound akin to a whimper passed from her lips as she slid across the slimy floor to huddle in the corner. Wrapping her arms about her knees, she stared numbly at the tiny ray of light that filtered through the crack in the door. She kept her eyes glued to the small glimmer as gooseflesh rose on her arms and a shiver raced down her spine. The light from the torch in the stone passageway beyond her dark world was all that served to remind Storm that she was in a cell in Newgate Prison instead of a crypt. The cold dampness that permeated the foul air and seeped through the threads of her worn gown made Storm think of death.

Death. In a short time she would hear the rattle of chains as Alisa was led past her cell door to meet the fate decreed by the judges. Squeezing her eyes tightly closed, Storm prayed the small pittance that had come from the sale of her hair would satisfy the executioner and he would end her mother's life swiftly before she endured the agonies of the flames.

Rubbing her fingers through the filthy stubble that was left of her hair, Storm bit her lower lip until she tasted the sweetness of her blood. Her thin shoulders shook with dry sobs as she pressed her forehead against her knees. Her mother would be executed that morning, and soon afterward Storm was to be escorted to the waterfront under armed guard and placed on a ship bound for the colonies.

Guilt at escaping her mother's fate tore at Storm's insides. She had been arrested with Alisa, but the authorities had been unable to prove her guilty of any crime beyond the fact that she was Alisa's daughter. Alisa was a known prostitute, and the self-righteous judges had unjustly assumed the same about her offspring. Instead of sentencing Storm to the pillory, which was the usual punishment for prostitution in England in the year of 1750, they had decided she should be deported and sold as a bond slave, bringing some recompense to the Crown for the trouble she had caused.

Storm's heart froze within her breast as she heard a distant rattle of chains. As it grew nearer, she forced herself to her feet, but it took all of her strength to move them forward to the door knowing what she would see when she peered through the tiny crack. The breath caught in her throat at the sight of her mother's tousled blond head. Alisa's hands were bound in front of her, the chain affixed to a cruel iron-studded collar fastened about her slender throat. Her ankles were manacled, hindering her movement, and she staggered against her guard, drawing a curse from him. "Bitch, you'll carry bruises to the stake if you don't have a care."

"Mother," Storm screamed, the word torn from her tight throat.

In agony she watched as Alisa hesitated, her frail, once-beautiful face turning in the direction of Storm's cell. She made an involuntary movement toward it, as if drawn by her daughter's cry, but the guard grabbed her roughly by the tangled mass of her hair and shoved her forward.

Over the thundering in her ears, Storm thought she heard her name, followed by "I love you," but she could not be sure. She slid slowly to the floor, splinters from the rough surface of the door pricking through the tattered fabric of her gown as she did so. Storm did not feel them. She sat rocking back and forth, her arms wrapped tightly about her chilled body as she keened her mother's death, the sound eerily echoing in the blackness of the cell.

Storm's grimy features were screwed up into a mask of pain as memories of Alisa flooded her mind. It had been only two short years, but it seemed a lifetime had passed since the day Storm had come from the virginal world of Mistress Simmons's boarding school for girls into a world that she had not known to exist.

The memory of the day she had stepped down from the public coach to meet her mother was still vivid in Storm's mind. And she knew that for as long as she lived she would never forget the shock she had experienced.

Overjoyed that she had finally been allowed to leave school to live with her mother, Storm had made the tiring two-day journey to London without complaint. She believed her future would be a happy one, and her young face glowed with excitement as she stepped down onto the crowded London street and searched the faces of those nearby for that of her mother. The woman who stepped forward to greet her was a shock to Storm. No longer was Alisa the well-dressed lady who had come once a month to visit her ever since she could remember. Before her stood a woman whose beauty had faded, the lustrous blond hair now dull and gray, the once-youthful, flawless complexion lined with tiny wrinkles. The sparkle had vanished from Alisa's gray eyes, and Storm sensed the smile that curved her mother's painted red mouth was only for her benefit; a sadness lingered in the distant depths of Alisa's eyes. The gown she wore was appallingly gaudy, the material cheap. Storm realized with a start that had Alisa not stepped forward, she would not have recognized her own mother.

It was another blow to her already-stunned senses when Alisa did not call for a coach but instead led her on foot not in the direction of the fine residences of London but toward the waterfront, where hastily thrown up tenements lined the muddy streets and provided meager homes for the less fortunate of London's citizens.

Unable to voice the questions that bubbled to her lips, Storm followed her mother in silence as she led the way up a flight of rickety stairs, the smell of damp rot and humanity permeating the air, and along a narrow corridor to the two small shabby rooms Alisa called home.

Storm could do little but gape at the grimy windows with their moth-eaten curtains and the rat-chewed feather ticks that sagged on the rope beds. The wobbly table was littered with dishes. Though the crockery had been washed, she noted several large repulsive bugs scurrying into hiding behind it as she stepped near. Nausea churned her insides, and she turned to look at her mother, praying that all this was a cruel joke. However, that hope was dashed as she saw the forlorn expression on Alisa's face.

Storm now pressed her fists against her eyes as she relived that horrible day. She heard the rustle of her own skirts in her mind as she mentally turned to Alisa once more and said, "Mother, we don't live here, do we?"

Storm would never be able to forget the look of raw pain that had etched her mother's gaunt features as Alisa slumped down onto the edge of the sagging bed and tightly clasped her hands in her lap before raising her eyes to her daughter's. "Storm," Alisa said, and then paused as if she was trying to gain the courage to go on. "I never wanted you to find out." Her voice trembled as she drew in a shaky breath before she continued. "I had hoped you would never have to know the truth about me, but I'm afraid I could no longer afford to keep you in school.'' Again Alisa's words halted, and her eyes seemed to plead for her daughter's understanding. ''This is my home, Storm, but if there had been another choice I could have made, you would never have set a foot in this abominable place.''

The look on Alisa's face twisted Storm's heart, and she quickly crossed to her side, placing a comforting arm about her mother's frail shoulders as she said, ''I don't understand, Mother. Can you think me so vain that I would not love you even if you lacked wealth?''

Alisa sadly shook her head as she pulled Storm down by her side and took her daughter's hand within her own. She raised it to her lips before clasping it tightly as if she feared Storm would flee as she spoke. ''Storm, what I'm going to tell you is not easy after all the years I have made you believe I was a widow with a small house in town. However, you are now sixteen, and circumstances have made it impossible for me to keep up the pretense any longer.''

Alisa's words bewildered Storm, and questions rose to her lips, but her mother shook her head again. ''No, I want you to first listen to all I have to say.''

Storm remained still as her mother cupped her chin in her hands and gazed down into her eyes. A rueful smile touched Alisa's lips as she said, ''Your eyes are like your father's, and you've also inherited the color of his hair. It was so silky, and in the sun it gleamed blue-black like a raven's wing.''

Storm noted the melancholy light that entered Alisa's eyes as she began to talk about her past. But when her mother came to Lyle Ashfort, the love she still felt for her husband glowed bright and new as if the past lonely and often brutal sixteen years had never existed.

''I was your age when I left my parents' small farm in the country,'' Alisa said. ''Mama begged me not to go, but there were too many mouths to feed, and the tiny plot of land in Kingsley would not produce enough food for all of us. I was tired of always feeling the niggling pangs of hunger and of the hard, backbreaking work it took to provide each of us with a few mouthfuls of food. I was young and full of dreams, eager to make my own way in the world, so I came to London. I was uneducated, and soon found my dreams tarnished by the fact that it was not easy to find work there, where the streets were crowded with so many like me, hungry and hoping for a better life. Fortunately, before I starved to death, I did find a position as a barmaid at the Golden Pigeon, and that was where I met your father, Lyle Ashfort.''

Alisa's eyes grew dreamy as she recalled her brief life with the man she loved. "Lyle was the young son of a nobleman. He had come to London fresh from Oxford and was enjoying his stay in the city as all young men do when out from under the watchful eyes of their guardians. He and his friends came to the Golden Pigeon for drinks and cards, but soon Lyle forgot all about them.

"I'll never forget the night he asked me to marry him. At first I was reluctant, knowing my position as a barmaid and his as a son of an earl; however, his kisses and stout avowals that he had little prospects of ever inheriting the family estate and could marry whomever he pleased soon changed my mind. With our passion to warm us and the winnings from his card games to provide food for our table, we were married at Gretna Green.

"Oh, how we planned our future, Storm. We would snuggle down in the soft mattress in our rented room, cuddling each other, imagining all the happiness we would share together. Even as Lyle's luck with the cards began to run out, we still dreamed. But the death of his father finally made Lyle realize he would have to live on the charity of his older brother if he did not make his own fortune. That thought stung your father's pride. Lyle was a proud man and refused to place himself in such a position. It was then he decided to go to the colonies to seek the wealth he had heard was easily attained there if a man was willing to work for it.''

Storm sensed her mother's more pleasant memories fading as Alisa's hand tightened about her own. When Alisa spoke again, her voice was laced once more with pain. ''I stood on the docks and waved farewell to Lyle until the river current took his ship from sight.'' She paused and drew in an unsteady breath before going on. ''That was the last time I saw or heard from your father, and it was not until two months later that I discovered I was carrying his child.''

Storm remained silent as she watched the vitality drain from her mother's eyes, to be replaced by the dull, beaten expression she had worn before speaking of her time with her husband. Storm saw the effort it cost Alisa to stay the sobs that clogged her throat, the muscles working convulsively as she swallowed. Her voice quavered as she said, ''I took the last of the money Lyle had left me and traveled north to his family estate of AshGlen, but his brother refused to receive me. His servant curtly informed me the earl did not recognize my so-called marriage to his brother and would see to it that I was sent to the workhouse if I dared bother him again with such preposterous lies. He vowed to see me punished if I went about spouting such nonsense about his family.

''His threats terrified me, and I did not know what else to do but return to London. You were born in the Foundling Hospital, Storm. The months I carried you were hard to endure, and I was soon to learn that my life would grow no easier. After your birth I again tried to find work so I could support us, but it was no easier than when I had first come to London. In fact, it was far more difficult, for no one wanted to hire a woman with no husband in evidence and a small child.''

Alisa paused and the silence lengthened, but Storm was loath to break it. She sensed from the look on her mother's face that Alisa had now come to the part of her life that she had wanted to keep from her daughter. Her gray eyes pleaded for her daughter's compassion, and her voice was so low that Storm had to strain to hear as she said, "Storm, I was young and pretty and had a new baby to care for. I had no means to survive except one: by using my body."

Storm saw the look of shame in her mother's eyes before she bowed her head, her thin shoulders drooping as she said, "I took the name of Kingsley, after the village where I was raised, so that I would not bring shame upon Lyle or you for what I had to do, and then I began to find lovers. At first they were only young men without the money to keep a mistress, but from what I earned I saved enough to send you away to the boarding school at the age of five so that you would be reared properly as an Ashfort. Gradually I managed to move up to the wealthy friends of the younger men, and over the years I lived well as the mistress to many of them. However, age and time take their toll. Men like youth, and my attraction began to wane for them. At thirty I was too old, and that was when my fortunes changed for the worst." Alisa seemed to cringe, and she squeezed her eyes tightly closed as if fearing the revulsion she would see on her daughter's face if she looked at her. "Storm, I never wanted you to know the truth, but now I have little choice."

Storm was stunned beyond speech, paralyzed by her mother's revelations. She could not believe what she had just heard. How could such a wonderful woman as her mother be a prostitute? Revulsion at the thought made Storm gag, and she quickly placed the tips of her fingers against her mouth to keep from spewing forth the bitterness welling up within her. She wanted to scream and cry out that it was all a cruel nightmare, but she knew for the first time in her life she was truly facing reality.

Storm had heard all the vulgar remarks made about women like her mother by the older girls at school, but still she could not relate them to Alisa. How could the woman she had loved so much over the years degrade herself in such a manner?

Storm opened her mouth to speak, but her stomach revolted and she ran to the window, throwing it open just in time to disgorge her morning meal. Trembling and pale, she wiped the beads of perspiration from her brow as she turned once more to Alisa. The look on her mother's face tore at Storm's tender heart, chastising her. How could she judge the woman who had given her life and had been forced because of circumstance into a way of living she found shameful? Storm knew girls who were well educated but who'd had to take husbands chosen for them by their parents because they could not take care of themselves. Was that any different from Alisa's case? Did not those girls' own fathers sell them off as if they were goods in the marketplace or, even worse, brood mares?

Alisa had done what she had to do to survive, and Storm could not hate her for it. She had been a loving mother, and that was all that counted. Tears of remorse brimmed in Storm's eyes and cascaded down her cheeks as she ran to Alisa and threw her arms about her. "Mother, I love you. I'll always love you no matter what you do. I don't blame you for what you've done, but I do hold Lyle Ashfort responsible, and I'll never forgive him, never."

With a start, Storm came back to the present. She sat staring into the darkness, trying to reorient herself to her surroundings. She hit the cold stone floor with her fist, feeling the sting of pain race up her arms from the impact. As she clenched her teeth against it, her face tightened with rancor. No, she could never condemn Alisa for the life she had led, but Storm still placed all the blame upon the man who had sired her and then departed without a thought to the wife he left behind, the woman who had still loved him until her death. Storm's bitterness toward Lyle Ashfort and all of his gender had begun on the day of her mother's confession, and ever since, she'd refused to use her father's name. She had rechristened herself Storm Kingsley. It was the surname Alisa had used when she sold her body to provide for her daughter, and Storm decided to use it as well. She would never acknowledge Lyle Ashfort by sharing his name.

The only fault Storm had been able to find in her mother was her undying love for Lyle Ashfort. Alisa had never given up the hope that he would someday return for her. Storm could have understood her mother's feelings for Lyle had she thought him dead, but they knew he still lived from an article they had read in the London paper nine months earlier. It had told of the fêtes given in honor of the new earl of AshGlen. Lyle had inherited the family estate after his brother had been killed in a hunting accident.

Storm remembered well the air of expectancy that possessed her mother after hearing that Lyle was in London. She'd waited for days for him to come and take them out of the squalor and back to AshGlen. It had never happened, but Alisa had still not given up the love she felt for Lyle Ashfort.

Watching men come and go from her mother's room during the past two years had deepened Storm's bitterness against all of the male sex. Her anger had manifested itself like some incurable disease, eating away all the girlish fantasies of love and knights on white chargers. Such things did not exist for her, and she vowed never to succumb to the illusion called love. It had served her mother badly, bringing nothing but humiliation and degradation. Now her mother had finally paid with her life for her mistake of loving Lyle Ashfort.

A moan of pain escaped Storm, and she quickly silenced it by pressing her fist against her mouth. Damn you, Lyle Ashfort; damn all men, she fumed. Men only want to throw a woman's skirts up over her head to satisfy their lust and then be on their merry way, forgetting about the pain they leave behind. I'll never make the same mistake as Mother did!

In her black Newgate cell, Storm reaffirmed the oath she had made so often after seeing men swagger from her mother's room without a backward glance, hitching up their britches as a smug self-satisfied smile played over their lips.

To hell with love. It's only a lie men use to get a woman into their beds, Storm thought as her eyes once more sought out the thin thread of light through the crack in the door. Mother is dead because of such idealistic folly.

Alisa's death sentence had no doubt been carried out to the gleeful cheering of the crowd. Without being there, Storm knew what the scene had been like. An execution was like a day at the fair to the multitudes of London. Sweets were harked while bets were made on how long it would take the victim to die. Everyone drank the wine and ale the vendors sold and made merry while the condemned person took his last breath of life. The image of her mother's death was so vivid in Storm's mind, she cringed back against the slimy stone wall and buried her face in her hands, her nails digging deeply into her newly shorn hair as she cursed into the darkness, "Damn you, Lyle Ashfort. If there is ever a way, I vow I'll see you pay for Mother's life with your own."

The guard settled his corpulent body on the rickety bench and picked up the cards that had been dealt to him by his long-faced companion, Sam Skaggs. The first guard's own fat face, with its bulging eyes and wide mouth, had earned him the nickname of Froggy. It was an accurate description; he looked much like a large toad as he sat eyeing the cards and chewing on a wad of tobacco. Tossing a coin onto the rough-hewn table, he jerked his balding head in the direction of the cell only a few feet away. "Have ye heard anything from the wench since the wigmaker left, Sam?"

Sam's narrow features screwed up, his thin lips pursing as he dug a coin from his pocket with long, bony fingers and then shook his head, causing several stringy, unwashed strands to fall over his bushy black brows. "Naw, ain't heard a thing from 'er since they took 'er mother away this mornin'." The coin clinked onto the table and rolled in a circle before finally stopping near Froggy's pence. "I'm glad she's finally quiet. I couldn't stand much more of 'er caterwauling."

Froggy chuckled as he laid his cards faceup on the table. "She be a feisty one, all right. 'Tis a shame I couldn't have had a little sport with 'er before she leaves us, but it looks like I'll not get the chance. We're to take her to the ship this afternoon."

Sam eyed Froggy's winning hand suspiciously before he threw his cards on the table in disgust. " 'Twouldn't have done you no good no way. Them that's lucky at cards ain't lucky in love."

Froggy pocketed the coins and began to shuffle the deck. "That may be, but I'd sure have liked to have given it a try. She was a real beaut when they first brought her in, though she was scratching and clawing like a little wildcat."

"Aye," Sam agreed, never taking his eyes away from the pudgy fingers moving the cards.

Froggy shifted his bulky body to a more comfortable position as he dealt. The crotch of his britches had become too tight as his thoughts dwelled upon the vision that had been Storm Kingsley when she had arrived at Newgate several weeks earlier.

The girl had been a true beauty, with waist-length raven tresses that reflected the torchlight with a blue-black sheen. Her complexion was flawless, lightly tinted with rose that only heightened the pink lusciousness of her delicately molded mouth.

That mouth, Froggy mused, was made for kissing. It made a man want to capture it with his own, tasting its heart-shaped sweetness. But it had been the girl's eyes that had made Froggy's blood rush through his veins. They'd reminded him of expensive jewels, flashing sapphires fringed with long, feathery black lashes that gave them a sultry air of mystery. She had been long of limb, with a luscious body that was rounded in all the right places. Ah, Froggy ruminated, I'd have had her before now had she not been such a screaming vixen. The girl had been named properly, Froggy decided. She was a tempest, a virago that would take more courage than he possessed to try to tame. A regretful sigh escaped his thick lips as he picked up the cards. It was a shame to lose such an enticing morsel.

A garish apparition swept out of the shadows of the dark corridor, causing the two guards to start nervously until they realized the vision in orange-and-purple satins was only a gaudily dressed woman. Her high-pitched voice grated on Froggy's ears as she braced her hands on her wide hips and said, "I've come to see Storm Kingsley, and I'll not leave until I do."

Froggy pursed his fat lips in annoyance as he placed both palms on the table and hoisted his bulky self to his feet. His bulging eyes swept over the obese woman with the flame-colored hair, and he shook his head. "Ain't nobody allowed to see the prisoner. Now, be off with you before you find yerself sharing one of them cells."

Big Nan, Alisa's friend and the only person who had helped see her through the past hard years, cocked her bright head to one side, regarding the two men with her small round eyes. From the experience she'd gained through her profession, Big Nan was an acute judge of men, and it took her only a moment to ascertain that she would have to use another tactic to gain her desire. "Now cuties, I ain't going to let yer threats dissuade me. All I want is a minute with the girl to give her this package. It ain't nothing but the Good Book. You'd not see the poor thing go all the way across the ocean without her mother's Bible, now, would you, handsome? You look the sort of man with a kind and generous nature."

Froggy's beefy features deepened in hue at Nan's compliment. "No matter, that be the rules. I'm just following me orders."

Big Nan's red mouth spread into an inviting smile as she moved her shoulder to give him a better view of her large breast, pushed dangerously high by the tight bodice. Giving a swish of her skirts to reveal her thick ankles, she winked. "Now, handsome, I'd be much in yer debt if you'd just let me slip this into 'er. I wouldn't even be seeing 'er, and you'd not be breaking yer orders. Then maybe after the two of you get off duty, we all could have a little fun together at my place. Nobody'd ever be the wiser. What do you say, good-looking?"

Froggy's earlier thoughts made Big Nan's suggestion even more appealing. Rubbing his crotch, he glanced at Sam, who nodded vigorously in agreement. "I guess we could let you drop the Bible through the bars on the door, but you can't see the wench. She's due to leave here anytime now."

Sam nearly stumbled over his long, ungainly legs in his hurry to unlatch the barred window in the door of Storm's cell. Swaying her hips provocatively as she moved by the guards, Nan slid the burlap package through the grate. "Good luck, love," she said before turning once more to the two men. "Now I'll be expecting you early tonight."

A smug look crossed Big Nan's face as she turned and sauntered back down the corridor, her mission complete. She'd be willing to bet it would not be until the two guards finished their day's work that they realized she had not told them where her place was.

Storm heard the commotion beyond the door but could not figure out what was taking place until the grate was opened and a package landed with a muffled thump on the floor at her feet. She recognized Big Nan's voice and realized the woman with a heart as large as her body had known she would want some small reminder of her mother.

Picking up the package, Storm recognized what lay beneath the coarse fabric without being able to see its contents. It was the only thing Alisa had kept from her past; her family Bible. Though she had been unable to read but a few words, Alisa seemed to gain comfort from leafing through the yellowed pages bound by the frayed leather binding.

Sinking to the floor, Storm clutched the book to her breast as if through it she could somehow touch her mother once more. Her eyes stung with the need to cry. The Bible was all that was left of Alisa, the once-beautiful woman whose life had been a tragedy until its end. Fate, never kind to her, had played one final cruel trick upon her; she had been found guilty of the murder of the rich planter Thadius Hollings from the colony of South Carolina. Alisa Kingsley had been convicted and executed for a crime she had not committed.

The day Hollings had died was branded upon Storm's mind. She had left her work as a seamstress's helper early that day because of her concern over her mother's health. Alisa had not felt well in several weeks, and Storm had stopped by the inn near their shabby dwelling to buy a pot of hot soup for her, spending the last of their hard-earned savings. When she came home, only to find their rooms empty, Storm's worry grew. She knocked on Big Nan's door to see if the big woman knew of Alisa's whereabouts. It was then that Storm learned her mother had gone to meet a man at the Silver Bull.

Concern and apprehension had squeezed Storm's heart as she rushed along the cobbled street on her way to find her mother. Common sense told her no good would come of Alisa trying to replenish their dwindled supply of funds. Alisa was not well enough to keep up her sordid life-style and needed to rest in a warm bed and have good food in order to regain her health.

Determined to see that her mother did just that, Storm made her way to the Silver Bull and banged on every door until she found the room where her mother was. Alisa quickly led her into the adjoining room so that their conversation would not disturb the man Storm saw writing at a desk. Once the door closed behind them, Storm launched into her protests over her mother's foolish actions, but nothing could sway Alisa.

Storm continued to argue with her until a loud explosion sounded from the other room. At the sound they rushed through the door, only to come to an abrupt halt at the sight of Thadius Hollings lying on the floor, a bright pool of blood spreading across the pegged boards, a smoking pistol at his side. Alisa foolishly picked up the weapon, and at the same moment the door was flung wide and the innkeeper and the young man who was traveling with the dead man charged into the room.

The hideous nightmare had begun. Storm knew she would never forget that young man, with his pale blue eyes and boyishly handsome face. He had worn a white wig, but from his sandy brows and golden lashes, she knew his hair would also be blond. But it was not his features that made Storm remember him; it was the lies he had told about Alisa to the innkeeper and later to the pompous judge. He had pointed his manicured finger at her mother as he lied. "There she is. She's the murderess. I heard them arguing through the door. She threatened to kill Thadius if he didn't pay her more than what he'd promised for her services."

His testimony had convicted Alisa and sentenced Storm to deportation.

Storm's throat felt clogged with guilt. She had not been able to save her mother. The judge had accused her of lying when she had told them the facts of what had transpired. Alisa had given her entire life to see to Storm's welfare, and when her mother had needed her, she had not been able to help her. Storm knew Alisa did not blame her, but she chastised herself for her inability to make the judge believe in her mother's innocence. It was something she knew she would always live with.

Storm felt she would never understand why the young man had lied, but marked it down as another black deed done by the opposite sex. The duplicity of men had led to her mother's death, and there was one man Storm dearly wanted to see pay for it: Lyle Ashfort.

Mutely Storm stared into the darkness as deep-seated anger began to seethe within her, burning away the numb state that had engulfed her since the previous day. I'll not let this prison or anyone else defeat me, Lyle Ashfort. I must survive to seek my revenge. Until I see you die for Mother's suffering, I will not be able to repay the debt I owe her. Storm's nails bit into the burlap covering of the Bible, her lips narrowing into a determined line.

Seven years is my sentence, but after that, beware.

Chapter 2

The cart swayed in its motion, jolting unevenly over the cobblestoned streets to the waterfront. Bracing herself in order to remain on her feet, Storm kept her face straight ahead, ignoring the jeers from the people who lined the street, seeking cruel amusement from the prisoners who passed on their way to the ships that would take them from England. She felt the sting of several clumps of dirt and refuse against the worn fabric of her gown but refused to acknowledge the hecklers' existence. Her eyes were like shards of ice, and her chin tilted proudly in the air as she traveled through the streets of London for the last time. She would not cringe at the invectives thrown at her. Such an action would only please the taunting crowd, and she was determined they would receive no pleasure from her misery.

After he had maneuvered the oxen through the bustling activity at the waterfront, Froggy drew the animals to a halt near the gangplank of the frigate called the *Sea Siren*. Storm stood taut and pale as she took in her surroundings. After so many weeks in the silence of her dark cell, the

21

noise and activity of the docks assaulted her senses as she watched the stevedores busily loading and unloading the tall masted vessels anchored at the wharf. Crates from all over the world crowded the pier, and the men worked feverishly at the never-ending job of sorting and shifting them.

The cart shook as Froggy stepped down and came around to the back. He spat a black wad of tobacco onto the cobbles and wiped his mouth with the back of his hand. "Bitch, yer here. Now, get yer ass down from there and up that gangplank without givin' me any trouble, or you'll regret it. Now get."

Storm's face was pinched and white as she held tightly to her mother's Bible and forced her shaky legs to take her over the end of the cart and down to the ground without the guard's assistance. With little thought to the pain he was inflicting, Froggy elbowed her in the back, prodding her forward as if she were no more than one of the thoroughbred horses that were also being led on board to make the long voyage to the colonies.

Storm's resentment boiled to the surface at the guard's cruel action, making her momentarily forget her mounting trepidation. She fought to stem the invectives that bubbled into her throat, but as she stepped down onto the polished deck of the *Sea Siren* and Froggy's fat hand clamped painfully around her arm, she was unable to restrain herself any longer. Jerking free, she turned on the guard, her eyes sparkling with ire, her lips curled back in a snarl as she spat out, "Keep your slimy hands off me, you bald-headed slug from the dung heap." Her hands curled into claws as she continued to shower abuse at him. "You bastard, I'll claw your bulging eyes from your fat face if you touch me again!"

Froggy's beefy features deepened in hue, and he took a menacing step toward Storm, but she quickly evaded him, backing away until her progress was halted by a hard male form behind her. Swinging about, her defenses ready for this new assault, she stared up at the man who towered over her. She opened her mouth to speak, but Froggy cut off her words, saying, "Here's the wench, Captain Wakefield, and here's 'er papers. She's all yers and ye're welcome to 'er. We're glad to be rid of 'er; she's got a tongue like a viper. Be careful that she don't slay ever' man on board with it."

After handing the papers to the tall man, Froggy quickly made his way back to the cart, wiping the beads of sweat from his balding pate as he went.

For the first time in her life, Storm felt awkward and small as she stood before the man called Captain Wakefield. Her fingers tightened protectively about her mother's Bible as she stared up at him. Taller than most women she knew, she had never considered herself petite until that moment, as she had to tilt her head back to look him fully in the face. His height dwarfed her, the top of her head reaching only to his shoulders.

Instinctively, Storm took a step backward to place as much distance between herself and the huge man as she could. His size awed her, and she felt a shiver race up her spine as she met his chilly, piercing silver-gray eyes. They caused a tingling in the nape of her neck, raising the silken strands of her hair on end. Annoyed by her own cowardly reaction to the stranger, she stared unflinchingly back at him, determined not to let the man intimidate her.

Thor Wakefield regarded the bedraggled girl, his keen eyes noting the proud tilt of her begrimed chin and the ashen hue of knuckles as she gripped the small book. As the captain of his own ship, Thor had learned through years of dealing with every type of person how to recognize trouble when it was presented to him. From the girl's stiff unyielding stance and the look in her diamond-blue eyes, Thor knew that he was faced with it once again.

Even in her tattered, soiled state her natural beauty was

visible. He suspected that once she gained a little weight and the rose came back into her complexion, the girl would have every man on board clamoring after her like a bitch in heat. That combined with the determined look in her eyes was a state of affairs he could well do without. Deciding he'd better resolve the problem before it could take root and grow, he unrolled the papers the guard had given him and perused them briefly, their contents only confirming his conviction that trouble lay ahead.

A muscle worked in Thor's clean-shaven jaw as his chilly gaze returned to the girl before him. "It says here you are Storm Kingsley and were convicted of prostitution. As the captain of this ship, I have been given the responsibility to see you and a group of your fellow prisoners to the colonies, since England breeds criminals in greater numbers than she can supply the ships to transport them. I don't enjoy the task but will do my duty to the Crown."

Thor paused, his gaze holding Storm transfixed as he gave his words time to sink in before continuing. "As of this moment, you are under my rule. I am judge, jury, and executioner on the *Sea Siren* and will have none of your whorish ways on my ship. Until I sell your papers, you are under my command, and I will abide no disobedience. You will remain in your cabin unless I order otherwise. You are to have no association with any member of my crew during the times you are allowed on deck or when you perform the duties assigned to you. Do you understand?"

Storm's eyes sparkled with hostility, adding to the illusion that they were precious gems as she stared up at him. Her cheeks flushed an indignant scarlet, and her chin jutted out at a mutinous angle at his commands. Her first instinct was to openly defy the condescending beast, but she stemmed the urge, biting her lower lip to hold back the bitter words that threatened to choke her. She knew little good would come of venting her rancor.

Thor easily read her rebellious expression and for one fleeting moment admired her for her pluck. Not many people left Newgate with their spirit still intact. Storm Kingsley was the only prisoner out of the ten brought on board the *Sea Siren* that had not been drained of everything. The rest were walking shells, hollow-eyed, their vitality completely vanished as if it had been absorbed by the granite walls of the prison. He had to respect her strength, but he could not let her silent defiance continue. As captain of the *Sea Siren*, he knew its safety lay in the way he controlled those on board. It would be dangerous to let even one person challenge his word. Men who lived their life at sea would only respect and follow a man who governed with a strong hand. Thor's voice was harsh as he said, "Mistress Kingsley, I expect to be answered when I ask a question. You are not deaf, are you?"

Seeing the hard line of his square jaw and the cold, forbidding expression in his eyes, Storm sensed the battle lines had been drawn between them. Like all men, he expected a woman to jump at his word, and it galled her to know she had little recourse but to obey. Her eyes reflected her bitter thoughts as she took a deep breath and said no.

"Then answer my question. Do you understand all I have said?"

Grudgingly she answered, "I understand."

Irritated with her belligerent tone, Thor rolled the papers and tapped them against his palm. "Then I suggest you remember my words and heed them. If you do, the voyage should not be unpleasant. Like the rest of the prisoners, you will be given duties while on board to help defray the expense of your passage."

The breeze changed direction, bringing with it the stench of Newgate. Thor's nostrils flared at the offensive odor.

"Another thing I require is that you bathe. I will not have the stink of prison fouling the air. You may be from the gutters of London, but on the *Sea Siren*, you will neither act nor smell like it. Fortunately for you, mistress, you are the only female making the voyage, so I have to give you one of the few cabins on board. My first mate, Joe Tyler, will show you to your quarters and see that hot water is sent to you. I suggest you make good use of it as soon as it arrives."

The slender thread holding Storm's volatile temper in check snapped at his last statement. She seemed to swell with indignity as she drew in a deep, angry breath. All of her life she had been considered odd for her fastidious habits. The girls at the boarding school had laughed at her daily baths, remarking that Storm was making her muscles weak from such frequent use of hot water. It had not been easy after leaving school and coming to live with her mother, but she had continued her habit until she'd been incarcerated in the filthy cell.

Storm was appalled as well at her offensive state, but it humiliated her to be reminded of it in such a high-handed manner. "Sir, I can assure you I do not come from London's gutters, as you so crudely put it. I have had little choice as to my physical state since entering prison and will welcome a bath. However, that does not give you the right to speak to me in such a manner." Her words were laced with venom.

Thor's lips narrowed into a thin line, his eyes glittering like newly minted coins. "You forget yourself, mistress. I will say whatever pleases me. I am the captain of this vessel, and you are my bond slave until I release you. I will have no more of your impudence while you are under my command. Now you are dismissed."

Glancing at the man who had been waiting patiently for his orders, Thor said, "Tyler, take her to her cabin before I send her below with the rest of the prisoners."

Uneasily, Tyler looked from his captain to the woman before him. There had been few times in his career on the *Sea Siren* that he had seen anyone defy Captain Wakefield, and it made him nervous to remember what had followed. This reckless wench was sorely tempting fate. Tyler's freckled face was suffused with a bright red that nearly matched the color of his hair as he uttered, "Aye, sir. Right away. Mistress, if you will follow me."

Giving Thor Wakefield one last hostile look, Storm clamped her lips tightly together and followed Tyler. Her eyes sparkled with ire as they made their way from the deck and down the short flight of steps to the small cubicle that would be her home for the next two months on the *Sea Siren*.

Thor's metallic gaze rested upon the stiff back of his new bond servant as she followed his first mate below. Trouble, he thought as they disappeared from view. Turning on his heel, he walked across the deck to the bridge. In two short strides he was up the ladder, the brisk breeze molding the white lawn shirt to his well-proportioned shoulders, the thin material revealing the hard outline of the muscles beneath. His gaze swept over the taut canvas as it filled with the wind that would take him home, home to Misty Rose. And at that moment he wished the next two months were already past and he was once more at Misty Rose, his rice plantation on the Ashley River in the colony of South Carolina.

Thor turned his eyes to the soot-blackened buildings along the waterfront. This would be his last look at London if he had any say in the matter. He intended to retire to his plantation after this crossing and become the gentleman planter like all of his neighbors. He had made his fortune during the past ten hard years and could now look forward to getting back to the parts of his life that he had had to neglect in his effort to succeed.

Planting his feet firmly apart, he crossed his arms over his chest, the matted curls revealed by the deep V opening of his shirt blending with the equally dark hair of his tanned arms. His deep voice carried easily across the bridge as he ordered his crew to up anchor and set sail.

As he felt the movement of the *Sea Siren* beneath his feet, Thor's eyes settled once more on the busy wharf. He would not miss England. Beyond London it was a beautiful country, but it could not compare with the rolling land of Misty Rose. The Ashley flowed slowly along the boundaries of the plantation, glistening silver in the early-morning sun, the dew making the petals of the roses along its banks appear as if they had been frozen in crystal. Their beauty had been the inspiration for the name of the plantation. The image of the roses was so vivid in his homesick imagination he could nearly smell the sweetness of their aroma. Each morning at Misty Rose he would awake to find their scent permeating the air, filling his bedchamber and assaulting his awakening senses like a seductive woman.

Tiny lines etched a path of worry across the smooth planes of Thor's forehead as he turned his gaze to the distant horizon. He needed the days to speed swiftly along. The rainy season would soon be starting, and if the new floodgates were not installed to protect the plantation, then he could lose much of his land back to the marshes if the Ashley overflowed its banks.

"Misty Rose," he whispered. The words fell softly from his lips and were swept away on the brisk breeze. After inheriting the land at the age of eighteen, when his father had succumbed to an inflammation of the lungs, Thor had worked to make the plantation into one of the richest holdings in the colonies. He had fought floods, mosquitoes, alligators, snakes, and the occasional Indian to make it productive.

In the beginning there had been nights when he had slept only three hours before resuming his grueling battle against nature to reclaim the marshland. It had been hard work, but it had been worth it. Misty Rose had prospered, and from the proceeds he had been able to buy his own ship to transport the valuable rice to Britain, gaining even more profits from the goods he brought back to the colony to sell. With what he'd earned from those transactions, he had managed to buy several more ships that sailed the oceans all over the world.

Thor had succeeded where his father had failed, and at twenty-eight he was a handsome, confident man who had molded his life into the form in which he wanted it. There was only one thing lacking now—an heir. He longed for a son to inherit all he had worked to achieve, but everything within him rebelled at the thought of marriage to gain his goal. He loved children but knew he could never have his son and heir without the encumbrance of a wife.

With a sniff of disdain, Thor braced his hands on the rail and stared down into the murky water of the Thames. His life did not lack women; his wealth and appearance had assured that fact. He knew there were plenty of beautiful females in Charleston who would gladly come to Misty Rose as its mistress. But the problem was, Thor found little to their credit. In his opinion there was nothing beneath their intricate coiffures but air. If a thought ever passed through their heads, it was of gowns and jewelry, nothing more.

The women he knew could flirt prettily behind their lace fans, and he had to admit their sultry smiles could arouse a man's passion, but he also knew that a man was a fool to give them his name. Once the vows were spoken, they became greedy termagants, possessive and demanding. That Thor could do without. He had enough experience of that type of woman to last him a lifetime. Such a female had left deep scars upon his heart at the tender age of five. He would never forget or forgive her.

Thor's expression clouded as he remembered the beautiful tawny-haired Angelina Wakefield, his mother. With the thought of her came the memory of his father, Raymond Wakefield. He had been a good man, if not an ambitious one, and had loved his son and wife. But that love had not been returned by the self-serving Angelina.

Thor remembered the day his mother had packed her bags and left Misty Rose as if it were the day before instead of twenty-three years earlier. He had cried and begged her to stay, but she had swept by him as if he did not exist. As she stepped into the carriage, she had turned to him, brushing his small hands from the hem of her skirt, her face hard and emotionless. "I want nothing to do with you or Raymond Wakefield. You'll inherit his laziness and never amount to anything either. I was not meant to live in poverty, and I'm not going to." With that she had slammed the door in her son's tear-drenched face, and the carriage had rumbled away from Misty Rose, leaving him standing on the dusty road with a broken heart.

Misty Rose had never been prosperous, but after Angelina's departure, Raymond Wakefield let it sink further into disrepair. He and Thor had survived, but meagerly, and at times they would have starved had Thor not learned to hunt at an early age to provide rabbits and other small game for their table. As he grew older, Thor had tried to arouse within his father some interest in the land, but Raymond had stayed submerged in depression, caring nothing about the plantation, until his death.

Thor blamed Angelina for all the hard years he had endured, but he did give her credit for one thing, his ambition. He had been determined to succeed because she had predicted otherwise. It had not been easy, but he had done it. Now he was one of the richest men in South Carolina and perhaps all of the colonies. He was also the most sought-after bachelor in the colony, but he had remained aloof to all the cunning ploys used by daughters and mothers alike to snare him into the trap of matrimony.

The belles flocked about Thor, but they reminded him too much of Angelina. Like her they cared for nothing beyond his wealth and position.

He had seen Angelina only once since the day she had left Misty Rose. He had been twenty-five and had finally achieved his goal of making his plantation one of the finest along the Ashley.

Angelina had come sweeping back into his life as if she had never left it, her mind filled with visions of new gowns and fripperies purchased at her son's expense. However, she had not expected to find Thor a man with none of his father's weaknesses. She had been at Misty Rose less than two days before she learned her son could not be manipulated as she had always done his father.

Thor had been coldly polite to Angelina. He did not refuse her his hospitality, but neither did he welcome her with open arms as she had expected. Angelina's visit to Misty Rose lasted exactly three days, and that was the last time Thor had seen his mother or ever hoped to see her.

He did not believe a female had been born that could make him walk to the altar meekly, because he knew he would never find a woman who would give freely of herself without expecting a man's soul in return. Such a woman did not exist.

He preferred the honesty of the waterfront prostitutes to those fine-bred ladies with their perfect manners and simpering airs. At least the whores did not try to make a man their slave by leading him to believe they loved him. Love was a ruse played out by women until they could sink their greedy claws into a man.

Love, Thor thought derisively, his mouth turning down at the corners, is for the idiots of the world. A man is a fool to fall under the spell of a woman, to be held an emotional prisoner for the rest of his life.

He scanned the *Sea Siren*'s deck, automatically checking his crew's actions to ascertain whether his orders were being carried out as he mused, I'll never let myself make that mistake.

Chapter 3

A hint of rose touched Storm's cheeks as she stood by the rail, savoring the brief time she was allowed on deck for fresh air. The *Sea Siren* had been at sea for over three weeks, and with each passing day the confines of her small cabin grew more unbearable. With her returning health also came a new surge of energy. In her effort to release a small amount of it, she had paced back and forth across the tiny cubicle until she felt certain there was a visible trail worn in the floorboards. There was only just so much pacing she could do within the narrow quarters before she drove herself mad. The inactivity combined with the isolation from other people played havoc with her nerves. Storm felt as if she were dry kindling ready to explode with only a tiny spark to ignite it.

In all of her eighteen years, she had never felt such desolation. Since the age of five she had been surrounded by people. Her imposed separation from the other members of the *Sea Siren*'s company made her feel like a deserted isle where ships passed but never dropped anchor. Everyone knew of her presence but ignored it. The only human contact she was allowed was with the silent, watch-ful first mate, Joe Tyler. At first she had tried to carry on a conversation with him when he accompanied her on deck, but she soon learned from his stoic demeanor that her efforts were useless. The man would not go against his captain's orders to appease her loneliness.

At the thought of the *Sea Siren*'s arrogant master, Storm's eyes were drawn to the tall figure on the bridge. He stood with his legs spread and his powerful arms casually clasped behind his back as he faced into the breeze. The current of air ruffled his white lawn shirt, making the material cling to the width of his chest, revealing the muscles banded beneath the mat of black hair that furred the garment's deep V opening. The wind had loosened his dark hair from the velvet ribbon that fastened it at the nape of his corded neck. Several strands curled naturally about his face, soft-ening his swarthy features somewhat with silken tendrils.

Each day Storm found her eyes unwillingly seeking out the magnificent man who ruled the *Sea Siren* with such a firm hand. Like some great noble beast, he seemed to exude power. Even from the distance she imagined she could feel it and was fascinated much like a child by a flame, knowing it would burn if touched but still unwit-tingly drawn to it.

Since the first day on board the ship, Storm had not spoken with Thor Wakefield, nor had she wanted to do so. She was intrigued by the man but also frightened by the strange sensations the sight of him aroused. She did not like the tiny butterfly feelings that fluttered in her stomach. They were totally foreign to her, and she could not under-stand why he had such an effect upon her. Nor could she understand why she could not put the arrogant man out of her thoughts. That in itself did little to aid her peace of mind.

As he sensed someone observing him, Thor's gaze swept the deck until it came to rest upon Storm. His mood was

light. They were making good time and would reach their
destination within the next month. Feeling amiable toward
the world, he tipped an imaginary hat to her and smiled,
the dimples in his cheeks deepening with the gesture. He
watched with amusement as Storm flushed a bright red at
having been caught staring, and he chuckled to himself at
the discomfort he saw on her lovely face.

Storm turned abruptly away, feeling the heat rise to her
cheeks. Nettled with herself for letting the man have such
an unsettling effect upon her, she muttered "Arrogant
bastard," as she trained her gaze on the distant horizon
and tried to focus all her attention on the waves rising into
white-tipped curls before breaking, only to begin the process all over. The effort was futile; no matter how hard she
tried, she could not get Thor Wakefield out of her mind.

Her thoughts thus turned to the *Sea Siren*'s captain, she
jumped as Thor's voice sounded close by her side. "I see
you are enjoying your time on deck."

Storm gripped the rail tightly and refused to look at him,
afraid that he could easily discern the agitation his presence stimulated in her. She kept her eyes glued to the line
where blue sky met green water as she said, "Yes, the day
is lovely."

Folding his arms over his chest, Thor relaxed against
the rail. "Aye, we're making good time, and if the weather
holds and we don't meet up with any Spanish ships, we
should nearly set a record for our speed."

Wondering at his amicable tone, Storm warily glanced
up at him. He certainly seemed a different man than the
last time they had spoken.

Unaware that she was again gazing at him, she was
disconcerted when he said, "Do you make it a habit to
stare, Miss Kingsley?"

Feeling the heat flood her cheeks once more, Storm
quickly averted her face. "No. Forgive me. I was only

trying to understand the reason for your coming to speak with me.''

Thor's voice reflected his amusement at her embarrassment. "Are you always so direct, mistress?"

Feeling she had suffered enough of his questions, Storm lifted her chin up in the air and looked directly into his metallic eyes. "I have found it serves little purpose to do otherwise. It is best to get to the matter at hand without all the insignificant preliminaries."

Taking a moment to study her features, Thor had to admit that Storm Kingsley was one of the loveliest women he had ever seen. From the first, he had suspected that beauty lay just beneath all the grime she had worn on boarding his ship, but he was amazed to find it present to such a degree.

He had known she was shapely from seeing her in the distance each day, but upon closer inspection, he could well understand why men had paid to have her in their beds. Her skin was flawless and tempted a man's hand. Her luscious pink lips made a man crave to taste them. Storm Kingsley was truly a beautiful, seductive woman.

He did not realize the effect she was having upon him until he felt his own wayward body reacting to the close proximity of her alluring form, and he quickly changed position to relieve the new tightness at his crotch. As he did so, he forced his eyes away from Storm and scanned the horizon. "I agree, mistress. It is best to get down to business, and I will do so. You have been relieved of your duties during the past weeks to give you time to recover sufficiently from your stay in prison. Now I see your health has returned, and there is no reason you cannot earn your passage as the other prisoners are doing. As of tomorrow morning, you will report to the galley and help the cook. McFergueson will give you any further instructions you may require, and I expect you to obey them."

Storm released the breath that had frozen in her throat as

she awaited Captain Wakefield's words. She had not known what to expect and was relieved by the order. For one fleeting moment she had thought she'd seen the same look in his eyes that had been worn by the men who had visited her mother. Grateful that she had misconstrued his expression, she felt the tension ease from her body. She gazed up at the fine line of his chiseled profile and said, "I will do my best to earn my passage. Now, if you will excuse me, I'll return to my cabin."

Storm had already turned away from Thor when his words halted her. "Mistress Kingsley, you puzzle me. How is it a prostitute from London's gutters speaks as a fine lady? At times you also possess the manner and bearing of one from much higher circumstances. That I can't understand."

Storm could feel the muscles in her back contract at the mention of her convicted profession. Though the claims stated in her papers were false, the insult still cut deeply, stirring her anger to the surface. Her eyes sparkled like cold, hard jewels as she slowly turned to face him, her chin tilted proudly as she said, "Sir, there are many puzzles in life. Has it occurred to you that there are some things that are none of your business?" With that she spun on her heel and walked with as much dignity as she could summon back across the deck and into the shadowy passageway beyond.

Thor was dumbfounded by her retort, and his mouth fell slightly agape as he stared after her retreating figure. At last he managed to recover sufficiently to see the humor of the situation. He threw back his head, the breeze waving the blue-black strands of hair about his face, his laughter sounding across the deck. "Damn me! She put me in my place."

Still chuckling, he strode back across the deck and climbed up to the bridge. He scanned the deep blue waters, his long fingers absently rubbing the cleft in his chin.

A wry grin tugged at his lips as his thoughts returned to Storm Kingsley. True, it's none of my business, mistress, but you have aroused my curiosity, he said to himself. You'll soon learn I've never been a man to leave a stone unturned when I want to find something out.

Storm's back ached as she rinsed the last of the suds from the galley floor. Her knees were sore from the constant kneeling, and her hands were red and chafed from the harsh soap the cook had given her to use. It was not that she was unused to hard labor, but it had been several months since she had done anything that required any exertion at all, and this physical labor wearied her to the bone.

With the back of her hand, she wiped a stray curl from her sweat-beaded brow and leaned back on her heels to survey her handiwork. The floor was sparkling clean, and now she could rest. It had taken all morning and nearly the entire afternoon to complete all the chores McFergueson found for her to do. She had washed dishes, cleaned potatoes for the stew, scrubbed pots and pans, helped prepare and serve the crew's lunch and breakfast, and the cook's final order had been to scrub the greasy floor.

After squeezing out the large rag, Storm tossed it into the bucket of dirty water and got to her feet. A sigh of relief escaped her lips as she rubbed the ache in her back, already looking forward to soaking her tired muscles in the wooden tub that had been provided for her use. Storm untied the apron, hung it on the peg by the door, and turned to leave the galley when the cook bellowed, "Wench, where do ye think ye're a-going? The day is not over yet, and ye've still not cleaned the capt'n's quarters. He be a real stickler fer things neat and clean, and he expects us to keep them th't away."

Storm's shoulders drooped as she leaned against the doorway. For one mad moment she considered telling the fat cook if the captain wanted his cabin cleaned, then he could do it himself. Squeezing her eyes shut, she managed to stem the urge. It would only serve to cause her more trouble. For the next seven years her labor belonged to others, and there was nothing she could do to change that fact.

Taking a deep breath, her cheeks puffing slightly as she blew out a resigned sigh, she wearily made her way up the steps to the passageway that led to Thor's cabin. Assuming that the captain's cabin would be unoccupied at this time of day, she did not knock before entering. As the door swung wide before her, she came to an abrupt halt on the threshold, her face reflecting her surprise to find Thor comfortably seated behind a large mahogany desk with his feet propped up on its shiny surface as he perused the small book in his hand.

Recognizing her mother's Bible, Storm gasped with indignation. Fury consumed her, making her forget her weariness of a moment before. Her blue eyes glinted with fiery lights as she quickly crossed the cabin and, without considering the consequences of her rash action, jerked the Bible from his hand. "How dare you! You have no right to invade my privacy."

The amusement Thor had felt at finding the only personal possession of a strumpet to be a Bible vanished as he came to his feet. His swarthy features deepened in hue as his blood began to rise at her temerity. His eyes were the color of shiny steel as he looked at Storm, the lines about his mouth etching grooves into his hard features. "Mistress, you go too far. I have been lenient with you until now, but it is time you learned your lesson. Bond slaves have no rights except those their masters give them. *I* am your master until I sell your papers." He extended his hand, palm upward for the Bible.

Storm glared at his hand and shook her head, her raven hair bouncing in a riot of untamed curls as she began to back away. "No! It's my mother's Bible, and I'll not let you have it."

Exasperated by her defiance, Thor strode around the desk and in two short strides reached her side, towering over her, his face stern, his eyes the color of a stormy sea. "Woman, you would try the patience of a saint, and I assure you I am not one. I'll have no more of your disobedience or you will suffer the consequences. Give me that book!"

Jutting out her chin at a mutinous angle, Storm clutched Alisa's Bible tightly to her breast as she spat out, "Never. It is mine, and I'll not let you take it from me."

All patience deserting him, Thor closed his hand over the book. No man had ever defied him in the manner of this one small bond slave. With one swift jerk, he twisted the book from her grasp, a look of triumph flashing in his eyes as he reiterated, "Bond servants own no property."

All the pent-up animosity that had been building over the years exploded within Storm. All her thoughts centered on the fact that it had been a man who ruined Alisa's life, men who had caused her death, and now this man was trying to take the only thing Storm had left of her mother. Storm's fingers curled into claws as she launched herself at Thor. She aimed for his eyes, and only his quick step backward saved him. She beat at his chest with her fists, releasing the bitterness instilled in her young heart from watching her mother degrade herself with so many men. Her fury made her heedless of her own fate. All she wanted was to inflict as much pain as she and Alisa had endured.

"Hold, woman!" Thor ordered as he managed at last to grasp her flying fists. Paying no attention to his command, she continued the battle even after her hands had been captured. She landed a sharp kick to his shin with the toe of her shoe and noted with satisfaction the look of pain that crossed his face before his features settled into a grim, foreboding expression.

"So you want to play rough? Then you'll have your wish." Jerking Storm against his hard body, Thor pinned her tightly to him with one strong arm in an attempt to subdue her struggles. Then he grasped both her wrists with his free hand, pulling her arms behind her. Pain seared up her arms, and she winced but did not cry out.

Breathing heavily from the exertion, he leaned away from her, assessing her flushed, angry face. His breath was hot on her cheek as he said, "Will you calm yourself now? I don't want to hurt you, but I will not let you inflict any more damage upon me, either. I have taken all I'm going to from you, Storm Kingsley. Since you're the only female on board, I have treated you kindly, though it seems my leniency was undeserved. I am repaid by you attacking me, physically assaulting me over a book. That is harsh retribution for my generosity. It seems you have not yet realized the truth of your situation."

Thor paused as he gazed down into her set face. "I had not thought you stupid, Storm, but since you can't comprehend your position, I will explain it to you. You are a bond servant, a convicted criminal, not a lady from George's court. Yet you act as if we should treat you as if you were on a pleasure cruise instead of being deported for a criminal offense. Rather than showing such belligerence, you should be on your knees, grateful that you have not suffered a worse fate than having to help in the galley and clean my cabin."

Reluctantly Storm had to admit the truth of his words, but they did not change the fact that he was determined to take Alisa's Bible, and she was just as resolved to keep it. No matter what threats Thor Wakefield made or what action he took to punish her, she would not relinquish her last link with her mother.

Thor's penetrating gaze never wavered from her face

while, still holding her prisoner with one hand, he tipped up her chin with the other. He saw the swift play of emotions across her features as well as the stubborn light that remained in her blue eyes.

His nostrils flared at the musky scent radiating from her heated body only inches from his own. The feminine fragrance stirred his senses, invading his mind and replacing his hot anger with other equally heated thoughts. Thor felt his muscles grow taut and fought the sudden rush of desire that throbbed into life. He drew in a deep breath, trying to stem the scorching tide as his gaze traveled over Storm's sculptured features, lingering on her smooth forehead where damp tendrils of stygian silk clung in wispy curls before moving down to her delicately arched brows and feathery black-lashed eyes. He peered into their dazzling depths, seeking a similar response but failing to find it. Drawing his eyes away, he moved his gaze along her slender nose down to her heart-shaped mouth. That was his undoing. His arms tightened about her, drawing her near as he released her hands and wrapped her within his strong embrace. "Storm," he murmured before his lips descended to capture the softness of her own, "you are a tempest indeed."

Paralyzed by this new turn of events, Storm stood transfixed. Thor's actions were so unexpected that it took her a few moments to comprehend what was transpiring. His lips seared her mouth like a red-hot brand, sending a shock wave through her. It jolted Storm to the very core of her being, shattering the thick wall of carefully constructed indifference, making her tingle with strange new sensations throughout her entire body, terrifying her. With a strength magnified by her fear of what would take place if she did not free herself from his ravaging kiss, she placed her hands against his chest and pushed herself abruptly out of his embrace.

Storm's breath came in ragged gasps, and her eyes were

wide, reflecting the panic welling within her, engulfing her until she felt as if she would faint for the first time in her life. Her features were ashen as she slowly backed away from the demon who had the power to bring forth feelings she refused to recognize.

Thor's chest rose and fell heavily as he looked into her frightened face. Her actions puzzled him, and he wondered briefly if it was a game she played. The girl was a convicted prostitute, yet she acted like an untried virgin. "Storm," he said, his voice husky with emotion as he took a step forward, instinctively trying to recapture his desire.

"No!" she spat, violently shaking her head from side to side. "Stay away from me. I want nothing to do with you. All I want is my mother's Bible, no more."

Resentment simmered through Thor at her rejection, and his face hardened as his gaze came to rest on the frayed leather binding of the book at his feet. In one swift, fluid movement he retrieved the Bible and held it up to her. "Is that the problem? I have not bargained for your favors? I had forgotten your profession and that you usually get paid for your services. Will you now haggle over the value of this book? Will it bring you to my bed, or will I have to sweeten the price with coins from my pocket?"

His words lashed Storm, making her wince at his assault. She swallowed convulsively, forcing her fear-constricted throat to work as she said, "Please, I'll cause you no more trouble. All I want from you is my mother's Bible; it's all I have left of her." She extended one trembling hand palm upward, tears brimming in her eyes for the first time since Alisa's death.

The expression on her face tugged at Thor's heart, but his fingers tightened about the Bible. He would not let himself succumb to her plea. In an unguarded moment, he realized, he could come close to believing the girl and might do so now if he did not possess the documents that attested to her trade. Like all women in her profession, Storm Kingsley was an accomplished actress.

Against his better judgment, Thor found himself deeply intrigued by her. Her methods were far different from those of any whore he had ever met before, and there were so many baffling contradictions about her still left unsolved. He knew he would not be satisfied until he knew the answers, and he decided that until that time he would keep the object she valued so greatly. Perhaps it would be the key that would reveal the true Storm Kingsley to him.

Seeing Thor's rigid expression, Storm realized he did not intend to return Alisa's Bible unless she prostituted herself for it. She could not force herself to do that, even if refusing would cost her the treasured volume. Like all men, Thor Wakefield wanted only one thing and did not care about the pain he caused to get it.

That thought pushed aside her fear of him, rekindling her old anger against all men. Resolutely stiffening her spine, Storm let her hand fall to her side, where it curled into a fist. She would not beg again. Staring unflinchingly at Thor, refusing to humble herself even with a downcast look, she thought, You might keep it now, but I'll get it back one way or another. But not by coming to your bed.

Thor watched the soft pleading expression fade from her face, to be replaced by one of hostility. He smiled to himself. Ah, my little Tempest, I was right, he mused. Your game will soon be over, and I will be the victor. Taking a key from his pocket, he strode to his desk and opened the top drawer. He dropped the Bible inside and locked it tightly. Then he smiled at her, his eyes mocking. "Think over my offer. When you decide to come to me willingly, you can have the book."

Storm's eyes narrowed as she regarded him, rancor flashing in the dark blue depths. "You do not own enough gold to get me to come to your bed willingly," she hissed through clenched teeth.

Dropping the key into his pocket and patting it reassuringly, he crossed to the door. "Perhaps not, but I do have your mother's Bible. Now you are excused, mistress. I have duties to attend to."

Suppressing a hot urge to try to kill the villain, Storm left the cabin as swiftly as her feet would carry her. Like her name, she raged down the passageway to her own small quarters and slammed the door behind her, the violence of her action doing little to relieve the wrath that boiled within her against the *Sea Siren*'s captain, Thor Wakefield.

As she wiped furiously at her damp eyes, her tears only heightening her anger and humiliation, she began to pace the small cabin. Her mind worked feverishly, seeking a means to regain the Bible without degrading herself and relinquishing the last things she possessed: her virtue and her pride.

Storm knew she had only three choices open to her, and she immediately discarded the first two. She had pleaded, to no avail, and she refused to consider the option Thor had given her. That left only one thing she could do: steal Alisa's Bible away from the heartless Captain Wakefield.

She stood thoughtfully tapping one finger against her lower lip as the idea took root. It should be a simple feat to accomplish, since she had been ordered to see to the cleaning of his cabin. She would have no trouble getting in, yet she knew she would have to wait until the right moment to make her move. She did not want the theft discovered too soon, or Thor would have the Bible confiscated again. As she pondered her course, a tiny smile curled the corners of her mouth. With a shrug of her shoulders, she thought, I've already been convicted of prostitution. What does it matter if I now add stealing to the crimes of which I've been accused. I'll be guilty of neither.

Settling the matter firmly in her mind, Storm curled up on the narrow bunk, tucking her legs beneath her as she made her plans. She would wait until they had reached their destination and it was nearly time for them to go ashore. That way her theft would not be discovered until after her papers had been sold. Thor Wakefield would be surprised when he returned to his ship to find the Bible missing, but by that time it would be too late to raise a hue and cry against her. She would already be safely out of harm's way.

Unaware of her actions, she absently traced her lips where Thor's mouth had left its brand. A tingle of pleasure crept up her spine to settle about her like a warm caress. Realizing where her thoughts had drifted, she jerked her hand to her side. Balling it into a fist, she hit the mattress, saying, "Damn the man and all men!"

Chapter 4

The *Sea Siren* swayed gently against the river current. From its rolling deck could be seen the settlement built on the sandy bluff above the twisting water course that divided the two colonies of Georgia and South Carolina. Like the river, the flourishing little town was named Savannah. This was the first port of call for Thor Wakefield's vessel. Here the *Sea Siren* would leave the ready-made goods she carried in her hold and the ten bond slaves before sailing on to Charleston.

To Storm, who sat twiddling her thumbs as she listened to the commotion on deck, it mattered little that they had reached Savannah. Nor did she care that within a few hours her papers would be sold and she would truly begin to serve out the terms of her indenture. Her entire being was centered on one thought: retrieving her mother's Bible.

Since the day nearly a month earlier when Thor had locked the book away, she had schemed to reclaim it. She had tried to maintain her vow to wait until the end of the voyage, but when she'd found herself alone in the captain's cabin, she had not been able to resist the temptation.

She had tried to force the lock, but it would not budge. She had threatened it, hit it, cursed it, and used the blade of a knife on it, but nothing had worked. Exasperated, she had come to the conclusion that her only chance with success was to find the key. She had searched every nook and cranny of Thor's cabin, but to her chagrin, she'd finally realized he carried the key on his person. From that moment on she had begun to try to find a way in which to get it away from him.

Hoping to find a time and place when she could search his clothing, she had observed his schedule each day and questioned McFergueson about his habits.

Her efforts had gained her little knowledge to help her achieve her aims. Events had conspired against her until that very afternoon. Just when Storm's confidence in her plans had finally begun to wane, McFergueson had ordered her to carry hot water to the small compartment adjoining Thor's cabin, stating the captain would want a bath before he went ashore to arrange the sale of the bond slaves the next day.

Buoyed up and sensing success once more within range, she had not been able to suppress a tiny smile of elation. The cook had misconstrued the gesture and gruffly informed her she'd not be so happy once she was toiling under the hot sun from daylight till dark. However, his dire predictions had not erased the glow in Storm's eyes.

She had willingly carried bucket after bucket of steaming water to fill Thor's tub, knowing when he settled himself in it, she would have the chance she had been so desperately seeking. After the chore was finished, she'd hurried back to her own small cabin and begun her nerve-racking vigil.

The hours had dragged by monotonously as she'd listened and waited all afternoon until now. She felt like screaming with vexation as she heard the crew's cheerful banter drifting down from the deck. They laughed and bustled about looking forward to going ashore when their chores were done. Storm did not share their jovial mood, and her depression deepened as Thor still did not come to take his bath.

The shadows of twilight dimmed the passageway when she finally heard his footsteps. As she crept to the doorway, her heart began to beat rapidly in her breast, pounding in her ears to such an extent that she was afraid it would be heard as she eased open the door and peered out. She caught only a glimpse of Thor's lean frame as he entered his cabin.

Trembling with anticipation, she closed the door again and leaned against it, praying that he would not order more hot water, since his bath had long since cooled.

Long agonizing minutes passed as she waited to hear his call for fresh water. When it did not come, she released the breath she had not realized she had been holding in, in a long sigh of relief. Her lips curved upward at the thought of Thor leisurely bathing himself while she found the key and retrieved Alisa's Bible without him ever suspecting her actions. The arrogant bastard won't feel so superior when he finds he's been outwitted, she thought. It gave her courage as her hand closed about the latch on her door.

Drawing in a deep breath, she slid stealthily from her quarters and crept along the shadowy passageway. She had nearly reached his cabin when his door opened, the lamplight spilling into the passage. With an agility born out of fear, Storm melted into the deepest shadows, pressing her back against the bulkhead as she prayed that she would not be found. Her stomach twisted into knots of apprehension as Thor's deep, angry voice penetrated her hiding place. "Damn it, Tyler. How can this have happened? It was your responsibility to see that the animals survived the journey."

Tyler's voice quavered nervously as he said, "Sir, the stupid oafs fed the horses hay that had soured. Every one of the prisoners comes from the gutters of London and don't know one end of a horse from the other. I didn't know anything about it until the filly could no longer stand on her own feet.''

Storm could imagine Thor running his fingers through his hair in his exasperation. She had often noted this unconscious habit of his when he was vexed.

"Tyler, I'll skin every last one of them if that horse dies. She's a thoroughbred from AshGlen. She's pure Arabian stock that the earls of AshGlen have bred for the past fifty years. Don't you realize that animal is worth more than all of the prisoners rolled into one? The Ashforts intend to continue breeding them over here. There's not another animal in the colony of South Carolina that can hold a candle to Ashfort's stock.''

Storm tensed as Joe Tyler backed away from the cabin, his face white and his hat in hand. The first mate's shoulders drooped under Thor's reprimand, and he tried to apologize. "Sir, I'm sorry. I know they're your neighbors and you are supposed to get the first foal for bringing their horses over. I'll do my best to keep the filly alive, but I can't guarantee it. She's mighty sick.''

Thor's tone seemed to rattle the timbers of the *Sea Siren* as he shouted, "Then damn it, man, go ashore and get a doctor or someone who knows about horses and bring him back here.'' With his words still ringing in the air, he slammed the door in Tyler's woebegone face. With a sigh, the first mate settled his hat onto his head and hurried down the passageway without looking once in Storm's direction.

As Tyler's steps faded into the distance, Storm stood transfixed, pondering the conversation she had just overheard. The import of it seemed to press her even more tightly against the bulkhead, weighing on her chest like a piece of heavy metal, choking the air from her lungs so that she could not breathe. The words spun dizzily about in her mind; AshGlen, Ashfort, it could be no other.

Lyle Ashfort, Alisa's husband—Storm could not say her father—owned a plantation in South Carolina. Suddenly a fury of turbulent emotions swept over her. Clenching her fist, she pressed it to her mouth and bit down on her ashen knuckles to keep from crying out with the rage that twisted her insides into vicious knots.

By accident she had learned the clue to Lyle Ashfort's whereabouts and knew she would let nothing stand in the way of her seeking vengeance against the man. She did not know where the colony of South Carolina lay but knew she would find it if it took the rest of her life. I will find you, Lyle Ashfort, she vowed. I know where you are, and I'll do anything I have to do to see you suffer the way Mother and I have suffered because of you.

Taking a deep steadying breath, she wiped away the beads of moisture that formed on her brow. Her hand trembled from the intense feelings the new knowledge had aroused.

It took all of her willpower to force her mind back to the present and the mission she had set for herself. Reclaiming Alisa's Bible was her paramount concern at the moment. After that was accomplished, she could then find a means to reach South Carolina and seek out her mother's husband.

Storm's hatred for the man that had sired her was all-consuming. Briefly the thought of her indenture surfaced as she moved out of the shadows, but she pushed it away; silently swearing, Nothing is going to stand in my way. She repeated, Nothing, as her hand came to rest on the latch of Thor's cabin door.

Taut with tension, she felt her breath catch in her throat as she slowly slid the metal bar back and eased open the door. Her heart hammered against her ribs as she peered furtively inside to ascertain whether the cabin was vacant. Seeing no one and hearing the sound of Thor splashing about in the adjoining room, she relaxed somewhat. Surreptitiously she moved into the cabin, her eyes scanning the area, coming to rest upon the burgundy coat laid carelessly over the back of a chair. With her full attention centered on the garment, Storm crossed the short space, her fingers frantically searching the satin-lined pockets before the coat was fully away from its resting place. A look of excitement brightened her face as she came in contact with the hard metal of the key. Her lips curled in triumph as her hand closed about it. Throwing the coat into the chair, she turned toward the desk, but her steps froze and her eyes widened at the sight that met them.

Before her stood Thor in all his naked splendor, his hair still dripping water, his eyes hard and shining as his lips narrowed into a grim line. His chiseled features were cold and without emotion, glistening in the lamplight with the moisture of his bath, reminding Storm of a statue she had once seen in London during a rainstorm.

She instinctively took a step backward, wanting to place as much distance between herself and the naked, hostile giant as possible. Thor appeared even larger without his clothing, and a tiny chill of fear tingled at the nape of her neck, making the short, silken strands there stand on end.

With the agility of a predator, his taut muscles rippling beneath his bronzed skin, he moved toward her without a word. Her mind cried out for her to flee, but she was unable to move. His steely gaze nailed her to the floor as he stalked her like a great angry beast. In one swift motion he grasped her wrist, his fingers biting into her flesh until her hand opened to reveal the key, its image impressed upon the pale skin of her palm.

Thor's voice rumbled from his chest, low and controlled, as he stared down into her wide, frightened eyes. ''I see you now add thievery to your crimes, Storm. Did you think I was such a simple wit that I would not suspect what you were up to? For a thief you leave too much evidence—I saw the marks on my desk after the first time you tried to pry it open. I suggest in future you keep to the trade in which you have more experience. Selling your body takes less talent than being a thief." His eyes held the look of polished steel as his gaze swept over her features, lingering briefly on her mouth.

Storm tried to quell the trembling that beset her at his nearness. Her throat was tight and her lips dry. She had to moisten them with the tip of her tongue before she could speak. Her voice was no more than a rustle on the still air as she said, "I was not stealing. The Bible belongs to me. You are the one who stole it."

His grip tightened about her wrist, and he drew her near. The heat of his breath touched her face as he said, "You and all you possess belong to me until I sell your papers tomorrow. It seems you have not yet realized the fact. I think it is time that you learn that lesson now, Storm."

The color drained from her face as she realized the danger in which she had placed herself. She saw the hot light glowing within his piercing eyes and recoiled. She tried to twist free of his hold, but his fingers dug even deeper into her tender skin to still her movements. Slowly, though she strained against his grasp, he drew her against his naked, sinewy body. The evidence of his passion was already very apparent.

"No!" she breathed frantically. "You can't."

His hot eyes swept over her features as his hand came up to caress the smooth line of her ivory throat. One dark brow arched quizzically over his thickly fringed eyes and he murmured, "I can't? Storm, you take my threats far too lightly. I can and will. I am no different from the other men you have served. I have paid for your services; I own you until tomorrow."

Nearly incoherent with fear, Storm violently shook her head. "No, I'm not what you think. I'm not a prostitute."

Thor chuckled as his fingers slowly traced her cheek. "You aren't? Your papers state otherwise, Storm. You should have gone on the stage in London. Your performance nearly makes me believe you, but I know differently. You have learned how to play the game well, my love; I give you credit for that. Rejection always spurs a man on, and that is what you intended, is it not? But I'm afraid you'll be disappointed in your dealings with me. You won't receive the high price you deem fit, because until tomorrow your body and soul belong to me."

In Storm's frightened state, Thor's words and the searing look in his eyes reminded her of the devil. With her free hand she pushed against his hard chest as tears brimmed in her eyes and began to make crystal paths down her cheeks. Her words came out in sobs as she pleaded, "Please don't do this thing. I beg of you, please."

Thor furrowed his forehead, his dark brows knitting across the bridge of his aquiline nose as he stared down into her terror-stricken face. Her plea had touched his heart, and the heat of his desire began to fade at the look of shimmering misery in her eyes. The tremble of her soft lower lip as she drew in a frightened breath quenched the last flames of his lust. Gently he enfolded her within his arms and held her close as he murmured against her hair, "I'm not a brute, Storm."

His temper had cooled with his passion. Had he not already been enraged about Ashfort's horses, he would not have reacted so harshly to finding Storm searching his pockets. He had known for several weeks that she had been trying to retrieve the book. It had become an amusing game to him to see the next ploy she would use to accomplish her aim.

He had expected no less from her, for the one thing he had learned of Storm Kingsley was the fact that she had too much spirit to come to his bed meekly without first trying by her own means to regain her mother's Bible.

Remorse swept through him at his having vented his frustrations upon her. Tipping up her chin, he saw his own reflection in her glistening eyes as he said, "I've never taken a woman to my bed that was not willing, Storm. No matter what you have done or by what method you choose to make your living, I'll not force even a prostitute to my bed."

Storm searched his face to find the falsity behind his words but could see none in the silver depths of his eyes. For one fleeting moment her expression revealed her astonishment at finding there were actually kind men in the world. Suddenly the dam of her emotions burst, loosing all her pent-up feelings, and she wanted to tell him the truth about herself. She opened her mouth to speak, but only a sob escaped. Thor's kindness had unlocked the door on all the heartache she had suffered during the past two years, and now it clogged her throat, impeding her words.

His warm embrace surrounded her once more, pulling her comfortingly to him. His tenderness unleashed her desperate need for human contact, and she clung to his chest. It had been so long since anyone had cared in even a small degree about her feelings. At that moment it mattered little that she stood within a naked man's arms. She did not consider the impropriety of the situation. She sought only the warmth of his lean body, wrapping her arms about his waist as she wept against his crisply furred chest. His gentleness was a balm to the open wounds in her heart.

The touch of his brown fingers running through her hair soothed her, and she did not protest as his lips lightly touched her brow. As if they were metal drawn to a magnet, Storm raised her lips to meet his. Unlike the previous kiss he had given her, this one was not searing but softly caressing, tentatively searching, allaying her fears and bringing forth a deep warm glow inside her. It gave as much as it took, and she greedily accepted the pleasure of it. The kiss filled her with wonder, and she did not want to lose the soft radiance it built within her. Her arms crept about his neck as she began to return his kiss.

Storm's response rekindled Thor's passion, and his arms tightened about her, drawing her close, pressing her against his hard body. He savored the sweetness of her mouth, gently probing with his tongue until her lips parted to let him taste the honeyed nectar that lay beyond the tender edge of the velvet cavern. He inhaled deeply of her feminine odor, his blood singing a siren's song wildly through his veins as the heat migrated to simmer in his groin.

His breathing grew heavy, the touch of Storm's responsive flesh stirring his senses into white-hot flames. His virile body demanded release, and he longed to lift her into his arms and lay her on the wide bed to satisfy the cry of his aching loins. Yet he held back, intuitively sensing he must proceed slowly if he wanted to obtain his desire.

His hands moved sensuously over her slender back, his sensitive fingers feeling her relax beneath their touch. He moved slowly, lingering in one spot and then another before languidly easing his caresses to her firm, round breast. He felt her small nipples respond through the thin material of her gown, her reaction making him more bold. His kiss deepened, his tongue stroking hers enticingly.

A shudder of pure pleasure rushed over Storm from the new sensations he was provoking in her. A torrid current seemed to radiate from his mouth to incinerate all of her rational thoughts, leaving only a fervid heat deep within her belly. Her young body sensed the need her mind did not recognize and pressed closer to his sinewy form, seeking gratification without her realizing the import of her own actions.

Thor's lips traced a scorching path from her mouth down along the sculpted curve of her cheek to the soft flesh beneath her ear before continuing their tantalizing trail to her white shoulder. His moist tongue tasted her

flesh, swirling seductively as his dark head lowered to the
soft mounds exposed above the neckline of her gown. His
fingers eased open the fastenings of the garment and slipped
the material from her shoulders to expose the hard pointed
peaks of her breasts. He buried his face in the satiny flesh,
inhaling her sweet fragrance before capturing one rose-
colored tip between his hungry lips.

The erotic sensations Thor's mouth aroused made her
weak. Her head fell back as she instinctively arched toward the source of the pleasure, her fingers entwined in
the silken strands of his raven hair. Her knees trembled
and threatened to give way beneath her. She would have
fallen had he not swept her up in his arms and carried her
to the wide, welcoming bed.

Laying her tenderly upon the soft down mattress, Thor
caressed her young body as he divested her of her gown,
leaving her alabaster flesh naked to his hot, searing eyes.
"You are beautiful, my Tempest," he murmured huskily
as he joined her on the bed.

Storm's blood raced through her veins like molten lava
as his hands and lips continued their sensual torture. His
mouth recaptured her breasts, suckling each taut peak
before languidly moving between them, his tongue teasing
her flesh as it burned a path down her flat belly, enticingly
moving through the silky meadow of curls to the mystical
valley below. Her body seemed to pulsate with the sensations Thor's lips aroused as he titillated her flesh before
attending to his own need. Her back arched to the passionate music building within her, rising into a crescendo until
she cried out for release.

No longer able to hold back his desire, Thor covered
Storm with his virile body, his mouth recapturing her lips,
his tongue devouring hers as he slid between her thighs
and plunged into the moist sheath of her womanhood. His
mouth absorbed her startled cry as her body arched away

from the sudden pain. Her eyes flew open, her fingers clawing at his bare back as she tried to free herself.

Stunned by her reaction, Thor lay still, his brow furrowing as the knowledge of Storm's virginity assaulted his mind. No, he told himself, it can't be! She is a convicted prostitute. Feeling the heat of her pliant body around him, he raised himself on his elbows and stared down into the glistening depths of her eyes, only to see there a look of shock and pain.

Cupping her pale face within his palms, he gazed at it, trying to find a lie behind her response but failing. He released a long, rueful sigh. His lips narrowed into a thin line, and he closed his eyes, shutting out the look of accusation in her eyes. Questions flooded his mind as guilt pricked his conscience. How could this have happened? he wondered. Was she arrested before she could ply her trade? Or was she unjustly accused? Damn it, he chided himself, I've been an idiot. I should have known something was wrong when she did not act like the other whores I've known. Guiltily he had to admit he had wanted to believe she could be bought, convincing himself that she was only a good actress, because of his attraction to her.

Storm's eyes were bright with tears, shimmering iridescent in the lamplight as she lay beneath him, watching the strange play of expressions cross his face. She felt him pulsating within her and knew his passion went unfulfilled. Knowing that he withheld it because of her pain touched her, and she tenderly laid her hand against his cheek. The stinging had eased, and another equally unfamiliar feeling had begun to invade her belly, making her feel the need to soothe away the troubled expression on his face.

Thor's lashes fluttered open in surprise at her touch. Gazing down at her, he sensed she understood the torment he suffered at that moment, and he turned his face into her hand, kissing her palm, his breathe warm, his voice husky, as he murmured against it, "Forgive me."

A tremulous smile touched her passion-swollen lips as she caressed his cheek and nodded. Her beneficence stirred Thor strangely, making him want to give as well as receive pleasure from the beautiful woman. His eyes smoldered anew as he began to respond to the heated flesh caressing his manhood. "Let me love you, Storm. There will be no more pain." Her answer came as a tiny quiver deep within her, and he began the ancient ritual, his lean body moving smoothly in rhythm with hers.

Storm's body flamed with each thrust, sending fiery tentacles along every nerve and making her gasp for air as the inferno consumed her. She clung to Thor's neck, her nails digging into his tanned flesh as she soared upward into the vortex of sensual release, her body shaken, tremors of rapture sending her to the brink of *petite mort* as ecstasy claimed her entire being.

Thor, too, had reached the erotic pinnacle, his muscles rippling as his dark head arched backward, his handsome features reflecting the overwhelming sensations that throbbed through him as he found his release and then collapsed over Storm, his sweat mingling with hers. He held her close for a moment, feeling both their hearts beat as they slowed to normal, before raising himself on one elbow and staring down into her love-flushed face. Tenderly he placed a light kiss on the tip of her nose before withdrawing from her to lie at her side, savoring the new feelings that had begun to blossom within his chest; at peace with the world.

Storm could not speak as the afterglow of passion faded and reality slowly began to encroach upon her once more. Her face suffused with color as the full impact of what she had let happen hit her with a devastating blow. Tears brimmed anew in her eyes and crept from their corners to dampen a path along her cheeks to her tousled hair. A sob

of humiliation escaped her before she could stifle it, and
she bit down on her swollen lip to hold back another. Like
a tiny wounded animal, she curled into a ball, staring
sightlessly at the cabin wall.

Hearing the wretched cry, Thor turned to her, wanting
to comfort her. He knew virgins often suffered megrims
after their first experience in lovemaking, and it touched
him. Knowing that few young girls understood their bodies'
responses to passion, he wanted to ease her feelings by
explaining that what had happened was nature's gift to
humanity and that there was no reason for her to be
ashamed. He reached out to bring her into his arms.

The touch of his hand shocked Storm from her dazed
state. Like a lightning bolt searing across a warm summer
sky, fury streaked through her at both Thor and herself.
With a cry of rage she rose from the bed, her eyes shooting daggers at him as she backed away from his outstretched hand. Her breast rose and fell heavily as she
balled her fists at her side, her small chin jutting forward,
ready to do battle with the man who had caused her to
forget her vows and succumb to the treacherous urgings of
her body. She had sworn never to degrade herself as Alisa
had done, and now to the first man who had offered her
kindness, Storm had given her virtue.

Her eyes were glassy with tears as she gathered her
worn gown from the floor and slipped it over her head.
She did not speak as she walked over to the tiny metal
object shining on the polished boards where it had fallen.
Picking up the key, she crossed to Thor's desk and unlocked the drawer. She had paid dearly for Alisa's Bible
and would have it no matter what the captain of the *Sea
Siren* said or did. Her eyes widened as the drawer slid
open; it was empty.

Frantically, unable to grasp the truth, Storm searched
the vacant space as if she could make the book reappear.
For one brief moment she squeezed her eyes tightly shut

before turning to face Thor. He stood barefoot in his britches, leaning casually against the poster of the bed, his muscular arms folded over his chest as he observed her actions with interest. One dark brow arched quizzically at the smoldering look she bestowed upon him.

"Where is it?" Storm ground out between clenched teeth.

Thor cocked his head to one side and gave an offhand shrug as his lips curved up at the corners. "As I told you, Tempest, I knew of your intentions and so took the precaution of removing the book from the drawer."

The memory of her foolish attempts to get the key settled about Storm like a heavy, suffocating mantle. Her insides writhed. It was nearly a physical pain, and she fought against it, laboring to keep her agony hidden as she said, "I want my mother's Bible. You have what you wanted from me in exchange."

The tender, almost loving feeling Storm's innocence had aroused within Thor faded with her words. His eyes grew cold, a tiny muscle twitching in his square jaw, as he realized she had paid him with her body to return the blasted book. She might have been a virgin when she came to his bed, but her papers had been proven correct after all. She was now a prostitute by her own words.

An icy contempt rose up to replace the warmth he had felt moments before for the girl staring at him with eyes filled with bitterness. He had felt a niggling guilt for misjudging her, but it died and was reborn as anger as he realized that she had played on her own innocence to gain her own ends. Like mother like daughter, he mused to himself as a forbidding light came into his own eyes. The vixen was clever and would have made a fortune by following in her mother's footsteps had she not been deported before she had a chance to ply her trade. You can take the whore out of the gutter, but you can't take the gutter out of the whore, he mused as he regarded her.

"I think, my little Tempest, that the book is worth much more than just one brief encounter in bed," he said, his gaze sweeping over her, judging her worth, as he tapped one finger against the cleft of his chin. "I've decided I will not sell your papers tomorrow. I think you will make a warm addition to Misty Rose."

Stunned, Storm stood with mouth agape and eyes wide. Thor's words echoed through her mind, setting off a tremor deep within her that steadily rose upward until her throat felt as if it were bound by a noose. She had to take several deep breaths to steady the sudden quaking that beset her limbs, and her tone reflected her uncertainty as she said, "You can't mean that. Please just give me my mother's Bible and be done with your torture. I have harmed you in no way to deem such punishment. Can you not be satisfied to know I have given you all I possess?"

Again Thor felt his heart stir betrayingly with pity at the look of pain in her eyes. Clenching his jaw against it and reminding himself of her origins, he resolved not to let himself be swayed again by her cunning tricks. Earlier he had foolishly let himself believe he had found a woman different from all the rest, who would give freely of herself without expecting something in return. That moment of madness had passed, and he would no longer be so easily duped by her ploys in the future.

Though he knew her for what she was, Storm still had the power to intrigue him, more so than all the other women he had met in the past. He was honest enough with himself to admit that fact. She was a girl raised in the gutters of London, the daughter of a prostitute burned at the stake, yet she possessed an air of mystery about her that he was determined to solve. She could hold her own verbally with any guttersnipe he had ever heard, yet she could also speak and act like a lady. None of it made sense.

Thor had always been fascinated by puzzles, and there

were few he could not unravel. It would be the same with Storm Kingsley. It might take a while, but he knew he would finally get to the bottom of her enigma. In the meantime, he would enjoy her beauty and passion. Perhaps by the time his curiosity was appeased, he would be tired of her and could sell her papers then.

"Mistress, I can see no reason for such protestations," he said aloud. "At Misty Rose you will be treated well, as are all of my people. I can assure you, your life will be much easier there, seeing to my needs, than it would be if I sold your papers tomorrow. At least you don't find my lovemaking repulsive. Your next master might not be so gentle and understanding of your vixenish moods as I have been. At Misty Rose you will be only my mistress, but with someone else you might have to labor in the fields as well as service him at night. With your unpredictable temperament, you would probably even suffer the lash."

Storm winced at his crude remarks but refused to let him see how they affected her. Raising her chin belligerently, her eyes glittering with rancor, she spat out, "I won't do it. I will not become your whore."

Casually Thor closed the space separating them, his wide hand coming up to cup her face as he stared down into it. "Mistress, you have little choice in the matter. As I have told you in the past, I own you body and soul for the next seven years and there is nothing you can do about it."

She glared back up at him. "Seven years is a long time. Beware you do not find yourself awakening in hell one morning."

Enjoying their contest of wills more than he would have imagined, Thor said, chuckling, "Your warning is taken, my little Tempest, but you had best beware also. I am not a man to let anything stand in my way when I want something, and woe be unto the one who tries." With the tip of his finger, he traced the sleek curve of her flushed cheek and smiled down at her. "I think from your response earlier, you will not mind as much as you say. Your body was made to be loved, Storm, and I intend to see it is not neglected. That would be a terrible waste."

Storm jerked away from his hand, moistening her suddenly dry lips as she argued, "But you said you had never taken a woman to your bed who was unwilling. I'll never come there again unless you force me."

Thor shrugged. "Time has a way of changing many things. Is tonight not proof of that?"

Storm could feel the heat mount in her cheeks as her face flamed with color. She could not meet his mocking eyes. She opened her mouth to protest, but before the words would leave her parched throat, a knock sounded on the door and Tyler called out, "Sir, I've brought the smithy. He knows about horses and has brought along some herbs to use on Ashfort's filly."

Thor's gaze lingered on Storm briefly as he shrugged into his white lawn shirt, then swung open the door. "I'll go down to check on the horses, Tyler. You see Mistress Kingsley back to her quarters. She'll be traveling on to South Carolina with us so make sure you lock the door and bring me the key."

Tyler's freckled face suffused with color as he looked past Thor and took in Storm's disheveled appearance. The tips of his pale ears glowing a vivid shade of scarlet, he nodded, "Aye, sir."

Noting his first mate's uncomfortable expression, Thor fought to suppress the grin that tugged at his mouth as he, too, glanced at Storm. "You are excused, mistress. We'll continue this conversation at a later date." Giving her a half-mocking bow, he strode from the cabin, leaving her no choice but to follow the embarrassed Tyler back to her own small cubbyhole.

*   *   *

Impotent fury seethed through her as she sat on the narrow bunk, her face set and her hands balled into fists in her lap as the tempest raged within her.

The urge to scream out her vexation and beat upon the locked door was strong, but she knew such actions would be futile. That would do her no more good than had any of her protestations since the horrible night in London when the fates had deserted her, leaving her to the mercy of brutal strangers such as Thor Wakefield.

Storm's red and swollen eyes attested to the tears she had shed since Tyler had obeyed his captain's orders and locked her in her cabin, but now there were no more tears left to cry. Her anger had dried the moisture, leaving her sapphire eyes hard and glassy as she sat contemplating the future Thor had described so vividly for her.

With no avenue of escape open to her, she felt trapped into the same life-style that her mother had lived. Alisa had chosen the path she would travel and Storm realized painfully that she had done likewise by succumbing to her emotions. For one brief moment she wondered if Alisa's weakness could be inherited. Alisa's emotional ties to Lyle Ashfort had been like a debilitating disease, ruining her life and leaving her defenseless. Her mother's love had made her vulnerable, beguiling her into believing Lyle Ashfort had cared for her; she had been convinced by his deceitful ways until her death. In Storm's opinion love had been Alisa's downfall.

Storm's expression hardened as she clenched her teeth, her delicate lips pursing as she fought back the memories of her moments with Thor. I'll never let myself be that foolish again, she told herself. Tonight I desperately needed someone. It was not love, only loneliness, that made me seek his arms. I don't love the man and never will. You'll see horses fly before that happens.

At the thought of horses, she tensed, her eyes widening as she recalled the conversation she had overheard earlier between Thor and Tyler. Until that moment she had completely forgotten about the Ashfort horses. Her mind had been in too much turmoil over what had transpired between Thor and herself to even consider the consequences. If what she suspected proved true, Alisa's husband owned a plantation near Thor's home. Storm was to be Lyle Ashfort's neighbor.

Pressing her eyes tightly together, she prayed, "Dear God, let it be so. Let me be there to see him suffer the way he made my mother suffer." Storm knew from the teachings of Mistress Simmons that it was sacrilege to beg for such a thing, but she cared little. Revenge was paramount in her thoughts where Lyle Ashfort was concerned, and she would gladly brave the fires of hell to know he would be there, too. Her face screwed up into a mask of pain as she thought, I began my payment tonight to the devil himself.

She felt a new stinging in her eyes and wiped them with asperity. She would shed no more tears; they were useless. From that moment forth, she resolved to concentrate all her efforts on her vendetta against Lyle Ashfort. At present she did not know how she would achieve her aims, but in time she would find a means to avenge Alisa. Perhaps then Storm could set her own life in order.

Chapter 5

The heat was oppressive in the tiny cabin. Glistening beads of perspiration dotted Storm's upper lip while others formed between her shoulder blades and trickled down her spine to dampen her gown. The worn fabric of the garment had been much too thin for England's climate, but for the hot, humid weather of the Carolinas it was much too heavy. The damp material itched her skin, and dark stains beneath her arms and about her waist visibly confirmed her mounting discomfort.

The *Sea Siren* had dropped anchor in the port of Charleston the previous evening. That much information she had managed to glean from her taciturn watchdog, Tyler. Scratching absently at the rash that had spread about her waist from the heat, she listened to the activity overhead. The shouts from the crew to the stevedores as they worked to unload the cargo from the hold filtered down to her small cabin. At times she could hear their laughter and knew their spirits were high. They were home after so many months away and were looking forward to seeing family and friends. Storm wished that she, too, could feel

67

some joy at reaching their destination but found she could not drag her spirits up from the deep quagmire into which they had sunk during the last days on the *Sea Siren*.

She could find little to look forward to in her future. It had been over a week since she had been confined to her quarters, and during that time she had not had to confront Thor again. For that she was grateful. She was not anxious for their next encounter. Each day she had prayed that his continued absence meant he had changed his mind about making her his unwilling mistress, but she had little hope that was true.

She had tried to come up with a way of extricating herself from his plans, but no matter how hard she thought, she couldn't find an answer to her dilemma. By law she belonged to Thor for the next seven years, and he had the right to do with her as he pleased. That knowledge did little to appease the anxiety that mounted with each passing moment. With the strain of knowing she was helpless to prevent Thor Wakefield from following through with his intentions, Storm had grown as tense as a mouse waiting for the cat to pounce and devour it.

At the sound of the key grating in the lock, she swung nervously about, her eyes glued to the door, her teeth worrying her lower lip as she waited for the portal to open. Their journey was concluded, and she knew her brief respite from Thor would also be at an end. As the door swung open to reveal the first mate, she released the breath she had been holding, grateful for another postponement of the inevitable.

Tyler carried a large burlap bundle in his arms and grinned sheepishly at Storm as he held it out to her. "The captain says you are to bathe and change into these. You'll be going ashore within the hour. I've brought water for your bath."

Puzzled, Storm accepted the package, a tiny frown etching a path across her forehead as she watched Tyler carry bucket after bucket of steaming water into the cabin and poured it into the round brass-bound tub. When he finished he wiped his hands on his britches and gave her an awkward smile before hurriedly leaving her alone to wonder at the bundle in her hands.

Never one to deny her curiosity, Storm laid the package on the bunk and knelt before it, her fingers swiftly working to untie the twine that bound it. Folding back the burlap, her mouth formed into a startled *Oh* of pleasure at the sight that met her eyes. Her face glowed with delight as she gazed down at a gown of sprigged muslin. In awe she touched the light and airy fabric the color of a robin's egg. It had been many years since she had owned a gown half as fine as this, and she savored the feel of the soft material, pushing away any thoughts of the man who had bestowed it upon her.

Getting to her feet, she felt her hands tremble slightly as she lifted the gown and held it against her. The design was exquisite. The heart-shaped neckline was trimmed in white lace and edged with sapphire velvet ribbon the same shade as her wonder-filled eyes. Tiny bows and silk flowers caught the hem up into a scalloped edge, while more lace peeped from beneath, giving the illusion of white frothy waves adorned by the glories of a spring garden.

The gown was a beautiful creation, but it was not the only surprise she found within the bundle. Beneath the folds of soft muslin lay a pair of soft blue kid slippers, white silk hose, and a sheer chemise edged with delicate lace, as were the petticoats that would make the gown flare bewitchingly. Ribbons to match those on the gown were also in the package, along with the most precious items of all, a tortoiseshell comb and mirror.

Needing no further invitation, she stripped off her old gown, leaving it in a gray, drab heap upon the floor as she quickly stepped into the tepid water. The nearly cool liquid soothed her irritated skin, relieving the severe rash that ridged her waist with angry red lines.

Storm scrubbed her body until it glowed, then dried herself with the rough towel before slipping on the batiste chemise. The airy fabric felt wonderful against her abused skin as she smoothed it down over her firm breasts before tying the pink satin ribbons on the bodice. Pulling the petticoats over her head, she wiggled into the fluffy, ruffled undergarments before settling down on the side of the bunk to pull the white silk hose smoothly on over her long, shapely legs.

After slipping on the kid slippers, she lifted the yards of muslin over her head, letting them fall in clouds of pale blue about her. She strained for several minutes in her effort to lace the gown but found she could not reach the tiny metal hooks at the back. She had forgotten the assistance it took to dress as a lady. The hard years had dimmed her memory of her friends at school helping one another to don their finery.

The thought served to dampen Storm's pleasure in her new clothing, for it also brought back the time she had had to sell the finery Alisa had bought her while at school, soon after Storm learned the true state in which her mother lived. The money had helped when Alisa was unable to find a man willing to part with a coin to quench his lust.

Forcing the ugly memories from her mind, Storm tried once more, unsuccessfully, to fasten her gown. It was no use. She would have to ask Tyler's assistance when he returned to escort her on deck. The thought of the poor man's reaction to such a request made a mischievous smile touch her lips. Tyler blushed when he had to speak to her, and she could imagine his freckled countenance turning an uncomfortable scarlet when he had to touch her in such an intimate manner. He'll probably have a seizure, she thought as she seated herself gingerly on the edge of the bunk so as not to wrinkle the fabric of her gown unduly.

Taking the mirror and comb in hand, she tried to bring some semblance of order to her locks. Since the wigmaker's shears had done their work, Storm's hair had grown back in its own style, with a natural tendency to curl in unruly ringlets about her head.

Making a moue of disgust at her reflection, she gave up the effort and tied a sapphire ribbon about her hair, making a tiny, pert bow just above her right temple. Regarding her image critically, she wrinkled her nose again in distaste. She did not realize the allure the provocative curls added to her features, accenting her cheekbones and drawing attention to her heavily fringed eyes and pink mouth.

With her toilette complete, Storm again found idle time upon her hands. The minutes ticked by at a snail's pace, and she was unable to stop her mind from turning to the expensive gifts from Thor. A blush suffused her cheeks at the thought of him choosing her intimate apparel. The thought disturbed her more than she would have liked to admit, for it brought back the memory of her last encounter with him and her own response.

The vivid mental picture caused a fluttery sensation in the pit of her belly. The man had the power to use her wayward body against her, and she knew she had to beware that she never let herself succumb to the needs of her flesh again.

Storm knew that in a short while she would see him, and she tried to brace herself for the meeting. She sought to rouse her anger but felt instead only mounting trepidation. It seemed to begin at the soles of her feet and spread in an ever-widening path, traveling the length of her body as she envisoned her future with the handsome sea captain.

Storm's stomach quivered, and her heart pounded violently against her ribs. She was treading on dangerous ground where Thor Wakefield was concerned. She could not put her feelings into words but only knew she had to avoid ever thinking he was different from the men she had known in the past. Intuitively she knew she had to keep up her defenses or she would find herself crushed beneath his overpowering masculinity.

Clasping her hands tightly in her lap, her palms damp from tension, she dropped her troubled gaze to the blue folds of her skirt as she muttered bitterly to the empty cabin, "Thor thinks I am nothing more than a whore." Her words reaffirmed the hatred of men that had grown within her during the past two years, and the pleasure she had found a short while earlier in her new garments died an abrupt death as she realized the circle was now complete. She was destined to follow in her mother's footsteps. The gown was not a gift from Thor; he would exact full recompense for it in his bed.

The acrid thought quelled the hollow feeling in Storm's stomach. Her eyes flashed with irritation as she suddenly realized that she had let fear make her into a cowering mass of quivering nerves. She might be far from confident about her future, but she'd be damned if Thor Wakefield ever knew how she felt. He was forcing her to travel the same road as her mother, but she would not do it meekly.

Her spine stiffened with sheer determination as she plucked up her courage and raised her chin mutinously in the air, ready to meet her future. Silently vowing to make Thor Wakefield rue the day he had forced his will upon her, Storm again spoke aloud. "Seven years, Captain Wakefield, and the day I am free, you will look upon it as a blessing."

She rose at the sound of the key in the lock. Expecting to see Tyler, she sought to find the right words to ease his embarrassment when she asked for his help with her gown. The attempt died, however, as the door swung wide to reveal the captain of the *Sea Siren.*

Storm tensed, her nails biting into the tender flesh of her palms as she watched him bend slightly to enter the cabin. She had tried to prepare herself for their meeting, but the sight of him made her courage desert her. As he crossed the short space that separated them, she was possessed with the urge to flee but forced the cowardly sensation away. She stood her ground and stared up at him, her face revealing none of her feelings.

Thor's sensual lips curled at the corners as his appreciative gaze swept over her from head to toe, taking in her beauty in the new finery. His body reacted instinctively to her allure. The muscles across his flat abdomen tightened as the unbidden thought of disrobing her came into his mind. The memory of her lying naked in his arms was still branded upon his brain—a vivid impression, one that he had been unable to rid from his thoughts since the night they had lain together.

During the past week it had taken all of his willpower to resist the urge to come to her. He had paced many miles around the deck of the *Sea Siren* as they sailed along the coast toward Charleston. The sea breeze had been strong on the clear star-studded nights, but it had done little to cool the heat in Thor's blood for the beautiful woman belowdecks.

It had been difficult to restrain himself, but he had wanted to give Storm time to accept the fact that she was to become his mistress. By the hostile expression on her face, Thor realized his patience had gained him nothing. Her determination to withstand him was clearly visible in her eyes. Thor's smile deepened as he regarded her. His own resolve was as strong or stronger than hers. Confident that she would soon come to understand that fact, he said, "I see you are ready to depart. I have ordered my carriage brought 'round so we will not have to travel to Misty Rose by horse. I thought it would be much more comfortable for you."

Storm fought to suppress the bubble of hysterical laughter that rose to her throat at his ironic statement. The man was mad. He wanted her to travel in comfort to his bed.

Ire sparkled in her eyes as she glared at him. "I would ask you to reconsider your plans, sir. Dressed as I am now, I'm sure you could regain the expense of my passage and clothing if you sold my papers. I am well educated, and that might be an added incentive to those interested in purchasing my bond."

A raven-colored curl fell over Thor's brow as he shook his head. "Storm, I have made my decision, and there is nothing you can say or do to change it."

Her face tightened with anger. "You would keep me, knowing that I loathe you?"

He chuckled. "Aye, that I would, Tempest. I do not ask for your affection, just your company in bed. If I wanted or needed love, I would seek out one of Charleston's scatterbrained beauties who would vow her undying adoration—at least until after the marriage ceremony was complete." Again he shook his head. "No, Storm, I prefer your physical charms."

Hoping against hope to find some further argument to sway him, Storm interjected, "But how will you explain my presence if you change your mind and decide to marry?"

The sound of his mirth filled the cabin. "Storm, I can assure you that you have nothing to worry about in that area. I have no plans to marry, now or in the future. There hasn't been a woman born who could change my mind about the state of matrimony. That is one encumbrance I can well do without. I've only met one woman whose unselfish behavior merited such an honor, and she is already married. There are few women like Miranda Ashfort, who devotes her life to her husband's welfare. So you see, Storm, that is a problem you do not have to concern yourself with."

Storm's stomach gave a sudden lurch at the mention of the woman who must be Lyle Ashfort's wife. Oddly, she found that she was most disturbed by the esteem Thor felt for Miranda Ashfort. Incensed by her own reaction, Storm drew in a deep breath to try to remain calm. It served only to bring to her nostrils the scent of Thor's masculine aroma, and with it came the vivid memory of the night spent in his arms. Shaken, she turned away, desperately seeking to hide the turmoil within her. The strange quivery feeling renewed itself beneath her rapidly pounding heart, and her throat was tight as she said, "Then if you propose to continue with this dastardly scheme, I can assure you your wish to have my body but not my love will be granted, because I shall hate you until my dying breath."

Thor chuckled at the sight of her smooth, bare back presented to his view. "Mistress, I would expect no less of you. Now come here and let me lace you up so we can be on our way. I have no objections to seeing your naked skin, but I'm afraid the ladies of Charleston will not appreciate your mode of fashion."

Chagrined, Storm glanced over her shoulder at him, her eyes sending a heated message. The movement made the sleeve slip off one shoulder, further goading her anger. Detesting the thought of Thor's assistance but knowing she had little recourse, she tilted her chin at a pugnacious angle and turned to let him act the lady's maid. Sensing his nearness as he closed the space between them, she could not stop her involuntary reaction to his touch. She jumped nervously as his warm fingers touched her skin, and she felt tiny tingles run along her spine, making gooseflesh form on her arms.

Amused, Thor chuckled near her ear, and his breath was hot against the back of her neck as he dropped a light kiss upon the sensitive skin before murmuring, "Ah, my little Tempest, our time together will be enjoyable, I think."

Forcing herself to contain the shiver that crept over her, Storm quickly placed as much distance between them as the small confines of the cabin would allow. She needed to regain some semblance of her composure, and his nearness did little to aid her. Swallowing back the tightness in her throat, she wet her suddenly dry lips as she looked at him. "I'm afraid you are mistaken, sir. There will be little joy between us. You may possess the papers that give you the right to do with me as you please, but I give you fair warning; I will do everything in my power to see you find little pleasure in this evil scheme."

In two short strides, Thor closed the space between them and captured her chin in his hand, tipping it up so he could gaze into her flashing eyes. "Tempest, if your words are meant to be the thrown gauntlet, then I accept the challenge. Your lovely lips speak one message, while the look in your eyes says another. Such pleasure as we found together is rare, Storm, and not easily forgotten. You are a passionate woman, and that will not be easy for you to deny. I am a man of much patience when it is merited, my Tempest, and I will wait. Time will see me the victor of this contest of wills."

Jerking away from his hand, Storm rubbed her chin as if to wipe away his touch. "Never! You can wait until hell freezes over, but it will do you no good."

A predatory look entered Thor's eyes, though his laughter was mildly pleasant as he took her arm to escort her on deck. "Storm, you have much to learn, and I am a very willing teacher."

The warm breeze ruffled the layers of lace on Storm's gown as she stood at Thor's side, awaiting their turn to depart the ship. Compared to her stifling cabin, the deck seemed cool, yet she took little notice of it. Her anger was in full bloom, heating her cheeks as she fumed silently over Thor's arrogance. His superior attitude exasperated her nearly beyond endurance. Like all men, he felt himself eminently superior to the women he bedded, assured that Storm was too weak to withstand his charms for long. His masculine vanity would never let him consider the idea that she would reject him. The thought added to her fury, and it was only with great restraint that she managed to control the urge to reach up and claw his handsome face into ribbons.

Her fingers curled unconsciously at her side as she glanced at him, only to find he seemed to have forgotten her existence as he concentrated on the activity on the docks. Following his gaze, she watched as the seamen tried to calm the horses that had traveled on the *Sea Siren* from England. Long of leg, with slender curving necks and small, wedge-shaped heads, the animals pranced nervously from side to side, unused to solid ground beneath their hooves after so long at sea. One sleek black mare reared on her hind legs and nearly trampled the sailor who struggled to restrain her. He fought to maintain his balance while trying to avoid the sharp hooves, backing closer and closer to the edge of the pier. With another step back the man would fall into the bay.

Seeing his crewman's difficulty, Thor released Storm's arm and rushed down the gangplank to give aid before the frightened animal could harm itself or the sailor.

Finding herself unguarded for the first time in months, Storm felt as if her prayers had suddenly been answered. While Thor's attention centered on quieting the mare, she saw her own chance at freedom. The instant the thought crossed her mind, her feet were already moving in the direction of the gangplank. Lifting the hem of her skirt, she sped down it and quickly ran in the opposite direction from the commotion on the docks.

Seeing several large buildings at the end of the street, Storm made for them. If she were fortunate, she would be able to hide in one of the alleys before her absence was noted. From that point she had no idea of what she would do or where she would go. At present all her thoughts were centered on evading Thor Wakefield.

The taste of success was already growing sweet as she neared the end of the ballast-cobbled street. Only a few feet more and she would reach her goal. Concentrating solely on gaining the shadowy alley across the way, Storm made a dash across the street, but her flight came to an abrupt halt as a shiny black carriage came careening to a stop before her, its wheels skidding as the horse reared from the rough treatment used by the driver as he pulled back on the reins. Shaken by her near accident, Storm turned wide, startled eyes toward the driver of the vehicle. She paled as she recognized Thor. Storm could nearly hear her hopes of freedom shattering about her on the cobblestones.

Thor's face was an angry mask as he stepped down from the carriage. His eyes were the color of a turbulent sky before lightning split the atmosphere, and his voice seemed to rumble like thunder from deep within his chest. "Storm, I told you I have patience when it's merited, but you have pushed me to the limit."

Never one to accept defeat meekly, her fear aiding her flight, Storm turned and began to run. She could hear the sound of Thor's boots as he gained on her but did not slacken her pace. Her last, desperate attempt to escape was brief. Thor's long legs soon shortened the distance between them, letting him capture her easily. Lifting her off her feet, Thor swung her up in his arms and strode back toward the carriage.

She pushed against his hard, rib-crushing hold, kicking and struggling. "Let me go!" she squealed in protest.

"Hold still, woman, or I'll turn you over my knee and give you a taste of what you deserve," Thor ground out as they came to the carriage. With little consideration to Storm's modesty, he tossed her onto the carriage seat as if she were a sack of potatoes, the action making her skirts fly up about her waist as she landed with a hard thump.

Gasping with indignation and embarrassment, she struggled upright and fought to cover her legs from view. "How dare you!" she spat as he casually climbed into the carriage and settled himself at her side.

A muscle twitched in Thor's clean-shaven jaw as he picked up the reins. His dark gray eyes settled on her, blazing with intensity as he said, "I'll have no more of your shenanigans, Storm. The law says I have the right to strip your fair back and beat you for your attempted escape. Don't tempt me further."

Fiery glints shimmered in her eyes as she glared back at him. "Then have me whipped now, for I will not stop trying to free myself of you until you sell my papers."

Thor's face settled into a grim mask as he abruptly slapped the reins down on the horse's back, startling the animal into action. His expression sent chills through Storm as he turned the carriage around and maneuvered it with ease through the crowded streets until he reached his destination, the slave market. Without a word, he stepped down and moved to assist Storm from the carriage.

Sensing that his intentions boded ill for her, she resisted until he grasped her wrist and jerked her forcibly from the vehicle in a less-than-gentlemanly fashion. She still did not give up the struggle as he began to pull her along behind him. She tried to dig her heels into the sandy soil to impede their progress through the maze of carriages and wagons in front of the large barnlike building, but his grip was too firm.

The dim interior of the building was crowded, but Thor pushed through the mass of people until they reached the front row of men clustered about a raised platform. Storm's eyes widened as she realized where he had brought her. Her nostrils flared as the offensive odor of human sweat reached her nose, but she paid little heed to it. All her attention centered on the cruel event taking place before her as the auctioneer went about his daily business.

She recoiled physically, but Thor jerked her back to his side, forcing her to view the auction block as a young black woman was led forward, the chains about her ankles rattling as she moved. Beads of perspiration broke out across Storm's brow as she watched and listened to the auctioneer point out the girl's better qualities. Vaguely Storm heard several questions directed to the man but did not comprehend their meaning until the auctioneer pulled up the baggy garment the girl wore to show she was unmarked by the lash or disease.

Storm cringed. The look of pain and humiliation she saw on the girl's young face as her nubile body was exposed to the ogling crowd twisted Storm's heart. With a start of fear, she realized that she had begged for the same horrible fate. The suffering reflected in the girl's onyx eyes could be hers if Thor chose to sell her at public auction. At the thought, the blood slowly drained from Storm's face as nausea churned her insides, rising in her throat to choke her.

Thor glanced down into her ashen face. The only color about her features was her wide, fright-filled eyes. Her expression tugged at his heart, and for one brief moment he regretted letting his anger coerce him into making Storm view such a degrading spectacle as the selling of human flesh.

Quickly reminding himself that she needed a lesson, he staunchly pushed the sympathetic thoughts from his mind. If the expression on her face was any indication, she would not soon forget the slave market. "Now, do you choose to go with me peacefully, or shall I render your papers to the auctioneer, Storm?"

Her eyes were the shade of violets as she looked up at him, the muscles in her throat working convulsively as she swallowed. She abhorred the words she had to speak, but the thought of being put on the block was even more horrible. "With you" was all that would pass her constricted throat.

Satisfied his cruel tactics had worked, Thor nodded and made way for them back through the crowd. A niggling guilt entered his mind, but he quickly suppressed it. He would not tell Storm that indentured servants were not sold in the same manner as the blacks of Africa. Their sale was conducted in a much more civilized, businesslike manner. The bond servants were not treated as animals like the negroes; during the transaction they were allowed to keep a small part of their dignity, while the blacks endured examinations as if they were prized stallions and brood mares. But to keep Storm in line, he would not divulge that bit of information.

As they stepped back into the afternoon sun, Storm gasped in the fresh air, trying desperately to forget the stench of the slave market. It was useless. She knew that for as long as she lived, she would always remember the smell of the place and misery it held.

As Thor helped her into the carriage, she glanced over her shoulder at the building. It seemed as if she could see the evil essence of the place seeping through the very cracks in the wooden walls. A shiver tingled up her spine, and she clasped her hands tightly in her lap to still the involuntary trembling that beset them.

She kept her eyes trained straight ahead as Thor slapped the reins, setting the carriage once more into motion. She did not note the beauty of the city as they passed along the cobbled streets lined with the magnificent two-storied townhouses that made Charleston the belle of the South. She cared little for the scenery; her mind could not eject the thought of the girl standing, head bowed in defeat, on the auction block. Storm remained silent, her stomach still quivering, as Thor drove through the city and onto the sandy road that ran along the winding Ashley River.

Tall live oaks adorned with gray-green spanish moss draped the roadway as they left Charleston behind. The trees' large rough-barked limbs gave a small reprieve from the hot summer's sun as the carriage sped along. Storm surreptitiously studied the chiseled profile of the man at her side. What type of man was Thor Wakefield? Arrogant and determined to have his own way and take his pleasure at her expense, she knew, but she had not judged him to be a cruel man. True, he was forcing her to become his mistress against her will, but he had never harmed her physically even when she resisted him. For that reason alone, she could not help but wonder if he really would have placed her in the same situation of the black girl. Without realizing she was speaking the words aloud until it was too late, she said, "Would you have put me on the block if I had said no?" She bit her wayward tongue, and her eyes widened with apprehension as he turned to look at her. The breath caught in her throat as he regarded her silently for a few minutes before reining in the horse to a more sedate pace.

"If you had preferred it," he finally replied. "But I assumed that after viewing what you seemed to want so desperately, you would change your mind."

Tiny furrows etched Storm's smooth brow as she considered his answer. Again he presumed to know her thoughts better than she did, and it enraged her to have to admit he had been right. A glint of anger flickered in her eyes. "You knew before you took me to that horrible place what my answer would be, didn't you? You only wanted to frighten me into submitting to you meekly. Well, you can go to hell, Thor Wakefield. I only agreed to come with you peacefully; I did not say I would welcome you to my bed."

Thor's eyes narrowed as he looked down into her angry face. "It was your decision to remain my bond servant, but I rule Misty Rose and you will do as I say." Giving a vicious snap to the reins, he urged the horse into a rapid trot.

Crossing her arms over her chest, Storm sat silently fuming, knowing she had little recourse but to go to Misty Rose as Thor's mistress. Glancing at him, she thought, However, that does not mean I will submit to your lust. He was physically stronger and he could force her to his will, but each time he took her he would know that she did not come to him willingly.

Thor's anger simmered just beneath the surface. The little witch had seen through his ruse within the first hour. Even after the experience at the slave market, she had not lost any of her stubborn hotheaded temperament. Where most would be cringing and begging him to take them to Misty Rose, grateful to share his bed, Storm Kingsley's attitude seemed to dare him to turn the carriage around and take her back to the auction block. Begrudgingly, he had to admire the quick-tempered vixen for seeing through his ploy to control her. He was beginning to realize that there might be something more than air beneath that unruly mop of curls.

The silence between them lengthened as the horse's hooves and carriage wheels made a sandy cloud behind the vehicle, layering the thick foliage along the roadway with dust. The shadowy tunnel of trees provided relief from the heat and sun, but there was a price to be paid for it. Mosquitoes buzzed about them, lighting upon Storm's exposed skin and drawing her mind away from her anger at Thor. The stinging bites soon had her concentrating on a different foe as she did battle with the vicious little insects that seemed intent upon devouring her.

She slapped them away from her face and neck but was not quick enough to stop one from biting her arm. She crushed the vile little creature beneath her hand as the carriage exited the cool tunnel of trees. Glancing at Thor to see how he fared, she saw one mosquito light upon the curve of his cheek. Her attention centered solely upon her war with the insects, she slapped his jaw without considering the consequences of her action.

Storm's fingers left their imprint upon Thor's skin, and it deepened in hue as he jerked the horse to a halt and turned to her, his eyes shooting sparks of fury. Used to the unpleasant aspects of living in the lowlands of South Carolina, Thor had paid little heed to the mosquitoes. His mind still lingered on their earlier conversation, and Storm's blow released the pent-up anger within him. In one swift motion, he gripped her by the wrist and pulled her violently against his hard chest, nearly knocking the breath from her as he gazed down into her frightened face.

She had not meant to strike him with such force and opened her mouth to apologize, but before she could utter the words, he ground out, his voice husky with suppressed rage, "Woman, never strike me again unless you want to be repaid in kind. I will stand many things, but I will not have man or woman raising a hand to me in anger."

Storm stared up at him, cringing from the pain inflicted by his fingers. It burned up her arms and made her gasp. She opened her mouth to speak, but her words were again cut off as his mouth descended over hers, his tongue plundering the soft cavern, cruelly tasting of its sweetness.

Thor had meant the kiss to punish her for striking him, but at the taste of her honeyed mouth, his anger faded. He had dreamed of her too many nights during the past week. The feel of her against him as he ravished her mouth inflamed his already acute senses. He could feel the heat of his desire as it settled in his groin and knew he could not mete out any punishment. All he wanted was to make love to Storm.

Sensing the change in his kiss, she began to struggle against him with fervor. She could not let herself succumb to him again. She had to resist with every ounce of willpower she possessed, or she would be lost. She fought desperately against the tiny fluttering sensation she could feel already beginning in the pit of her stomach from the touch of his lips upon hers.

She pushed against his chest but found herself imprisoned in his embrace. His lips left hers and traveled along her cheek to the slender column of her throat as he murmured, "Ah, my Tempest, you were accurately named. I hear the thunder of my desire pounding in my temples, and the merest touch of your skin is like lightning in my blood, sending sparks to fire my flesh into an inferno of need to possess you."

He nibbled at the sensitive skin of her neck, then with a voice husky with emotion he said, "I want you, Storm."

Before her dazed mind could clear, he released her and stepped down from the carriage. In one fluid motion, he lifted her in his arms and strode from the roadway, down toward the shining river. Storm's muslin skirts swept the top of the thick lush grass as he carried her to a moss-covered bower beneath a large live oak. The breeze from the river kept the insects at bay as he laid her gently upon the primeval bed, his fingers losing her gown as his lips once more possessed her.

Storm fought against her own feelings as well as Thor, pressing her palms against his wide chest, trying to free herself from the kiss that was bringing back too many pleasurable memories. She wanted to deny the hunger that began to spread from the junction of her legs up through her belly, where it quivered with a life of its own, refusing to be rejected by her mind. The touch of his warm hand upon her breast as her gown came loose only intensified the yearnings until, with a moan of protest at her own weakness, she felt her arms creep up about his neck, drawing him near.

Feeling her resistance ebb, Thor began a leisurely assault upon her senses. His hands roamed over her, stripping away her garments as well as his own while his lips sent a trail of fire careening along every nerve in her heated body.

The glade was cool, yet Storm felt herself consumed by the fiery touch of his mouth as it closed over a hard, round nipple, suckling it before moving to the other rosy peak to further arouse her. His hand played a sensuous game along her flat belly, kneading the silken flesh before enticingly moving to her hip and along her thighs. Rubbing slowly in small circles, he caressed the sensitive skin before making his way slowly to the jewel hidden beneath the forest of silk. Feeling the invitingly moist warmth there, he could no longer contain his own desire to possess her. He had dreamed of it too often in the past week. Moving over her, his hot mouth recapturing her lips, he thrust himself deeply within her, savoring the feel of her satiny warmth about his quivering manhood.

Wanting to prolong their ecstasy for as long as possible so he could carry them both to the peak of fulfillment, Thor moved with long, slow strokes. He watched Storm's expression as she abandoned herself to passion. Her thick lashes cast feathery shadows upon her flushed cheeks as her lips curled with the pleasure coursing through her entire being.

Thor's bronzed hands contrasted vividly with her white breasts as he stroked the rose-tipped globes, inflaming her senses all the more. Her back arched to receive all of him, her legs coming up about his waist as she clung to his bare shoulders, her fingers biting into his sinewy flesh, urging him onward toward the rapids of swirling, searing passion. A small cry escaped her lips as they tumbled over the brink into ecstasy together.

Tenderness welled within Thor as he moved to Storm's side and kissed away the beads of perspiration that formed on her brow. He cradled her gently in his arms as if he feared she would break like fragile china. Burying his face in her curls, he savored their silken texture as he inhaled deeply of her sweet, heady female scent. He felt content, and knew she satisfied him more than any woman he had ever bedded. He opened his mouth to tell her of his feelings, but his words went unspoken as she stiffened in his arms and then jerked abruptly away from him.

Within moments Storm had managed to slip back into her clothing and stood glaring down at Thor in all his naked glory, her eyes full of accusation as she braced her hands on her hips and spat venomously, "You have now received your payment for the gown you bought me." Her lips trembled and a suspicious brightness shimmered in her eyes as she turned and ran back to the carriage.

Storm's chest felt heavy and tight as she clambered back into the vehicle. Impotent fury boiled within her at her shameless behavior. She had again fallen prey to her emotions and had let Thor make love to her. Not *love*, she thought bitterly; he used me.

Hot tears of remorse burned the backs of her eyelids, but she refused to give way to them. It was much too late to cry. Today had confirmed her worst fears. Thor Wakefield was her weakness, one she found she could not fight against. He possessed the magnetic masculine appeal that assaulted her senses and made her forget her resolves no matter how firmly she vowed to withstand him. For that reason Storm could not forgive herself or him.

The carriage swayed under Thor's weight as he climbed in and settled himself at her side. He picked up the reins, his fingers fiddling absently with the leather as he turned to Storm, who sat silent and withdrawn. He studied her set face, trying to understand her reaction to him.

She seemed to have erected an invisible fortress about herself, and no matter how hard he tried, he could not make a dent in the barrier. He knew he could arouse her passion, making her body betray her mind, but as soon as the glow of desire faded, she turned cold and hostile.

Storm was as complex and unfathomable as the sea, her moods changeable, like the currents. After each encounter with the beautiful woman, Thor was never exactly sure how to navigate the turbulence that followed. Where most women cooed and cuddled after making love, she became a spitting cat, lashing out as if rejecting the very image of the previous moments from her mind.

Her reaction left Thor feeling as if he stood on emotional quicksand, never sure of his own footing. That uncertainty annoyed him. He was a man who had always kept his life and emotions under control until he met Storm Kingsley. Since he had come of age, he had experienced few rejections where women were concerned. His wealth and appearance had assured that. Storm's response puzzled him and pricked his vanity.

Damn, he thought as he gazed at her face. It revealed none of the emotions she was experiencing. She stared straight ahead, refusing to look at him. Does she have no heart? he wondered.

Exasperated for letting her have such an unsettling effect upon him, he said with a voice tinged with anger, "Turn 'round and let me lace you. I'll not have you appear as if you'd just come from a brothel on your entrance to Misty Rose."

Storm swung sharply about to face him, her eyes glittering with rancor. "I cannot see what difference my appearance should make. Everyone will soon know you are forcing me to be your harlot."

Thor's face darkened with his mood. He reached out and jerked her about before roughly lacing up her gown. His fingers bit into her shoulders as he turned her to face him once more. His eyes held her transfixed as he said, "I gave you a choice, Storm. You knew what I expected from our relationship when you chose to come with me. I can see no reason why anyone has to know about what takes place between us unless you tell them. You will be introduced at Misty Rose as my new housekeeper, but I'll leave the decision up to you as to whether or not to reveal the truth of our relationship. And I will stand no more of your sharp tongue and vixenish ways."

Storm's eyes never wavered from his as she spat,

"You have never given me a choice. You've forced me to come with you from the beginning. First you used my mother's Bible to coerce me into obeying your dictates, and then you showed me the slave market, knowing all along what my decision would be once I saw it. Now you leave it up to me to tell the world I am your whore. I do not call that a free choice, Thor."

Rigid with anger, he said, "Remember this, Storm: I still possess your mother's Bible, and at any time I can take you back to the slave market. I was not responsible for your deportation, but I do hold your papers now. I'll not sanction any more of your disobedience, Storm. At Misty Rose I insist you be on your best behavior. Is that understood?"

Stubbornly Storm turned her face away, refusing to answer.

Thor fought the urge to shake her until her teeth rattled. Releasing her before he gave in to it, he picked up the reins and slapped them sharply against the horse's back. "You will be treated in the manner that befits your own actions, Storm. My household runs smoothly, as does the rest of Misty Rose. I will not have the peace of my home disrupted by a tempestuous woman who does not think before she acts. If you remember all I have said, you will find Misty Rose a pleasant place to live. Much better, I assure you, than you would have found on the streets of London peddling your body to one and all."

Fury burst within Storm like an explosion of fireworks. She opened her mouth to refute his last remark and to let him know once and for all that she had been decently reared and would never have followed in her mother's footsteps no matter what the circumstances. But reason intervened, and she stubbornly clamped her mouth tightly shut, biting the inside of her lip to keep the words in check. Silently fuming, she mused, What does it matter about the truth of my past? It would change nothing now even if he believed me.

Considering that Thor might also learn of her connection with his neighbor Lyle Ashfort, Storm quickly decided it was best to let him think what he pleased and be damned. She had to keep her secret until she was able to fulfill her vendetta. After that it would not matter what Thor knew of her past.

Growing aware of Storm's continued silence, Thor glanced uneasily at her, receiving a view of her delicate profile, her chin tilted in the air. Suspecting things would not go as smoothly at Misty Rose as he had dictated, he thought, If I had any sense I would turn the carriage around, head back to Charleston as fast as the horse can travel, and sell her papers to the first person to make an offer. But, damn it, I still want her.

Thor knew he was acting the fool, but he also knew Storm Kingsley was in his blood and he could not rid himself of her until he managed to rid himself of his desire for her.

The gates of Misty Rose lay only a short distance ahead, and he urged the horse to a faster pace, eager to be home after so many months away. There would be much to do in the next few weeks. He would have to settle his shipping business in Charleston, turning the *Sea Siren* over to another qualified man to captain, and then he had to see to the rice harvest. If he was fortunate, he would have Storm out of his system by the time things settled down, and then he could think rationally about what to do with her without being distracted by the heat in his loins.

Chapter 6

Climbing roses nearly obscured the tall mortar pillars crowned with intricately carved stone lions that stood guard at the entrance to Misty Rose. Storm caught only a fleeting glimpse of the lions' fierce countenances as the carriage passed through the gates and onto the crushed-shell drive. Like a white ribbon on green velvet, it wound with serpentine grace for a quarter of a mile through the manicured grounds to the two-storied mansion that sat magnificently upon the highest point of Misty Rose overlooking the Ashley River and the rice fields that had made the plantation rich.

Storm's anger at Thor faded as she stared about her new surroundings with eyes wide with wonder. She was immediately captivated by the beauty of Misty Rose. The sight and smell of Thor's home assaulted her senses as they sped along the winding drive lined with profusely blooming rosebushes. Their sweet musky scent permeated the warm afternoon air, their velvet blossoms creating a rainbow of color along the carriage path from the palest pink to the deepest scarlet. It was intoxicating and entrancing to Storm's young soul, starved for beauty after the years spent in the dismal, poverty-ridden section of London.

Her face was transparent, revealing her feelings as Thor reined the horse to a halt before the stately mansion fronted by a spacious veranda, its roof supported by six grecian columns. She had seen elegant houses in England but nothing to compare with the simple grace of Misty Rose.

Her gaze swept over the exterior of the house from the shingled roof painted gray to resemble slate, since the stone was a rare commodity so near the ocean, to the high-backed rockers made of latticed cane and fine southern pine, resting upon the bluish-gray cypress boards of the veranda.

Her eyes lingered on the half balcony that spanned the length of the manor, and she took note of the rails made of rod-iron intricately designed to resemble climbing roses. Stained-glass panels echoing the rose design accented the set of double doors that opened onto the balcony and veranda. Thor's home had been accurately named; it was dominated by roses.

A husky male voice drew Storm's attention away from the manor, and she looked to see a tall sandy-haired man striding toward the carriage. Until that moment she had been so engrossed with the beauty of Misty Rose that she'd been totally unaware of his presence. She watched as a slow smile spread his full lips and he said, "Thor, welcome home. It is about time you came back." The man's cinnamon-colored eyes swept over the occupants of the carriage, briefly lingering on Storm as Thor laughed and stepped down.

"It's good to be home, Matthew." The two men clasped hands in fond greeting. "How has everything been going?" Thor asked.

Matthew grinned wryly as he cast another quizzical glance at Storm. "Everything has been fine at Misty Rose, but I'm not sure about AshGlen." Digging into his pocket, he withdrew an envelope and handed it to Thor. "This came a short while ago."

At the mention of AshGlen, Storm tensed, and her eyes never wavered from the letter as Thor tore it open and perused it briefly before placing it in his pocket. His face clouded and the affable smile faded as he looked at Matthew. "Miranda wants me to come to AshGlen as soon as possible. Lyle's anxious to hear about the horses."

Suddenly aware of Storm's steady gaze, Thor glanced at her and realized she presented another problem. He needed to see her settled, but he also had to go to AshGlen. Miranda's note sounded urgent.

At the present moment he was too uncertain of Storm's intentions to like the idea of leaving her in Matthew's charge. If she took the idea into her cunning little mind, the vixen could have his overseer wrapped about her little finger and be on her way back to Charleston before he reached AshGlen.

Pondering his dilemma, Thor released a long breath and knew he had little recourse in the matter. If Storm was to live here under the guise of his housekeeper, he could not ask Matthew to guard her to ensure she remained at Misty Rose. Finding himself caught in his own tangled web, Thor could only hope she would heed his earlier warning and behave. Extending his hand to assist her from the carriage, he said, "Matthew, this is Storm Kingsley, my new housekeeper. Storm, my overseer, Matthew Boone. I'd appreciate it, Matthew, if you would show Storm to the Petite Maison and see her settled. I have to go to AshGlen. From the tone of Miranda's letter, Lyle is upset, and she's worried about his health."

A sandy lock of hair fell over Matthew's brow as he gave Storm a courteous nod and said, "It's a pleasure to have you at Misty Rose, mistress." His eyes sparkled with devilment as he glanced at Thor. "When you said you were going to get another housekeeper to take Spinster

Murdock's place, I never dreamed you'd find someone so lovely, Thor. You go attend to your business and, as usual, I'll stay here and take care of your dirty work." Matthew gave Storm a charming grin. "With pleasure," he added and winked flirtatiously.

The rose in her cheeks deepened in hue as she blushed at Matthew's compliment and extended her hand graciously. "Thank you, Mr. Boone."

Matthew's large hand swallowed hers and held it longer than necessary. "It's Matthew to my friends, and I'm sure we'll become friends while you are at Misty Rose."

Thor missed none of this exchange. His guts twisted with something akin to jealousy as he looked sharply at Matthew. Thor didn't like his overseer's tone or Storm's friendly response. She had never bestowed such warmth upon him. Matthew Boone could charm the devil himself when he set his mind to it, and few could resist his boyish grin. Noting the look in his eyes, Thor knew Matthew had decided to do so with Storm.

Thor knew his overseer too well. Matthew was more like a brother to him than an employee. Over the past ten years they had worked closely together, and a deep bond had grown between them. They had shared defeats and triumphs and often the same women, when after a long day's work they had gone to Charleston to visit the whores on the waterfront. Matthew was a loyal friend, and Thor would gladly have given him anything he desired, with one exception—Storm.

Vexed at the ease with which Matthew could gain a smile from her, Thor said in a voice that was tinged with annoyance, "Mistress, I expect that you'll find that the Petite Maison is to your liking and you will be there when I return. Now, if you'll excuse me." He flashed her a look of warning before he strode toward the stables.

Mystified at Thor's abrupt manner, for he had never heard his friend use such a tone with a lady before,

Matthew furrowed his brow as he watched Thor disappear from sight. Unable to solve the puzzle, Matthew looked down at the young woman at his side to find that her brow also wore a perplexed frown. Sensing some unspoken message had been transmitted between Thor and his house-keeper, Matthew mentally shrugged. He might not under-stand it, but it was none of his affair. Extending his arm gallantly to Storm, he said, "Well, mistress, it looks as if I will have the honor of showing you your new home."

A winsome smile tugged at the corners of her mouth as she visibly relaxed under his congenial manner. "Thank you, Matthew, but if you will only tell me where I might find the Petite Maison, as Captain Wakefield called it, I'll not impose upon you further."

Matthew's crooked grin returned as he took her hand and placed it on his arm. Patting it reassuringly, he said, "It's no imposition on me to aid a lovely lady. Come and I'll show you where your new home is located. It's at the end of the gardens, slightly away from the main house."

As Matthew led her along the flag-stone path that curved through the rose garden, Storm felt as if a heavy burden had been lifted from her shoulders. Glancing up at the large manor house as they passed, she was grateful for the small favor granted her; at least she would not be living under the same roof as Thor Wakefield.

Matthew paused some distance away from a small white-framed house resting in the shade of several tall oaks. With a flourish, he waved his hand toward the Petite Maison and said, "Mistress, your home."

While Storm had found the main house of Misty Rose entrancing in its elegance, she now found the Petite Maison, small house, equally enchanting. Compared to Thor's home, it looked like a tiny dollhouse, but its size did not matter. To her it was perfection.

A sweet scent that she did not recognize reached her nostrils as they stepped upon the porch. She inhaled deeply, savoring the delicate aroma. Noting her reaction, Matthew picked a twig covered with tiny star-shaped yellow flowers from the green vine that entwined the pillars of the porch. Handing it to her, he said, "It's jasmine. Thor loves roses, but I prefer the heady fragrance of this small plant. It grows wild here in South Carolina."

Holding it to her nose, Storm sniffed the sultry odor and nodded. "I think I agree. It's lovely, as is the Petite Maison."

Matthew's gaze swept thoughtfully over the exterior of the house before he opened the door for her to enter. "Aye, I've always preferred this house to that grand monster Thor built once he could afford it. This is where he was born. After building the main house, he considered tearing this one down, but I argued him out of it. I told him he could always use it as a guesthouse, but after Spinster Murdock came to Misty Rose, it became the housekeeper's residence."

Matthew chuckled at the memory. "Spinster Murdock refused to reside under the same roof as an ummarried man. Poor woman. She didn't realize she had nothing to worry about. She was at least fifty years old and as thin as a sapling pine." Shaking his head, Matthew grinned. "Now, if she had looked half as lovely as you, then I could have understood her reasons."

Blushing again, Storm turned to look about her new home. A smile of pleasure touched her lips at the sight of the polished pine floors and mahogany furnishings. The Petite Maison was not richly decorated but was pleasingly comfortable. It lacked grandeur, but that simplicity agreed with her. She could feel at home here.

The thought caused her a pang of sadness. Petite Maison possessed an unpretentious charm, a sense of tranquility to soothe the troubled mind. Storm knew that was not to be. Her relationship with Thor and her vendetta against Lyle

Ashfort would destroy any peace she might find at Petite Maison.

Her face clouded as an inexplicable longing welled deep within her. She couldn't understand her sudden melancholy in such pleasant surroundings, but she felt like bursting into tears. Her eyes burned with her need to cry for something she had lost or had not gained. At the moment she did not know which.

Matthew Boone was a large man; his strong muscular physique reflected the years of hard labor he had endured. Yet he was possessed of a tender heart and could easily sense pain in others. His sensitive nature had been the reason for his long friendship with Thor. He understood Thor's drive to succeed and the pain his friend still kept locked within him. In the same manner, he now read Storm's expression and instinctively sensed her need to be alone to sort out the things that troubled her.

Matthew's heart urged him to take the small woman into his arms and comfort her, but he suppressed the impulse. Storm Kingsley was battling demons within herself, and until she turned to him, he knew he could not help her. Someday when their friendship had grown, the time would come, but not now. He would have to gain her trust first.

"Mistress, I'll leave you now to rest and get acquainted with your new home. I'll stop by the kitchen and tell Mamie to have your evening meal sent over on a tray so you won't have to be disturbed."

Touched by his kindness, Storm could not suppress the slight tremble of her lips as she said, "Thank you, Matthew. I would appreciate that. The drive out from Charleston was quite wearying." She did not add that it was not the journey that had exhausted her but the emotional strain from all that had transpired since she had left the *Sea Siren*.

Noting her tremulous lips, Matthew knew there was much left unsaid and nodded his understanding before touching his brow with the tips of his fingers giving her a jaunty salute. "Rest well, mistress."

As he turned to the door, his hand already on the latch, she said, "If we are to be friends, Matthew, you must call me Storm."

He glanced back over his shoulder and a pleased grin curved his lips. "Rest well, Storm." The foundation of their friendship had been laid.

Storm released a long, tired sigh as the door closed behind Misty Rose's overseer. Her muscles ached from head to toe. Stifling a yawn behind her hand, she turned to the narrow hall that led to the two bedchambers of the Petite Maison.

She inspected both with a careful eye and chose the larger of the two rooms. It was spacious, and after the months in her tiny cabin on board the *Sea Siren* she welcomed the feeling of freedom the austere chamber gave her. The room contained only a dressing table and large cherry-wood tester that was draped in white mosquito netting and a lace counterpane. The simplicity was refreshing.

Giving in to another yawn, she kicked off her slippers and pulled back the counterpane. She tried unsuccessfully to unlace her gown before giving a shrug. Climbing into the bed fully dressed, she sank down in the soft mattress. Her head no more than touched the pillow before sleep claimed her.

A featherlight touch upon her lips roused Storm from her sound slumber. Her thick lashes fluttered open in the dark room. Disoriented, she lay still, trying to clear the hazy clouds of sleep from her mind.

Drowsily she recognized the heady scent of brandy and tobacco and inhaled deeply of the masculine aroma as she turned her head in the direction from which it came. She managed to control her start of surprise as she saw Thor sitting on the side of the bed, a dark silhouette against the moonlight that filtered in through the window.

The shadows obscured his features, but Storm sensed his silent regard upon her. A tingly sensation crept up her spine, making her shiver in the cool night air. Moistening her suddenly dry lips, she asked, "How long have you been here?" Her voice quavered with uncertainty.

His hand came up to trace gently the curve of her cheek as he said, "Long enough."

As if his touch burned her, she jerked away and pushed herself upright as she ordered, "Get out of my room or I'll scream."

Ignoring her command, Thor chuckled, pulling off his boots and settling himself more firmly on the bed. Leaning back against the pillows with hand braced behind his head, he said, "Scream all you like, Tempest. There is no one at Misty Rose to come to your rescue. You forget I am master here."

Storm moved to the edge of the bed, ready to flee if necessary. "I think you forget about Matthew Boone. He doesn't seem like the type of man who would approve of your method of seduction."

At the mention of his friend, the muscles contracted across Thor's flat belly. Against his will he felt the green-eyed monster raise its head for the first time in his life. A muscle twitched in his jaw, and he reacted before she could utter a protest. His arms snaked out and captured her in one swift movement, and he pinned her beneath him. He seized her raven head between his hands, his fingers playing through the silken strands as he cupped her face in his palms. His voice was icy and filled with contempt as he said, "Scream now all you like and bring Matthew to your rescue. But do you think he'd be so interested in protecting your virtue if he learned where you came from and how you came to be at Misty Rose? I doubt it seriously. More than likely, he would offer me a few coins to share your bed. We've often shared the same women in the past. How would you like that, Storm?''

She recoiled as if he had struck her. Tears brimmed in her eyes, and she blinked rapidly to stem their flow. She was grateful for the darkness that hid her misery from Thor; seeing it would give him too much pleasure. Anger welled within her at herself for letting him have the power to hurt her, and she struggled valiantly to keep her voice steady as she spat, ''I hate you, Thor, you son of a she dog.''

His fingers pressed more tightly about her skull as if he would crush it. ''True, that I am, Tempest, but I would think you'd know the correct word to use. If you don't, let me refresh your memory, Storm. It is bitch. My mother certainly was one, but that does not concern you. As for your feelings toward me, you know my reply. You can hate me all you like, but do not attempt to refuse me your bed. I'll not stand for it.''

''You bastard,'' she shouted as she began to struggle in earnest. She beat at his chest and shoulders with her fist and would have clawed his face had he not moved quickly to avoid it. Capturing her hands within his own, he jerked them over her head, ordering, ''Hold still, woman, or I'll give you a taste of your own medicine. I did not come here to fight with you. In fact, I did not even come here to make love to you, but if you keep squirming beneath me, I'm afraid I'll not be responsible for my actions.''

Storm froze instantly, his words dampening her spirit for battle. Guardedly she looked up into his shadowy features. ''Then why did you come?''

Releasing her hands, Thor eased his weight from her and propped himself up on one elbow, his chin resting on his fist as he gazed down into her wary eyes. They caught and reflected the moonlight, reminding him of a blue velvet sky studded with stars. He felt the heat rise in his loins but strove to quench it. He had several items he wanted to discuss with her and knew he would be unable to do so if he gave way to the urgings of his body.

Clearing his throat, he said, "I was concerned that you had not heeded my warning and had run off. When the servants told me they could not rouse you when they came earlier with your meal, I thought it best to ascertain your whereabouts."

Storm absently rubbed her wrists where the prints of his fingers were still visible. "Then you have no reason to stay. As you so crudely put it, I have not 'run off.' I was resting until you disturbed me."

A wry grin tugged the corners of Thor's mouth upward. "I had already guessed as much, but I'm not inclined to leave so quickly. There are several more things I have to say to you." Running his fingers through his hair, he sat up and swung his long legs off the bed. His bare feet made no sound as he crossed to the window. Folding his arms over his chest, he braced himself against the windowframe and stared thoughtfully out over the silvered gardens of Misty Rose. After several long moments, he turned his head back to look at Storm, his sensual lips pursing. "Since this afternoon, I have been considering your position at Misty Rose."

Storm pushed herself upright, her eyes bright with expectancy as hope rose from the ashes of despair. The breath caught in her throat as she waited anxiously, praying he would grant her desire and free her from being his mistress. She learned at his next words how easily the walls of air castles crumble with the shifting of the wind.

"Storm, you are now established at Misty Rose as my housekeeper, but that will not change our relationship. It will continue as before. However, this afternoon has reminded me of certain proprieties that I had forgotten while at sea.

"At times you will be required to act as my hostess, and due to the sensibilities of my female guests, if they knew of your past, they would never accept you. If you agree, I see no reason for anyone to learn of your indenture. When it is served out, you will have a chance to make a better life for yourself than the one you had in England.''

As if jolted from the bed by lightning, Storm came to her feet. Her chest rose and fell rapidly as she braced her hands on her hips and spat, her voice laced with venom, ''You cold, unfeeling bastard. Thor Wakefield, you can go to hell if the devil will take someone as despicable as you. You want me to agree to be your whore at night and then pretend to be a chaste housekeeper during the day so as not to sully some scatterbrained twit who is fool enough to set her cap for you.'' Storm's eyes misted with tears and her voice began to tremble. ''I hate you.''

In two short strides, Thor closed the space between them, his hands capturing her shoulders and jerking her against his hard body. His eyes smoldered like molten lead. ''Damn it, Storm. You will do as I say. I've tried to consider your future in this matter, but you don't have enough sense to see it for yourself.''

She glared up at him, her eyes glistening like sapphires in the moonlight. ''Consider my future? You have thought of nothing beyond your own pleasure and your reputation. You care nothing about how I feel.'' Her voice broke and she gulped in several deep breaths, but she could not go on. With head bowed, she let her tears flow unheeded down her cheeks.

Thor felt the hot droplets on his arm, and his anger was dampened by her misery. Instinctively, his arms came about her, cradling her close to his heart as he tried to soothe the pain he had caused. He had not meant to hurt her. He had been contemplating her future and in truth had thought to give her something to look forward to. When her indenture was served, she could find another position or a good man who would never know of her past indiscretions and love her for herself. A man like Matthew Boone.

The thought constricted Thor's chest, and his arms tightened about Storm. He was not willing to give her up at present.

His body responded to the feeling of her soft form pressed against him. He clenched his teeth and pressed his eyes tightly closed, trying to stem the urgent need that swept over him. The sweltering heat of his desire settled in his loins, making them throb painfully. God, how I want her, he thought, but he was determined not to take her. He had caused her enough misery for one night. He had to get away from her before his willpower burst into flaming cinders.

Tipping up her chin, he meant to tell her he would leave, but the words went unspoken as he gazed down into her shining eyes. Within their depths, he saw a need to equal his own. Her tears had drained away her defenses, leaving her vulnerable to her emotions.

The brimming ponds of her soul reflected not only physical desire but a much deeper need that neither she nor Thor would admit as he lowered his head and murmured, "I want you, Tempest." Then his lips captured hers.

Together, they set out on a sensual quest, exploring, seeking fulfillment. They sailed the torrid seas and scaled the peaks of passion until, joined, Thor and Storm found the golden chalice of ecstasy. They drank deeply of its loving nectar, savoring each exquisite moment of heady rapture. Returning from their blissful voyage, they lay with limbs entwined and bodies glistening as they drifted into a peaceful slumber.

Chapter 7

Storm awoke to find herself bathed in the golden rays of the morning sun. Her body moved with feline grace as she stretched her arms lazily over her head, a smile of contentment playing about her delicate lips. Her mind was still languid with sleep as she turned on her side to find herself staring into Thor's silver eyes. Shocked, she sat upright. Suddenly aware of her nudity, she gasped and jerked the sheet up to cover her nakedness.

Thor's laughter broke the stillness of the morning as he raised up on one elbow, totally relaxed and unconscious of his own naked body. His eyes twinkled with mirth as he saw her gaze travel the length of his lithe form before her cheeks flushed crimson with embarrassment. Enjoying her discomfort, he said, "Good morning, Tempest. How did you sleep?"

Storm kept her eyes focused on the distant wall as she struggled to compose herself enough to speak. Her distress mounted by the moment as the memory of the previous night returned to haunt her in the light of day. Her knuckles were white as she clenched the sheet to her breast, and her mouth grew dry with remorse.

Again she had let her body betray her. Feeling sick at her own shameless behavior, she swallowed back the bile that rose in her throat. She wet her parched lips with the tip of her tongue, and her tone reflected the despondency she felt as she answered truthfully, "I slept well."

As she spoke, she realized that it had been the first night in months when her sleep had not been disturbed by terrible dreams of Alisa's death. That in itself added to Storm's guilt. She had succumbed to her passion while she should have been concentrating on repaying the debt she owed her mother. Galled by her own weakness, she pursed her lips, bitter against both Thor and herself. He aroused her senses until nothing else mattered except the pleasure she found in his arms.

Wondering at Storm's capricious nature, Thor eyed her curiously as he sat up and combed back his tousled hair with his fingers. God, she is an enigma, he thought, vexed at his own inability to understand her. Finding his britches crumpled with the bed linens, he pulled them on and shrugged into his shirt. He paused at the foot of the bed, silently regarding her. He sensed her dejection but could not comprehend the reason behind it. Their encounter had been a beautiful interlude, and it annoyed him to think she had not found the same pleasure with him that he had experienced with her.

His insides coiled into tight knots at the thought. He wanted Storm; he wanted all of her, not only her body; not just when he aroused her passions until they overcame her mind. He wanted to destroy the barriers she had erected about herself so he could possess her totally.

His pride and fear would not let him voice his feelings to Storm. He knew if he spoke of his emotions, he would leave himself defenseless and she could destroy him. He had survived one rejection by a woman he loved and was determined never to open himself up to such pain again.

A derisive smile curled his lips, but his ridicule was directed at himself for even thinking of the word *love*. No, it was not love he felt for Storm, he staunchly told himself, but passion for the challenge she represented.

Glancing at the window, he wondered what had happened to the pleasant day. The sun still spilled into the room in all its bright glory; however, to his mind it seemed to have dimmed. The golden glow that had filled him upon awakening with Storm had faded until it was no more than a shadow.

Looking back at her sitting with head bowed and shoulders hunched, he said, "Storm, have you considered what we spoke of last night regarding your responsibilities as my housekeeper? If you do as I ask, then you have a chance of living a decent life in the future."

She did not answer. Bending, he took her chin in his hand, his eyes the color of flint as he stared down into her pale face. "I would have your answer."

Storm's eyes burned with the need to cry, but she managed to control the threatening tears as she returned his gaze. Ruefully she acknowledged that she had little choice in the matter. Thor might ask for her decision, but he had already made up his mind, and she would have to accept it. Storm had to force the words past her lips. "I will behave as you ask."

Relieved that she had come to her senses at last, Thor smiled. "I'm glad to hear it. Though you do not like it, you will see someday that I was right and perhaps thank me."

His superior attitude rekindled some of Storm's spirit. Fiery glints sparkled in her eyes as she jerked away from his hand. "I'll never thank you, Thor Wakefield. I'll not offend the delicate sensibilities of your friends by letting them know your whore is serving them, but it's not because of your offer to see me respectably placed after my indenture is served. It's because I wouldn't want anyone to know that someone as detestable as you has touched me.''

Thor's face clouded. ''Don't you think it's time to pull in your claws and dress so you can begin your duties as the housekeeper of Misty Rose?''

Taking note of the fury on her face, he decided it was also time for him to make his exit. Many more words between them would only lead to another fight, and he was in no mood to put up with her vixenish temper, because he felt hard put to control his own.

''I have to ride out to the fields this morning,'' he said. ''I'll tell Mamie to show you about my home and see that you are acquainted with what is required of your services beyond this room. Good day, mistress.''

Fuming, Storm clambered from the bed when she heard the front door shut loudly behind him. Muttering curses upon his head, she jerked on her undergarments and did likewise with the muslin gown, caring little about the open back that she could not lace. Running a comb through her short curls, she wrinkled her nose at her reflection and stamped from the Petite Maison, slamming each door behind her. She knew her actions were childish, but the sound of the door banging against its frame helped alleviate some of her ill humor.

By the time she reached the rear entrance to Thor's home, she had managed to conquer her bout of temper. Pausing at the door, she drew in a deep breath and stiffened her spine. If she was going to be Thor's housekeeper in actual fact, she was determined to do the job well.

She didn't like to admit that he was right, but she was honest enough to recognize the truth of his words about her future on one account. She would need some kind of trade to survive once her indenture was served out. However, she would rather have the tongue severed from her mouth than concede the fact to that arrogant man.

Grasping the brass knob, she opened the door and stepped into the manor. With her thoughts centered on Thor and her new role as housekeeper, she failed to see Matthew Boone nearby, in the shade of a large willow.

Matthew's sandy brows lowered, shadowing his brown eyes as a frown made a deep path across his forehead. A muscle twitched beneath his right eye as he stared at the vacant space where Storm had stood only a moment before. He had been standing beneath the willow for more than an hour, feeling as if a great beast chewed on his insides, leaving him raw and bleeding from what he had learned. He had been on his way to see Storm when Thor had left the Petite Maison, buttoning his shirt and tucking it into his britches before he strode toward the kitchens.

In that instant, Matthew understood Storm's tormenting demon. It was his friend Thor Wakefield. Thor had made Storm Kingsley his mistress, and from the expression Matthew had seen on her face the previous afternoon, it was not exactly to her liking.

Pondering his new knowledge, Matthew scratched his head in bewilderment. It was not like Thor to force a woman to his bed. The pieces of the puzzle did not quite fit together. Something wasn't right here, and Matthew resolved to get to the bottom of it. Too much lay at stake.

"Damn right," he muttered to himself as he placed his hands in his pockets, staring down at the dark sandy loam beneath his feet. He strove to extinguish the sudden boiling resentment that seethed within him at the thought of Thor taking Storm to his bed, but it was a futile effort.

Matthew realized he had met Storm Kingsley only the previous afternoon and knew nothing about her past, but there had been something in her eyes that had touched him deeply. As any man would be, he was attracted to her beauty, but that alone was not the reason he felt as he did. He sensed a vulnerability about her that made him want to hold her close and protect her from the world.

Matthew loved Thor like a brother, but he was not blind to his friend's faults. Storm would serve Thor's purpose for a while, and then he would discard her as he had done in the past with so many others. Thor Wakefield would never love a woman; he only used them. His mother's rejection had left deep wounds that were still raw, and until he was able to let them heal, he could not trust enough to love.

Matthew's tender heart twisted inside his chest. He could not condemn Thor for being wary of caring deeply for a woman, and he knew his friend's actions were really none of his affair. However, in this instance Matthew wanted to interfere. The thought of Storm lying beneath Thor tore at him.

He kicked at a loose pebble, sending it skipping across the grass, and turned toward the stables. Thor was expecting him at the construction site for the new floodgates. Mounting the bay stallion his friend had given him on his thirtieth birthday, Matthew urged the horse in the direction of the rice fields.

He knew that the conflict within him would not be easily solved. He owed Thor much, but he still did not approve of his actions with Storm. Suddenly realizing that his resentment stemmed from a certain degree of jealousy, Matthew tightened his grip on the reins. His sandy brows lowered once more over his eyes as he pondered the thought and admitted the truth of it. Storm Kingsley was a beautiful, desirable woman, and he wanted her. The thought did not hearten him but served only to add to his growing turmoil. He had never been a man to act on impulse, but if given the chance in this matter, he would give Storm something she could never have with Thor Wakefield—marriage.

Taking his hat from the pommel of the saddle, Matthew clamped it down on his head and kicked the bay in the side. He was now faced with a dilemma that could sever his friendship with Thor forever. He had two choices. He could take Storm away from Misty Rose, perhaps only to find she could never come to love him, or he could wait until Thor tired of her and then pick up the pieces.

Turning over the options in his mind, Matthew decided to wait. There were too many unanswered questions. He could still be wrong about the relationship between Thor and Storm and their feelings for each other, though he suspected that he was not at all mistaken.

Storm could find no other word to describe the black woman who bustled forward to greet her except round. From the top of her turbaned head to her sandaled feet, the cook's well-padded body resembled a large plump ball.

Mamie's round cheeks spread to reveal startling white teeth as she welcomed Storm warmly to Misty Rose. Storm responded in kind, instinctively sensing that in Mamie she would have a friend. The look in the woman's onyx eyes revealed her warmhearted nature and reminded Storm of Big Nan. That resemblance made her like Misty Rose's cook instantly.

Storm did not feel the least bit disturbed as Mamie eyed her disheveled gown critically. Clicking her tongue, she turned Storm about and laced it as if she were a mother hen with a new chick. Finishing the task, Mamie dusted her hands together and said, "Now, Missy, Master Thor told me to show you about his home. But from the looks of your peaked cheeks, I think we had best begin in the kitchen and get somethin' into your stomach before you collapse."

Giving Storm no time to protest, Mamie ushered her through the rear entrance and along the covered walkway to the board-and-batten building sitting to one side of the main house. Smoke rose from the large brick chimney, and the scent of fresh-baked bread drifted through the doorway to greet them.

At the smell Storm's mouth watered. Until that moment she had not realized how ravenously hungry she was. Her stomach began to grumble in protest, reminding her it had been more than a day since she'd had her last meal. She didn't have to be urged to take a seat at the rough-hewn table. Nor did Mamie have to encourage her to eat the hot biscuits and fresh ham the cook placed before her. Storm devoured the delicious meal, leaving no crumbs upon her plate.

Replete, she leaned back and released a satisfied sigh. Her cheeks flushed lightly with embarrassment as she glanced up to find Mamie smiling at her. She had gobbled the food down like a member of the *Sea Siren*'s crew, giving no thought to her manners.

Mamie chuckled, her round belly quivering beneath the black material of her dress, at Storm's evident discomfort. "Now, Missy, that's all right. I like to see a person with a good appetite. It makes me feel appreciated."

In response to Mamie's generosity, Storm's lips curved upward in a smile. "Thank you, Mamie. I feel much better now."

The cook nodded with approval. "Good, then I expect it's about time we got to carryin' out Master Thor's wishes."

Mamie gave Storm a guided tour of Misty Rose, introducing her to the various servants as they passed through the elegant house. She proudly displayed the linen, silver, and china closets as if she were the owner instead of only Thor's cook.

As Storm followed her guide, she soon came to realize that Misty Rose was well staffed with servants who knew what was expected of them and carried out their duties with a minimum of supervision. There would be little for her to do if overseeing the staff was all that was required of her.

She soon learned otherwise. The last room on Mamie's agenda was a small office located near Thor's study. This,

Storm learned, was where she would spend much of her time. Mamie tried to explain the housekeeper's duties, pulling one of the heavy ledgers from the shelf, placing it on the desk, and flipping it open. "Master Thor said I was to show you what to do, but I just don't know nothin' about all this scribblin' on paper. All I know is that Spinster Murdock used to work in this room, sometimes all day. If you can't figure it out, I'm sure Master Thor can tell you all about it." Mamie face reflected her bewilderment as her eyes scanned the cluttered shelves. Clicking her tongue, she shook her head, as if resigned to the mysteries presented by the ledgers. "Missy, I'll leave you with all these hen scratchin's and get back to the kitchen. It'll soon be time to have the men's midday meal fixed. They're powerful hungry after a mornin's work."

Storm took the cook's dark hand within her own, pressing it gently to convey her gratitude as she said, "Mamie, you've been a great help to me. Thank you for all you've done."

Giving Storm's cheek a motherly pat, Mamie said, "If you need anythin' else, I'll be in the kitchen, Missy."

As the door closed behind Mamie, Storm settled herself before the desk piled high with papers and account books. She began to dig through the large heap, trying to sort out and arrange the clutter so she could make heads or tails out of it. Time passed swiftly as she became engrossed with the ledgers. There was much more to being the housekeeper at Misty Rose than she had imagined.

It was the housekeeper's responsibility to see to the household accounts as well as to the needs of the plantation's slaves. She had to keep accurate records of each birth and death as well as see to the allotment of food, clothing, and the other necessities that ensured their welfare.

As Storm studied the record books, she realized that it would take a great deal of work to do the job properly. She was grateful for that. It would keep her hands and mind occupied, so that she would have little time to brood over things she could not change.

Much depended on her ability to be equal to the task, and she could not help but wonder at the faith Thor had placed in her to see to his people's welfare. It pleased her as well as puzzled her. Since their first encounter she had sensed nothing but his contempt. Now he had placed her in a position of trust, apparently thinking her worthy of such responsibility. Considering this new turn of events, Storm wondered if she had misjudged Thor. Perhaps she'd failed to see this side to his personality because of the animosity that had built within her toward men over the years. The thought caused a warm glow to settle about her like a gentle caress.

Feeling more like herself than she had in months, she delved into the account books, determined that she would prove Thor's faith had not been in vain.

Spinster Murdock had kept the records like a diary, adding small tidbits of information about the everyday affairs of Misty Rose. At times Storm found herself laughing out loud at some small incident that had transpired months earlier. And then, when a death was recorded and she read of the grief suffered by Misty Rose's people, tears stung her eyes.

A knock on the door interrupted her train of thought, and she glanced up at the tiny porcelain clock on the shelf. She had not realized the hours had passed so quickly. Rubbing the small ache in the back of her neck and stretching out her cramped muscles, she called, "Come in."

A pert little black face peeped around the edge of the door, and Storm had to search her memory for the girl's name. Finally seizing upon it, she smiled. "What can I do for you, Perle?"

A sheepish grin came to the girl's full lips. "Ma'am, Madame Ashfort's here to see Master Thor, but he's not yet come in from the fields. I jest wanted to know what you'd like me t' do."

Caught unaware by this unexpected visit from Lyle Ashfort's wife, Storm drew in a sharp breath, her knuckles turning white as she gripped the edge of the desk, her heart pounding against her breastbone. She fought to keep her voice steady as she said, "Perle, show Madame Ashfort into the drawing room. I'll be there directly."

As the door closed behind the maid, Storm held out her hand and watched it tremble. Then she took several deep breaths and squeezed her eyes closed. Balling her fists at her side, she told herself that she had to calm down. She could not face Lyle Ashfort's wife trembling like a feather in a brisk breeze.

As Thor's housekeeper, she had to be composed and courteous to his guest no matter how she felt. It would not do to let herself fall apart on this first encounter. Her actions might raise suspicions. Though she despised anything or anyone connected with Lyle Ashfort, she knew she had to keep her feelings under control until she was actually ready to exact her vengeance upon the man she hated.

Bile rose in her throat at the thought of meeting Miranda Ashfort, but Storm forced it back and raised her chin in the air. Telling herself that this was the first step on the road to avenge Alisa, she walked resolutely from the office.

She paused in the doorway of the drawing room, and a look of surprise flickered over her face as her gaze took in the woman sitting upon the striped-satin Queen Anne sofa. Miranda Ashfort was beautiful. She wore an emerald-green riding habit that emphasized her golden hair and creamy white complexion.

Storm had expected the woman to be of a similar age to her mother and was not prepared to meet a woman that could be no more than a few years older than she was. She found the thought of Lyle Ashfort marrying a woman young enough to be his daughter disgusting. In Storm's eyes it added another black mark to his long list of misdeeds.

Pushing her bitter thoughts away, she forced a smile to her lips and entered the drawing room. "I'm sorry to have kept you waiting, Madame Ashfort. Would you care for tea while you wait for Captain Wakefield?"

Miranda raised her chin haughtily in the air as her pale blue eyes coolly appraised Storm Kingsley. They swept over her from head to toe, assessing her and immediately disliking what she saw. The girl Thor had hired to be his housekeeper was far too beautiful in Miranda's opinion and might even prove to be a rival for his affections.

Determined to keep Storm in her place, Miranda said in an icy voice, "My dear girl, you are mistaken. You have not kept me waiting, because I do not wait for servants. Now, if you would kindly run along and have Mamie prepare my special blend of tea, you can then return to your duties or whatever it is Thor requires of you to do." Waving her hand in Storm's direction as if shooing away an insect, Miranda continued, "Now, be off with you."

Storm's face tightened as rage swept over her at the woman's ill-mannered arrogance. Sparks danced in her eyes, and she quickly lowered her lashes to hide her emotions. It was all she could do to control a sudden urge to slap the superior, condescending expression off of Miranda's flawless features. Invectives rose in Storm's throat, but she squashed them before they could be spoken. Instead she said politely, "I'll see to it right away."

She turned toward the door, but Miranda's words stayed her steps. "Girl, have Mamie send some of her lovely tea cakes as well. I feel quite famished from my ride."

Girl, Storm fumed, her restraint shattering into a million tiny fragments as she turned back to Miranda. She opened her mouth to give Lyle Ashfort's bitchy wife a proper setdown, when Thor's voice behind her checked her words.

"Miranda, it's good to see you. I see you have already met Mistress Kingsley, my new housekeeper."

An angelic smile quickly replaced the disdainful sneer of a moment before as Miranda gave Thor an innocent, beguiling look. "Yes, I have made the acquaintance of Mistress Kingsley. I was just telling her I would love some of Mamie's delicious little tea cakes and tea if it would not be too much of an imposition. The ride over has made me quite ravenous, but I would not want to cause Mistress Kingsley any undue trouble."

The transformation from devil's handmaiden to angel bewildered Storm until she glanced at Thor to find his eyes resting upon her, glaring in disapproval at her lack of courtesy to his guest. A look of triumph flashed across Miranda's face but was quickly hidden as Thor turned back to her and took her hand, brushing his lips against it. "I'm sure Mistress Kingsley will find it no trouble to see that you have a cup of tea to quench your thirst." Casting a stern look in Storm's direction, Thor added, "Would you, mistress?"

Again Storm lowered her lashes to hide her resentment and another unidentifiable emotion that swept over her. "No, sir. I'll see to it now." With that she fled the drawing room, seething with rage. Spying Perle in the hall, she gave her orders to serve Madame Ashfort tea and cakes and then hurried back to her small office, damning Thor Wakefield and Lyle Ashfort's wife with every step she took.

Storm remained secluded in the office until she heard the sound of a horse's hooves upon the crushed-shell drive. Unable to stop herself, she crossed to the window and watched as Thor accompanied Miranda away from Misty Rose.

Storm's nails bit into the wood of the windowsill as she saw the two ride down the drive. Even from this distance, she could read the sultry invitation in Miranda's eyes as she smiled sweetly up at Thor. A scalding current ran through Storm as she saw Thor throw back his dark head and laugh at some witty remark Miranda made. Damn you, Thor Wakefield, for a fool, Storm thought. The witch has you exactly where she wants you.

Through narrowed eyes, she stared after the receding figures. Had she not met Miranda in private before seeing them ride off together, their heads intimately close in conversation, Storm would have placed all the blame on Thor. But after seeing the metamorphosis that had taken place in the woman when he entered the drawing room, Storm knew well who was at fault. Miranda Ashfort was not satisfied with her rich older husband. She wanted Thor Wakefield as well. A person had to be blind or a fool not to see it. Since Thor's silver eyes seldom missed anything, Storm considered him the latter.

The tiny office suddenly seemed to become stifling. Beads of perspiration broke out across her brow, and as she mopped them away, she envisioned Miranda in Thor's arms. Nausea churned her insides, and she swayed, her knees turning to jelly beneath her. She clamped her hand over her mouth and forced her legs to move as she hurried from the manor into the coolness of the rose garden. She gulped in great breaths of air, trying to quell her queasy stomach, then sank weakly onto the rod-iron bench beside the fountain with cupids entwined in a lover's embrace. The sight did little to ease her tumultuous mind. Instead of the carved stone images, she invisioned Thor and Miranda, their lips pressed together in a passionate kiss, their arms and legs entwined as he made love to her. Revolted by the vivid picture her imagination painted, Storm once more had to clamp her hand to her mouth to keep back the bitterness.

Tears stung her eyes, and she tried to stem their tide, but the effort was futile. They brimmed and flowed unchecked in a glistening path down her pale cheeks. Giving

way to the misery that engulfed her at the thought of Thor
with another woman, she bowed her head and wept. Despite all that she had vowed, at last she could put a name
to the strange yearnings and emotions that had possessed
her since she had met Thor Wakefield. Seeing the pleasure
on his face as he looked at Miranda had made Storm
realize she had committed the same folly as Alisa had done
with Lyle Ashfort. She had fallen in love with Thor.

New tears filled her eyes with the thought. She wanted
to scream out her anguish and vexation to the world but
knew it would do no good. She did not want to love Thor;
he had given her little reason to do so. He was a man who
would never love her in return, for he considered her little
better than a prostitute from the gutters. To Thor she was
only a vessel to appease his lust and nothing more. She
was as much a convenience to him as were the utensils on
his table. He used them when necessary and then thought
nothing of them until needed again.

No, she did not want to love Thor Wakefield or any
man. But something had gone awry within her. She had
staunchly declared that such a thing as love did not exist,
and now to her own bewilderment, she found herself
suffering because she had finally recognized it in herself.

It was an agony she vowed to endure in silence. She
could never let Thor know of her feelings; her pride would
not allow her to be that foolhardy. Seeing him with Miranda had made Storm aware of her love for him, but she
also knew she would not reveal it to him unless it was
returned, and that would never happen. Storm well knew
Thor's position on marriage. He wanted only a mistress,
and though she loved him, she was resolved to fight with
every fiber in her body against that. She might be asinine
enough to crave his arms about her, but she would never
accept him fully until he told her he loved her in return.

Storm's shoulders drooped as she gazed down at her
tightly clasped hands and thought, I might be foolish

enough to have fallen in love with you, Thor Wakefield, but that doesn't mean I believe in miracles.

Drawing in a ragged breath, she wiped the moisture from her cheeks and looked about her. She was surprised to see the last rays of the sun peeping through the tall pines. Caught up in her misery, she hadn't realized that she had stayed so long in the garden. It would soon be time for dinner, and she had as yet to return to the Petite Maison to freshen up. Her fingers were still stained with ink and dust from going through the ledgers.

Rising, she went to take the flagstone path that led to the Petite Maison. A startled gasp escaped her lips as she nearly collided with Matthew Boone. Giving him a wobbly smile of apology, she said, "Matthew, I didn't see you."

The muscle beneath his right eye twitched as he studied Storm's tearstained face. His expression remaining solemn, he said, "Yes, I know. I suspect you had too many other things on your mind to notice my presence."

Uncomfortably aware that Matthew had seen her misery and not wanting him or anyone to know the reason behind it, Storm looked quickly away from his somber eyes.

Sensing her distress, he took her arm. "I'll escort you home. It's the least I can do after nearly frightening you to death."

Keeping her eyes glued to the path before them, she said, "You didn't frighten me. I just didn't know anyone was near, and it gave me a slight start."

Remembering what he had learned that morning, Matthew remained silent, his natural quick wit dampened by the fact that he was falling in love with Thor's mistress. Conflicting emotions battled for supremacy within him; his loyalty to Thor against the new feelings that Storm aroused. In all his thirty-two years, Matthew had never felt such an overpowering need for a woman. He wanted to take her into his arms and tell her of his feelings but knew he could not.

The muscles across his abdomen contracted sharply as he glanced once more at her sad face. Had anyone told him two days earlier that he would fall in love with a woman at first sight, he would have laughed. Forty-eight hours later, he knew it could happen. The thought was not comforting, because to gain a love, he would have to lose a friend.

As they reached the Petite Maison, Storm forced a smile to her lips and turned to Matthew. "Thank you, kind sir, for escorting me to my door." She tried to make her tone light but failed miserably. Her voice trembled, and she looked away, hoping he had not noted it.

Matthew's work-roughened hands settled on her shoulders as her hand touched the latch, and he turned her to face him. Looking directly into her eyes, trying to convey his understanding, he said, "Storm, I am your friend, and if you ever need me, I'll be here." At the present time that was all he could offer.

Storm's throat constricted with emotion at his kindness. She gave him a feeble nod to assure him that she understood and was grateful.

Touched by the look in Storm's eyes and unable to restrain himself, he gently caressed her cheek, cupping it tenderly in his palm as he said, "Remember, Storm, friends help each other. All you have to do is ask."

Again she nodded and turned away, a new flood of tears blinding her as she pushed the door open, leaving Matthew staring after her.

As she closed the door, he dug his hands into his pocket and with head bowed strode toward his own small dwelling near the slave quarters.

Thor stood in the distance, his jaw clenched and knuckles white as he gripped his riding crop until it almost snapped under the pressure. He had rushed back from AshGlen to dine with Storm after seeing Miranda safely home. The memory of the previous night had been still vivid in his mind as he galloped home—only to find Storm and his best friend in an intimate encounter.

Thor's nostrils flared as he drew in a deep angry breath and he turned back to the stables. Mounting his black stallion, he kicked the animal in the side and galloped furiously down the crushed-shell drive toward Charleston.

Chapter 8

The full moon rose lazily over the tops of the tall pines, its light frosting the rose garden beyond Storm's room in silver. The heady fragrance of rose and jasmine wafted in upon the sultry breeze that stirred the lace curtains. Pale moonbeams illuminated her pensive features as she leaned her cheek against the glass and stared up at the shining sphere that lit the night.

Absently, she rubbed the back of her neck to try to ease the niggling ache that had built there through the afternoon. She was tired; the past two weeks had been hectic. It had taken several days for her to learn Spinster Murdock's method of keeping the books. Once she had accomplished that feat, she'd had to record everything that had transpired at Misty Rose since the woman had left the plantation. Between that and organizing the office, plus seeing to the various other duties she had found to be part of her job, Storm was exhausted.

Glancing over her shoulder at the tall poster bed, she knew well that she needed to seek its comfort and rest. But the night was too hot, and her mind would not let her find the sleep that would help her be fresh for the next day's duties.

Storm's fingers curled about the edge of the curtain, crushing the delicately woven fabric. Since her meeting with Miranda Ashfort, her vendetta against the woman's husband had fermented until Storm's nerves were stretched taut. Her inability to fulfill her vow of vengeance wore upon her mind, making her restless and irritable. That served to make her mercurial temperament even more volatile. She felt herself to be a tinderbox sitting upon a keg of black powder.

The heat of the South Carolina summer did little to ease her mood. Used to the cooler climate of England, she found that the humid weather also helped fray the thin thread that bound her composure.

The stillness of the night was disturbed by the sound of a horse approaching the main house. From her vantage point Storm recognized Thor as he circled the drive and reined the horse to a halt before Misty Rose. She stepped away from the window, lowering the curtain back into place as she watched him dismount and toss the reins to the groom before striding briskly up the walk to the manor.

The pale moonlight illuminated Thor's powerful physique, giving her a clear view of his figure from the tips of his shining black boots to the rakish wide-brimmed hat that obscured his features. The white silk of his lace cravat and cuffs gleamed against the dark velvet of his coat. The sight made her pulse begin to race wildly, and the heat of the room seemed to intensify.

Since the day when Miranda Ashfort had come to visit, Storm had not encountered Thor. She had seen him from a distance as he strode to the stables or along the pathway to the white building that she had learned was his office. She had also seen him ride in the direction of AshGlen and knew he was going to meet Miranda.

Knowing his destination, Storm had felt jealousy churn

her insides. Thor had not sought her out, and she knew Miranda Ashfort was the reason. Like a toy that no longer amused him, he had cast Storm aside in the same manner that Lyle Ashfort had done Alisa.

For the first time, Storm was able to feel compassion for Alisa's love toward Lyle. She now understood it all too well. She, too, had fallen into the same emotional trap; she loved Thor Wakefield even knowing he sought out another's bed.

Feeling a large drop of perspiration roll down the graceful curve of her spine, Storm turned away from the window, annoyed with herself for even thinking of Thor. It had only added to her agitation.

She strode determinedly to the door. She needed to be free of the confinement of the house, to walk alone in the gardens, to feel the cool breeze from the river upon her hot skin. Then perhaps she could put him from her thoughts and center her attention on Lyle Ashfort.

She knew she had to find a way to make the man pay for her mother's sufferings, but as of that moment, she had no idea how to go about it. She was Thor's servant and had no reason to venture from Misty Rose to AshGlen on any pretext. That was the first obstacle in her path to vengeance. Once she overcame it, she would find a means to exact the rest.

As she moved through the dark rooms of the Petite Maison without lighting a candle, her bare feet made no sound upon the polished floors. She opened the door and stepped out into the sultry night, feeling the breeze from the Ashley ruffle the lace on her night rail as she crossed the flag-stone path. Mamie had brought the soft cotton gown to her several days after her arrival. Several day gowns followed, along with their accessories; all delivered without any explanation. The garments fit her perfectly, and Storm knew they had come from Thor. She was grateful for his beneficence, and it pleased her to think that at least he had taken the time to remember her lack of clothing.

The dew had already fallen, and the lush, green grass felt cool beneath her feet as she left the path and crossed the rose garden to the tall willow at the edge of the lawn. Brushing aside its indolently swaying limbs, she entered the dark haven, instantly feeling the difference in temperature beneath the graceful branches.

Safe from the world, in her little haven, Storm felt herself begin to relax. She savored the cool breeze that molded the thin night rail to her body. Her white throat arched as she rested her head against the rough bole of the tree, her firm breasts pressing against the fabric of her gown as she breathed deeply of the intoxicating aromas of the night. The scent of jasmine, rose, of damp earth, and of the river filled her senses.

Drawing in another breath of the sweet air, she felt her nostrils flare as another smell drifted to her. Jerking sharply around, she saw Thor casually leaning against the opposite side of the willow, smoking a cheroot, his eyes focused on the distant river.

The muscles in her stomach tightened, and her heart began to beat a rapid tattoo as a pale sliver of moonlight crept through the thick branches illuminating his features. Fighting the sudden rush of feelings that swept over her, she demanded, "What are you doing here?"

Thor dropped the cheroot to the dark loam and crushed it beneath his boot before he replied, "As I recall, I live here." As he spoke, he moved to her side.

His nearness unsettled Storm, and she quickly stepped back, imagining she could feel the heat radiating from his hard body. The breeze shifted, bringing with it his male odor. The scent of leather, tobacco, and verbena, the herb Mamie put in the soap, filled Storm's senses, further distracting her. Angry with herself for letting him have such an effect upon her, she said, "That does not give you the right to invade my privacy."

One corner of Thor's sensuous mouth curved upward in a mocking half smile. "I beg to differ with you, Tempest. I have the right to do as I please at Misty Rose."

All the frustration and resentment that had been building inside Storm over the past weeks boiled to the surface. Tilting her chin in the air, her eyes sparkled as she said, "All I wanted was a breath of cool air. Can I not seek that small pleasure without your permission or your presence?"

Before she could avoid it, Thor's hand captured the back of her neck, drawing her near. She could feel his hot breath upon her face as he bent closer, his lips only inches from hers.

"Are you sure a breath of cool air is all you require, Tempest?" he murmured.

She tried to pull away but found his long fingers entwined in her hair, imprisoning her head like a vise. She balled her fists against his chest, trying to push free, but her actions had little effect upon him as his other arm encircled her waist, bringing her body into contact with his muscular frame.

Storm tried to twist free, saying, "No, all I want—" Her words were absorbed by Thor's mouth as he captured her tender lips, searing them with a kiss that brought back vivid memories of the ecstasy they had shared, memories her mind had tried desperately to bury but her body refused to forget. It reacted even as she fought against the assault on her senses. The war was waged and lost as his fiery kiss engulfed her, bombarding her reserves, draining away her defenses, as wildfire raced along every nerve in her body. Her slender hands uncurled and inched their way up his wide chest before encircling his neck, her fingers playing in his blue-black hair.

Storm's breathing grew heavy as Thor's hand molded her against him. Through the thin fabric of her night rail, she could feel the hardness of his desire pressed against her belly. His lips left hers, traveling slowly to the sensitive spot beneath her ear as he murmured, "I need you, Tempest."

His husky words laid siege to the last wall of her resistance. It crumbled away, leaving her vulnerable to the passion rushing through her, rumbling like the center of a volcano before erupting into a sensual explosion.

Thor's arm swept down her body, clasping her beneath the knees, lifting her off the ground to cradle her against his chest as he strode into the moonlight. His lips recaptured hers while his long legs carried them into the fragrant garden.

There among the silvery roses, he laid Storm gently upon the glistening grass, his hand brushing tenderly against her heated flesh as he removed her night rail, baring her satiny body to his gaze. He paused, savoring her perfection. The pale light made her skin appear translucent, while tiny shadows emphasized her softly rounded curves. Thor knew that if he were an artist and could have captured upon canvas this unadorned loveliness amid the roses, he would have created a masterpiece.

The moment of reflection evaporated into the cool night air as the heat in his loins intensified. Disrobing, he lay down beside her, his long fingers cupping her chin as he gazed down into her passion-glazed eyes. He tasted the honeyed nectar of her mouth, and then his fingers moved sensuously along the curve of her throat to the smooth planes above her breasts, before molding themselves to the silken globes. His thumb teased the rose peaks, feeling them contract and grow hard beneath his touch before his mouth followed the path set by his hand. His lips closed over the rigid nipples, his tongue circling them enticingly before he began to suckle their sweetness.

Storm felt her breast crushed against Thor's mouth and reveled in the sensation it aroused. She cradled his head, her fingers smoothing the silken strands of hair before slipping down to his tanned shoulders. The touch of his warm flesh inflamed her senses, creating a deep, quivering need in the pit of her belly. She arched against him, yearning for her hunger to be sated.

Instinctively knowing that her arousal matched his own, Thor covered her pale body with his own sensuous male form. Her thighs spread voluntarily, welcoming the thrust that would take them to ecstasy. They moved in unison, equal in the ancient ritual, no longer a man and a woman but one soul joined by desire. They rode on a shooting star until it burst into a shower of rapture, sprinkling their lithe bodies with liquid diamonds that glistened in the moonbeams that caressed them amid the roses.

Thor did not withdraw from Storm but lay with his head on her breast, enjoying the peace and beauty of the moment as her fingers tenderly brushed the damp tendrils of hair from his moist brow.

Quiescent, she lay beneath him, stroking his brow and savoring the feeling of his lean flesh pressed against her sated body. Her gaze lingered on the dark head that contrasted boldly with her milky skin, and her heart swelled. She loved this man. She knew that for him this moment of bliss was only temporary, but she was loath to give it up. She wanted to remain in the fragrant garden, wrapped in Thor's arms, and forget about the past and the future. But that could never be. He did not love her. Tears burned in her eyes, and she turned her face away, feeling them mingle with the dew on the grass.

Though they lay with limbs entwined, Thor sensed the distance that came between them as Storm buried her emotions once more in the secret place in her heart. He could feel the subtle change that came over her body, the slight tension in her muscles, the coolness of her skin. Puzzled, he propped himself up on one elbow and stared down at her. He saw her tears and could not understand them. He knew she had experienced the same enthralling ecstasy as he had; her response had proven it.

Vexed at her reaction, he moved away from her and began to jerk on his britches. The sight of her tears was like a slap in the face, and he could nearly feel his cheek stinging from the blow of her rejection. Annoyed beyond endurance, he fastened the buttons on his britches and turned to glare down at her, his eyes reflecting the pale moonlight. "Damn it, Storm, I've had about enough of your hot and cold spells. I'm tired of feeling like a schoolboy after each time I make love to you. I never know what to expect. One moment you are ablaze with passion and the next as frosty as a winter's morn. You can deny your attraction to me until you are blue in the face, but it is there, if only you would recognize it and accept it for what it is."

Embarrassed suddenly by her nakedness, Storm sat up and pulled on her night rail. She brushed the tousled curls from her forehead as she looked up at him towering over her. Her heart urged her to tell him how she felt, but her pride stayed her. "I will neither recognize nor accept something that does not exist. You have forced me to become your mistress. That is the only thing I will concede to you."

Thor's features darkened as he shrugged into his white silk shirt, leaving it open to expose the fine mat of black hair on his chest. "Force be damned!" he lashed out, his anger overcoming his reason. Her cool rejection hurt him and he wanted to return it in kind. "I have paid well for your services and intend to make use of them. I can't touch the virginal little airheads in Charleston when they flaunt their charms at me, trying to lure me to the altar. But I see no reason why I should have to come home and take a cold swim in the river to cool my blood when I have you."

As if to protect herself, Storm folded her arms over her

breast and bowed her head against his cruel onslaught. His words struck her like a whip, ripping open new wounds in her already-scarred heart. The beauty she had found lying in his arms vanished into the still night as she realized he had used her as a surrogate. He had spoken of the ladies of Charleston, but she knew he had meant only one lady, Miranda Ashfort. Thor had used Storm to release the lust Miranda had kindled within him. The thought left her feeling soiled, and her stomach churned.

Fighting to retain her evening meal, Storm struggled to her feet and looked up at him. Her eyes glistened with pain and self-loathing for giving her heart to a man such as Thor Wakefield. All the bitterness she had felt over the years of watching Alisa degrade herself coupled with Storm's humiliation, magnifying her folly at ever feeling anything but hatred for any man. Turning, she fled the garden before she could further disgrace herself by vomiting.

Blindly she ran toward the Petite Maison, stumbling over the lacy hem of her night rail. As she reached the small front porch, she could no longer contain the bile, and she leaned weakly over the railing and retched. Finally Storm sank to her knees and leaned her head against the jasmine-covered post. She gulped in ragged breaths of air while her mind shouted, Fool, fool, as tears of shame coursed down her pale cheeks.

It was in that position Matthew Boone found her. He had ridden to Charleston that evening hoping to take his mind off of Storm Kingsley. He had not succeeded. On his return to Misty Rose, he had taken the path that led past the Petite Maison on his way to the overseer's cottage.

Kneeling at Storm's side, he took her into his arms, cradling her like a small child, whispering soothing words against her hair. Needing his comfort, she clung to him as he lifted her into his arms and carried her into the Petite Maison. Without a word, he strode through the dark hall to her bedchamber and laid her gently upon the bed. Then he settled himself at her side, stroking her tousled curls as if he were her father, murmuring words of comfort until he felt her breathing become even.

For a long while Matthew sat gazing down at her sleeping features. An angry scowl formed across his brow. Something had happened tonight between Thor and Storm that had left her devastated. Matthew did not have to have been present to know that his friend lay at the root of her troubles. During the past weeks he had observed her from a distance and had seen her expression as she watched Thor ride toward AshGlen. Unaware that anyone was watching her, she had let her feelings show. It was then Matthew had realized he had been correct in his decision to wait to reveal to Storm how he felt about her. On her beautiful face he had seen written the love she felt for Thor. Matthew knew what caused her remorse. She had given her heart to a man who did not return her affections.

Since the day he had discovered Storm's secret, Matthew had avoided her. Being with her was too painful, knowing of her feelings for Thor. They only added to his growing resentment toward his friend. Had Thor also cared for Storm, Matthew knew he would not have felt such animosity. He would have let nature take its course and wished them both well, though his own heart ached at the thought of them together. But Matthew knew he could have lived with that fact as long as Storm was content.

Matthew's heart went out to her as he looked down into her lovely face. It was clear that she was not happy at Misty Rose. He wanted desperately to help her but knew there was nothing he could do. He could not force Thor to love her, no more than he could stop himself from caring for her. All he could do was be there when Storm needed him. That Matthew was determined to do, even if he had to throttle Thor Wakefield in the process.

At the thought, Matthew's lips formed a narrow line and his sandy brows knit over his eyes. His fists curled at his side. He wanted to go and beat some sense into Thor. His friend was a fool to use Storm so callously while catering to Miranda Ashfort's every whim. Thor could not see the true Miranda; he was tricked into believing she was the devoted wife. He couldn't see that she sat preening and sharpening her claws and would pounce when the time was right.

Bending over, Matthew placed a light kiss on Storm's brow before pulling the counterpane over her sleeping form. Turning, he left the Petite Maison, knowing his life at Misty Rose would no longer be easy. It would be hard to face Thor each day without venting his exasperation and resentment at his friend's stupidity.

With head bowed, his thoughts still lingering on Storm, he strode along the path toward his cottage. He did not see Thor standing in the shadow of the willow, nor could he avoid the hands that clamped down on the front of his jacket, jerking him around and slamming him with force into the trunk of the tree. Matthew's head snapped back, making contact with the rough bark surface, the impact staggering his senses.

Stunned, he shook his head, trying to focus on his assailant. The blow to his head coupled with the darkness hampered his vision, yet he recognized Thor's voice instantly.

"What in the hell were you doing at the Petite Maison?"

Anger surged through Matthew as all of his tumultuous feelings boiled to the surface. Bringing both arms up between Thor's, he knocked them away. "Damn it, if you want a fight, then you'll get it. I'll not explain my actions to you. I work for you, but you don't own me."

Thor stepped back, his chest heaving as his rage ran like white-hot lava through his veins. His fists were clenched at his sides, ready and waiting for Matthew to make a move toward him. He had come to apologize to Storm for his rash words, only to find her in Matthew's arms. He had watched as his friend lifted her up and had seen Storm cling to him as he carried her into the house. It had been all Thor could do to keep from following them and throttling his overseer for taking what was his by right.

The thought of Storm with Matthew was a gut-ripping agony to Thor. His blood boiled as he glared at his friend. "By God, you will explain. I may not own you, but I do own Storm. You'll not trespass upon my property."

Matthew straightened, his feet splayed wide as he braced himself for another assault. "Is that all she is to you, a piece of property?"

Thor felt his stomach knot. He could not and would not answer Matthew's question. He didn't know the answer to it himself. "Damn it, that's none of your business. You are paid to oversee Misty Rose, not my housekeeper."

Matthew took a step forward, his face hard and angry. "I'm making it my business. If she is nothing to you beyond a piece of flesh to quench your lust, then I'll take her away from Misty Rose. Storm deserves better than that, Thor."

Suddenly Thor's anger evaporated, and his shoulders slumped as he looked at the man he had grown to love over the years. A moment before he would have killed Matthew without any qualms. Running his hand through his hair, he sadly shook his head. "Matthew, I'm sorry to have treated you in such a manner. I don't know what's gotten into me lately."

Matthew's anger was not so easily cooled. "I forgive you your actions toward me, but that doesn't mean I've changed my mind, Thor. I'll take Storm and leave Misty Rose if she gives me the slightest indication that she wants to go."

A sliver of moonlight peeped through the branches and illuminated Matthew's face. Thor saw his friend's determination upon it and knew he was not jesting. "You'd be

stealing my property, Matthew. Storm is indentured to me
for the next seven years.''

"I don't give a damn about indentures. She could be
your slave, and it wouldn't change anything. I'll be honest
with you, Thor; I want the girl more than any woman I've
ever met. I've tried to keep away from her because I've
known since the first morning she was here that she was
your mistress. But I'll not stand by and watch her be
abused by you or anyone else.''

Thor smiled derisively at Matthew. Shaking his head
again, he said, ''You might change your mind if you knew
of her past.''

Matthew eyed his friend dubiously. ''What are you
trying to tell me, Thor?''

Disgusted that Storm should have caused such dissension between them, Thor said, ''Matthew, her past is not
very reputable. She's from the streets of London, and her
mother was executed for prostitution and murder. Storm
herself was charged with prostitution.''

The muscles across Matthew's abdomen contracted as if
someone had slammed a fist into them, knocking the wind
out of him. ''I don't believe you,'' he said.

The fact that Matthew doubted his word rankled Thor all
the more. ''Ask Storm if you don't believe me. She was
transported by the courts on the *Sea Siren*; that's how I
came to possess her papers. I was supposed to sell them
but decided to bring her to Misty Rose instead. Now do
you still want her?''

Matthew glared at Thor. ''It changes nothing. I don't
care a thing about her past, and I'm warning you. I won't
hesitate to make her mine if I have the chance.''

The green-eyed monster roared within Thor as he stared
at his friend's determined face. ''Stay away from her,
Matthew. I treasure our friendship, but where Storm is
concerned, I will not tolerate your interference. She belongs to me, and I intend to keep her.''

Bracing his hands on his hips and cocking his sandy head to one side, Matthew regarded him skeptically. "Does that mean you care for her?"

Exasperated that his overseer would not take his warning and let the subject die, Thor said, "Blast it, man. You know how I feel about all women. Why should this one girl be any different?"

Rubbing his chin thoughtfully, Matthew pondered Thor's words as he studied his set face. In the ten years they had been together, Thor Wakefield had never reacted so violently about a woman before. They had often shared the same women without a qualm. Now Thor was putting Storm off-limits. That in itself told Matthew a great deal more than his friend's words. After working, drinking, and fighting alongside a man, you come to truly know him, and Matthew knew Thor. He could say he felt nothing but physical passion for Storm, but after tonight Matthew knew better.

Smiling ruefully to himself, he realized he had lost the battle before it had begun. Thor cared for Storm, and she loved him. That left Matthew with a relieved mind but a troubled heart. It also raised another dilemma: how to get them to recognize their feelings for each other.

Hunching his shoulders, he dug his hands into his pockets and kicked at a small pebble with the toe of his boot. Eyeing Thor, he decided it would not hurt him to believe the worst.

"Since she means so little to you, I see no reason why I should stay away from her. As a matter of fact, I can offer her more than you can." Smiling to himself, Matthew watched a dubious expression flicker over his friend's face. "You see, Thor, I can offer Storm marriage. You may have the riches of Misty Rose, but what is that to your mistress? I can offer her my heart and my name, where you never will. Which of us do you think Storm will choose, Thor?"

Thor's face grew livid, his eyes glittering with anger once more. "Damn it, Matthew. I'm telling you one last time to stay away from her."

Matthew chuckled, the sound further inflaming Thor's jealousy. "Thor, we've been friends for a long time, but in this I'll make my own decision. I give you fair warning now; I will do everything within my power to sway Storm's heart in my direction. In the event that she should choose me, I'll agree to purchase her indenture from you."

Thor ground his teeth together, his lips narrowing into a harsh line as he fought to restrain the urge to strangle Matthew Boone. "The hell you will! Matthew, you are pushing me, and I've never been a man to let another run over him. Heed what I've said, or you'll find yourself gone from Misty Rose."

Giving a careless shrug, Matthew said, "It's a free world, Thor. You can let me go as your overseer, but that doesn't mean I'll forget about Storm." With that he turned and left Thor fuming in the shadows of the willow.

Thor watched his friend saunter away as if nothing had transpired between them. Damn it to hell! he thought as he turned on his heel and strode angrily in the direction of the main house. Reaching it, he stamped into the foyer and slammed the door behind him with such force that the sound echoed eerily through the entire manor. Taking the winding stairs two at a time, he made his way to his bedchamber. He jerked at his lace cravat, tore it loose, and tossed it to the floor. Matthew had left the decision up to him. He could either get rid of his overseer, the man he loved as a friend and brother, or chance losing Storm.

Not liking either choice, Thor ran his fingers irritably through his hair as he stared at his reflection in the mirror. Suddenly his eyes lit and his lips curled. He would not lose Matthew or Storm. He would see that Matthew never had the chance to be alone with her long enough to make his suit.

Pleased with himself and his idea, Thor poured himself a brandy from the crystal decanter on his nightstand. Kicking off his boots, he relaxed back on to the bed. Bracing one arm behind his head, he sipped his brandy and stared up at the ceiling, feeling in control of the situation once more.

Chapter 9

The scratch of quill upon paper was the only sound to disturb the peace of Storm's small office as she bent over a ledger itemizing the material it would take to make new winter clothing for the people of Misty Rose. Concentrating on the task at hand, she did not hear the door open, nor was she aware of Thor's presence until he said, "Good morning, Tempest."

Startled, she jerked about to see him standing in the doorway. At the sight of his immaculately clothed body and the charming smile playing over his lips, she felt her mouth go dry. Completely unsettled, she quickly turned back to her work. "Good morning, sir."

Noting her use of *sir*, Thor chuckled to himself as he strolled across the office and leaned negligently against the desk. Folding his arms across his chest, he gazed down at the dark head bent industriously over the heavy leather volume. "Ah, it's a beautiful morning, Tempest. I thought today you might enjoy a ride."

Though Storm kept her eyes glued to the paper, she could no longer concentrate on the words before her.

Moistening her lips, she shook her head. "I'm sorry, but I must finish this today so the seamstress can begin to make the slaves' winter garments."

In one swift motion, Thor flipped the ledger closed, and she had to pull her hand back to keep from being caught. Turning startled eyes upon him she saw him smile indulgently. "I don't think my people will freeze to death this winter if it takes you one more day." Seizing her ink-stained fingers, he drew her from the chair and placed her hand on his arm. "A ride will do you good. You're a little pale today, and it will help bring the color back to your cheeks." Leading her toward the door, he asked, "You do ride, don't you?"

Bewildered by his strange behavior, Storm could only nod as they walked through the wide front doors and down the steps to the pretty roan mare that waited at the mounting block.

Thor eyed Storm critically for a moment and he shook his head. "That gown will have to do for today, but I'll see you have a proper riding habit as soon as one can be made." Without waiting for either her protest or approval, he grasped her about the waist and lifted her onto the sidesaddle.

She stiffened as his hands closed about her, lingering slightly longer than necessary. As he felt her response to his touch, his amicable smile faded. "Storm, if you try hard enough, you might enjoy today." His features reflected his annoyance as he strode to his ebony stallion and mounted. Urging it alongside Storm's dainty mare, he said, "I'm sure your lovely face would not break if you chose to smile once in a while."

The gall of the man! Storm fumed silently as she urged her mare forward. *He forces me to obey his dictates and then expects me to enjoy them.*

Thor glanced at her and could easily read her heated thoughts in her face. He grinned to himself. *You may not* enjoy this outing, he thought, but from now on, I'll keep an eye on you so that there'll be no meeting Matthew when I'm not around.

Wanting to avoid having to speak with Thor, Storm lagged behind, keeping the distance between them just great enough to hinder conversation.

They rode in silence along the sandy road until Thor finally reined his mount to a halt before an ivy-covered archway. Turning in the saddle, he folded his arms as he waited for her to come alongside. Having no other recourse, she halted her mare and calmly looked up at him, wondering what next to expect of his odd behavior that day.

Seeing the question in her eyes, Thor smiled. "This is AshGlen. I thought you might enjoy seeing it, since it is built in the fashion of your English homes. I'm sure Lyle and Miranda would wish us to stop by for a visit, since we are so close."

Something akin to fear snaked up Storm's spine as she realized that only a short distance away was the man she had vowed vengeance against. Suddenly her courage seemed to desert her. She had planned for this moment, but it had come upon her so unexpectedly that it left her shaken. At the thought of finally meeting Lyle Ashfort, she felt her hands grow clammy on the reins and her heart begin to pound in her chest.

Mistaking her silence for agreement, Thor urged his horse forward, and she had little choice but to follow him along the winding drive to the magnificent manor. It was built in the Georgian style and boasted three stories with ivy-covered walls and rolling lawns manicured to perfection and edged with English boxed hedges.

Storm's eyes widened and her mouth fell slightly agape as she took in the beauty of her surroundings. A tiny pang of homesickness swept over her. Had she not known better, she would have believed she was once more in England.

Watching her reaction to AshGlen, Thor smiled to himself as he dismounted and helped her from the mare. "Welcome to AshGlen. I thought you'd be surprised when you saw it. It's my understanding that Lyle took the design from his family's estate in England, bringing a little piece of his boyhood home to South Carolina when he decided to make his life here."

As Storm's gaze swept over the elegant exterior of the manor, she could not help but think of the two dilapidated rooms she and Alisa had called home and the reason they'd had to leave them. The man who had been at the root of all her troubles resided within this fine Georgian mansion. He might have wanted to bring a little of his home to the colonies but never his wife and child, she thought bitterly as she let Thor escort her to the door.

His sharp rap upon the gleaming brass knocker was answered by a black man with graying hair who wore the Ashfort livery. His ebony face spread into a wide grin of welcome at the sight of Thor. "Master Thor, it's good to see you. Master Ashfort and the madam are in the study. I'll tell them you're here."

"Thank you, Zachery," Thor said as he handed him his wide-brimmed hat.

Within moments the butler had returned to show them into Lyle's study. Those few feet across the foyer were the hardest Storm had ever had to travel. She felt her knees turn to jelly and she stumbled slightly as they neared the door. The color drained from her face, leaving her ashen.

"Storm, are you ill?" Thor asked as he glanced uneasily down at her.

Taking several shaky breaths, she tried desperately to regain her courage as she shook her head. "No, I'm just a little unsettled from the heat and the ride. It's been a long while since I've ridden."

"I'm sure you'll feel better after a cool drink and a little rest," he said, and smiled, satisfied with her answer.

Giving him a weak smile in return, Storm swallowed convulsively as Zachery opened the study doors. Drawing from all of her reserves, she raised her chin in the air and stiffened her spine as they entered Lyle Ashfort's presence. She had long awaited this meeting and was determined not to cower when she met the man who had caused her so much misery.

Miranda rose and gracefully swept forward, her hand outstretched to Thor in greeting, her satin skirts rustling against the thick turkish carpet that silenced her footsteps. "Thor, I'm so glad you've come. Lyle has been wondering when we'd see you again. It's been days."

Puzzling over the strange conversation, Storm regarded Thor and Miranda suspiciously. Thor came to AshGlen nearly every day on some pretext or other, or so she had assumed from the direction in which he rode when he left Misty Rose.

He took Miranda's hand and brushed his lips lightly against it. "Well, I'm here now and have brought a guest for Lyle. Since Mistress Kingsley is so recently from England, I thought Lyle would enjoy meeting a fellow countrywoman."

"Ah, yes, I'm sure he would," Miranda said, her icy gaze sweeping insultingly over Storm as she gave her a frosty smile.

A craggy voice came from the chaise lounge near the window. "You two can quit speaking of me as if I'm deaf. There is nothing wrong with my ears, only my legs."

"I know that very well, you rascal," Thor said as he took Storm's arm and led her forward. "I'd like to present my new housekeeper, Mistress Storm Kingsley."

Storm felt numb as she stared down at the man who had sired her and realized the reason he had not risen to greet them. Lyle Ashfort could not walk; he was a cripple. Her gaze swept the lap rug that covered his legs and up over the thin blue-veined hands, to finally come to rest on the face she had never been able to visualize, though over the years she had tried often to do so.

She took in the features of a man who could not have been over forty-five years of age, but who looked much older. His parchmentlike skin was nearly translucent because of his ill health. She took in the high cheekbones and aquiline nose and the once-shapely lips now tinged with a bluish palor. However, what drew Storm's attention most were the sapphire eyes that were so much like her own. They had not aged and still sparkled with the apparent vitality of his mind.

"Welcome to America and AshGlen, Mistress Kingsley. In what part of England did you reside?" Lyle asked as he extended his hand to Storm. He had to repeat his question a second time before she could pull herself out of her dazed state and realize that he was speaking to her.

Storm hesitated only briefly before taking his hand and managed to force her throat to work as she said, "Thank you for your kind welcome, sir. I come from London."

Lyle clasped her hand gently for a moment before waving her to a chair near his lounge. Leaning back, he drew in a ragged breath and said, "Ah, London. I was there only last year, right before my accident, to clear up my family's estate. It had changed much since my previous visit."

Thor noted Storm's mounting discomfort. Her lovely face was tight with tension, and she sat stiff and straight on the edge of the chair seat. Her forced smile did not hide her distress from his keen eyes. He assumed the change that had come over her was caused by the fact that she feared Lyle's questions might lead to answers she would rather keep secret. He could well understand that, for he too wanted her origins to remain a mystery. Taking a seat by Miranda, he tried to change the subject to safer ground. "Lyle, how have you been feeling recently? Has the doctor said when you might walk again?"

Lyle gave a disgusted snort and said, "He keeps trying to tell me I'll never be on my feet, but that fool doesn't know enough to treat my horses, much less to treat me."

Thor chuckled at Lyle's spirit. He had to admire the man for his courage after all the disheartening predictions the doctor had made since his accident. "Speaking of horses, have you had anyone show you the new stock I brought over on the *Sea Siren*?"

For a moment Storm thought she saw a flicker of suspicion in Lyle's eyes as they rested upon his wife's face, but then he shook his head and said, "No, I've not felt up to it; but I've heard you've been over quite frequently to check on them. Miranda said I slept through each of your visits."

Feeling suddenly uncomfortable for a reason he could not explain, Thor glanced at the beautiful woman at his side. "Ah, yes. I've been concerned about one of the fillies. When we docked at Savannah, she wasn't feeling up to par, because the prisoners who were seeing to the stock had fed them some bad hay. I had the smithy take a look at her, but I've also wanted to keep an eye on her myself. I know you've got some of the best stable hands around, but for my own peace of mind, I've stopped by to make sure nothing else happens. She seems to have come through it all just fine, however. I think all that was wrong with her was seasickness. She's done well since we landed."

Lyle's fondness for Thor was reflected in his smile. "Good, I'm glad to hear it. That filly's line has been in my family since a Turkish prince gave a magnificent pair to my grandfather over fifty years ago. I'd hate to see something happen to it now."

A bored expression played over Miranda's features as she flipped open her painted-silk fan and slowly moved it back and forth, stirring the warm air and wafting her perfume in Thor's direction. As Lyle paused, she glanced at Storm, her lips curling before she snapped her fan closed and said, "Thor, since you mentioned the horses, I just recalled the stable boy said the stallion had a slight limp this morning. Would you mind seeing to it before you return to Misty Rose?"

A look of concern knit Thor's brow as he glanced from Lyle to Miranda. "Of course. I'll check him now while Lyle visits with Mistress Kingsley."

With the rustle of satin Miranda rose from the sofa as Thor stood. "I think I should go with you, since my brother, Geoffry, isn't here to see to it. I don't trust the servants to keep me well informed. Since Lyle's accident, it seems I must see to everything personally because of the laziness of the help." The tone of Miranda's voice implied the heavy burden she carried as the wife of a cripple.

Thor's eyes softened with sympathy for Miranda's plight. He could well understand the pressures that were placed on her since her husband was unable to see to his holdings. Thor admired her for the courage she had shown during such a trying time. There were few women who could take on the responsibility of managing a plantation as Miranda had done. Most would have crumbled under the weight of it all. "When will your brother be back?" he asked.

"Geoffry returned from Europe yesterday," Miranda said as a smile flashed across her face and her eyes glowed with happiness. "But he has business in Charleston that will keep him there for a few more weeks. He visited us last night and stayed until only a short while before you arrived."

Pleased that Geoffry Chatham had finally decided to come home and would be there when Miranda needed him, Thor said, "I'll look forward to seeing your brother when he returns to AshGlen, or perhaps I'll look him up in Charleston when I go there next on business."

Lyle's face darkened at the mention of his young brother-in-law. His bluish lips thinned into a narrow line as he murmured, "Yes, Geoffry is back," but did not elaborate further.

Miranda glanced over her shoulder at her husband, her eyes glinting with animosity, before she turned once more to Thor and took his arm. She gave him an enchanting smile as they left the study together.

Storm had caught the hateful look on Miranda's face and sensed an undercurrent of dissension between Lyle and his beautiful wife over her brother. She gazed thoughtfully through the window as Thor and Miranda passed by on their way to the stables. All was not right at AshGlen.

Dragging her eyes away from the scene beyond the window, Storm turned to look at the man lying so quietly on the lounge. He, too, was watching Thor and Miranda stroll along the path, his wife clinging to his friend's arm, gazing up at Thor as if held by his every word. Lyle's parchmentlike skin seemed pinched with annoyance, and his fingers fidgeted nervously with the fringe on the lap rug.

Using the moment to study the man her mother had loved until her death, Storm realized that even with his ill health, Lyle Ashfort was attractive. She could imagine how Alisa's heart had fluttered at the sight of the handsome young nobleman nearly nineteen years before. Storm had experienced the same sensation when she looked at Thor. Though she now understood her mother better, her resentment of Lyle had not dissipated. He was still the man who had left Alisa to bear his child and survive the only way she could on the streets of London.

Storm jumped with a nervous start as Lyle suddenly turned to her and said, "You say you come from London? Did you live there all your life?"

Swallowing back the urge to tell him exactly how she and her mother had lived, she said, "No, I spent the major part of my life in Somerset. I lived in London only two years before coming to the colonies."

The need to vent all her animosity upon Lyle Ashfort rose within her but she knew the time was not right. Her rage would not hurt him enough. He would only order her from AshGlen and then forget about the depraved young woman from Misty Rose. She had to wait until she could make him suffer.

To her relief, Lyle did not seem to note her reticence as he stared down at the plaid lap rug and absently flicked away small pieces of lint from it. "Yes, London has changed considerably since I had seen it last. I didn't remember it being such a dirty city, but youth has a way of making things appear more beautiful and exciting, especially to a young man fresh from school and on his own for the first time in his life." He chuckled as he looked up at Storm. "Or it could be that I have grown used to the clean air of the colonies and the open spaces of the AshGlen that I built here."

A rueful smile touched his lips as he continued. "Miranda's brother, Geoffry, accompanied me to London last year, and where I detested the crowded streets and smokey air, he seemed to thrive on them. So much so he decided to take an extended tour of Europe this past winter after I had my accident."

Storm mused bitterly to herself as she listened to Lyle ruminate about his visit to London. Do you remember the young girl and the vows you spoke at Gretna Green? she asked silently. Or did Alisa grow less beautiful and exciting with time? What was the reason you left her? Was it because your boyish fantasies began to fade? Why, Lyle, why? The questions boiled in Storm's mind, but she did not voice them. Looking away from him so that he could not tell from her face the turmoil of her thoughts, she said, "I can see why you prefer AshGlen to London. It is lovely."

A pleased smile lit Lyle's thin features. "Yes, it is. I modeled it after my family home in northern England.

Most assumed it is called AshGlen because it rests on the banks of the Ashley River, but in fact AshGlen was also the name of my family's estate. Had I settled in Georgia or further north, my plantation would still have been called after my ancestral home.''

Lyle's evident pleasure faded as he looked once more out the window and watched Thor and Miranda stroll up the path from the stables. Something akin to pain flickered in the dark depths of his eyes before he quickly veiled it and said, ''I see Thor and my wife are returning. I hope there was nothing amiss with the stallion.''

Storm seriously doubted that there had been anything wrong with the horse in the first place. She suspected Miranda had used the ploy of the horse's limp to be alone with Thor and away from her invalid husband. Miranda's intentions were clear to Storm, and from the expression on Lyle's face, they were also apparent to him. She saw Lyle purse his lips at the sight of Thor and Miranda laughing together as they paused in the garden. That small action revealed much to Storm. Lyle knew his wife had set her sights on his young, handsome neighbor.

A spasm of pity for Lyle Ashfort swept over Storm, and she glanced uneasily down at her tightly clasped hands. She had no reason to feel sorry for the man. He did not deserve any compassion from her after all he had done to her mother. Pushing the unexpected emotion to the back of her mind, she thought vindictively, You deserve what you're getting and worse.

Surreptitiously, she glanced at Lyle to see his eyes still on the tall man and the beautiful woman. Possibly fate is seeking its own retribution for the wrongs you have committed in the past, Lyle Ashfort. You lie here a cripple and have to watch your young wife flaunt her charms at your friend. I know from your expression that you suffer. Perhaps I will have to do nothing at all to fulfill my vendetta for Mother. Thor and Miranda will carry it out for me.

Storm found little comfort in the thought. If what she suspected was true, Lyle's debt would be paid in full, but her own heart would be broken in the process.

She could not take her eyes away from Miranda's flushed, happy face as she and Thor entered the study. Her ripe mouth looked as if it had been recently and thoroughly kissed. Her eyes were bright and seemed to glitter with triumph as she looked at Storm, conveying a silent message: He belongs to me.

Storm could feel her cheeks burn with anger as Miranda dropped a perfunctory kiss on Lyle's brow and cooed in a syrupy voice, "Darling, I'm sorry to leave you so long, but Thor wanted to be sure that there was nothing truly wrong with the stallion. Thank goodness he didn't find anything out of the ordinary. I'm going to give the stable boy a good setdown for worrying us for no reason."

Lyle assessed Miranda's flushed features before his gaze came to rest on Thor. "I'm sorry for the trouble, but I appreciate your concern. Will you and Mistress Kingsley be our guests for the midday meal?"

Suddenly feeling somehow at fault, Thor glanced away from Lyle's knowing eyes. "Thank you for the invitation, Lyle, but I'm afraid we have to get back to Misty Rose. I need to check on the progress of the new floodgates Matthew is installing."

A flicker of relief seemed to pass over Lyle's features. "Certainly; perhaps another time," he said graciously before turning his attention to Storm. "Mistress Kingsley, I have enjoyed your company. I hope you will come often to visit me. We seldom have many guests now, since I have to spend a great deal of time in my bed. Will you come again?"

Lyle's sincerity and apparent loneliness provoked a bout of confusing emotions within Storm, making her uncertain how to reply. Before her lay the man she had vowed vengeance upon for causing Alisa's death, but she found herself responding to him with sympathy. A part of her mind still cried out for justice, while the gentler side of her nature was repulsed at the thought of heaping more misery upon a cripple.

Over the years she had envisioned a strong, cruel man and knew she would find satisfaction by bringing him to his knees. Now she was suddenly finding herself unable to proceed with her vendetta. She knew she would find little contentment in harming a man who was unable to defend himself. Life claimed its own type of justice for the offenses of man, as Lyle's disability proved.

With this reasoning, Storm managed to settle the turmoil in her mind to a certain degree, but she still did not know how to reply to Lyle's invitation. Because of her position at Misty Rose, she was not free to come and go as she pleased. Hoping Thor would help her solve the dilemma, she glanced at him, only to see a look pass between him and Miranda. That small intimacy snapped Storm's tenacious hold over her temper.

Damn them, she fumed as her innate sense of justice rose to Lyle's defense. She had no love for Lyle Ashfort—far from it—but everything within her rebelled at Miranda's sordid treatment of her crippled husband.

Storm had never been a person who could tolerate abuse of any kind toward man or beast. She instinctively reacted to defend Lyle in the same manner she would a mangy cur that was being beaten. He could not battle against a strong man like Thor for his wife's affections. If Storm's presence helped Lyle in some small way, she would come to AshGlen.

Flashing a look of defiance at Thor, she rose from the chair, hoping her words would place him in a position where he could not deny Lyle's request. "Certainly. I will come as often as Captain Wakefield permits me."

A teasing light entered Lyle's eyes. "Permits you? My dear, surely Thor cannot keep you burdened with so much work that you can't spare a few hours to cheer an invalid's day." He paused as his gaze came to rest on his neighbor. "Can you, Thor?"

Thor saw the trap awaiting him with doors open wide. He had brought Storm to AshGlen this morning to keep her in his sight, and now he was being maneuvered into having to give her more freedom and perhaps giving Matthew the opportunity he sought to further his suit. The thought irritated him.

Thor knew it would be impossible for him to escort Storm on every visit to AshGlen in order to keep Matthew at a distance along the way, but he also knew he could not refuse to let her come without revealing his reasons. Hiding his annoyance, he said, "Mistress Kingsley is free to visit as often as she likes. However, I would suggest she wait until I can escort her to ensure her safety. She is not yet familiar with our country."

Miranda broke into the conversation. "I fully agree. Mistress Kingsley needs an escort. I can understand Thor's concern, because I know the area well, but still feel much better when I have a groom with me." Giving Thor a beguiling smile, Miranda continued, "And it would also be nice to have you visit us more often."

Lyle snorted. "Ridiculous. Thor is much too busy to escort Mistress Kingsley on every visit. Perhaps he would let Matthew come with her on the days he can't. I haven't seen that rascal in a long while."

Storm noted the tension that seemed to hover about them as Miranda watched Thor's reaction to Lyle's suggestion. The woman's lovely features seemed to harden as she slowly turned to look at Storm. No one else saw the jealousy and hatred that shimmered in Miranda's pale eyes. Storm had known from the beginning of Miranda's dislike for her, but now it seemed to have deepened. Then the evil expression was gone from Miranda's face, and her red lips curved prettily as she said, "I think Lyle is right,

Thor. We cannot expect you to take time out for our pleasure. I'm sure Matthew wouldn't mind taking a few hours from his work to accompany Mistress Kingsley to AshGlen.''

Obviously pleased that his wife agreed with him for once, Lyle smiled. ''I think that finishes this discussion, Thor. I'm sure you cannot deny Miranda's request.''

Mentally hearing the doors of the trap swing closed, Thor gave a resigned sigh and nodded as he took Storm's arm, his fingers bearing down with more pressure than necessary. ''Then we'll bid you good day.''

Fuming, he did not release his firm hold on her until he had placed her once more in the saddle. His face was dark with anger as they left AshGlen behind. He silently rode at her side until the ivy-covered arches were no longer in sight.

Storm sensed the impending explosion but was unable to contain her involuntary start when Thor leaned over and grabbed the reins of her mare, jerking it to a halt.

''Storm, I have been coerced into giving you more freedom, but I will not tolerate any more of your sly manipulations. Lyle is a good man, and I'll not see him used for your benefit.''

Storm gripped the pommel until her knuckles grew white, her face flushing scarlet as the anger that had been simmering within her now exploded into full-blown rage. It rippled in a shock wave along every nerve in her body, making blue sparks of fire flash in her eyes as she turned on him. ''You odious bastard! You condemn me at every opportunity, though I am innocent of all the crimes of which I have been accused. You have the audacity to censure me when *I* am not the one who has manipulated Lyle Ashfort. Damn you, Thor Wakefield, for a fool. You're too blind to see it is Miranda who is using her husband, not me.''

Tossing the reins back at her, Thor growled angrily.

"That's enough. You can say anything you want about me, but I'll not have Miranda's name slandered by a conniving wench from the gutters. She is a lady in all respects."

Storm's sarcastic laughter drifted through the air. "If she is such a lady, then why did she let you kiss her? Your guilt was written all over your face, Thor, as well as on her smug little mouth. I'm not blind, nor is Lyle Ashfort. How does it feel to cuckold a cripple? Does it make you feel like a man?"

Everything that had transpired since the previous night suddenly came rushing back to Storm. She felt tears burn in her eyes and quickly bit down on her lip to stay them but failed in the attempt. She tasted her own blood, and nausea churned her insides as she gave the mare a sharp kick in the side. She had tried to bury the pain Thor had so carelessly inflicted during the night but realized she had not succeeded. It had returned, strengthened by his condemnation.

Ashamed of giving in to her emotions before him, she urged the horse into a gallop, caring little in which direction the mare went as long as it was away from Thor Wakefield. Storm rode hard and fast, trying to flee her feelings as well as Thor. At that moment she despised him, but not as much as she loathed her vulnerable heart.

Blinded by tears, she let the animal have its head, paying no heed as it left the roadway, sprinting across a newly turned field and into the thick underbrush on the other side. She heard Thor calling from behind her but could not make out his words.

The sharp edge of a low-hanging limb lashed her, the impact bringing back her reason and making her realize her own stupidity. Gripping the reins tightly, she tried to halt the animal, now frightened by the slaps and stings of the underbrush. Her effort was fruitless. The mare dashed recklessly forward, her eyes rolling wildly as the trailing spanish moss brushed her head, adding to her fear.

Storm clung to the pommel, trying desperately to maintain her balance as her own panic engulfed her. If she fell, she knew she would be lucky to escape severe injury or worse. Frightened for her life, she felt her anger vanish into the wind. When she felt Thor's arms about her, lifting her from the saddle, an overwhelming feeling of relief swept over her. She clung to him, her arms going about his waist as she buried her face against his chest and wept openly, releasing all her pent-up terror.

Thor slowed the stallion to a walk as he cradled Storm in his arms and murmured soothingly against her wind-blown curls, "Hush, now, you're safe." His long fingers brushed several unruly locks from her forehead before gently raising her chin to allow him to peer down into her tear-bright eyes. "Storm, what on earth possessed you? Don't you realize you could have been killed? Damn it, have you no brains at all in that beautiful head of yours?"

Storm's soft lower lip trembled. She blinked rapidly to try to stem a new rush of hot tears as she straightened up and tried to put as much distance between herself and Thor as being mounted on the same horse would allow. She drew in a tremulous breath as she glared up at him. "I've enough brains to know that I don't want to ride on the same horse with you. You are despicable. You pretend to be Lyle's friend while you bed his wife, and you use me when she is unavailable to quench your lust. I loathe you, Thor, with every ounce of my being."

He jerked back as if she had slapped him. His expression darkened and his jaw grew rigid with anger. He pulled her roughly against him, his hands biting into her arms as he glared down at her. "Damn it, Storm, hold your wayward tongue or you will regret it. I did not bring you to Misty Rose to meddle in my affairs, nor will I tolerate it. I brought you to my home for one purpose, and that alone stands between you and the auction block. If you treasure the smooth flesh of your back, you'll not repeat such slander again.''

Forgetting her precarious seat in her anger, Storm brought both hands up against his chest and gave a hard push. She tasted freedom for but a moment before she began to fall.

Thor reached out to save her but found himself off-balance as well. He slipped from the saddle and landed with a hard thump at her side. Unhurt, he drew in a deep angry breath, ready to give her the beating he had promised, but as he turned to her, his face paled. She lay still, her face white, her thick lashes lying like dark shadows upon her ashen cheeks.

He knelt beside her, his fingers unsteady as he touched her throat to find a pulse. Relieved at the steady beat beneath his fingertips, he gently lifted her into his arms, cradling her in his lap as he tried to revive her. He patted her cheek, and he placed light kisses on her brow, murmuring, ''Tempest, what is it about you that brings out the devil in me?''

He gazed down at her pale features and wondered at his own sanity. He had never let another woman intrude upon his life the way Storm had. Like her namesake, she had swept into it, turning it upside-down, creating turmoil in its every facet. He had argued with Matthew over her and had even threatened him with dismissal. That in itself was a new experience for a man who had always been able to keep women at a distance, mocking them, while he took what they offered and then went his own way, never looking back but always onward to a new conquest. He had scoffed at his friends when they declared undying love for their ladies, reaffirming in his own mind that only fools fell under that deceptive spell. Storm had called him a fool, and he feared she was right. She was in his blood, fermenting it like a heady wine, and even during their torrid arguments, all he wanted to do was to make love to her. He shook his head at himself in dismay.

Seeing her lashes begin to flutter open, he smiled down at her with relief. Perhaps he was a fool, but the vixen in his arms would never know it. She loathed him, and he would never give her the satisfaction of learning of his feelings. He might be a fool, but he would keep it to himself.

Storm's hand came up to her brow as she squinted at him. "What happened?" she asked, rubbing her aching head.

"You fell from my horse, Tempest. How do you feel?"

As she tried to sit up, her face twisted in a mask of pain, a streak of lightning searing across her skull, bursting into flashes of light before her eyes. She fell limply back against his arm and groaned, "I feel as if someone has taken an axe to my head and rendered it open."

Concern etched a deep furrow across Thor's brow. "Do you think you can ride? We need to get you back to Misty Rose so Mamie can take a look at the lump on your head."

Tentatively Storm explored her hair until she found the bump from her fall. "I think I can," was all she could say as another pain ripped through her head. She felt the bile rise in her throat from it and knew she was going to disgrace herself in front of him. Clamping her hand over her mouth, she managed to scramble from his lap and onto her knees before her stomach gave way.

Tremors shook her body as she succumbed to the sickness. Beads of perspiration broke out across her brow and upper lip as a sudden weakness invaded her limbs. She would have collapsed had Thor not placed his hand to her head and his arm about her waist as she retched.

When the spasms of nausea passed, he wiped her brow with his handkerchief before lifting her into his arms and placing her on the stallion. Climbing up behind her, he turned the animal into a shortcut through the woods. The path would not be as easy for the horse to travel, but it would get them to Misty Rose much more quickly than if they took the sandy road. Storm needed attention as soon as possible. Her face was deathly pale as she leaned weakly back against him and closed her eyes.

Matthew tethered his horse to the hitching post near the kitchen. The breakfast he had consumed before dawn had been used up with his hard labor that morning, and his stomach rumbled hungrily. Thinking of the delicious meal Mamie no doubt had prepared, he turned in the direction of the white board-and-batten building.

Striding along the flagstone path, his mind centered on appeasing his hunger, he caught a glimpse of Thor out of the corner of his eye. Pausing, he waited as his friend approached the manor, thinking he might join him during the midday meal. However, Matthew's thoughts of food vanished as he saw the pale form lying limply in Thor's arms.

Shaken at the sight, Matthew ran to give his friend assistance. He took Storm gently from Thor's arms, then strode up the walk and into the house without considering his actions. Taking the winding stairs two at a time, Matthew carried her to the bedchamber across from the master suite. Tenderly he laid her upon the large bed and smoothed back the hair from her brow, worry marking his own brow as he bent over her.

Hearing Thor order Perle to find Mamie, Matthew knew from his friend's tone of voice that he, too, was very concerned about Storm's welfare. Matthew looked over his shoulder as Thor strode into the room. "What happened?" was all he could say at the sight of his friend's haggard expression.

Running his hand through his hair, Thor shook his head. His eyes filled with anxiety as he looked past Matthew to the still form on the bed. "She fell from my horse. She didn't take a hard fall, but her head must have hit a stone or something."

Matthew's face grew hard. "What in the hell was she doing on your horse, Thor? I thought you had the small roan saddled for Storm."

A muscle twitched in Thor's jaw. "I did, damn it, but she made the animal bolt. She fell after I managed to rescue her from the roan."

Matthew turned to face him, his fists clenched at his side, his eyes suspicious. "Are you sure nothing else transpired between you?"

Thor's face flushed with rage. "Are you calling me a liar?"

Knowing he was letting his jealousy overcome his reason, Matthew shook his head. "No; I'm sorry, Thor. I didn't mean that. All I wanted to know was how she managed to fall from your horse."

Before Thor could answer, Mamie came waddling into the room, huffing and puffing from climbing the stairs. Sensing the tension between the two men, she said, "Now, you get. If I needs you later I'll call. I got to see to this youngun' now, and I ain't got time to put up with your little-boy squabblin', like two dogs with a bone. This child is what's important, if you ain't forgot it."

Both men gave Mamie a sheepish look before obeying her orders. She clucked in disgust as she closed the door on them and then turned back to her patient.

Mamie examined Storm from head to toe to see if anything was broken or bruised. She found only a small lump on the back of her head the size of a bird's egg. Mamie knew such a tiny bump should not have caused the girl to lose consciousness. She had seen much worse lumps on the heads of the plantation children when they got into mischief.

Placing her hands on her wide hips, Mamie clucked

again as she stared down at Storm, trying to solve the mystery. Knowing she would not find the solution by just standing beside the bed, she shook her turbaned head and began to undress the girl.

The cook's keen eyes came to rest on Storm's slightly protruding abdomen as she removed her undergarments. As she placed her pudgy black hands on the swelling mound, Mamie's fat cheeks spread into a wide, knowing smile. Satisfied, she nodded to herself. "Yes, siree, Master Thor is going to be a pappy." Chuckling, she pulled the sheet up over Storm. "I do declare it's about time, too."

Mamie stood gazing down at Storm a moment more as she considered the girl's condition. The pleased smile began to fade. From the look on Storm's white face, it was not going to be an easy term. Mamie had known women who fainted at the least little thing, and it always seemed to foretell a bad time ahead with the pregnancy.

Her lips pursed, she folded her arms over her melon-sized breasts. She needed to tell Master Thor, but it wasn't her place. The young Missy should be the one to let him know he was going to be a father. Mamie's brow furrowed as she said aloud, "I got to tell Master Thor somethin', but what?"

Storm's lashes fluttered as Mamie spoke. Confused to find herself in new surroundings with the cook hovering over her, she said, "What do you have to tell Thor?" As the words left her mouth, she was quickly reminded of her fall by the sharp pain that seared through her head.

"Lawd, child, you is awake, and I'm glad to see it. You had us all worried half to death." Mamie took a vile of white powder from her pocket and poured it into a glass before adding water. Stirring the mixture until it dissolved, she then raised Storm's head up enough so the girl could drink it. "This'll help your head. When Perle said you'd taken a fall, I figured you'd wake up with a terrible headache.''

Storm swallowed the bitter liquid gratefully and settled back on the pillow. "You never answered my question, Mamie. What were you going to tell Thor? If it concerns my health, there's no need. I'll be fine when my head quits pounding.''

Settling her corpulent body next to Storm on the side of the bed, making it sag with her weight, Mamie fiddled with the edge of her white apron as she said, "Child, I think it is your place to tell him, not mine.''

Puzzled, Storm looked up at Mamie. She had no idea what the woman was talking about. "Mamie, I just told you I'll be fine when my head stops aching. I see no need to tell Thor anything more.''

Mamie's double chin sank to her collarbone as she gave Storm a dubious look. "Child, it ain't somethin' you can keep a secret for long. And the way you been actin', it's best that he knows right away.''

With her head feeling as if a little man with a sledge-hammer were pounding his way through her temple, Storm was in no mood for riddles. All she wanted was peace and quiet to help ease her pain. Exasperated, her temper growing shorter by the moment, she said, "Mamie, for the life of me, I have no idea of what you're talking about. If you think my headache is that important, then by all means tell Thor and be done with it. Please don't badger me until I'm screaming with pain.''

Bewildered by her outburst, Mamie jutted out her bottom lip and lowered her brows over her dark eyes. She studied Storm silently for a few moments before shaking her head, a look of sympathy entering her eyes as she reached out and patted the girl's hand. "Child, don't you know what I'm talkin' about?''

Storm winced as she shook her head.

Mamie's mouth curled up at the corners. "Tsk, tsk, I

don't know what this here world is comin' to when a woman don't know she's carryin' her first babe.''

Storm froze, her eyes widening and the blood draining from her face, leaving her the same color as the sheets she lay upon. She stared at Mamie in disbelief. Babe, babe, echoed through her mind, but she could not accept it. It could not be. Her lips moved several times before she could force the words from her throat. ''No, Mamie, you're mistaken. I'm not going to have a baby. No, not that, never that.''

Mamie's expression grew serious, her tender heart going out to Storm. ''Missy, are you sayin' you ain't been with Master Thor in his bed?''

Storm could not look at her. Covering her face with her hands as she shook her head from side to side. ''No, Mamie, I've been, I mean—'' Her words broke off; she could not voice her humiliation.

Mamie soothed Storm's tousled curls as if she were her mother. ''There, there, Missy, I understand. We can't always fight it. But a babe is somethin' you can't ignore.''

Tears glistened in Storm's eyes as her hands fell to her lap and she looked at Mamie, trying to deny the truth. ''It can't be. It just can't be.''

The cook's eyes reflected her pity as she moved her head slowly up and down, her fat chin quivering with the motion. ''If it can't be, it can't, but if there's a chance, you'd best think on it, for you got all the right symptoms. I heard you be sick several mornin's when you thought nobody was around.''

Storm shook her head again, rapidly, still resisting the truth of Mamie's words. ''That was just nerves; nothing more.''

Mamie stood and wiped her hands on her apron as she gazed solemnly down at Storm. ''Missy, you can't change things by denyin' 'em. But I'll hold my tongue until you decide it's time to tell Master Thor he's goin' to be a pappy. I'd bet he'll be proud enough to bust when he learns it.''

Storm's eyes brimmed, and her lips trembled as she said, "Thank you, Mamie."

The cook hugged her to her huge breast. "Child, you have to take care. I won't say nothin' unless you have another faintin' spell. That ain't a good sign. You got to think of the little 'un now, too." Giving Storm a motherly peck on the brow, Mamie waddled to the door. Pausing, she looked back at the girl. "I'll tell Master Thor you is restin' and don't need to be disturbed for a while."

Giving Mamie a greatful smile, Storm managed to hold her tears in check until the door closed. As the latch clicked, she gave way to them, letting crystal droplets course freely down her cheeks as she stared blindly up at the ceiling.

The only sound in the room was the porcelain clock on the mantel. Each tick seemed to say, Babe, Babe, Babe, in her mind, and her tears came faster. She wept until there were no more tears to shed.

Finally Storm's hand crept to her slightly rounding belly, experimentally passing over the soft surface as she began to accept the truth. Within her grew Thor's seed. Conceived in love not for her but for another woman.

The thought seared her mind, and she felt for a moment as if her head would fly from her shoulders as agony split her skull. Clamping both hands to her temples, she rolled her head on the pillow, asking the silent room, "What am I to do? What am I to do?"

Mamie's powder slowly began to take effect, easing Storm's pain. As the throbbing receded, she drew in a ragged breath and turned on her side to gaze out through the window. Below her lay Misty Rose, Thor's home and her child's heritage. But like herself, her babe would never be recognized by its father. Thor would neither marry her nor accept her offspring. And even if he would, she was not at all sure that she could accept him on those terms. Her life would be hell, married to Thor and knowing he loved Miranda Ashfort.

The thought made a new pain twist in Storm's heart. It would be far better if she left Misty Rose and Thor never knew of their child. Taking another deep breath, she closed her thick lashes over her red and swollen eyes. She now knew how Alisa must have felt when she learned she carried Lyle Ashfort's babe but would have to bear it alone.

Again the fates had manipulated Storm's life so that she would tread the same rocky path Alisa had traveled nineteen years earlier.

Before Mamie's powder made her drift into a restless sleep, Storm murmured, "But I'll be the one to leave this time."

Chapter 10

The amber liquid sparkled in the glass as Miranda handed a brandy to Geoffry. "Well, brother, it's good to have you home. We had so little time before you went to Charleston to discuss your trip. How was your tour of Europe? I especially want to hear how you enjoyed your time in London."

Geoffry swirled the brandy in his glass as he regarded his lovely sister for a few moments before he answered. The sun streamed through the window, highlighting her golden beauty, its rays creating an ethereal glow about her as they shimmered on her bright hair and the satin of her gown. A twinkle of mirth came into his eyes at the thought. His sister was far from an angel and would be offended if compared to one. Smiling, he said, "Ah, my trip. I do think the best part was the little extra service I was able to perform for you along the way."

Settling herself gracefully at her brother's side, Miranda cast a quick glance about the drawing room to ascertain that all doors were closed to ensure their privacy. A malicious light gleamed in her pale eyes as they came to rest once more on his boyishly handsome face. "Were there any problems?"

"None that I would consider major," Geoffry said as he stretched his lithe body lazily. A smug and cunning expression played over his fine features as he shook his head and added, "But I do bear sad tidings. Poor Thadius was murdered by a prostitute by the name of Alisa while we were in London."

Miranda's ripe mouth curled upward with cold-blooded pleasure. " 'Tis sad to hear. I do hope the woman was punished for such a terrible crime."

Chuckling, Geoffry nodded. "Aye, that she was. The young man traveling with Thadius testified against her to ensure she was sentenced to the stake." Raising his hands palm upward in a helpless gesture, he said, "What else could I do? I had to see justice done; as a good citizen it was my duty."

Miranda leaned back against the Queen Anne sofa and let out a sigh of relief. "Good. I was worried that you might not find her. We would have lost everything if she turned up here to claim her rights."

Giving her an offended look, Geoffry said, "My dear Miranda, I'm not the incompetent fool your dear husband deems me. I beg you to remember that in the future. You should know by now that I have never failed you."

A look of remorse crossed Miranda's face as she took her brother's hand. "I'm sorry, Geoffry. I've just been upset of late. I know I owe everything to you for finding Lyle's first wife. I shudder to think what might have happened to us had you not gone with Lyle to London last year."

Tossing down the last of the brandy, Geoffry set the glass down and wiped his mouth with a lace-edged handkerchief. "That would have put both of us in quite a bind. I'm afraid if poor Lyle doesn't succumb to his injuries soon, so you can get your hands on his money, I'll be in a fix anyway. My gambling debts keep mounting.''

A rueful smile touched Miranda's lips as she patted her brother's arm sympathetically. ''I understand completely how you feel. I wish to God we had cut the saddle strap all the way. Perhaps then Lyle would have broken his neck as we planned, instead of only his hip. But at least you managed to return to England and solved one problem for us. That eases my mind a great deal.''

Geoffry grinned. ''That I did. I wonder what your dear husband would think to know he was the one to lead us in that direction?''

Remembering the day Lyle and her brother had returned from England, Miranda gazed thoughtfully out the window, a vicious little smile playing about her lips. She well recalled the state Geoffry had been in upon their arrival home. He had been completely overwrought as he told Miranda she was not the legal Madame Ashfort. Poor Geoffry could see his future crumbling about him and the gates of prison opening wide to welcome him because of his gambling debts.

Miranda had been stunned by his disclosure but had had the sense of mind to keep her own hysterics at bay as she calmed her brother and ordered him to tell her all that had transpired. Through his garbled explanation, she had gathered that he and Lyle had gone to the Golden Pigeon, an inn Lyle had frequented in his youth, and her husband had imbibed too much wine, trying to drown the memories London revived. He had begun to talk about his first wife and how she had died in childbirth while he was trying to make his fortune in the colonies. Before passing out, he had revealed the guilt he still felt about not being with Alisa at the time of her death.

It had not been Lyle's disclosures that had led Geoffry to learn that Alisa Ashfort still lived. He had received that startling bit of information from the innkeeper, who had

helped him lift Lyle's unconscious form and carry him up
the stairs to the rooms they had secured for their stay. The
innkeeper had recognized Lyle Ashfort even after so many
years had passed. He easily recalled the man who had left
the pretty barmaid, forcing her to turn to the streets to
make a living.

After the innkeeper had finished his gruff story of Lyle
and the woman he had run out on, Geoffry had packed
their bags and had carried his brother-in-law back to the
ship, telling him the next day that he had done so out of
concern for Lyle's condition. However, his main purpose
had been to get Lyle away from the Golden Pigeon before
he, too, learned from the innkeeper that Alisa Ashfort still
lived.

On the day of her husband and brother's return, Miranda
had begun to scheme of how to rid herself of Lyle before
he found out about his wife in England.

Her first plan had failed dismally. Lyle had survived the
accident she and Geoffry had contrived for him. Afterward
she knew she would have to use another tactic to ensure
her inheritance of AshGlen. She could not make another
attempt on her husband's life without raising suspicions,
so she had sent Geoffry on a presumed tour of Europe.
Actually he had gone to England, to find Alisa Ashfort and
kill her.

Geoffry had been most creative in the enterprise. He had
rid them of Lyle's first wife without any problems. Thadius
Hollings had been sacrificed, but she did not regret the
part he had served. That fat, lecherous pig deserved to die,
Miranda thought. Jennifer Hollings, his little mouse of a
wife, should thank us for freeing her from him.

Turning her thoughts back to the present, Miranda glanced
once more at her brother. "I'm glad you didn't have any
problems to keep you away longer. I need you here now."

A blush swept over Geoffry's fair face as he looked
nervously away from his sister's penetrating gaze. "I had

one slight problem that I failed to mention, Sister. You know Alisa's child who was to have died at birth? Well, uh, she didn't.''

Miranda's features tightened with fury, her eyes flashing fire as her mouth narrowed into a line. "You fool! Damn it, Geoffry, now of all times I don't need this new worry. Why didn't you get rid of her, too?"

He suddenly looked like a little boy who had stolen a pie and got away with eating the whole thing as he gave her an impish grin. "I did. I—pardon the play on words, Sister—killed two birds with one stone. Though they couldn't find enough evidence to sentence her to the same fate as her mother, they convicted the girl of prostitution. She's now in Newgate, and from what I hear of the place, she won't live long there."

Miranda drooped with relief, then slapped her brother playfully. "Geoffry, you nearly frightened me to death."

Lounging back against the arm of the sofa, he grinned. "I can't resist teasing you a little, Miranda. I like to watch the sparks in your eyes. I'll never settle down until I've found a woman who can match you."

She smiled at her brother's compliment. "Then prepare yourself for bachelorhood, Geoffry."

Brother and sister laughed together, enjoying their evil comradeship. As their mirth died, Geoffry eyed his sister quizzically for a moment before asking, "You've mentioned several times that you didn't need a new problem now. What is it that troubles your pretty head?"

Agitated, she rose from the sofa and began to pace back and forth across the drawing room. At last she paused in front of her brother. Her eyes gleamed with hatred for the girl who at first had seemed only her rival in beauty but who now threatened all the plans Miranda had made for her future. "We do have another problem, and I'm afraid we must solve it soon or I'll lose everything we have worked so hard to gain. Thor has a new housekeeper, and if what I suspect is true, then there is much more to the girl's duties than overseeing his home.''

"Do you think it's more than a casual affair?" Geoffry asked, cocking one blond brow curiously.

"From Thor's reaction when Lyle suggested Matthew Boone escort her to AshGlen when Thor could not, I think it could develop into much more, but I intend to see that it does not." Miranda's voice was laced with malice as she recalled the look of jealousy she had seen in Thor's eyes at Lyle's mention of Matthew Boone and Storm.

Digging into his pocket, Geoffry withdrew a gold snuff-box and flipped it open. He pinched the brown powder and sniffed. Giving a light, gentlemanly sneeze, he patted his nose delicately as he eyed his sister's worried face. "Haven't we always solved your dilemmas in the past? I'm sure this will be no different.''

Tiny lines fanned Miranda's eyes, flawing her beauty, revealing the years she had subtracted from her age. "Yes, we have, but I don't know if it will be so easy this time. Thor is not as easily manipulated as Lyle. At times I think I have him where I want him, but then I'm not sure.''

Trying to reassure his sister, Geoffry pulled her down beside him and placed a comforting arm about her shoulders. "I have as yet to see you go after something and fail to get it, Miranda.''

Her eyes glittered as she cocked her head to one side and grinned up at her brother. "Rest assured that I will not disappoint you this time. I intend to have Thor Wakefield to myself, but there are two things that have to be disposed of first. That's where you come in.''

Geoffry was not at all pleased by the thought of his sister with Thor Wakefield, but for the moment he would hold his peace. He needed the money Miranda would give him and soon. Reaching inside his coat pocket, he withdrew a glass vial filled with crumbled dry leaves of fox-glove. A cunning light crept into his pale eyes, so much like his sister's. "I assumed as much. That's the reason I brought you this small gift. My debts keep growing by the day, and if I don't get some money soon, I won't even be able to afford a whore. What is your plan, Miranda?"

Her hand closed about the vial as her gay laughter filled the drawing room. "My plan, dear Brother, is to see us rich."

"I would expect no less of you, Sister," Geoffry said as his laughter joined Miranda's, and they began to plot to bring Misty Rose and AshGlen together.

Storm paused to rub the back of her neck, where a small ache had begun to form. It was her first day back at work since her fall two weeks earlier, and it had taken nearly all morning to bring the ledgers up to date. She wondered briefly how Thor managed to run a shipping firm as well as Misty Rose if two short weeks could pile up the work to such an extent.

As she placed the tips of her fingers against her burning eyes, her thoughts lingered on Thor. At his insistence she had remained in the guest chamber, letting Mamie coddle her with rich foods and motherly affection. The cook's care had done wonders for her. Storm had bloomed; her cheeks were again tinted with rose, and her eyes sparkled with vitality. She felt well physically and knew if she could find a solution to her other problems, her world would once more be set right.

Picking up the quill, she dipped it into the inkwell and bent once more to the task of recording household expenditures. It was a relief to be able to work again. At least it kept her mind occupied with something other than her pregnancy. Thankfully, she felt, Mamie had kept her word and had not told Thor of Storm's condition. For that small favor Storm was grateful. She knew Mamie was keeping a close watch on her health, but she never mentioned her condition outright.

Surprisingly, Storm found she had not felt nauseated again since she had accepted her state. And without the constant churning in her stomach, she had begun to feel well enough to start looking for a way to leave Misty Rose before anyone else was aware that she carried Thor's child. She had considered slipping away during the night but knew Thor would soon find her and bring her back. Each time a new idea occurred to her she rejected it. It always came back to the fact that without help, she would easily be prevented from escaping.

As her options dwindled, she came to the conclusion that there was only one person who might help her— Matthew Boone. He had often come to visit her while she was recuperating, and their friendship had deepened in the short time they were allowed to be alone.

Thor always seemed to choose the same time of day for his visits. That in itself was a mystery to Storm. She found Thor's behavior strange, as well as the undercurrent of tension she sensed when the two men were in the same room. She couldn't understand it. Each was polite to the other, but their actions seemed stiff and restrained. She knew of the bond that existed between Matthew and Thor, but now each seemed on edge in the other's presence.

Storm had pondered the reason for the sudden coolness between the two men, but no matter how hard she thought, she failed to find the answer to their odd behavior. Nor was she able to find the proper time to speak with Matthew about taking her away from Misty Rose. Thor's constant presence ensured that she did not have the chance.

She knew time was her enemy. Soon she had to find the opportunity to make her plea to Matthew, or all her efforts would be in vain. For that reason, she hoped Thor would not insist that she stay on in the guest chamber. Since she had returned to her duties, she also hoped to be allowed to return to the privacy of the Petite Maison. There she could find a way to broach the subject to Misty Rose's overseer.

Storm's brow knit as she forced her mind away from the two men and tried to concentrate on the ledger before her. A sharp rap on the door interrupted her train of thought, and before she could answer, Mamie hurried into the office. Her ebony face was lined with worry as she said, "Missy, a groom jest come for Master Thor. He says Master Ashfort is dying, and Master Thor is needed at AshGlen. Master Thor says for you to come, too, in case Madame Ashfort needs a woman to give her comfort."

The quill fell from Storm's suddenly numb fingers. Her face paled at the thought of Lyle Ashfort dying. Her heart constricted with a spasm of pain. No, she thought, it can't be. He can't die before I know why he left mother and me. I won't let him!

A fierce urgency possessed her to be at Lyle's side before he took his last breath. Without a word to Mamie, she lifted her skirts and ran from the manor. Her feet sped down the flagstone walk to find Thor waiting there with the carriage. His face reflected the anxiety she felt as he lifted her into the vehicle and climbed in beside her. He did not speak as he whipped the horse into a rapid gallop down the crushed shell drive and onto the sandy road to AshGlen.

As he reined the carriage to a halt before the Georgian manor, Storm did not wait for him to assist her to the ground. She scrambled down from the vehicle and hurried to the door. Her hand already rested on the knocker by the time he was able to catch up with her. However, before she could bring it down, the door opened, and a tearful Miranda flung her arms about Thor, weeping piteously.

"Lyle is dying. Oh, Thor, what shall I do?" the woman sobbed.

Thor cradled Miranda in his arms, trying to give her comfort as he said, "Hush, my dear, you'll make yourself ill, and you know Lyle would not want that."

Sniffling, Miranda dabbed at her nose with a white lace

handkerchief and looked up at him, her eyes wide and glassy. "Yes, I know you're right, but I can't stand the thought of losing him." New tears brimmed in her eyes, and her lips quivered. Her actions had the desired effect upon Thor; his arms came about her as he looked over her golden head at Storm. "Perhaps you should go up and see Lyle. I'll be there as soon as I get Miranda calmed down."

Knowing well Miranda's feelings for her husband and seeing that she would even stoop to use his dying to be in Thor's arms, Storm said disgustedly, "Yes, I'll do that."

Casting one last acrid glance at the couple, she made her way to Lyle's bedchamber. The room was in shadow, the heavy velvet drapes drawn over the windows as if to hide the white figure on the bed from death.

Zachery, the butler, rose from his vigil at Lyle's bedside as Storm entered the room. His shoulders were hunched in grief, and a half-hearted smile of welcome touched his deeply lined face. His eyes glittered brightly with unshed tears as he said, "Mistress, it was good of you to come."

Since she had come to AshGlen, Zachary's was the first sign of true grief Storm had seen. It kindled a sudden sense of loss within her, and her throat tightened. She made an attempt to give him a reassuring smile but failed. Swallowing back the tears in her throat, she said, "Thank you, Zachery. How is he?"

The butler's aged countenance reflected the sorrow in his heart as he looked down at Lyle. "Master Ashfort is took real bad this time. I fear it is in God's hands now."

Storm could easily sense the truth of Zachery's words. Death was in the air, hovering about the large bed, flapping its great black wings like a vulture. "What did the doctor say?"

Zachery's shoulders drooped even further as he shook his graying head. "Ain't been no doctor here. He ain't had time to get here from Charleston. Master Lyle took sick so suddenly after his midday meal that the madame was afraid he wouldn't last until Master Thor got here. We sent for the doctor just after the groom left for Misty Rose."

Wondering at Miranda's decision to send for Thor first, Storm placed her hand against Lyle's forehead, finding his brow clammy but cool. Pushing all thoughts of Miranda and Thor from her mind, she turned her complete attention to the invalid before her. Ruling out fever, she wondered at the cause of such a severe attack. Glancing at Zachery, she asked, "What have you done for him?"

Again the servant shook his head. "Madame done everything she knew to do, but nothing helped. Everythin' she gave him come right back up."

Touching Lyle's wrist, Storm felt for his pulse and found it irregular but not that of a dying man. Suspecting he had eaten meat that had been tainted, she asked, "Zachery, how did Master Ashfort act just before his attack?"

Zachery's ebony face screwed up thoughtfully, and he scratched his head. "He seemed fine when he finished his meal, but after he drank his tea, he began to sweat and to complain about a headache. He grabbed his stomach as if it pained him something terrible and then started to retch."

The butler's description confirmed Storm's suspicions. She had once seen Big Nan react the same way after she'd eaten something that had poisoned her system. Alisa had come to her friend's aid, forcing her to drink milk to help kill the poison after each time she vomited. When that was over, she had given Big Nan wine mixed with peppermint to soothe her stomach.

Knowing there was no time to wait for the doctor to agree with her diagnosis, Storm said, "Get one of the maids to go to the spring house for fresh milk, and then bring a bottle of wine and some fresh peppermint from the garden. Hurry, Zachery. There's no time to waste if we're going to help Master Lyle."

Hope seemed to shine again in Zachery's eyes as he

hurried to do her bidding. Inexperienced in matters of sickness and healing, she did not feel the same optimism. She only knew she could not sit by and do nothing. She had to make an effort to save Lyle.

She settled herself in the chair Zachery had vacated and lifted Lyle's limp hand, clasping it tightly as if to relay some of her own strength to him through her touch. Her voice was low and pleading, only a whisper in the stillness of the shadowy room. "You can't die, Lyle. I need you to live. There are too many unanswered questions. I find I can't reap the vengeance I sought against you because of your condition, but neither can I go through life never knowing the reason you left Mother."

Storm's words came from the heart. She had to learn why Lyle had not returned to Alisa before she could put the past behind her and look toward the future. Soon she would leave Misty Rose, but before she did, she wanted all the questions answered so she could build a new life for herself and her child. Too much old bitterness had ingrained itself in her heart, and she knew it would haunt her like a specter in the night, leaving her vulnerable when she would need all her strength for the babe that grew within her womb. Storm knew she had to learn the truth once and for all.

Zachery was huffing and puffing from his exertions as he entered the bedchamber with the items she had requested. Eagerly he bent to the task of helping her lift Lyle so that she could administer the simple remedy of milk to soothe his stomach. At first it would not stay down, but after several attempts, it remained within him.

Relieved, she crumbled the peppermint into the wine and set it aside to give the mint time to seep into the ruby liquid. Zachery hovered anxiously at her side as she waited for Lyle's system to adjust to the milk. Feeling as if enough time had passed, she asked the butler to lift Lyle's shoulders once more and she rubbed his throat to help him swallow the peppermint mixture.

Lyle's stomach did not revolt, and Storm released a sigh of relief as she turned to Zachery. The look that passed between them said much. They had done all they knew to do and could only wait and hope the doctor would arrive soon.

Time seemed to hobble by on crutches until the balding, reed-thin man, layered with dust from the road, rushed into the room. His watery eyes swept over Storm and Zachery questioningly, but he did not speak as he bent to listen to Lyle's heart.

The doctor's shiny pate wrinkled as he straightened and looked at her again. Pulling thoughtfully at his ear, he said, "I don't understand it. From Miranda's message, I thought Lyle was dying, but from what I can see, he is sleeping peacefully."

The doctor's words lifted the heavy burden resting on Storm's shoulders, and her face brightened with hope and relief. Flashing Zachery a happy look, she told the doctor how she had found Lyle and her own diagnosis of his illness. The doctor shook his head in wonder as he grinned in approval. "Well, young lady, it seems you have probably saved Lyle's life. It certainly sounds as if he suffered from some type of food poisoning. It's fortunate for him that you had the foresight to see it. If he had kept vomiting, it might have put a strain on his heart, and then he would not have pulled through."

Picking up his black bag, the doctor turned to leave. He paused at the door, saying, "I'll speak with Miranda before I leave and let her know that she can stop worrying, because she's not going to be a widow today."

Nodding gratefully, Storm said, "Thank you," before her knees suddenly turned to jelly and she sank into the chair. It was a delayed reaction from the past few hours of tension. Until that moment she had not realized the toll her effort to help Lyle had taken. Her hand shook unsteadily as she placed it over his and said, "You'll live, Lyle, you'll live."

An inexplicable sense of joy swept over her as she gazed at the pale countenance of Lyle Ashfort. Fate was truly a fickle thing. Before her lay the man she had vowed to see pay with his own life, and she had saved him from death. Storm knew she would never understand the twists and turns of life. They were strange indeed, but she did not regret her actions toward the man her mother had loved so deeply.

A sound drew her attention away from Lyle, and she looked up to find Thor and Miranda standing in the doorway, Miranda's face nearly the same ashen shade as her husband's had been. Her eyes flickered nervously about the chamber as if dreading to view the still figure on the bed. She clung helplessly to Thor's arm, a perfect picture of an aggrieved wife needing his support to see her through the crisis.

Storm sought desperately within herself to find a small amount of sympathy for Miranda. She failed. She could not feel sorry for the woman, whose vapid exhibitions did no one any good. When Lyle regained consciousness, he would need his wife's strength, not weakness.

To hide her annoyance, Storm lowered her eyes to her hands. A prickly sensation crept up her neck as she sensed someone's gaze upon her. Unable to keep her eyes lowered, she looked up to meet Miranda's eyes. In that brief moment Storm read all the animosity and resentment the woman felt toward her. And with a start, she realized the reason behind it; Miranda had not wanted Lyle to live.

A chill swept over Storm. She had known Miranda cared nothing for her husband. Her actions with Thor had proven that fact. Storm had been able to see through the woman's little games, but she had not considered Miranda so coldhearted that she would wish her husband's death.

You bitch, Storm thought, you wanted Lyle to die and leave you free to further your pursuit of Thor.

Feeling her face flush from the heat of her blood boiling through her veins, she rose, her hands clenched tightly at her sides to keep from striking out at Miranda. A white line formed about her lips as she said, "I'll leave you with your husband." Storm knew her limits and realized she had to get away now before she exploded.

As she swept by Miranda and Thor, his hand halted her. His eyes glowed warmly with approval as he said, "The doctor told us that if Lyle lived, we would have you to thank for it. He said there was nothing he could do that you had not already done and your quick thinking saved Lyle's life. For that we are grateful."

Fiery sparks danced in Storm's eyes as her gaze swept over them both. Her voice was icy with contempt as she moved away from Thor's touch. "I did only what was necessary. There is no need for your gratitude." Flashing another scalding look at Miranda, she continued, "I'm sure anyone would have done the same in my place."

Miranda's words were glazed with honey, though her eyes were hard, as she said, "We owe you our thanks for saving Lyle. I hope someday to repay the debt in full."

The fine hair at the nape of Storm's neck stood on end as she sensed a hidden message in Miranda's words. "I assure you there is no need. If you'll excuse me, I'll wait downstairs until it's time for us to return to Misty Rose."

Thor sensed the hostility in Storm's voice. Puzzled by it, he called out her name, but she swept by him and left the room without a backward glance. The words he wanted to say went unspoken.

He felt the need to go after her but suppressed it. For now Miranda needed him more than the vixen with the hellish temperament.

Storm's feet sped along the carpeted hall and down the stairs to the drawing room. She felt the urge to smash something and had to restrain herself from picking up one of the delicate porcelain figurines that adorned the mahogany table and throwing it at the fireplace. She knew just hearing it crash against the stone would have helped appease some of the fury she felt toward Miranda Ashfort.

Unable to do as she wished, she began to pace the room instead, needing to work off some of the anger that twisted her insides into tight knots. Fuming, she thought, That woman is the devil in disguise. She looks like an angel but is far from it, and Thor is too stupid to see it. She would do anything to have him.

Suddenly she froze, her eyes widening as the horrible accusation began to form in her mind. Miranda wanted Lyle dead. Could she have poisoned him herself?

Beads of tension formed on Storm's brow as the thought haunted her. She knew Miranda did not love Lyle, but could she be vile enough to stoop to murder?

Storm's hand trembled as she wiped her brow and sank to the sofa, her lower lip held pensively between her teeth while she mulled over her suspicions. She despised Miranda for taking advantage of every opportunity to ingratiate herself further with Thor and wanted to believe the worst about her. But Storm was honest enough to admit to herself that much of her own hostility stemmed from jealousy.

Miranda was heartless and calculating, but that did not mean she actively sought to murder her husband. From her observation of Miranda Ashfort, Storm quickly surmised that if the woman truly wanted to kill Lyle, he would no longer be breathing. Miranda was the type of woman who would achieve what she wanted at all costs.

Storm's cheeks colored guiltily as Thor and Miranda entered the drawing room. She had no right to pass such biased judgment on the woman, no matter how she felt about her. Lowering her eyes to hide her thoughts, Storm kept her gaze on her tightly clasped hands as Thor continued to soothe Miranda. Storm paid little heed to his words until he said, "I see no reason why my housekeeper can't help you nurse Lyle back to health. I know you have servants to aid you, but it would be better if Storm were here to oversee them when you need to rest. It's too much of a burden for you to carry alone."

Storm's head snapped up, her mouth falling slightly agape as she stared at Thor in disbelief. She could not credit the fact that he was making her a servant to the woman she detested. Bile rose in her throat at the thought, and she could feel the heat of anger sting her cheeks. Words of refusal rose to the tip of her tongue, but she bit them back. She could not voice her objections. She had no right. She was Thor's bond servant, and there was nothing she could say or do to prevent him from using her services as he saw fit. Her hands balled into fists as she saw Miranda's eyes flicker over her, a glint of triumph in their pale depths before the woman turned a winning smile to Thor and said, "You think of everything. I don't know what Lyle or I would do if you were not nearby. It seems I can never depend on Geoffry to be here when I need him."

Storm had to suppress the urge to tear out Miranda's blond hair by the roots as she construed the look bestowed on her to say, See, you are not good enough for him. He's making you my servant because I'm the one he cares for.

Thor patted Miranda's hand and without even asking Storm said, "Then it is settled. Until Lyle is better, she'll come during the day to help you."

Chapter 11

Storm sat on the window seat, her head bent and her feet curled beneath her as she read the volume of verse she had found in AshGlen's library. The afternoon sun spilled in through the leaded panes, making her curls shimmer the blue-black of a raven's wing. It danced in a halo about her as she glanced up from the book. The room was quiet. The only sound to disturb the stillness was Lyle's even breathing. Glancing at her patient, Storm closed the book and stretched her tired muscles from their cramped position. Storm massaged the back of her neck as she turned to view the scenery of AshGlen. The day was waning, casting lengthening shadows across the manicured grounds and gardens. Soon it would be time to return to Misty Rose.

For a moment she closed her eyes against the view. She was exhausted from the double burden of nursing Lyle and then returning to Misty Rose in the evening to resume the duties required of her as housekeeper. But she knew it had to be done. Miranda had taken Thor at his word. She had turned Lyle's care completely over to Storm, seldom venturing into the sickroom even once a day to see how her husband faired. Though it required every ounce of energy she possessed to nurse him, Storm knew that without her, Lyle would not have received the care he needed. Hiding a yawn behind her hand, she rose and crossed to the bedside.

Each day for the past month and a half, she had sat by Lyle's side. At times he seemed to be recovering, but soon after, he would suffer another of his strange attacks. His illness puzzled Storm. She knew it could not be food poisoning on every occasion, though she treated him each time as she had done after his first seizure. Beyond that she could do little to help him. The doctor had come several times, but he had little advice to give her.

Lyle slept a great deal, but there had been times between his seizures when he had been able to talk with Storm coherently. To her surprise, she found herself growing fond of him. That left her badly confused. She felt she was betraying her mother and breaking her vow to avenge Alisa's death.

Gazing down into Lyle's pale face, Storm realized things were not turning out at all as she had planned. Due to Thor's insistence that she tend Lyle, she had found no time in which to speak with Matthew Boone.

Storm knew her time was growing short. Her waist was thickening, and soon she would be unable to keep her secret hidden from Thor. If she waited too long to leave Misty Rose, she might not be able to carry out her plans. For a few moments she thought over the scheme she had been so sure would succeed. She would get Matthew to help her escape from Misty Rose, and then she'd assume a new identity and find some type of position until the babe arrived. She would tell everyone that she was a new widow whose husband had died on shipboard while traveling to America. However, if she did not get away soon, no one would hire a woman who was heavy with child, and that in itself could mean the difference between life and death for both herself and her babe.

Dragging her thoughts away from her problems, Storm noted the tiny bit of color that had come into Lyle's cheeks. It was a good sign. Soon, she prayed, he would be well enough not to need her constant care. Then she could turn her thoughts to her own future far away from AshGlen and Thor Wakefield. The idea caused her heart to twist against her will.

Her brows knit, and a frown furrowed her forehead as she considered Thor's odd behavior of late. Since her accident, he seemed to have changed toward her. He no longer forced his attentions on her, and for that she was grateful, but he always seemed to be nearby.

She pursed her lips. He was always hovering near as if he suspected her intention of leaving Misty Rose and was determined to thwart her efforts. If that was his plan, he had succeeded. The only time Storm found herself alone was when he was unable to escort her to AshGlen.

In her attempt to find a means to speak with Matthew, Storm had reminded Thor that his overseer could ride with her on the days he himself was too busy. Thor had abruptly and bluntly stated that Matthew did not have the time. He was much too busy in the fields. After that conversation, Thor had provided Storm with a small woven cart pulled by a meek little mare, saying she could see herself to AshGlen without any problem.

Storm had been thwarted again when she had asked to return to the Petite Maison. Though Thor did not come to her bed, he had insisted she remain in the guest chamber so Perle could see to her needs, using the excuse that Storm was exhausted from nursing Lyle each day. She had protested that she could care for herself, but Thor had been adamant. Fearing he might grow suspicious as to her reasons for wanting privacy, she had not pushed the matter further.

Storm's reverie was broken as Lyle mumbled in his sleep. Unable to understand his words, she bent near as he murmured once more. The blood slowly drained from her face as she realized that he was calling for Alisa. Storm's heart constricted in her breast when Lyle's lashes slowly fluttered open and he gazed up at her, confused. Tiny lines fanned his eyes as he squinted up at her and after a long moment a smile slowly spread across his bluish lips. The muscles worked in his throat as he cleared it and said, "For a moment I did not recognize you, Storm. I was dreaming of someone I knew years ago and briefly thought you were her."

The skin along Storm's spine prickled and her heart began to pound furiously against her ribs as she sensed the time had arrived to solve all the mysteries of the past. For a moment she didn't know if she wanted to hear what he would say. She feared it would make her hate him again, but she also knew she had to learn the reasons for his actions all those years ago.

Steeling herself, she settled herself on the bed at Lyle's side and took his parchmentlike hand into her own, urging him to speak. "Do I look like her?"

The eyes so much like her own assessed her face slowly. After a long moment, Lyle said, "Yes, to a degree, but she had golden hair, where yours is touched by midnight. Her eyes were a soft dove gray." He paused as he mentally brought forth Alisa's image, seeing her as he had left her nineteen years earlier. "Eyes that mirrored her gentle soul and all her emotions."

To hear Lyle describe her mother unnerved Storm. But he did not note her reaction, nor did he feel the slight tremor that shook her or see the muscles work in her throat as it tightened with emotion.

Lyle gazed at Storm but did not see her as his eyes softened with memories of his love and he focused his thoughts on the distant past. He mused aloud without realizing he had spoken. "It was nearly twenty years ago. How time flies. It ages us but not our memories." His lips pressed tightly together, and the wrinkles in his face deepened, showing his pain.

Seeing the distress on his lined face and fearing it might bring on another attack, Storm said, "If you prefer not to speak of it, then please let it rest. You shouldn't be upset." She spoke honestly. No matter how much she wanted to know about the past, she did not want to risk Lyle's health in the process.

Pulling his thoughts back to the present, Lyle looked up at her concerned face. A fond smile tugged at his lips as he said, "Storm, since the first day Thor brought you to visit me, I have felt we would become friends. I'm grateful it has come to pass. You saved my life and have nursed me devotedly over the past weeks. I could ask no more from friend or family and see no reason to keep secrets from you."

Drawing in a ragged breath, he paused briefly, his eyes never leaving her face. "It's strange I should have grown so close to you in such a short time, when I have not felt this way for more years than I care to remember. For the first time I feel a need to speak of my past, because I sense you will understand. Perhaps it's my age or that I've come so close to meeting my maker during the past weeks; I don't know. I truly can't explain why I want to tell you of the things that brought me to my AshGlen on the Ashley."

Storm felt tears prick the backs of her lids at Lyle's candor. He, too, must feel the bond that had begun to grow between father and daughter, though he had never suspected the reason for it. Moistening her dry lips, she said, "Then I would be honored if you would tell me."

Lyle's bony fingers tightened about her hand. "Storm, it was so long ago, before you were born, but it seems to me as if it was only yesterday."

Storm remained quiet as his gaze seemed to drift into the past, seeing once again all that had transpired. His words came slowly as he spoke of the days that would never return. "Miranda is not my first wife. I think now it was her golden beauty that first attracted me to her because it reminded me of the woman I loved in England so long ago."

Storm's heart lodged in her throat, choking her as she bit the inside of her lip to suppress the rush of tears that burned her eyes.

Lyle paused, and a rueful smile came briefly to his mouth. "Alisa was my first love. Ah, my beautiful Alisa. The moment I first saw her my heart was lost. I loved her so much and wanted to give her everything, but I had few prospects. My father was still alive at that time, and when he died, my older brother was to inherit the estate. I knew my family would never approve of Alisa, since she was not of the peerage, but I cared little for that and swept her off to Gretna Green, where we were married. That was the happiest day of my life."

Lyle's voice grew hoarse with emotion, and he had to clear his throat before he could continue. "Alisa and I lived and loved for several months without a care in the world. I was a reckless young man in those days, enjoying life to its fullest, using the small allowance from my family carelessly, feeling I could conquer the world. That was until my luck with the cards disappeared. Seeing no future for Alisa and myself in England, I decided to come to America and make my own fortune as I had heard many had done. I went to my family for help, but they would not give it; they considered my venture a boyish prank. They said they would not throw good money after bad. That did not stop me. I took what little money we had and bought passage for America. I was to come first and then send for Alisa when I could afford it."

Tears clouded Lyle's vision. "I'll never forget watching her wave until my ship sailed from view. I didn't know then that it would be the last time I ever saw her.

"When I arrived in America, I worked day and night to

earn enough to secure a small piece of land. I had just begun to see my way clear to send for Alisa when I received a letter from my brother.''

Lyle drew in a ragged, tremulous breath. ''When I read it, I thought my heart would burst with grief. My lovely Alisa had died in childbirth. During our last nights together she had conceived my babe, and until this day I have not forgiven myself for not being with her.'' His voice broke, and he could no longer suppress the tears. They streamed down his face unheeded.

Storm's first reaction to his revelation was to deny it, but she could not. She knew Lyle spoke truthfully, though what he said contradicted everything she had believed since she had learned of him. All the years of misery the three had endured had been because of one evil man who wanted to control his brother's life.

Guilt assailed her for hating her father for events over which he had no control. He, too, had been a victim and had suffered greatly, as had his wife and daughter.

Storm's face also glistened with tears as she looked at Lyle. At last she knew the answers, and her heart swelled with sympathy for the two people who had loved each other so dearly and, because of a lie written so long ago, had been torn apart.

She had to fight the longing within her to throw her arms about Lyle and comfort him in his misery and be comforted in return as they shared their grief. She wanted to tell him she was his daughter, that a part of Alisa still lived within her, but she could not. She could never reveal their relationship without telling Lyle of the years Alisa had waited for him to return for her. Storm knew from the agony she saw in his eyes that his heart would not stand the strain of knowing what Alisa had endured because of his brother's vicious lie.

Futilely, Storm realized that even if she told Lyle her true identity, she had no proof of it. He would think she was lying to insinuate herself into his life and gain a portion of his wealth. That would destroy the slender bond that had formed between them. Without evidence to confirm she was his daughter, she would have to keep the knowledge of it to herself.

With the back of her hand, she wiped the moisture from Lyle's cheeks before brushing away her own tears. Her voice quavered with emotion as she sought to give some small bit of solace to ease the guilt he had lived with for so long. "Lyle, I think it's time for you to forgive yourself. From what you've told me about Alisa and the love you shared, I'm sure she never placed any blame on you. She would not rest peacefully knowing you suffered such anguish over something you could not control. Fate seems to play cruel tricks on all of us. Would you have blamed Alisa if she was not able to be with you and some tragedy had befallen you?"

Lyle considered Storm's words, his eyes never wavering from her tearstained face. A hesitant smile crept to his lips as his fingers brought hers to his lips. Placing a light kiss upon the back of her hand, he said, "How can one so young be so wise?"

Her cheeks flushed with pleasure. "Perhaps it's not age but experience that gives a person wisdom. I understand your feelings because I lost my mother before I came to the colonies, and there was nothing I could do to help her."

The pressure of Lyle's hand conveyed his sympathy and understanding. It tightened about her own, comforting her as she had done him a few moments before. "I'm glad Thor was wise enough to choose you for his housekeeper. You are a remarkable young lady, Storm Kingsley, and I am proud to consider you my friend. Had Alisa's and my child lived and had it been a girl, I would want her to be like you."

Storm felt she would burst with suppressed emotion.

Her eyes glistened brightly once more as she said, "Thank you, Lyle. I could ask for no better compliment. I am honored to be regarded as your friend." Feeling the tears clog her throat and knowing she could not hold them back much longer, she said, "Now it's time for you to rest. Zachery will be bringing your evening meal soon, and I expect you to eat all of it so you can soon leave this bed."

Putting the past behind him once more, Lyle smiled, the charm that had won Alisa's heart now claiming her daughter. A mischievous twinkle flashed into his eyes. "For one so young, you are certainly a bossy little thing."

Storm nodded and wiped her eyes as a wobbly smile touched her lips. "I agree with you, and I intend to continue to be bossy until you are completely well." She bent and brushed her lips against his brow. "It's getting late, and I must return to Misty Rose. Rest well, Lyle. I will come again tomorrow."

She remained at his side until he drifted once more to sleep. In the silence of the still room, she studied his sleeping countenance thoughtfully. His face reflected an inner tranquility that had not been present earlier as he slept, and she hoped she had helped bring about the change by relieving the guilt he had carried over the years. It was time for all the pain to be put away; for them both to be rid of the guilt and bitterness caused by things none of them had been able to control.

Tiptoeing so as not to awake Lyle, Storm crossed to the door. She paused briefly and glanced back at the form on the bed. He had been the man her mother had believed him to be after all. Alisa had not been the fool Storm had considered her. Lyle had loved her mother deeply and still loved her. In his folly, he had tried to recapture that love by marrying Miranda but had failed and knew it. Storm's heart went out to him as she closed the door behind her and whispered, "Rest well, Father." She savored the word as it passed her lips.

The demons that had haunted her since she had learned of Lyle Ashfort's whereabouts had been slain that afternoon. Unknowingly, he had freed her from the vendetta that had ruled her life for so long. The bonds were broken at last, and she knew it was time to try to set her own life to rights.

It would not be an easy task leaving the man she loved and the father she had just found. It would tear her heart asunder, but she had no other choice in the matter. She could not remain at Misty Rose and have her babe labeled a bastard; nor could she turn to her father for help in his present condition. Out of the friendship that had grown between them, Lyle might try to give her aid, but his health could not stand another burden. He faced enough as it was, suffering from his wife's lack of love. Storm's decision to flee was the only course she could take for the benefit of her child and her peace of mind.

The shadows of twilight enfolded Misty Rose as Storm stepped wearily down from the small cart and walked up the flagstone steps to the veranda. Her slim shoulders drooped with fatigue as she paused at the wide double doors. Until that moment she had not realized the true extent of her exhaustion. The day had been mentally as well as physically tiring, and now all she wanted to do was to seek her bed and give herself up to sleep.

As she reached for the latch, the door swung open and Mamie stood in the doorway, her arms crossed over her melonlike breasts and her foot tapping with vexation. Her eyes sparkled with annoyance as her gaze swept over Storm, inspecting her from head to toe. "Lawd, child, you do worry a person to death. I thought somethin' had happened to you."

Again Storm was reminded of a mother hen whose feathers were ruffled because her chick had misbehaved. Under Mamie's reproachful gaze, she felt exactly like that wayward chick. Giving Mamie a slightly weary but reassuring smile, Storm stepped into the foyer. "Mamie, you shouldn't worry about me."

Seeing the shadows of fatigue beneath her eyes, Mamie clicked her tongue dubiously. "Not worry about you? Now how's a person not supposed to be concerned when you leave at the crack of dawn and don't get yourself back here until nearly dark. I declare, Missy, I told you before and I'll tell you again that you is going to have to take care of yourself. It ain't good in your condition to be gallivantin' across the countryside all the time. You doin' too much by takin' care of your job here and then tryin' to see to them at AshGlen. It ain't your job to take care of Mis' Miranda's husband. Tha' woman should look after him herself. You've got yourself and the babe to think of now. Lawdy, it ain't right."

Uneasily, Storm glanced about to make sure that no one could overhear the cook's mention of her pregnancy. "Hush, Mamie, before someone hears you."

Unappeased, the woman braced her pudgy hands on her hips and cocked her head to one side. "Maybe if they did, you'd take better care of yourself. Now, I want you to get up them stairs and go straight to bed. I won't hear of you doing anythin' else today. I'll bring your supper to you myself. I ain't going to let you make yourself sick no matter how hard you try. Now, get."

Knowing well Mamie's annoyance with her stemmed only out of concern, Storm threw her arms about the cook's plump shoulders, giving her an affectionate hug. Mamie had become like a second mother to her during the past weeks. Dropping a light kiss on the woman's ebony cheek, Storm said, "All right, Mamie, I'll do as you ask. To be honest, I can think of nothing that would suit me more at this moment."

Mamie watched Storm's retreating back as the girl hurried up the stairs. Poor thing, the cook mused to herself as she turned toward the kitchens, her mind already on what she would prepare for Storm's meal. Humming under her breath, Mamie did not see her master standing in the shadows of the doorway to his study as she passed.

Thor stood transfixed, his swarthy complexion paling as he clenched his fists tightly at his side, his mind repeating Mamie's words, *You've got yourself and the babe to think of now*.

Abruptly he swung back into the study, his mood as black as the approaching night. Picking up a glass and the decanter of brandy, he slumped into the leather chair behind his desk, taking no note of the gloom as he poured himself a stiff drink. Gulping it down, he refilled the glass and again drained it. The fiery liquid burned its way to his stomach, but it did not ease the sudden anger that took hold of him. The vixen is pregnant, he thought, and his hand clenched the crystal glass until it shattered, spraying him with droplets of brandy.

A sharp fragment cut his palm, and it stung as a few stray drops of the liquor found their way to it. The small wound served only to inflame Thor's senses further. He jerked his handkerchief from his pocket and wiped his hand. After wrapping the white lawn about it in a make-shift bandage, he reached for another glass, his fingers unsteady as he poured himself a third drink.

Leaning back in the chair, he propped his feet up on the shining surface of the desk and sipped the fiery liquid. His eyes were the color of a stormy sky as he mulled over what he had just learned. The knowledge seemed to pound in his temples, and he felt suddenly as if a noose had been placed about his neck. Unaware of his actions, he worked his cravat loose with two fingers, then downed the last of his drink.

A surge of rage swept over him, and he threw the glass at the fireplace, smashing it into crystal fragments as he fumed silently, Damn it to hell! I'll not be trapped so easily by the wench. She may think I will, but I have news for her. I won't be forced into marriage, especially to a woman who cares nothing for me. I won't put myself or my child through the same misery I endured because of a scheming woman.

The twilight deepened into night, and the decanter of brandy slowly emptied as Thor sat brooding and drinking. The alcohol finally mellowed his anger to a degree, making him realize that Storm carried the child he wanted more than anything else on earth. He had accomplished all he had set out to do with the exception of that one thing. Now he would also have an heir. A crooked grin tugged at his lips as he considered the thought. He would have Storm and his child without being bound by matrimony. She would soon learn he could not be trapped into marriage, if that was her devious plan.

As if a streak of lightning had lit a dark room in his mind, Thor abruptly realized that Storm had not asked him to marry her, nor had she even seen fit to tell him she carried his babe. The insult of it burned into his gut. His body went rigid, and a stricken look crossed his face as he sat up with a start. Recalling the expression of fear on Storm's face when she had glanced about the foyer, he became painfully aware that she had no intention of revealing her condition to him. She had often told him she hated him, and with a certainty that caused his heart to ache, he knew she planned to keep his child from him.

Renewed fury swept over him like a tidal wave. He roared at the outrage. It was his child, and he had a right to it. No matter how Storm felt, he would not let her keep his babe away from him. It was the heir of Misty Rose, and he would see to it that nothing prevented the child from accepting the heritage he had worked so hard to build.

Thor slammed his fist down onto the hard wood surface,

making the desk tremble with the impact. "I won't let her take my child from Misty Rose!" he vowed even as he wondered how he would be able to stop her once her term of indenture was served.

Unless he relented and married Storm, he would have her and his son or daughter for only seven years. No, he thought; I won't marry her just for the sake of the child. It would be unfair to the babe and cause nothing but misery for all concerned. He had learned that lesson the hard way by watching his own mother leave him.

Irritably, he ran his fingers through his hair and stared into the darkness, trying to solve the dilemma facing him. Storm carried his child but detested him. What could he do to keep her at Misty Rose? Propping his elbows on the desk, he rested his face in his hands, seeking an answer.

It glimmered to life deep within the recesses of his mind, and he froze as he pondered the thought. He would make Storm see the benefits of letting him adopt the child. That would solve the problem. Releasing a long breath, he leaned back in the chair. If he could convince her to see the benefits in what he asked, she would be free at the end of her indenture without the encumbrance of a child to bring up, and he would have the heir he desired.

Thor relaxed only briefly before another niggling question rose to plague his mind. How would their child feel when Storm left Misty Rose? For leave she would; she had spoken too often of it in the past. Again his face clouded at the thought of his own flesh suffering as he had when Angelina had decided to leave his father. Thor's protective instincts rose in defense of his unborn child, but he did not know how to shield his offspring against the same pain he had endured.

He rubbed his forehead with his fingers, knowing there was only one solution to the problem, and he did not like it. His heart twisted in his chest from what he had to do, but he knew it was the only way. He would give Storm her freedom soon after the babe's birth. In that way the child would not grow to love her, only to have her torn away from him. It was a radical thought, one Thor found little pleasure in because he would lose Storm in only a few months' time, but he had to put the child's welfare before his own feelings.

Determined to see the matter settled that night, he rose unsteadily to his feet, the brandy he had consumed making his movements awkward. He fumbled for the tinderbox and after several minutes found it at the base of the lamp. Lighting the wick, he lifted the lamp and staggered from the study and up the stairs to Storm's chamber.

Without knocking, he opened the door, to find her curled on the bed clad only in a thin night rail. Her graceful arms hugged a fluffy pillow to her breast, and her lips were slightly parted as she slept. The carpet muffled his steps as he crossed the room and set the lamp on the bedside table, its light casting a soft, warm glow over her sleeping features.

Moments stretched into minutes as Thor stood gazing down at Storm. He perused her lovely face, unabashedly admiring the new radiance that made her complexion glow. It tinted her cheeks a vibrant rose and made her lips seem like dew-kissed petals of the flower.

Thor felt his senses stir and shifted his weight to try to ease the tightness that had invaded his loins. He had come here not to make love to Storm but to let her know that he would never allow her to take his child away from Misty Rose. But the sight of her scantily clad body made his blood run hot.

It had been well over two months since the last time he had held her in his arms, and his wayward body was forcibly reminding him of his self-imposed denial. Since the day she had lain unconscious after her accident, he had determined to keep his distance. By denying himself, he had hoped once and for all to get her out of his system.

He had spent many nights during the past weeks in his lonely bedchamber, tossing and turning, with visions of Storm tormenting his thoughts. Instead of crossing the few feet that separated them and fulfilling his needs, he had resorted to late-night swims in an attempt to cool his blood. The chilly water of the Ashley had been only a momentary reprieve. No matter what he did, his desire for her always returned to haunt him.

As he gazed at the woman who had turned his world upside-down, his fury dimmed and gradually faded away. Settling himself on the bed at her side, he gently brushed a silken curl from her brow. He realized with a start that it had been fear that had kept him from her. He had been afraid of his feelings and had shied away from her because of it.

An avalanche of unwanted emotion swept over him as he finally acknowledged the truth—he was in love with her. He found no comfort in the knowledge; it changed nothing. His wide shoulders drooped as he gazed down at her. In that moment he knew he would offer her marriage if he thought she returned his feelings, but she did not. All that was left for him to do was exchange her freedom for their child.

Needing to be close to the woman he loved, Thor disrobed and slipped beneath the sheets, taking care not to awaken Storm. Gently he lifted her into his arms, cradling her against him as he placed his palm over her slightly rounded belly. The muscles in his throat stretched painfully taut, and it seemed as if his heart were trembling in his chest. Beneath his hand grew his seed, within the womb of the woman he loved, and he was desperately afraid he could never keep them both.

The brandy released the restraints he usually kept upon his emotions, and tears brimmed in his silver eyes as he slowly drifted off to sleep. Dreams came to disturb his slumber, carrying him back to the day that he stood in the dusty road and watched the black carriage carry his mother away. Then the vision changed, and he saw a small child toddling across the lawns of Misty Rose, calling, Mama, Mama; only to have no one answer. As the nightmare continued to torment him he saw Storm in the black carriage before the images altered again and the woman inside became Angelina once more, while he was the child left weeping in the dust.

Thor began to toss and turn as the demons of the night haunted him. Beads of sweat formed on his face, glistening in the lamplight. He shook his head back and forth upon the pillow, his hands gripping the sheet as he had held his mother's gown, crying, "No. No!"

Storm awoke with a frightened start, her eyes flying wide with fear as she heard his agonized cry. She did not stop to wonder why he was in her bed; all her thoughts centered on the fact that the man she loved was in agony. Instinctively wanting to protect him, she put her arms about him, cradling his head against her breast as she crooned, "Thor, Thor, wake up. You're all right. It's only a nightmare. Hush, my darling, hush."

Thor stiffened, his eyes flying open, reflecting his confusion as the horrible dream kept its strong grip upon his mind. His heart pounded against his ribs, and he drew in several shaky breaths before he gave an anguished groan and wrapped his arms tightly about her, burying his face in the soft cleft between her breasts. He crushed her to him, needing desperately to fill the huge void that seemed to engulf him. He held her as if he feared she would vanish into the night air and leave him all alone.

Lovingly, Storm caressed his dark head, her fingers moving soothingly through his hair while her other hand massaged the tautness from the muscles of his neck and shoulders. She did not know what demons terrified him; all she understood was that he needed her. She did not protest as his lips began their slow ascent of the ivory column of her throat to find her waiting mouth. His touch stirred the senses that had lain dormant in her since their last encounter, and she could find no argument to use against the tingling excitement coursing through her as he began his gentle exploration of her mouth and body. Relaxed by sleep, she was defenseless against her love for him.

Laying her back against the pillows, Thor gazed down at her, his eyes and heart pleading with a burning intensity as he whispered, "Love me, Storm, please love me."

She sensed his vulnerability for the first time, and her heart opened to him completely. She responded freely, returning his caresses and reveling in the tremor of excitement she felt rush over his sinewy body at her touch. It added to her own pleasure, creating and heightening the sensations that rippled along every fiber of her body as her hands traveled over his lithe form. She explored his tanned flesh as he had done hers, savoring the feeling of his supple skin as her fingers moved over his muscular shoulders and down to the crisply matted hair on his chest. Her breathing became labored as she began to follow the narrow trail of silken hair along his flat belly to his aroused manhood. A thrill of pleasure coursed through her as she touched him and felt him throb in response. She heard his moan of pleasure as she stroked the satiny warmth of him and felt his body quiver as he arched toward her caress.

Sensing her sensual assault had pushed him to the limit of his endurance, she moved slowly back up along the trail she had followed earlier, placing enticing little kisses along the way. The taut peaks of her breasts brushed against him, adding to her pleasure. She was surprised for a moment as his hands cupped her round bottom and brought her astride him, but other sensations soon held sway as he guided her down, his manhood sinking deep within her. His hands went to her breasts, his thumbs caressing the rose-colored nipples as he moved beneath her.

Storm pressed herself into his palms as she arched her back and gloried in his lovemaking. She moved with him, her fingers biting into his chest as wave after wave of pleasure washed over her. Weak with ecstasy, her body glistening with moisture, she lay against him, thinking she could endure no more of the sweet torment until, their bodies still joined, he gently rolled on top of her.

His lips captured hers as he began to move within her again, arousing her passion to new heights. The rapture she had reveled in a few moments earlier dimmed in comparison as he again took her beyond the stars, where her world burst into a fiery explosion of fulfillment.

Cradling her against him, Thor felt the warm quivering pulsations deep within her as she experienced the final throes of passionate release. Contentment welled up inside him and was expressed in the gentle curve of his mouth and the tender glow in his eyes as he lay over her, savoring the feeling of their bodies united.

His wide palms framed her flushed face as his gaze lovingly caressed each of her features. He reveled in the knowledge that she had responded to him without his first having to batter down her mind's defenses and assault her sensuous nature. He had been welcomed inside the walls of her fortress, and his victory tasted sweet, satisfying the ache in his bruised heart. As he felt the tender essense of his love bubble to the surface, words rose to his lips to tell her of his feelings and to let her know that he had learned of their child, but he checked them. He was still wary of the newfound emotions Storm inspired in him. He first had to be sure that her feelings toward him were the same before he could venture onto the path that might end in heartbreak again.

Placing a light kiss on her damp brow, the tip of her nose, and finally her soft lips, he moved to her side, still holding her in his arms as he rested his face against her tousled curls and whispered, "Good night, Tempest. Sleep well, my love." For now he would hold the woman who carried his child and held his heart, and he would be satisfied.

Thor's words sent a thrill of happiness through Storm. "My love" echoed through her mind as she snuggled against his lean body to ward off the chill of the early autumn night. He had not actually said he loved her, but for now she would be content with the words he had spoken. They were more than she had ever hoped to hear from him. Forcing everything from her thoughts except her love for him, she murmured, "Good night, Thor," then whispered beneath her breath, "my love." Content with the world, Storm drifted off to sleep, her body curved against Thor's and her head cradled on his shoulder.

Chapter 12

Time was a bandit stealing away the halcyon days of autumn. It moved much too swiftly for Thor, who sat hunched over his desk, pondering the decision he would soon have to make. His face reflected his grim mood as he picked up the piece of paper that proclaimed Storm Kingsley a prostitute and his bond servant. For the past two hours he had sat thus, reading and rereading the bond of indenture. Each time he thought it over, he liked his plan even less.

Things had been beautiful between Storm and him since the night he had learned of her pregnancy. He'd decided then that he would wait until she felt free to tell him of their child, hoping they could share the miracle of the new life together. But that had not happened. Often as they lay together with limbs entwined, savoring the ecstasy of their union, he had wanted to speak of the secret she carried beneath her heart, but his fear of breaking the spell that blanketed them kept him quiet. He also shrank from broaching the subject because, though he sensed a change in her feelings toward him, he could not bring himself to tell her of his own in fear of her rejection.

That was the only dark cloud upon the horizon of their happiness. As each balmy day and sensuous night passed, it darkened Thor's mind with doubts, making him unsure and afraid that once more he was being a fool for giving his heart to a woman.

He had pretended he did not note the changes in Storm's body as the child grew and thickened her waist and her breasts swelled in preparation for motherhood. Secretly as she lay sleeping in his arms, he would place his hand on her rounded abdomen and feel the babe stir beneath his palm. Each time, his spirits soared but then would plummet back to earth with the knowledge that she did not care enough for him to reveal she carried his child.

"Damn," he muttered under his breath as he let her bond of indenture fall to the polished surface of the desk. He did not know if he could go through with his plan. He could barely tolerate the thought of coercing Storm to agree to give up their child.

Propping his elbows on the desk, Thor put his face in his hands and slowly shook his head from side to side. "God, if she could only return the love I feel for her, then all would be well. I would go down on bended knee and beg her to marry me."

A melancholy sigh escaped his lips as he once more looked at the paper. Tonight he would confront her with the knowledge of their child and then let her reaction make his decision for him. If her feelings toward him had changed, they could be married, but if not . . . if not, then he would be prepared. Tense with apprehension, he picked up the bond. Within his hand lay the paper that could tear his own heart asunder. If he had to force Storm to give up her child, then he would do so. The babe she carried was the heir to Misty Rose and had to be protected at all costs.

Thor was startled from his burdensome reverie as Miranda swept into the study, a vision of loveliness in a teal-blue riding habit and a hat with a large red ostrich feather curling provocatively from its wide brim. An enchanting smile was on her lips as she said, "Since you have been neglecting your neighbors, I thought I would come to see you."

Thor rose and stepped around the desk. Taking her hand, a smile of welcome on his lips, he said, "Miranda, it's good to see you. How is Lyle today?"

Miranda's golden lashes fluttered downward, and a tiny, sad sigh escaped her as she shook her head. "Thor, I've been so upset. At times Lyle seems to be recovering, but then he has another of his strange attacks. I'm near my wit's end. That's the reason I've come to see you. I've missed your company, since you're the only person who seems to understand what I've been going through." She looked up at him, her eyes tear-bright. "I've been so afraid that Lyle is going to die. I don't know what I would do if that happened."

Unable to stand the sight of her distress, Thor took her into his arms and held her close. "Miranda, Storm thinks Lyle will recover, but you know if you ever need anything all you have to do is ask. I'll always be here for you."

Miranda's mouth curved into a smug grin, and she hid a look of triumph as she wrapped her arms about him and pressed her face against his chest. Dramatically she feigned a sob. "Thor, I'm so grateful for your friendship. Since Lyle is ill, there are times when I feel I have no one. Geoffry seldom comes to AshGlen, and Mistress Kingsley has little time for me when she visits Lyle." Miranda paused for effect, gazing up at him, her eyes reflecting her need and her lower lip trembling as she whispered brokenly, "I'm so lonely, Thor."

His heart went out to Miranda. Her pain mirrored his own. Both were afraid they would lose the person they loved. Feeling a need to comfort and be comforted in return, he lowered his lips to hers.

Unaware that it was the sound of Miranda's horse that had stirred her from sleep, Storm opened her eyes to the golden ribbons of sunlight spilling through the window across her bed. Feeling at peace with the world, she stretched her graceful limbs, flexing her supple muscles like a contented feline who had licked up all the cream.

Well-rested from her night spent in Thor's arms, she blinked against the brightness as she sat up, squinting as she brushed the tousled curls from her brow. She suppressed a lazy yawn behind her hand, then she drew her knees up and dreamily laid her cheek against them. Her gaze sought the imprint on the pillow where Thor's head had rested, and she touched it lovingly, a warm glow filling her.

Only a few short weeks before, she never would have believed she could find happiness at Misty Rose. Since the day Lyle had slain the ghosts from the past, everything had changed for the better in her life. Lyle was slowly recovering, and a bond had grown between her and Thor.

A sense of euphoria swept through her at the thought of all they had shared during the past weeks. They had acted like lovers, spending hours together, laughing and, most important, making exquisite love that filled her heart until she thought it would overflow. She loved Thor Wakefield and had no regret about the time they had spent in each other's arms. Though he had spoken no other words beyond "my love," she sensed he also felt the deeper bond between them. For that reason alone she refused to let herself feel any remorse for the passion he aroused within her.

Basking in the knowledge of her love, Storm slid her bare feet to the floor and padded across the thick carpet to the window. The day was beautiful, as were the emotions that stirred within her heart. No dark clouds marred either the azure sky or her hopes for the future. The sun-drenched landscape of Misty Rose lay before her as she rested her head thoughtfully against the velvet drapes and gazed out over the land that would someday belong to the tiny life within her.

Unconsciously, she rested her hand on her rounded abdomen as she thought back to the wonderful night Thor had come to her bed while she slept. It had been then that she had given herself totally to him for the first time. Their lovemaking had not been a one-sided affair in which he assaulted her senses until she was unable to resist him. She had not felt used as she had done on previous occasions. Thor had given of himself, instead of selfishly taking his pleasure. After that night she had been able to understand why her love for him had caused her such turmoil in the beginning. Until he had been willing to give, she could not open her heart and accept him completely.

Storm was suddenly jerked out of her reverie by a sharp kick that reminded her she was not alone. A tender smile came to her lips as she gazed down at the swelling beneath her night rail. Strangely Thor had not questioned her sudden weight gain but seemed to enjoy her new roundness as he cradled her against him at night. It had been all she could do during the past weeks to keep from telling him her secret, but she had kept quiet, wanting nothing to upset their happiness.

Reflecting on her reasons for not speaking to Thor about the babe, she realized that to a certain degree her motives had been selfish. She wanted him to love her for herself and not because she carried his child. She had waited, hoping to hear him say he loved her. But time was slipping away, and soon her pregnancy would be apparent to everyone.

An overwhelming need to tell him of their child suddenly possessed her, and she turned from the window and crossed to the cherry armoire, where she selected a sunny-yellow gown of sprigged muslin. Its color matched her mood. She dressed quickly before any shadow of doubt could encroach upon her euphoria. Thor cared for her, though he had never spoken the words, and he had a right to know of his child. After today there would be no more secrets between them. Her steps were light as she made her way down the stairs to Thor's study, and a smile tugged at her lips as she envisioned his happy reaction to her news.

The door stood slightly ajar, and she pushed it open, thinking he would be alone and buried in his work. At the sight of Miranda in his arms, Storm froze, her smile fading as her eyes widened with shock. Reality descended upon her with brutal force, leaving her shaken and feeling more vulnerable than at any other time in her entire life. The blood slowly receded from her face, and a groan of pain escaped her before she could suppress it.

The sound startled Miranda and Thor apart, and they quickly turned to look at her. Thor's swarthy features reddened as he stepped away from Miranda. He opened his mouth to speak, but before he could begin, Storm mumbled a hurried "Excuse me, I—I didn't mean to intrude." In a flurry of yellow muslin, she spun on her heel and ran from the study.

Tears blinded her as she fled back up the stairs to her room and slammed the door behind her before falling across the bed, covering her head with her arms. She buried her face in the satin counterpane, trying futilely to shut out the vision of Thor's mouth upon Miranda's. She could not erase the image; it was branded into her brain, mocking her for her own foolishness.

A taunting voice rose in her mind, ridiculing her. What a great fool you are, Storm Kingsley. You love a man who cares nothing for you. You fall eagerly into his arms, knowing full well he is only using you to relieve his lust for another woman. You knew it from the first time you met her, and even Thor threw it in your face, but you blinded yourself into believing otherwise.

Storm placed her hands over her ears in an effort to shut out the jeering voice, but the mental demon relentlessly continued. See where your folly has gotten you? His seed grows within your belly, and soon everyone will know you are nothing but his harlot. You are weak, Storm Kingsley. You have let your traitorous body overrule your mind. You dreamed of things that you knew from the beginning could never be.

Then Storm's pride surfaced defensively. Clambering from the bed, she dashed the tears from her eyes with the back of her hand and glared at her reflection in the mirror of the dressing table. Her chin jutted out at a pugnacious angle as she braced her hands on her hips, ready to do battle. "Yes, I've been weak, but no more," she said aloud. "He'll not use me again as a surrogate for that witch Miranda Ashfort. I'll soon leave Misty Rose, but until that time, if he attempts to touch me again, I'll fight until there is not a breath left in my body. I might be fool enough to love Thor Wakefield, but I will never accept anything less than his love in return. He has used me for the last time!"

Thor felt everything he had hoped for between himself and Storm fade away when he saw the hurt in her sapphire eyes before she fled the study as if the demons of hell were after her. He opened his mouth to call her back, then clamped it shut. It would be useless. Exasperated by his own foolishness for bringing about such a compromising situation, he turned to his desk and poured himself a large drink of brandy. He drained the fiery liquid, gulping it down in one swallow, hoping it would relieve the tightness that constricted his chest.

Miranda watched the scene through narrowed eyes. She had seen the look on Storm's face and the involuntary

movement of Thor's hand as it came up as if to catch
Storm before she fled. Keen jealousy ripped through Miranda as she realized there was more between Thor and his
housekeeper than she had believed. She had suspected as
much from the first but had let her suspicions wane over
the past months while Storm saw to Lyle's needs.

Miranda's nostrils flared with anger, and her pale eyes
sparkled with malice. Thor belonged to her, and the little
black wren would soon learn that, she vowed silently as he
turned to her.

Running his fingers through his hair, he irritably shook
his head. "I'm sorry, Miranda. I'll explain to Storm that
what she observed was only an innocent kiss between
friends."

Miranda's ire only rose further. "Thor, I see no reason
to explain our actions to a servant. Let her think what she
will. We know the truth of the matter, and that is all that
counts."

Again he shook his head, and his shoulders drooped.
"No, you don't understand. If it had been anyone but
Storm, I would agree with you, but I have to make her see
that there is nothing between you and me except friendship."

Sensing the meaning behind his words, Miranda said,
"Thor, if there is some problem, surely our friendship
merits that you share it with me as I have shared my
sorrow with you."

Thor poured himself another drink before slumping into
the chair. His features were haggard, reflecting his turmoil. Tiny lines fanned his silver eyes and etched a path
about his shapely mouth. "Miranda, Storm is carrying my
child. I had hoped she was beginning to feel something for
me and that we could work things out between us, but
today ruined the chance of that ever taking place."

Hiding her shock, Miranda crossed to him and placed
her arms about his shoulders as if to comfort him in his
time of distress. Her mind worked fervently, trying to find

a means of ridding herself of this new impediment to her
scheme to see AshGlen and Misty Rose joined. Leaning
her head against his, she lied convincingly. "Thor, I'm so
sorry. I had no idea our friendship would cause you this
problem."

He took her hand and pulled her around to face him. He
gazed up into her lovely face, feeling torn between the two
women. Giving a weary shake of his head, he tried to
smile but failed. "You did not cause the difficult, Miranda. I did. I was fool enough to bring Storm to Misty
Rose and then let myself become involved with her when I
knew she would never stay here after her term of indenture
was over."

Realizing his slip, he tightened his hand about Miranda's. "I trust you will not repeat what I have just said. I
never meant to tell anyone of it."

At his disclosure, she felt a sudden jolt to her flagging
spirits, and she smiled to herself. There was much more to
Storm Kingsley's past than she had ever imagined. Miranda gave no sign of her feelings; her face showed only
feigned sincerity as she said, "Thor, I would never repeat
what you have told me. I only wish I could help you solve
the problem."

He managed at last to smile and patted her hand. "I
know you do. You and Lyle have always been good
friends to me."

Returning his smile, Miranda picked up her gloves
and riding crop. "Speaking of Lyle, I need to get
back to AshGlen. I don't like to leave him alone too
long."

Thor rose and draped his arm about her shoulder. "I'll
escort you to your horse."

As he helped her into the saddle, she gave him a radiant
look calculated to enchant the hardest of hearts. "I hope
everything works out for you, Thor." Bending, she placed

a light kiss on his brow before giving her mare a sharp
kick in the side and cantering down the crushed-shell
drive.

Storm watched the intimate scene being played out below her window, feeling a cold, hard fist grip her heart
and squeeze it until she thought it would burst with the
pain. It was agony to watch Miranda caress Thor's cheek
before placing a brief kiss on his brow. Storm could not
hear their conversation but knew from Miranda's expression that the witch was satisfied with her day's work.

Storm's cheeks burned with humiliation as Miranda's
actions vividly recalled the intimate caresses she herself
had bestowed upon him during the past weeks. She could
well imagine how he had laughed to himself at her wanton
response to his masculine allure.

Her gaze lingered on his dark head. Had it been less
than an hour since she had decided to tell him she carried
his child? It seemed an eternity had passed since she had
stood at this same window and foolishly dreamed of a
happy future for herself and her babe.

Fool, she chided herself as she turned away from the
scene. And I considered Mother a fool. At least Father
cared enough to marry her before he took her to his bed.

The thought stung, and Storm squeezed her eyes tightly
closed, hoping the excruciating pain she felt would pass. It
did not. It magnified and mingled with her humiliation
until she was seething with anger. That was her only
defense against her feelings for Thor.

Folding her arms over her breast, she hunched her shoulders as she began to pace back and forth across the bedchamber. Every muscle in her body was taut with rage as
she ranted, "Why should he care anything about me? I am
nothing to him but a piece of purchased flesh. For seven
years I belong to him, but damn it, I won't be used in such

a manner. I'm not what he thinks, and I intend to let him know it!''

Fuming, she strode from her chamber and down the stairs to Thor's study. Again she did not knock but swept into the room, prepared to do battle. Slamming her fist on the top of the desk, she leaned forward, glaring hostilely at him. ''I've come to speak to you about the last few weeks.''

Noting the fiery light of combat in her eyes, Thor arched one dark eyebrow. His voice held no emotion as he said, ''What did you want to say about them?''

His detached manner added fuel to Storm's wrath. How could he sit there without a flicker of feeling after all they had shared? she asked herself, outraged. Her voice was laced with ice as she said, ''Since the day I was brought to the *Sea Siren*, I have let you abuse me, Thor, but as of this moment, that has come to an end. I have fulfilled my duties as your housekeeper to the best of my ability, but from now on, that will be the only role I serve in your household. If you intend otherwise, I suggest you take me to Charleston and put me on the block, because I will not submit to you again.''

Sparks seemed to crackle in the air about them as fiery sapphire met molten gray. Thor bristled under her attack, letting his own anger mask the pain of knowing he had lost her. His face grew stormy; his nostrils flared as he inhaled sharply, and the papers beneath his hands crumpled as his fingers curled into fists. A vein throbbed in his forehead, but his voice was deceptively low and even as he stood and faced her. ''Tempest, shall I take you to the block before or after you deliver my babe into the world?''

The breath seemed to leave Storm in one great whoosh, and she had to gasp to regain it. Paling, she fought to remain calm, hoping desperately to brazen her way through the situation. She had to make him believe his suspicions were false. Moistening her suddenly dry lips, she said, "I don't know what you're talking about."

A caustic smile came to Thor's lips. "I find that hard to believe, Storm. Has your memory deserted you since your conversation with Mamie a few weeks ago?"

A tremor shook her. She felt as if every bone in her body had suddenly turned to jelly. The room swayed before her eyes, and she gripped the edge of the desk for support. Her mind cried out for her to flee before it was too late, but Thor's piercing gaze held her pinned to the spot. Her throat was tight, and her words barely stirred the air as she said, "You overheard?"

Noting her reaction, he picked up the brandy decanter and sloshed a small amount into a glass. Handing it to her, he said, "Drink this and sit down before you fall. I would not want anything to happen to my heir."

Storm gulped the amber liquid, and feeling as if her legs would no longer support her, she slumped into the chair. She watched mutely as he came around the desk and leaned negligently against it.

He folded his arms over his chest as he studied her coldly. "To answer your question, yes, I heard your conversation with Mamie. Though you must truly consider me a simpleton to think that I would not realize you were pregnant after a while. You know that's one thing that is hard to hide."

The brandy soothed Storm's nerves to a degree, and she struggled to find a lie Thor would believe. None came to mind. She knew it was hopeless to even try to lie her way out of the situation. He knew of her condition, and there was nothing left to do but face it. Drawing in a quavering breath, she fought to recall her anger to give her the needed strength to do battle with him. Her palms grew damp as she looked up into his harsh face, but she could not let him intimidate her. "I saw no reason to speak of the child to you. It's none of your concern."

Lightning flashed in Thor's eyes as he slammed his fist violently down on the desk. His chest rose and fell heavily as he ground out through clenched teeth, "None of my concern? If the child is mine, then it is most certainly my concern."

He paused, a niggling suspicion beginning to take root in the back of his mind. Until that moment he had never doubted that the child belonged to him, but the memory of Matthew Boone leaving the Petite Maison combined with Matthew's threats to take Storm away came vividly to his mind. "Or does the babe belong to Matthew?"

Storm came to her feet, trembling from head to toe with outrage at Thor's insult. Had he slapped her across the face, she would not have been more affronted. Seething, her face flushed with indignation, she spat, "You bastard! You'd like to think the child I carry is Matthew's so you would not have the responsibility for it, wouldn't you? But it is you who sired my babe, Thor Wakefield, and no other. You are the only man that has ever come to my bed, whether I was willing or no. You might want to ease your conscience and pretend to believe I act like a prostitute, but I'm not one and have never been."

Storm fought to control the tears that threatened, and her voice quavered as she continued venomously, "You have treated me like a whore, knowing well all the while that you took my virginity that night on the *Sea Siren*. I'll stand no more of your abuse, Thor. And as far as the child I carry is concerned, you have no right to it. Do you hear me? The babe that grows within my body is mine, not yours."

Her words lashed Thor like the stinging tip of a whip. The muscles across his chest constricted, making it hard for him to breathe as he realized the reasons Storm had never come to love him. His insides tied themselves into intricate knots, though he was outwardly calm. The only indication of his turmoil was the white line about his lips as he pressed them tightly together.

Finally recognizing his mistakes, he knew it was too late. He could not blame her for the way she felt toward him, nor could he convince her to feel otherwise. But that changed nothing where his heir was concerned. He would not let her keep his child from him and would stop her at all costs. His voice was low and controlled, revealing none of what he felt as he said, "Sit down, Storm."

Seeing her make no move to obey, he let a low growl escape him, and he again slammed his fist down on the desk, the force of the blow seeming to make the entire room tremble. "Damn it, Storm, I said sit down before I break that lovely neck of yours. At this moment you are tempting fate. It would not take much more for me to throttle you."

Though her chin jutted out at a pugnacious angle and she eyed him belligerently, Storm sank into the chair once more. She did not want to obey Thor but knew she could not fight him physically.

A long, angry breath escaped him as he strode back around the desk. Shuffling through the papers, he found what he sought. After reading it over and resigning himself to what he had to do, he looked back up at her. "Now that your tirade is spent, we can talk calmly. Since the child you carry is mine, I will take full responsibility for it." He paused as he seated himself in the leather chair, trying to gain the courage to say the next hated words. "Since marriage is out of the question, I have come to the conclusion that there is only one thing left to do. I will adopt the child in exchange for your freedom with one stipulation. And that is you must leave Misty Rose soon after you have given birth."

The blue of Storm's wide eyes was the only color left in her face. Thor's words shattered her and left her heart withered in her breast, shriveled into a cold stone. Drawing in a deep breath, she shook her head slowly from side to side. "No, Thor, you'll never take my babe. My child belongs to me, and I will not give him up to you."

Thor's eyes blazed like red coals as he came to his feet. He would not let her thwart him. "Damn it to hell, Storm. It's my child you carry, the heir to Misty Rose. By now you should know me well enough to realize I will not let anyone take what belongs to me. Either you agree to my terms, or I will see the child taken from you by the courts. What judge would rule against me, one of the richest men in the colonies, in favor of a convicted prostitute? I'm offering you your freedom, Storm. Accept it and be grateful that I do not sell you after the child is born."

She came to her feet and leaned on the desk, her face only inches from Thor's as she glared at him, her eyes glassy with unshed tears. "No, Thor, the freedom you offer costs too much. I would not accept your terms if you were to give me your entire fortune."

She could feel his hot breath on her face as he leaned closer and said threateningly, "Storm, I intend to have my child one way or the other; be certain of that."

Glaring defiantly back at him, she spat, "You and your intentions can go to hell, Thor Wakefield. I'll fight you every inch of the way. You'll never take my child away from me as long as there is breath left in my body. I'll see you dead first."

A derisive smile curled Thor's lips as he gazed down into her flashing eyes. "For one who has little choice in the matter, you speak bravely, Storm. But we shall see who comes out the victor. The child is mine, and no one will keep him away from me. You have solved a problem that has plagued me for some time. I now have an heir to inherit Misty Rose without being forced to marry to get my desire. For that I'm grateful to you."

Storm recoiled as she realized Thor had been using her in a far more devious manner than she had ever suspected.

She was nothing to him but a brood mare. Without thinking, she drew back her hand and slapped him across the face with all the strength she could muster as she spat, "You low, vile bastard. You planned all this, didn't you? Even to the point of acting like you cared for me so I would come willingly to your bed. In that way your chances of my conceiving your babe would multiply." An acrid smile touched her lips as she looked at him through narrowed eyes. "But you did not plan well enough, Thor. I will not meekly give up my own flesh and blood as you assumed. So keep your gratitude; it is misplaced."

The imprint of her fingers was livid against his pale, rigid jaw as he grabbed her by the shoulders. "Storm, you go too far. I warned you to never strike me again. I suggest for your own welfare you return to your duties at once. I have been pushed to the limits of my endurance and will not be responsible for my actions if you don't get out of my sight right now."

He released her so abruptly she nearly stumbled back into the chair. Her face was tight with hatred as she rubbed her shoulder where his fingers had bruised her skin. "Nothing could please me more. I would prefer it if I never had to lay eyes on you again!" With that she walked haughtily from the study, mentally naming him after every vile creature beneath the sun and in the depths of hell.

Chapter 13

Miranda pushed her dapple-gray mare to its limits in her haste to reach Charleston and Geoffry. The animal's sides were lathered white, and it trembled from exertion because of the strenuous pace set by its owner. Thinking nothing of the horse's welfare, she jerked it to a halt before the house her brother rented in the city. Sliding from the saddle, she tied the reins to the hitching post and ran up the small flight of stairs, the heels of her riding boots clicking against the boards. She did not pause to knock on the door but opened it and strode in, heedless of the fact that Geoffry was seldom alone when there was an available female nearby whom he could entice into his bed.

Without a qualm, Miranda strode directly into his bed-chamber. Her red lips curled in disgust at the sight of two naked sweaty bodies struggling in the throes of passion. The air was heavy with the odor of strong whiskey and heated flesh, causing her to raise her hand to her nose in distaste. Seeing that her brother and his companion were too enthralled to note her entrance, Miranda said, "For the

love of God, Geoffry, hurry up with the wench so we can
talk.''

The couple on the bed froze in their awkward position
as she stood tapping her hand with her riding crop, annoyed that his amusement was detaining him when she
needed him to come to her aid in this new and unexpected
development at Misty Rose.

Geoffry glanced over his shoulder at his sister as he slid
away from the heavy-breasted, painted-faced woman. Without a flicker of embarrassment about his own naked, excited body, he grinned wickedly at Miranda as he lay back
against the pillows and propped one arm behind his head.
He did not try to cover his aroused manhood as his other
hand went to fondle the woman's thigh and the shadowy
triangle at the apex of her legs. His companion made to
cover herself, but he brushed her efforts aside as he said,
''Miranda, won't you join us? It's been a long time since
we enjoyed that kind of excitement together.''

Unamused by her brother's invitation, Miranda said, ''I
haven't the time for such play at the moment. I suggest
you finish with the wench so we can talk without your
mind wandering to that member between your legs. The
wench looks as if she will flee at any moment, so I would
advise you to take advantage of the situation quickly,
before it is too late.''

Geoffry cocked a brow at his sister. ''Will you stay and
enjoy the show, since you won't participate, or would you
prefer a glass of wine in the adjoining room?''

Miranda gave him a wicked grin. ''I believe I will
watch. It's been so long since anyone has made love to me
that I've nearly forgotten how it's done.''

Geoffry threw back his golden head and roared with
laughter. ''Then enjoy your lesson, Sister, while I finish
the task I started before I was so rudely interrupted.''

Without batting an eye, he returned between the woman's thighs as Miranda settled herself in a chair and watched

his lean body plunge into the flesh of the waterfront whore. It had been years since she and Geoffry had frolicked with one of his women in the same bed, all three sharing one another's pleasure. Though she had pressing matters on her mind, she could not suppress the sudden rush of excitement the memory brought forth as she observed the couple on the bed. It was nearly too tempting for her, and she tried to quell the erotic side of her nature by recalling her reason for rushing to Charleston.

Though she fought to stem her arousal, by the time Geoffry arched his back to slake his lust, Miranda was breathing heavily, her lips slack and her tongue darting about their dry surface.

Geoffry glanced at his sister and saw the effect his performance was having on her. He feigned even more rapture than he felt for her benefit, enjoying the look of excitement on her face as much as his own release.

It had always been so between them. Only ten months separated them in age, and their relationship was as close as that of identical twins. They had grown up on the family plantation in Virginia, and where Miranda led, Geoffry followed. It had been so as children and was still the same.

The first time the two had come to realize they possessed a side to their nature that leaned toward the perverted aspects of sexual pleasure was when they were twelve. Their mother had gone to visit relatives in Charleston, and they had been playing in the hallway outside her bedchamber when they heard strange sounds coming from the room.

Envisioning ghosts, the two had crept stealthfully to the door and opened it. At first they had been embarrassed by the scene within, but their curiosity kept them glued to the spot as they watched their father with the upstairs maid. They stared with bated breath as their father used the young girl in a manner he would never have considered doing with his wife.

On that afternoon, as their father forced the young girl to service him from head to toe, front and back, Miranda and Geoffry became conscious of their own sexuality. Their young blood was excited by what they had seen, and they had slipped away after their father collapsed over the maid, anxious to experiment with each other in the same manner. That had been the beginning of their erotic explorations, which had continued until Miranda had married Lyle Ashfort.

After their mother's death, their father had squandered away everything he possessed by gambling, drinking, and whoring, leaving Geoffry and Miranda in desperate financial straits. The only thing left for the two to do was find Miranda a rich husband.

At first Geoffry had not objected to their plan, because otherwise they would have been reduced to begging unless he found employment. That idea had little appeal to Geoffry, who possessed the same lazy, self-serving, pleasure-seeking disposition as his father.

It was not until Geoffry watched Miranda kiss Lyle Ashfort at the altar in the church that his hatred for the man had bloomed. He had willingly taken Lyle's money, but his feelings toward him had never changed during the five years of Miranda's marriage. Geoffry's jealousy had made him eagerly agree to help his sister rid herself of her husband.

Now a new problem had arisen to inflame his jealousy: Thor Wakefield. Where Lyle had never managed to replace Geoffry in Miranda's affections, her brother feared Thor would. He knew Miranda had fallen in love with Thor, and as soon as she was free of Lyle, she would marry him.

Geoffry was determined to keep his animosity to himself, however, until after the ceremony, so Miranda could inherit Misty Rose as well as AshGlen. After that he would dispose of Thor without Miranda's ever knowing of it. Geoffry swore he would not make the same mistake he had with Lyle; Thor's accident would be fatal the first time.

Geoffry's nearly feminine lips spread into a wide grin at the thought of Thor's demise. Stepping from the bed, he patted the round behind of the whore and tossed her a wad of bills as he ordered, "Now, get out. I'll call for you when you're needed again."

The woman glanced nervously at him and Miranda as she quickly gathered up her earnings and her clothes before fleeing the room. She had seen many things during her life on the waterfront but never a lady of quality watching as her brother took a whore.

Picking up a towel, Geoffry wiped the sweat from his body before draping it about his waist. Pouring himself and Miranda a glass of wine, he asked, "Now, what is so urgent that you don't have time for a moment of pleasure? From the look on your face you could use a man between your thighs, Sister."

She grinned at her brother as she accepted the glass. "I think you're right, and that's my problem. I'm having an awful time getting Thor to accept what I nearly throw in his face. To add to my dilemma—just when I thought I was gaining ground—I learned today his housekeeper is carrying his child."

Geoffry eyed his sister with wry amusement as he lounged back in the chair and stretched his long, golden-fleeced legs out before him. "Damn, Miranda, you must be losing your touch if the man's housekeeper can oust you from his bed."

Her face tightened with annoyance. "Geoffry, I see little humor in your remark. I've not lost my touch. You know as well as I that it's the friendship between Lyle and Thor that has stood in my way. But now if we are not careful, the little hussy will ruin all of our plans to unite AshGlen and Misty Rose.''

Geoffry cocked a golden brow. ''Is that the only reason you're interested in Wakefield?''

Lowering her lashes to hide her true feelings, Miranda lied. ''You know it is. AshGlen and Misty Rose are the richest plantations along the Ashley, and I will not stop until they are mine; I mean ours.''

Knowing she lied, Geoffry downed the last of the wine and set the glass on the table as he stood. ''Then what do you plan to do about the housekeeper?''

Miranda eyed her brother thoughtfully, and without a flicker of emotion she said, ''We've got to get rid of her before she entices Thor into marriage.''

Geoffry strolled across the room and propped his arm on the mantel of the fireplace as he gazed at Miranda speculatively, watching her face. ''I surmised as much, dear Sister. What do you suggest we do?''

Her fingers tapped against the dark wood of the chair arm. ''I would like nothing better than her death, but I'm afraid people might grow suspicious if there are too many untimely demises in the area. The only other thing I can think of at the present moment is to try to turn Thor against her so he will do the job for us.''

Geoffry rubbed his stubbled chin as he regarded his sister dubiously. ''How do you plan to do that? If she is carrying Wakefield's brat, I doubt that he will send her away on any pretext.''

Miranda's eyes glittered with malice and cunning. ''Perhaps that is where you can be of service. If we can convince Thor the child is not his, then he will gladly be rid of her. She is nothing to him but an indentured servant.''

Geoffry shook his head in bewilderment. ''Miranda, your plan sounds fine, but I'm afraid it will take more than your or my telling Wakefield the child is not his. He will need proof.''

A wicked gleam glowed in her eyes and one corner of her mouth curved upward in a superior little smirk. "Perhaps we can arrange for him to view you and Storm Kingsley in bed together. That should be all the proof he'll need. When he confronts you, you can say it's not the first time you've been with her, nor are you the only man to have slept with her. It would be your word against hers. And who would believe a servant before a gentleman? You can even add a little spice by telling Thor you purchased her favors. That would settle everything nicely."

Geoffry's face lit at the exciting thought. "How do you intend to arrange my seduction?"

Pleased that her brother had again fallen into her schemes, Miranda laughed. "Geoffry, it should not be hard to do. She is often at AshGlen, and who is there to thwart you when you take her to your bed? Lyle can't come to her aid, and I would be forced to admit I heard her proposition you. You just leave it to me. I'm sure a nice cup of tea would arrange things for us when the time is right, don't you?"

Geoffry threw back his golden head and laughed. "I should have known you would think of something. You plan well, Sister, as you have always done."

Miranda's face clouded. "I haven't always succeeded with my plans. Lyle is recovering."

Unable to stand the look on his sister's face, Geoffry crossed to her and pulled her into his arms. He kissed her, and the gesture was far from brotherly. Miranda could feel his arousal against her belly. She pushed against his chest until he released her and stepped away. His eyes lingered on her mouth briefly before he gave a sigh of regret and picked up the gray coat resting across the back of the chair. Digging into the pocket, he withdrew a small glass vial of crushed foxglove and held it up. "Since Lyle has been recovering so well, I took it upon myself to purchase a small quantity of this. I thought you would need it to complete the task.''

Miranda's hand closed about the vial, and she quickly stuffed it into the pocket of her riding habit. Patting it, she smiled up at her brother. ''That's the reason I love you so much, Geoffry. You understand me and know all my needs.''

He cupped her face in his hands, and a look of utter longing filled his eyes as he studied her beautiful features. ''It's been a long time, Miranda. Shall I go and fetch back the whore so you, too, can have a little enjoyment?''

Her heart showed in her eyes as she stepped away from her brother and shook her head. ''No, Geoffry, that is all in the past. The only person I want in my bed is Thor Wakefield, and I will wait until I have him.''

For one brief moment all of Geoffry's feelings flickered across his face, but he quickly veiled his expression. His jealousy bubbled in a hot current through his veins as his plans for Thor firmed into certainty. Drawing in a resigned breath, he said, ''Very well, we'll just have to get him for you.''

Miranda threw her arms about his neck, giving him a radiant smile. ''I knew I could count on you. I love you so much, Geoffry.''

The book of verse lay unopened in Storm's lap as she sat by Lyle's bed while he slept. She had fled to AshGlen, seeking to be near someone who cared for her. Her first thought had been to go to Lyle. He did not know of their relationship, but it helped her battered emotions to be in his presence. Now she worried her lower lip with her teeth and tried to avoid thinking of her confrontation with Thor. But it was useless. Her mind kept returning to it.

Storm drew her gaze from the distant spot on the wall that she had been staring at unseeingly, back to her father's pale face. It seemed to her that years had passed since the day Lyle had told her of his past and she had thought she was free to look forward to her own future. It had been a beautiful illusion, one that had made her forget all her plans to leave Misty Rose and Thor. She had been blinded by love, failing to see the deception she brought upon herself by believing Thor cared for her in return. But reality had infringed abruptly on the fantasy world she had constructed about herself, crushing beneath its heavy heel all of her romantic dreams.

A hollow ache formed in her breast. All that was left of her moments with Thor was the babe that stirred within her. And if she remained at Misty Rose, she would lose even her child to him. That fact alone made it paramount for her to find a means to flee Thor's clutches before he could carry out his threats.

The turmoil of her thoughts made it impossible for her to sit still. She rose and moved about the room, absently touching the objects her father treasured while her mind dwelt on a means to leave Misty Rose. She knew she had only one hope: Matthew Boone. If he refused to help her, then all would be lost. There was no one else to whom she could turn. Her future and that of her babe rested on Matthew.

Storm paused at the window and drew the drapes against the brightness of the afternoon sun. For a moment she was silhouetted against the glaring light, and her pregnancy was clearly evident. She was unaware of being observed until she turned back to the bed to find Lyle watching her curiously. She smiled as she crossed the room to settle herself once more in the chair. "How are you feeling today?"

Lyle's bony fingers plucked at the sheet as he regarded her thoughtfully before he spoke. "Have you told the father yet?"

Storm could feel the blood drain from her face. Every

muscle in her body grew rigid as she moistened her dry lips. "How did you find out?"

Lyle gave her a sad little smile. "I have eyes, Storm. It's not hard to see you are carrying a child."

Storm lowered her lashes to hide the sudden mist of tears that rushed into her eyes. Her voice was low and filled with shame as she said, "I didn't want you to know."

"Why?" was all Lyle said.

The muscles in Storm's throat worked convulsively as she swallowed back the tears. She kept her eyes glued to her tightly clasped hands. "I didn't want this to hurt our friendship. I knew that once you learned of my condition, you would not approve of me anymore. I'm sorry, Lyle."

His heart went out to her, and he shook his head sadly. "Storm, my dear Storm, don't you think we are good enough friends to share this? It doesn't change how I feel about you. I'm only concerned. Have you told the father yet?"

Her brimming eyes rose to Lyle, and she bit her lower lip as she nodded.

His expression grew grim at the stricken look on her face. "Won't the bastard marry you and give the babe a name?"

Storm burned with shame as she lowered her head once more, unable to look at him. "No. Marriage is out of the question. He doesn't love me."

Lyle's blue-veined hand curled into a fist, and his lips pursed ominously with anger. "By God, something can be done to force him to marry you, the scoundrel. Who is it, Storm? I'm sure Thor will see that the man does the right thing by you."

She gave an involuntary start, and her eyes flew up to meet Lyle's gaze. The hurt, lost look in them told more than words, and he swore under his breath before he said, "It's Thor's child?"

Storm's nails bit into her palms as she nodded once more.

"Damn," Lyle said. "I've known Thor Wakefield for over ten years and would not have believed this of him. Storm, I'll speak to him and make him realize the wrong he is doing you. Thor is a good man, and I'm sure he will agree to the marriage once he thinks it over."

Storm took Lyle's hand and gripped it as she shook her head. "No, Lyle, you mustn't. Thor doesn't love me and has already said marriage is out of the question." Her lower lip trembled as she pleaded, "Lyle, if you care anything for me, you must not speak with him. I beg you."

Unable to cope with the look of raw pain on her face, Lyle reluctantly agreed. "If that's what you want, Storm, but I still think Thor should marry you. It's his child also."

A wave of relief swept through her as she leaned back in the chair, a timid, grateful smile touching her lips. "Thank you, Lyle."

Though he had agreed to keep silent, that did not make it easier to understand, and Lyle muttered under his breath, "But damn it, he should do the honorable thing by the girl." Giving Storm's hand a reassuring squeeze, he regarded her solemnly. "Storm, do you love him?"

She brushed at the dampness of her lashes with the back of her hand, answering truthfully, "Yes, I do."

The forlorn note in her voice tapped Lyle's protective instincts more than ever before in his life. During the past weeks he had begun to look upon Storm as the daughter he and Alisa might have had if she and the babe had lived. He would have wanted a child from their union to possess the same generous nature as Storm. He also owed her a debt that would not be easy to pay. Had it not been for her care, he would have died. Damn, he thought, Thor will marry her or I'll know the reason why. But to Storm, Lyle said, "If you ever need anything, you have only to ask."

She brushed her lips against his cheek. "I know, and I'll remember. Thank you, Lyle, for being my friend."

He pressed her hand, his eyes full of concern. "You need to take care of yourself. You've got to think of your child now."

A shadow seemed to pass over her features. "I know, and you must believe me when I say that whatever I do in the future will be for the welfare of my babe."

Sensing a hidden meaning in her words, Lyle furrowed his brow, and his eyes searched her face for an answer. Failing to find it, he pushed the doubt from his mind. "I do believe you, Storm. Your gentle heart would not let you do otherwise."

Storm's throat grew tight with the emotion that welled within her for the father she could never claim as her own. Lightly kissing Lyle's brow, she said, "I'll see you tomorrow. Rest well and don't worry; I will be fine."

Lyle pretended to drift off to sleep until he heard the door close softly behind Storm. At the sound, his lashes fluttered open, and he stared up at the ceiling without truly seeing it, his mood thoughtful. He had agreed to say nothing to Thor, but his conscience would not let him keep that promise. He had to try to make his friend see that he should be honored to have a woman such as Storm Kingsley in love with him.

You're a fool, Thor, Lyle thought. Storm is like my Alisa. Once she has given her heart, it is yours forever. Few men can say they have been loved so deeply by a woman.

As Storm descended the stairs, Miranda strode briskly into the foyer. Without a glance in Storm's direction, she patted her windblown locks, tossed her plumed hat to the servant, and turned toward the drawing room.

Storm paused on the bottom step, hoping Miranda would not see her. After she had interrupted the woman's intimate interlude with Thor, the idea of facing her so soon held little appeal. The wounds Thor had inflicted that morning were still too raw.

Luck was not with her as Miranda suddenly glanced toward her. Miranda's pale eyes narrowed as they swept over Storm insultingly and her red mouth curled into a mocking smile as she strolled across the foyer to stand in front of Storm. "I see your pregnancy does not prevent your visits to AshGlen."

The color receded from Storm's cheeks, but she refused to respond. She feared that if she did, the pain she carried would be audible in her voice. The knowledge that she suffered would give the witch too much satisfaction. Storm had lost the man she loved to Miranda, but her pride would not let her wallow in her misery or give the woman any pleasure at her expense. Storm's chin inched upward, and she attempted to step past her.

Miranda was determined not to let Storm off so easily, however, and threw an arm across her path. The woman's overbearing manner pricked Storm's temper, but she did not give way to it as she said coldly, "Let me pass, Miranda."

A sneer lifted Miranda's upper lip as she shook her head slowly from side to side. "Not before I know the reason behind your devoted concern for my husband. I hope you do not think I'm fool enough to let you try to worm your way into Lyle's heart and get your hands on AshGlen the way you are trying to take over Misty Rose."

Storm fought the tempest building within her, managing to speak calmly only with great effort. "You know the reason I'm here. Thor insisted I care for Lyle. If you will remember, you agreed to the arrangement."

Miranda's face tightened with hatred. It seemed to emanate from her and hover about them like a black cloud.

''That was fortunate for you, wasn't it? However, Lyle is recovering, and I can only assume you have other devious reasons for coming so often to AshGlen.''

Feeling her hard-won control begin to slip, Storm drew in a deep breath and clenched her hands in the folds of her gown. ''Miranda, Lyle's health is the only reason I come to AshGlen. Now, if you will excuse me, I need to get back to Misty Rose.''

Miranda still did not move from Storm's path. Her icy eyes glittered with malice, and her red mouth narrowed into a thin line, marring her angelic features and making her look like the witch Storm considered her to be. ''Not so fast; I have a few things on my mind that I want to say to you.''

Storm could feel the heat of her anger sting her cheeks, and her voice was tinged with sarcasm as she said, ''Then tell me everything that's on your mind, Miranda. It should not take long.''

Miranda's sense of self-importance failed to let her take note of Storm's implied insult. ''I most certainly will. I don't need permission from Thor's bond servant to speak, mistress, nor will I let some little tart from the gutters of London ingratiate herself into my household.''

Too late, Storm saw that Miranda had noted her involuntary start of surprise upon the woman's disclosure that Thor had revealed everything about her past. Miranda smiled maliciously up at Storm. ''Yes, I know you are nothing more to Thor than his indentured servant. He and I are *very* close, and he has told me everything about you. Did you think him gullible enough to marry someone like you? I can assure you he has no such intention. He is not that big a fool.''

Clamping an iron hold on her temper, Storm barely managed to suppress the urge to slap the sneer from Miranda's face. Fraught with anger, she pushed the woman's arm out of her way and stepped past her. Storm's eyes sent sparks in Miranda's direction as she spat, "Nor will he be fool enough to marry *you* when he learns what a witch you truly are."

Miranda gasped at Storm's audacity. "How dare you speak to me in such a manner, you—you little tramp."

Storm's spine stiffened, her muscles screaming with tension in her fury. "I would say that is the pot calling the kettle black." With that she spun on her heel and strode to the door without a backward glance.

Miranda sputtered with outrage and rushed after Storm. Her manicured nails bit into Storm's upper arm as she jerked her about. "You slut, I'll see you punished for that remark."

Storm's control raveled and snapped as she jerked free of Miranda's grasp. "Keep your hands to yourself, or I'll scratch your eyes out. I'll take no more of your abuse. You are a witch, Miranda Ashfort. We both know what you are. I've seen the little game you play for Thor's benefit, and I've also seen your complete lack of concern for your husband when Thor is not in attendance. I'm not a fool, Miranda. I know you're just waiting for Lyle to die so you can hook your claws into Thor. So don't tempt me too far. I would have no regrets about telling Thor his little angel is really a she-devil in disguise. How do you think he would feel about you then? I would think your loving-wife image would be slightly tarnished if he knew how you neglect Lyle, hoping his next seizure will be his last. And from the way you behave, I wouldn't put it past you to try to help matters along."

Miranda's eyes widened in astonishment as the meek little mouse turned into a lioness before her. She took an involuntary step backward as she said, "Your impertinence knows no bounds, mistress. Thor would never believe such slander against me. He knows you for the whore you are. I can assure you of that."

Tired of dueling, Storm said, "You can keep your assurances, Miranda. To be honest, I don't give a bloody damn what you or Thor thinks of me. But I will most certainly tell him everything if you refuse to let me come to visit Lyle.

"Your husband is a kind man and deserves much better from you than he has received. Since you, his wife, refuse to see to his needs and make an effort to help him survive, I will do so, because he has become my friend. I have seen the pain in his eyes when you fawn over Thor. It does his health little good to know his wife wishes him out of the way so she can pursue his best friend. If I can ease his mind at all, I will do it, and you had better not try to stop me." Storm spun on her heel, stalked through the door, and with a loud bang, slammed it in Miranda's face.

Miranda stood frozen to the spot, her eyes glued to the closed door as her hand came up to her throat. "She suspects," she breathed, unconsciously touching the glass vial in her pocket with her other hand. Storm Kingsley could ruin everything she had planned and would have to be stopped right away.

Forcing her numb limbs to move, Miranda strode into the drawing room, directly to the brandy decanter. Her hand shook as she poured the amber liquid into the glass and raised it to her dry lips. Her plans for Storm had taken a radical turn in the past few minutes.

Storm's fury stood her in good stead until she maneuvered the small cart out of the winding drive of AshGlen onto the sandy roadway. Then a small tremor began in the soles of her feet and moved upward with the force of an earthquake, making her tremble from head to toe. Her hands shook so badly she felt she no longer had the strength to control the mare. Reining the animal to a halt beneath a tall live oak, she let the impact of everything that had transpired engulf her.

Tears blinded her as wave upon wave of humiliation and

pain descended upon her, battering her unmercifully. No longer able to fight her despair, she gave way to it, great sobs racking her slender frame as she bent forward over her knees with her head pressed against her folded arms.

Miranda's words echoed through Storm's mind and made her realize Thor had begun to carry out his threats even before they had spoken of the child she carried. From past experience, she knew Thor had once again pretended to give her a choice and, anticipating her answer, had moved ahead to ensure that everyone knew of her conviction and believed the worst of her. It was a clever scheme, because she would have no defense against him. He had power and strong allies. No one would argue in favor of a convicted prostitute and bond slave. Storm sat still. Her tears were spent, and all that was left was a feeling of utter helplessness.

The sandy loam muffled the sound of the horseman as he rounded the bend and drew his mount to a halt beside the cart. Storm was unaware of his presence until she felt the touch of his hand upon her shoulder. Startled, she jerked abruptly upright and turned to face the intruder. New tears sprang into her eyes at the look of concern on Matthew's face. Without thinking, only wanting comfort from him, she threw her arms about his neck, and her voice cracked as she said, "Oh, Matthew."

Automatically, his arms came about her, and he held her against his chest until her bout of weeping subsided. When nothing was left but sniffles, he gently eased away from her and peered down into her damp face. "Storm, what on earth has happened? Are you ill? Have you had an accident?"

She drew in a tremulous breath and shook her head. "No, Matthew, I am physically fine."

Matthew regarded her thoughtfully as a frown etched a jagged path across his forehead and his brows lowered suspiciously over his cinnamon-colored eyes. "Then this has something to do with Thor, doesn't it?"

Like a small, lost child, Storm wiped her eyes with the back of her hand, and her voice quavered with hopelessness. "He—he has threatened to take my babe away from me when it is born, Matthew."

Matthew blanched. "Babe?"

Seeing his stunned expression, Storm suddenly realized she had not reckoned on Matthew's feelings when she made her plans. In the short time they had known each other, she had found him to be a decent man, but there were few men who would not look askance at an unmarried pregnant woman.

The heat of her embarrassment flooded her cheeks, tinting them a deep rose. She could no longer look him in the face and lowered her eyes to her hands, waiting tensely for his judgment and condemnation.

"Damn!" Matthew swore loudly, his curse disturbing the birds in the live oak, making them chatter with fright and take wing across the evening sky.

Storm was also startled by his oath and raised wide eyes to his angry face.

Seeing her fear, Matthew ran his hand irritably through his hair, fighting to control his fury. With an effort he mastered his temper and released a long, exasperated sigh as he gave her an apologetic look. "I should have known this would happen. It's my fault for not obeying my first instincts."

"Matthew, none of this is your fault. You could not have done anything for me. I'm Thor's bond slave, and you would have been breaking the law to help me."

The muscle beneath Matthew's right eye twitched as he looked at her. "I know, Storm. Thor told me the same thing when I threatened to take you away after I found out he had made you his mistress against your will."

"You told him you would take me away from Misty Rose?" Hope surged to life within Storm's breast, overriding all else as she waited for Matthew's answer.

His shoulders drooped as he nodded. "Yes, and I should have done it. If I had, you wouldn't be in this predicament now."

Storm's face brightened as excitement welled within her like a pool, each moment a drop of new hope rippling the surface to make it grow larger. Feeling as if all her prayers had been answered, she clutched his brawny hand, and her words rushed out breathlessly. "Matthew, will you take me away now? If I don't leave Misty Rose before my child is born, Thor will see it taken from me. You are my only chance. If you don't help me, I don't know what I'll do."

Noting the edge of hysteria in her voice, Matthew squeezed her hand reassuringly. "I will help you, Storm, but it won't be easy. Thor has kept me away from you since the night I told him I would take you away."

Unaware that she had been holding her breath, Storm gave a great sigh of relief as she released it. Exuberantly, she squealed with delight and like a small child threw her arms about Matthew's neck, raining kisses enthusiastically down on his craggy cheeks as she said, "Thank you, Matthew; oh, thank you."

He enfolded her in his strong arms, holding her close as he mentally cursed Thor for being a fool. The man was too stubborn to admit he cared for Storm, and because of it he was putting her through such useless agony. Remembering his vow to bring them together, Matthew felt his conscience begin to nag at him, and he grew hesitant to help her leave Misty Rose. Tipping up her chin, he held Storm's gaze with his own solemn one as he said, "Are you sure this is the right thing to do? Perhaps it's all a misunderstanding."

The happiness faded from Storm's features, and she shook her head. "There has been no misunderstanding. Thor has made his intentions quite clear, and Miranda reaffirmed it only a short while ago. I know how he feels about me. The only way I can keep my child is to leave

Misty Rose. I have no other choice, Matthew, and I will do it one way or the other. Can't you see? Thor has the power to do as he wishes, and if I stay, I will have no say in the matter at all.''

Still undecided as to the best course of action to take, Matthew asked, ''Do you still love him, Storm?''

A lost, pain-filled look came into her sapphire eyes as she moistened her suddenly dry lips and whispered, ''Yes, Matthew, I still love him, though that makes me a great fool, because he feels nothing for me. He planned this all along. He has used me to gain the heir he wanted. To Thor I'm but a brood mare.'' Seeing the doubt flicker in Matthew's eyes, she raised her hand to his cheek, cupping it as if she were his mother instructing him about something he did not understand. ''I know Thor is like a brother to you. You love each other, and it is hard for you to comprehend the cruel streak that lies within him. He is heartless, Matthew. He was pleased I was to bear his child because it would save him from marriage.''

Emotion constricted her throat, and she had to swallow several times before she could go on. ''Matthew, I could have accepted the fact that he did not want to marry me, if only he had cared a small bit. But that was a dream. Thor cares only for himself and for Miranda Ashfort. He wants the seed of his loins because it belongs to him, not because he has any other feelings. He is selfish, and why I love him is beyond my own reasoning, but I do. However, it does not matter how I feel, because I can't accept him on his conditions. I will not stay here and have the child I labor to bring into the world taken from me to be one of Thor's possessions. I would see him in his grave first or me in mine.''

Unable to completely reconcile the Thor Wakefield he knew with the one Storm described, Matthew found himself placed in an untenable position. He knew he had to make a decision and prayed it would be the right one for all concerned.

Pondering the predicament, he rubbed his stubbled chin has he lowered his gaze to the roadway and absently kicked at the small stones with the tip of his boot. Finally, still undecided, he looked once more at Storm, hoping in some way to find the answer he sought. He found it in the determined light in her blue eyes and the stubborn line of her jaw. They told him that her course was set. With his help or without it, she was resolved to leave Misty Rose. At last he said, "Then we had best begin to make plans. If Thor has an inkling of our intentions, he'll put me off Misty Rose at gunpoint and lock you away until the babe is born."

Matthew and Storm were too engrossed with their plans to note the rider that traveled toward AshGlen from the direction of Charleston. At the sight of them, he reined in his mount, his eyes narrowing speculatively before he urged his horse from the road and into the underbrush.

Curious, Geoffry pushed back the thick foliage, wanting to get a better view of the couple. He had recognized Matthew Boone but not the young woman with him. However, she fitted the description Miranda had given him of Storm Kingsley.

Wanting to get a better look at the girl his sister hated, Geoffry slid from the saddle and secured his mount before he made his way stealthfully along until he was near enough to hear their conversation. A grim smile played about his mouth as he watched Storm and Matthew embrace and begin to make plans for their departure from Misty Rose. He chuckled to himself as he gathered the ammunition for his sister to use against the girl. Miranda should be pleased with this day's work, he thought. She was closer to the truth than she even realized.

Satisfied he had heard enough and would be back with

his whore in Charleston before nightfall, Geoffry began to ease quietly back through the tangle of vines and bushes. Wary of being discovered, he kept his gaze on Storm and Matthew, watching their every move for any indication that his presence had been noted. It was not until Geoffry was about to turn away that he caught his first clear view of Storm's features. He froze as she glanced toward the side of the road. His breath left him in one great whoosh, and his already-pale features turned a deathly white. Miranda's rival was the girl from London, Alisa Ashfort's daughter.

Geoffry stood paralyzed, his mind trying to comprehend what his eyes saw. The girl before him was the one he thought safely out of the way in Newgate. His eyes widened, and his hands began to shake. At his best he had never been a brave man, and now he felt as if the earth had opened up before him and a great void lay only inches from his feet.

Fear churned his insides as he realized that all he and Miranda had worked to gain could be destroyed if Storm Kingsley recognized him and began to put the pieces of the puzzle together. Beads of sweat broke out across his forehead as he watched her scan the underbrush as if searching him out. The dark future loomed before him as he envisioned himself climbing the steps of the gibbet. He could feel the rough hemp noose placed about his neck by Storm Kingsley for his part in her mother's death. His hand trembled as he wiped the perspiration from his brow, then quickly made his way back to his horse. There was no time to lose; he had to warn Miranda.

Miranda eyed her brother contemptuously as he sloshed the amber liquid into a glass and raised it shakily to his lips. "Damn it, Geoffry, get hold of yourself. Now is not the time for you to have a fit of faintheartedness. You can't turn into a nervous wreck because of something you think you saw. I suggest you lay off the wine for a while, Brother.''

Again the decanter clinked against the glass as Geoffry refilled it and then turned to her. "I'm sorry if I haven't your iron constitution, but I don't believe you've heard a word I've said, Miranda. The girl is the same one I saw in London. She is Lyle and Alisa's daughter, the legal heir to AshGlen!"

Her hands braced on her hips and her foot tapping a rapid tattoo against the polished floorboards, Miranda's stance reflected her irritation at her brother's behavior. Since they were children, she had known Geoffry often put on a bravado he did not feel, but to be so starkly reminded of his cowardliness when she needed his help infuriated her. "I've heard what you think you believe, but how can you be so sure Storm Kingsley is the same girl?"

Geoffry slumped into a chair and looked up at his sister, his eyes pleading with her to believe him. "For the love of God, Miranda, she is the same one. As much as I enjoy women, you should know I would not forget someone that lovely."

Miranda eyed him dubiously. "Then why hasn't the little witch come forward? If she is Lyle's daughter, why has she remained at Misty Rose?"

Geoffry downed the last of his drink and shook his head slowly as he gave a slight shrug. "I don't know the answer to that, Miranda. Perhaps she doesn't know Lyle is her father."

A thoughtful expression crossed Miranda's face as she digested all her brother had told her. "Or perhaps she does know and for some reason is waiting to reveal her identity."

Geoffry looked up at her in bewilderment. "What reason would she have?"

Exasperated that she could not answer his question, Miranda began to pace the drawing room, her mind working feverishly to solve the riddle. Failing, she turned once

more to her brother. Her pale eyes narrowed with cold
malice as she said, "I don't know what devious little
scheme the wench has in mind, but I do know she'll not
have time to carry it out. She already suspects I'm trying
to poison Lyle, and that in itself has sealed her fate. This
new bit of information about Matthew Boone may be just
what we need. I think we can use it to our advantage."

Unable to follow his sister's cunning reasoning, Geoffry
asked, "How?"

Miranda gave him a look that clearly spoke of her
superiority over him. "You amaze me sometimes. I don't
believe you can see anything beyond the tip of your nose,
Geoffry. Don't you realize no one will suspect us of
anything if they believe Storm Kinglsey has fled with the
overseer? All it will take is a few properly dropped hints at
the right time and place and all our problems will be over.
Once Storm is out of the way, poor Lyle will finally
succumb to his strange illness and everything will be
ours."

Finally comprehending her train of thought, Geoffry
relaxed for the first time since he'd discovered Storm's
identity. Giving Miranda a warm smile, he said, "I should
have known you would figure out what to do."

Incredulous that he could believe otherwise, Miranda
arched one golden brow. "Have I ever failed in the past?"

Sensing his sister's silent reprimand, Geoffry lowered
his head sheepishly. Miranda had never failed once she'd
set her mind on what she wanted. He did not doubt she
would also succeed with her plans to rid them of Storm
Kingsley and her father.

Chapter 14

Dark clouds billowed on the horizon, warning of the storm to come. Gusts of cold wind whipped the dead leaves into piles before another blast of chilly air destroyed them, sending the leaves scattering across the lawn. Winter had come early to the lowlands of South Carolina, and with it came the heavy rains that swelled the Ashley until it overflowed its banks.

Thor's mood matched the weather as he sat before the blazing fire, a chessboard between himself and his host, Lyle Ashfort. They had begun the game upon Thor's arrival an hour earlier, but the ivory playing pieces were hardly touched. A muscle worked in his lean jaw as his ill humor grew by the moment. Before the first move could be made, Lyle had broached the subject that chafed Thor sorely: Storm Kingsley.

Of late it had taken little to spark Thor's temper in matters that concerned his housekeeper. The past two weeks had been hell. He had done everything in his power to keep his distance from her, hoping to quell the ache in his heart and the desire that raged in his loins but to no avail.

That in itself had added a keen edge to his temper. He had tried to be patient with his friend as Lyle praised Storm effusively for her kind and gentle nature as well as her beauty and charm. Now Thor had reached his limit; he could stand no more.

Abruptly he pushed the board to one side and stood. A scowl etched his brow as he crossed to the fireplace and placed his palms on the mantel. For a moment he studied the dancing flames before looking over his shoulder at Lyle. "For one who can't walk, you tiptoe prettily about a subject. I would appreciate it if you would just say what's on your mind instead of drowning me with praise for my housekeeper."

For a few long minutes Lyle regarded Thor thoughtfully. He had tried to keep his word to Storm but Thor was too muleheaded to take his subtle hints. Shaking his head sadly, knowing he would have to take the direct approach to make the young rascal realize the mistake he was making, Lyle said, "Then, Thor, I will say it so you can understand. For the past hour I've been hoping to make you see Storm as she really is: a beautiful loving woman who should not have to bear the shame you seem determined to inflict upon her."

Thor tensed, and his hands curled into fists upon the flat surface of Italian marble. His lips thinned into a line as he drew in a deep breath and turned to face his friend. "Lyle, I don't know what you've been told, but obviously you are the one who does not understand."

Lyle cocked one graying brow. "How so? Do you mean to say you have agreed to marry Storm and give your babe a name?"

Thor's expression was guarded, though he felt his insides twist into painful knots. "No, and I'll not agree to it. I intend to adopt the child, but that is all I will do."

Lyle's pale features flushed a dull angry red. "You're a fool, Thor, and if I were able, I'd take a strap to your

backside to try to beat some sense into you. The girl is
carrying your seed, and you have the audacity to say you
will be magnanimous and adopt the babe when it is born.
Do you know what such an act will do to a woman like
Storm? Do you even care? Thor, I'm disappointed in you.
I thought you were a man instead of a sniveling brat.''

Thor blanched under Lyle's attack. His nostrils flared as
he drew in a deep breath in an effort to maintain control
over his own temper. "Lyle, this is none of your affair. I
treasure your friendship, but I will not let you sit in
judgment of me. I will not be forced into a loveless
marriage no matter what. I know firsthand what it can do
to the child of such a union. I'll not have my heir suffer
the same fate.''

Lyle gripped the lap robe, and his lined face grew taut
with fury. "Damn it, Thor, I'm making it my affair whether
you like it or not. I care for the girl and owe her a debt I
can never repay. I can't just sit meekly by and let you use
her in such an abominable fashion. You are treating her
worse than one of your slaves.''

Thor's control snapped. His silver eyes glinted as he
said, "Damn it, I've heard all I'm going to from you about
Storm Kingsley, friend or no. I've made my decision and
intend to see it carried out.''

Lyle's heated gaze never wavered from Thor's face.
"You are a bigger fool than I first thought. Storm is a
beautiful, sensitive woman, and she will never agree to
your terms no matter what you say.''

A determined light glimmered in the depths of Thor's
eyes as his face hardened. "She has no other choice. I
own her bond of indenture. If she agrees to my demands,
then I will give her the freedom she craves. But if she
refuses, I will see the courts settle the matter for me.''

Dumbfounded by Thor's disclosure, Lyle stared at him,
unable to comprehend that his friend could be so heartless.
Finally regaining his voice, he said, "My God, Thor, I

can't believe this of you. Release the girl or let me buy her papers. Don't do this thing. You can't truly expect to use Storm as you have and then take her child away when it is born. What kind of man are you to even consider such a thing?''

Thoroughly exasperated, Thor ran his fingers through his hair and shook his head. "Lyle, I'm the kind of man who has no other choice.''

Puzzled, Lyle studied the young man briefly before he said, "Is the reason behind your objection to marrying Storm the fact that she is a servant?''

Wearily Thor rubbed his hand over his face. His shoulders drooped as he looked at Lyle, his eyes pleading for the older man's understanding. "No, that has nothing to do with my decision. I love Storm, Lyle, but she has made her feelings plain to me ever since we first met. She hates me. So you see, I can't have her, nor can I let her take my child away from Misty Rose. The babe is my heir. You of all people should be able to comprehend how I feel about that.''

Lyle felt the urge to shout for joy at Thor's admission of his love, but he quickly suppressed it and lowered his gaze to the lap robe as he considered the future of the two young people that were so dear to him. If Storm and Thor both loved each other as they had said, then things would work out for the best.

Glancing up at Thor's haggard expression, Lyle knew he could end the younger man's misery with only a few words, but he would not. It was not his place to speak of things that only lovers should tell each other. If their love was to survive, they would have to come to terms with their stubborn pride and recognize each other's needs and be willing to share. It could not be a one-sided affair, nor could anyone force them to face their feelings until they were ready.

A smug little grin touched Lyle's lips as he thought,

From their attitudes toward each other, it will probably be sometime in the distant future.

Feeling better by the minute, Lyle said, "Then I'll say no more. This is something you and Storm will have to work out between you. I just hope you remember that time will not stand still and wait for you, Thor. The thing you desire most may slip through your fingers if you don't make an effort to keep it."

The muscles in Thor's chest rippled as a wave of emotion rushed over him. His voice was painfully tight as he said, "I know what you're trying to tell me, and I appreciate your advice, but I'm just afraid that what I want most has already been lost to me because of my own stupidity."

Lyle smoothed the fringed edge of the lap robe absently as he regarded Thor. "You must remember, my friend, it is never too late to try to win the war until the last battle has been fought."

Those few words were the sparks that ignited the dry kindling of Thor's hopes. They burst into vivid flames as a boyish grin tugged the corners of his shapely mouth. "I think it's time for me to start planning my battle strategy instead of wallowing in this self-pity that will gain me naught. I may eventually lose the war, but it will not be from lack of effort."

Lyle could no longer hide his look of pleasure as he said, chuckling, "Now, that is the Thor Wakefield I know. He has always been a man who wouldn't let anything stand in his way when he set his mind to something." Lyle paused, his face growing serious. "I wish you victory in this war, Thor. If you fail, I'm afraid to think of the consequences."

Thor's smile faded as a fleeting shadow passed over his face. "If I don't succeed in this quest, I'll have to continue as I had planned."

Fearing to even consider such an outcome, Lyle reached for the crystal decanter on the table at his side. He filled two glasses with ruby wine and handed one to Thor, raising his own in toast. "Then let us drink to your success." The red liquid sparkled in the light from the fire as Lyle brought the glass to his lips and sent a silent prayer heavenward, begging aid for his friend in this battle to win Storm's love.

With hopes buoyed by Lyle's encouragement, Thor was eager to return to Misty Rose and Storm. His steps were lighter than they had been in weeks as he descended the stairs and crossed the foyer. Tossing his great cape about his shoulders, he picked up his hat and gloves. His hand was already resting on the brass doorknob when Miranda called out to him, "Are you so preoccupied these days that you can't stop and say hello before you leave?"

Thor turned to the beautiful woman, a warm smile of pleasure playing over his features. "Forgive me, Miranda. I was unaware that you had returned from your ride."

Miranda pouted prettily before bestowing him with her most provocative smile. "I will forgive you if you will stay and have tea with me. I had to cut my ride short because the day was so chilly. A nice cup of hot tea will do you good before you venture out into it."

Thor was anxious to be on his way but could find no excuse to turn down the invitation. Resigned, he followed Miranda into the drawing room. Removing his great cape and tossing it over the back of a chair he settled his lean frame in a striped-satin chair across from her, watching her pour the golden liquid into translucent china cups. He did not realize his mind had drifted away from his hostess's conversation to Storm until Miranda offered him a cup of tea for the second time. Giving her an apologetic smile, he said, "I'm sorry, Miranda. What was it you were saying?"

Used to having Thor's full attention, Miranda was annoyed by his distracted air, but she managed to hide her feelings behind an air of concern. "Thor, is something wrong? You seem as if your thoughts are a million miles away.''

Taking the proffered cup, he shook his head as he stirred the tea with a silver spoon. ''No, there is nothing wrong, Miranda. For the first time in weeks I feel as if everything may be going to turn out right.''

Her curiosity piqued, Miranda arched one golden brow at him. ''Is it something you might share with a friend?''

Thor chuckled, unable to contain his good humor. Tiny lines fanned the corners of his gray eyes as his smile deepened. ''Gladly. Lyle has made me see that things may work out between Storm and me after all.''

Miranda's heart seemed to freeze in her chest, and her throat grew dry as she fought to remain calm. No, her mind cried, this can't be! But she only said, ''How very kind of my dear husband. What did he say to change things?''

Years seemed to lift from Thor as his face lit with hope. ''As of yet nothing has changed, but Lyle has made me see the situation differently. If all goes well, I intend to ask Storm to be my wife.''

The blood drained from Miranda's face, and she could not hide the trembling that beset her hands. The cup rattled on the saucer as she set it on the table and quickly clasped her hands in her lap. She searched furiously for a ploy to stop his plans and settled on what Geoffry had seen. She had intended to use the information later, after she had time to prepare her story convincingly. Now she could only hope Thor would believe her without question because of their friendship.

A grieved little sigh escaped her lips as she looked up at him. Her eyes reflected her pity. ''Thor, I feared that something of this nature might happen. I wanted to come to you as soon as I found out, but I felt I owed Storm a debt for saving Lyle's life. I did not think my silence would cause you any pain, since it was my understanding

that there was nothing between you and your housekeeper."
Miranda's eyes pleaded for understanding as she continued. "Thor, I hope you will forgive me. You know I
would never hurt you intentionally."

A perplexed frown etched a furrow across his brow as
he looked at her, his suspicions beginning to grow. "What
are you trying to say, Miranda?"

She paused for effect, biting her lower lip as she looked
down at her hands. "We are friends, Thor, and I would do
anything to keep from seeing you hurt, but I must tell
you."

Miranda's hedging exasperated Thor. "Damn it, out
with it. This beating about the bush is driving me insane.
What is it you know?"

As she raised tear-bright eyes to his face, Miranda's lips
trembled slightly as she said, "It's Storm. I'm afraid you
have raised your hopes for nothing. Geoffry saw her with
your overseer, Matthew Boone."

Thor's stomach muscles contracted sharply as if he had
been kicked in the gut. His hand clenched about the dark
wood of the chair arm, his knuckles white from the pressure. Fury mingled with jealousy to make his body taut as
Miranda's words filled his entire being with a hot current.
"What are you saying? What did Geoffry see?"

Miranda withdrew a lace-edged handkerchief from the
pocket of her burgundy wool gown and hid the smug smile
that played over her lips behind it before dabbing dramatically at her eyes. "It grieves me, Thor, to have to speak
against Storm. I have never been one to carry malicious
gossip, but now your feelings have to come first." She
paused, drawing in a shaky breath, to give her words time
to have the desired effect. "Geoffry saw Storm and Matthew in each other's arms. They were kissing and making
plans to leave Misty Rose."

Thor's anger made him fail to wonder how Geoffry had
managed to gain so much information without being privy

to the conversation between Storm and Matthew. With his thoughts centered only on what Miranda had said, he came to his feet, his face dark with fury as he jerked his cape from the chair once more and threw it about his shoulders. His voice was no more than a low growl as he swore, "Damn the bitch to hell! I suspected something between them but believed their lies when they denied it."

Miranda's devious mind worked quickly as she saw her chance to further disillusion him. Feigning shock, her eyes wide and one hand pressed to her breast as if she felt faint from such a thought, she said, "Thor, you can't mean to say you suspect the child to be Matthew's? I don't believe Storm could be that evil, not after all she has done for Lyle."

Thor's head snapped about as he looked at Miranda, considering her words. His eyes narrowed, and his face grew granite-hard. "The thought had crossed my mind, but I believed Storm when she said the child belonged to me. I'll not be that big a fool again."

Satisfied that she had set the hook and Thor had taken the bait she had dangled enticingly before him, Miranda fully intended to reel in her catch as she crossed to him and looked up at him with eyes filled with compassion. "Thor, I'll not let you call yourself a fool. You are a good man who believes there are honest people in the world. You are not the first man who has been deceived by a devious woman. What do you know of Storm Kingsley beyond the fact that she is your bond slave? Her past could not be spotless if she was transported by the English court. No, it would not be the first time a heartless woman has lied and schemed to gain a man's wealth by using the excuse of what grows in her belly."

Thor considered Miranda's words, letting his pain and anger make him forget that Storm had asked nothing of him. It was true that he knew little about her beyond what had been stated in her papers. Storm had never revealed

any of her past to him. Suddenly he realized how he had
fallen prey to her schemes. He had much experience in
avoiding the ploys used by the belles of Charleston, but
she was no doubt a more devious type of woman, since
she had been reared in the gutters of London, where her
very survival would depend on her own cunning. She
could easily have found out from Matthew how he felt
about greedy women and acted accordingly. She could
have pretended that she wanted nothing from him but in
reality thought to gain it all.

A white line formed about Thor's lips as he pressed
them tightly together at the thought. His agony intensified
as he considered Matthew's part in Storm's schemes. How
could the deep bond they shared be severed by one woman?

Drawing his mind away from such hurtful thoughts,
Thor gazed down at Miranda and saw the love she felt for
him openly displayed. He mistook it for the compassion of
a friend and thought, Miranda is the only woman I have
ever met who does not have a greedy bone in her body.

Cupping her chin in the palm of his hand, he said,
"Miranda, there are few women as good as you in this
world. I envy Lyle his good fortune."

Demurely, Miranda let her lashes flutter modestly downward and blushed at his compliment. "Thank you, Thor. It
means much to me to have you say such a lovely thing."

He brushed a kiss against her brow before he released
her and picked up his hat and gloves. "There is no need to
thank me for speaking the truth, Miranda. I only wish
there were more women like you. It would make my life
much easier." Giving her a wry grin, he strode from the
drawing room, his mind turning once more to the two
people he loved most in the world and who had betrayed
him.

A smug, self-satisfied look crossed Miranda's face as
she settled herself once more in the chair, spreading her
skirts about her. As she picked up her cup of lukewarm

tea, her eyes glowed with triumph. The groundwork had been laid, and soon Storm Kingsley would be out of her life forever.

"Good work, Sister," Geoffry said as he strolled into the room and poured himself a brandy before taking the seat Thor had vacated only moments before.

Miranda's red mouth curled into a malicious little smile as she eyed her brother. "You heard? Then you know all is now ready, and if it goes as we have planned, we will soon be rid of both Storm and Lyle before anyone knows of the connection between them."

Geoffry nodded, his pale eyes gleaming with a predatory light as he raised his glass to his sister in silent tribute.

Comfortable for the first time since he'd left his cabin before dawn, Matthew sat before the blazing fire with his long legs outstretched before its warmth, sipping a hot cup of mulled wine to take away the chill.

He was tired. He had worked all day to make sure the floodgates were open so the excess water from the rising Ashley would not damage the rice fields. They had managed to open the last one just as the downpour began. Already damp and muddy from his work, Matthew had been drenched to the skin by the rain, so that his weary body ached from head to toe. When the work was finished and he was making his way home, the only thought in his mind had been a blazing fire and hot drink.

Now that he had his desire, his thoughts turned to the beautiful woman he had vowed to help flee Misty Rose. Since that day he had had little time even to consider how he would provide Storm with the assistance he had promised her. The day after he had found her weeping on the road, the weather had changed abruptly. Winter had descended with force, bringing with it the torrential rains that had kept him too busy in the fields to contemplate much else. Even had he not been needed to oversee the workers, the weather would have hindered any attempt they might have made to leave Misty Rose. He could not ask Storm in her condition to travel in such weather on horseback. It would be far too dangerous.

Thoughts of her slowly drifted from Matthew's mind as he grew drowsy watching the flames leap and swirl to the music of the drumming rain that beat furiously against the board-and-batten walls of the cabin. As he gave in to the mellow warmth surrounding him, his chin dropped to his chest and his eyes fluttered closed.

The threats the black clouds had made all day were now fulfilled with a vengeance. The steady downpour drowned out the sound of Thor's horse approaching the cabin, and Matthew was unaware of his arrival until Thor kicked the door open with the heel of his boot and strode into the room, his face dripping rain and dark with unabated fury.

Startled awake by the sound of the door crashing open, Matthew spilled the hot wine down the front of his shirt as he came to his feet and turned to confront the intruder. He had to blink several times to clear his drowsy vision before his eyes widened in surprise at the sight of Thor standing in the middle of the room, a puddle of water forming about his feet. Wiping at the wet stain on his shirt, Matthew eyed his friend warily, sensing Thor's black mood. "Has something happened in the fields to make you come bursting in here like a madman?" he asked.

Thor brushed the dampness from his face as he crossed the short space that divided the two men. With one swift movement, he gripped the front of Matthew's shirt, jerking him forward. Thor's teeth were clenched together as he growled, "I should throttle you. I thought you were my friend, and all the while you were lying to me and slipping around behind my back to meet Storm after I warned you to keep your distance."

Matthew's face flushed a deep, angry red as he glared at

Thor and jerked free of his grip. "I told you once that your order could be damned. I'm your friend, Thor, not your slave."

Thor's eyes glittered with sparks of lightning, and his voice held the rumble of thunder as he said, "Call yourself no friend of mind, Matthew Boone. I want you to collect your belongings and be off Misty Rose by dawn. I'll not have a liar and sneak in my employ."

Matthew's cinnamon-colored eyes glowed red as he looked at Thor, taut with rage. "I'll leave Misty Rose, but I'm taking Storm with me."

Thor drew in a deep breath in his effort to control the violent emotions ripping through him. "Storm belongs to me for the next seven years, and she will remain at Misty Rose."

Belligerently, Matthew shook his head. "No, Thor. I'll not leave her here to be abused by you any longer. The girl has suffered enough at your hands. I'll not let her stay here so you can inflict further misery upon her by taking away her child. When I leave this plantation, Storm goes with me whether you like it or not."

A muscle worked in Thor's jaw, and his chest rose and fell heavily. "Don't tempt fate, Matthew. I'm warning you; you're pushing my patience to the limit, and it would take little for me to beat you to death with my bare hands."

Unyielding in the face of his threats, Matthew thrust out his chin as if offering it to Thor's fist. "If you think you can, just try it. After everything you've done to Storm, I would enjoy beating the hell out of you."

"Damn you, Matthew. Get off Misty Rose and never show your face here again," Thor said as his rage exploded in a shower of fireworks in his brain. "And as far as Storm and the bastard she carries are concerned, you can rest assured I have no further intention of adopting the child you tried to foist off as mine. In seven years you can have the wench and your brat, but until that time, never let me see you on my property again.''

Matthew's brows lowered as he regarded Thor warily. Had the man gone mad? Had he taken a blow to the head and lost all reason? Does Thor honestly believe the child Storm carries belongs to me? Matthew asked himself. He considered Thor thoughtfully a few long moments more, until the light of understanding flickered to life in the back of his mind. He knew what had aroused his friend's odd behavior—jealousy. Somehow Thor had learned of their meeting on the road and had come to the conclusion that he and Storm were lovers.

Understanding did not mean forgiveness. Matthew's own anger did not lessen but instead was kindled hotter with the knowledge that Thor had so little trust in him. His rage made him forget that he had gone against Thor's orders and agreed to help Storm.

''Have no fear that you will see me at Misty Rose again, Thor. Nor will you see Storm and *your* babe. You don't deserve a woman like her or the child she carries. At least I will love her, and I'll not hold it against the babe that it was sired by a fool.''

Before Matthew could raise a hand to defend himself, Thor's fist slammed into his jaw, knocking him backward against the table. It toppled over with his weight, and Matthew landed on the floor.

Thor stood over him, his body rigid, his hand resting on the butt of the pistol beneath his cape. ''Don't get up, Matthew, or I'll kill you. Be gone from Misty Rose at first light, or you'll live to regret it.''

Matthew eyed him hostilely as he rubbed his jaw. ''I'll leave, but I'll be back for Storm. You may have the advantage now, but you can't watch her every moment. I told you a long time ago that if she asked for my help, I would give it, and I intend to do exactly that. Nothing you can say or do will stop me. You may be too blind to appreciate her, but I'm not. I will happily accept your child as my own if she will have me. And as far as I'm concerned, you can go to hell.''

Jealousy raced through Thor, and his fingers tightened about the butt of the pistol, but he forced himself to regain some measure of control over his temper. A sneer curled his upper lip as he glared at Matthew. ''Spare me your noble intentions. If you are fool enough to be snared by the witch, then you are more than welcome to her once her time is served.'' He regarded Matthew thoughtfully for a moment. ''I should be grateful to you for helping me to see Storm for what she really is. You called me a fool, but I'm afraid you are the only fool present at the moment. The two of you deserve each other.''

''Then let me take her away from here tonight,'' Matthew said quickly.

Thor smiled grimly and shook his head. ''No, Matthew, I'll not make it that easy for you two after your treachery. Storm will remain at Misty Rose until her term is served or I tire of her.''

A malicious light glittered in the depths of his silver eyes, and his lips curled into a cruel smile as he watched Matthew's face harden with impotent rage. ''Did you think because of her lies that I would not still desire her, Matthew? Rest assured I don't have to trust or believe a woman to bed her.'' Wanting to further hurt Matthew in the same manner in which he suffered, Thor taunted him, ''It should be several months still until her condition hinders my sport.''

''Damn you,'' Matthew ground out, and made a move to rise but reconsidered his action as Thor's hand again closed over the gun.

Thor's steely eyes narrowed, and a muscle twitched in his jaw as he ordered, ''Get off Misty Rose and for your own good forget about Storm Kingsley. I hold what is mine, as you well know, and will abide no trespass.'' With that Thor strode from the overseer's cabin.

A streak of lightning split the black sky and thunder rolled in its wake as Thor urged his mount into the dry haven of the stable. The smell of hay and horseflesh permeated the air as he shook the rain from his cape and removed his hat. Finding the flint to light the lantern, he struck it near the wick and watched as it bloomed into flame. Holding the lantern high to light his way, he crossed to the tack room, where the stableboy slept on a small cot in the corner. Bending, he gave the youth a rough shake on the shoulder. ''Jeb, wake up.''

Jeb mumbled in his sleep and buried his head in his arms, unconsciously rebelling against having his rest disturbed after a hard day's work. Giving the stableboy another shake, Thor ordered, ''Damn it, wake up. I've things for you to do, and I don't have all night.''

Jeb came awake with a start, eyeing the figure towering over him groggily. As the sleep began to clear from his mind, he recognized Thor. His dark eyes grew round in surprise, and he struggled to sit up as he apologized. ''Master Thor, I's sorry I didn't wait up on you.''

Thor reached for the rain slicker behind the door and tossed it to the youth. ''Never mind that now, Jeb. I want you to go to the quarters and get Zeus and Dom. Tell them to go to the overseer's cabin and stand guard.''

Jeb yawned widely and scratched his curly head. ''What you need them to guard, Master Thor?''

Thor's mouth narrowed into an unforgiving line as he said, ''Matthew Boone. Tell them there will be an extra ration of rum if they make sure Boone is gone from Misty Rose by dawn.''

Jeb eyed his master curiously as he slipped the oversized slicker on. Questions bubbled to the tip of his tongue, but he refrained from asking them. From the expression on Thor's face, Jeb knew it was in his own best interest to do as he was bidden and quickly. Hunching his thin shoulders against the blowing rain, he hurried out into the wet night.

Another bright flash of lightning illuminated Thor's stony features as he stood in the doorway of the stable, eyeing the dark facade of his home. Only one window on the second floor glowed with light, and he knew it came from the room where Storm sat, unaware that all her devious schemes had been ruined.

Purposefully, he strode across the muddy lawn and into the house. He had settled one problem that night and would solve the other when he confronted her with her deceit. Stamping the mud from his boots, he wiped the rain from his face and tossed his wet cape onto a satin upholstered chair without considering the damage he wrought.

His intentions were firmly rooted as he stamped determinedly up the stairs and along the hall to Storm's chamber. He paused on the threshold, then pushed the door open and with one swift glance took in his surroundings before his eyes came to rest upon her. She sat with her feet tucked beneath her and was clad in a demure white silk night rail, stitching the lace edge to the neckline of a tiny garment. Thor's face hardened, and the muscles across his chest constricted at the sight. Acrid bile rose in his throat when he realized it was a christening gown.

Like the night, his brow clouded with thunder and his eyes flashed with lightning as he closed the short space between them. He towered over the wide-eyed Storm, and his voice was low with menace as he said, ''I see you are already preparing for the birth of your bastard.''

Before she could make a move to stop him, he reached down and took the small gown from her hand. A cruel semblance of a smile played over his lips as he eyed the tiny garment. ''But I'm afraid the babe won't be able to wear this. They do not christen bastards in the Church. And since I've put a stop to your plans to leave with Matthew, that ends any chance the brat had of being born in wedlock.''

A chill raced up Storm's spine, and a cold hand of fear gripped her heart as she watched him. It was not the hard expression on his face that frightened her, but the burning, satanical light that glowed in the depths of his eyes. It reminded her of a man who had lived in their tenement in London. His eyes had possessed the same mad light when he'd been arrested for murdering his wife in a fit of jealousy.

Fighting to quell her trepidation, she came to her feet and jerked the gown from Thor's hand as she said, ''I have no idea what you're talking about. I have no intention of marrying Matthew, and what I do for my child is none of your concern.''

Thor lazily arched one dark brow. ''Storm, your memory seems to desert you at the most opportune moments. You failed to remember your pregnancy when I first asked, and now you seem to have forgotten your plan to marry Matthew Boone once the two of you were free of Misty Rose.''

Hoping to hide her apprehension, she turned away from him and tucked the little gown back into the woven basket that held her sewing articles. She fought to keep her voice calm as she said, ''Thor, you're mad. I have no plan to marry Matthew now or ever.''

Tiring of the cat-and-mouse game, Thor crossed to her, his wide hands clamping down on her shoulders like a steel vise as he turned her to face him. ''I'm glad to hear it, because it would do you little good after tonight.''

The heat of his anger shimmered in his eyes, causing Storm's heart to pound against her ribs as she looked up into them. A new fear rose in her as she realized he had discovered her scheme to run away and had put a stop to it. Suddenly she was afraid for Matthew. Her anxiety mounted by the moment, and she gripped the front of Thor's jacket, demanding, "Matthew? What have you done to him?"

Thor's fingers curled about her wrists as he pulled her hands roughly from him. "I took the measure I should have taken several months ago when I suspected there was something between the two of you."

Storm's face grew ashen with worry, and her eyes brimmed with tears as she repeated, "My God, Thor, what have you done to Matthew?"

Thor's steely gaze never wavered from her pale face as he said, "I've only ensured that what belongs to me stays mine. No man, friend or foe, trespasses on my property without suffering the consequences, Storm. By morning, Matthew Boone will be only a bad memory at Misty Rose."

Knowing herself to be responsible for Matthew's troubles, Storm said, "Thor, he is your friend."

A caustic smile came to Thor's mouth. "A friend no more, my dear. You ensured that when you bedded him behind my back and conceived his brat."

Dumbfounded, Storm stared up at him as if he had suddenly grown two heads. "Thor, you are mad. Matthew has done nothing against you. If you must blame someone, then let it be me. I was the one who begged Matthew to take me away from Misty Rose. He is guilty of nothing else."

A cold, cynical light glimmered in Thor's eyes, and his words were laced with sarcasm. "Do you honestly expect me to believe you, Storm? I swallowed your lies once, but I will not be so foolish again. I didn't have any proof to base my suspicions on before, but I do now. I'll not fall prey to any more of your lies. You can plead and beg for Matthew and protest his innocence all night long, but it will do no good. At daybreak he will leave Misty Rose, and he will not return to help you escape your indenture. You will serve out your full sentence, and then you and your bastard will be free to find him, if he will still have you after all that time."

Before Storm could avoid him, his hand snaked out and captured the back of her neck, drawing her near. She could feel his hot breath on her skin and saw the smoldering light in his eyes as he said, "But he may not want you after I've enjoyed the pleasure of your body for so long."

Her hands came up flat against his chest, and she tried to shake her head, but his hand held it captive. "No, Thor, never again. I've told you I'll take no more of your abuse."

He brushed his lips seductively against her brow, murmuring, "Abuse, Tempest? You have railed abuse after each time you withered beneath me in passion. Does not your game begin to grow tiresome? At least while you carry Matthew's babe, I do not have to fear you will conceive mine."

Storm stiffened as a tiny ripple of anger surfaced and began to magnify into a tidal wave of fury. Thor's insult washed away every emotion within her except the need to lash out at him. With a cry of sheer, undiluted rage, she struck out at him with both fists. "You bastard! You spawn of the devil! I hate you, Thor Wakefield."

Her anger gave her strength and she managed to free herself from him at last. Without thinking, she grabbed the first object that came to hand, a hairbrush. She threw it at him and then proceeded to hurl everything within reach. After a crystal perfume bottle crashed against the wall behind him, leaving nothing more on the dressing table, she searched for more objects to sail at his arrogant head. With each missile, a curse followed, each one more damning than its precursor. Seeing the dainty French porcelain clock on the mantel, she made for it, her intention clearly visible on her flushed features.

In that moment of slack in the barrage, Thor managed to collect his wits enough to dive after her. Her hand had already closed about the timepiece as he spun her about. Along with her came the clock, and it crashed against his skull with a bone-shattering impact. His eyes widened momentarily in shock before his knees buckled and he crumpled to the floor at her feet, a trickle of blood making a scarlet ribbon along his temple.

Aghast at her own actions, Storm let the clock fall from her nerveless fingers. Her own knees gave way, and she sank to the floor at Thor's side. Her hand trembled violently as she tentatively touched the bright streak of blood. A cry of terror escaped her as she covered her face with her hands and wept. She had killed the man she loved.

She keened her misery, rocking back and forth. She had murdered the father of her child. The fates again had guided her down the rock-strewn path her mother had followed, but where Alisa had been innocent, Storm was guilty.

Giving way to her grief, she collapsed over his body, her wet cheek pressed against his chest, her tears dampening the white lawn of his shirt. She was too consumed with anguish to note the slow rise and fall of his chest. Until he gave a moan, she did not realize he was not dead.

Relief swept over her, and she scrambled to her knees at his side, raising his head to her lap as she whispered, "Oh, Thor, thank God."

Tenderly, she brushed the damp tendrils of raven hair from his brow and dabbed at the blood with his handkerchief as tears of happiness flowed unheeded down her cheeks. A wobbly little smile touched her lips as his lashes fluttered open.

Thor squinted up at Storm and blinked several times as pain slashed across his skull. He tried unsuccessfully to suppress another groan as he lifted a hand to his head. As the pain gradually faded, he managed to push himself upright, waiting for his vision to clear. Drawing in several deep breaths, he turned his head to look at Storm. His voice was a coarse whisper as he said, "You nearly killed me."

Storm's insides quivered nervously. She knew well Thor's feelings about anyone who dared raise a hand against him. He had warned her before, and now she expected him to mete out the punishment he thought such an action merited. She feared his reaction, but she would not cringe away in a cowardly manner. Her own guilt at having come so close to murdering him made her feel as if she deserved his anger. New tears brimmed in her eyes as she said, "I thought I did."

Thor braced his arms over his knees and propped his forehead against them. He stared down at the floor, confused by the grief and regret he read in Storm's eyes. After several long minutes, he looked at her again, searching her face for an emotion he desperately wanted to see there. "Why did you stay if you thought I was dead? You could have had your freedom before anyone found me, Storm."

She crumpled the bloodstained handkerchief in her hand as she bit her lower lip and shook her head. She could not look at him as she said, "I would not want it at that cost."

Thor sensed all he had to do to have his desire was to take her into his arms, but he could not. There was too much left unsaid between them, and he knew it would never be spoken, because it was now too late. Had it been earlier in the day or even the day before, he would have eagerly grasped the chance to have her, but things could not now be changed. Storm carried Matthew's child, and he could never forgive her for that betrayal.

The thought stung as much as the cut on his temple. Frowning, Thor got to his feet and looked down at her, his hand going experimentally to his tender head to test the extent of the damage. "Storm, Matthew has been ordered from Misty Rose, and from this day forward I forbid you to have any contact with him. Heed my orders; I will not tolerate the slightest infraction. Unless you want to see Matthew Boone in his grave, I suggest you keep your distance from him. If he returns to try to help you escape your indenture, it is my right to defend my property, and I will do so.'' Wincing at a new flash of pain, he said, ''Now I'll bid you good night. My head deems it imperative that I seek my bed.'' With that he strode from the room without a backward glance.

Amid's the clock's porcelain fragments, Storm sat staring at the closed door. She longed to rush after Thor but knew it would do no good. He believed the child she carried was Matthew's, and no matter what she said or did, he had and always would believe the worst of her.

Strangely, the thought did not provoke her temper. She felt totally drained by his cold attitude toward her. She had expected his rage at the blow she had inflicted upon him but had received nothing but his curt orders. Thor was a passionate man in all areas of his life, and to Storm his distant attitude only proclaimed the truth of what she had known all along; he cared nothing for her.

For a brief moment when he had regarded her so intensely, she had sensed that all could be resolved between them, but the moment had passed, creeping stealthfully by, taking with it her opportunity to tell him of her feelings.

That knowledge left a barren ache within her breast. The weight of despair rode heavily upon her shoulders as she resigned herself to living the next seven years in Thor's household and keeping her love for him a secret buried deep within her heart.

Slowly she rose to her feet and crossed to the dark window. The rain still beat furiously against the panes as she leaned her forehead against their cool surface and stared out into the dark turbulent night. She also had another burden to bear, Matthew Boone. Were it not for her, he would not have to leave Misty Rose. Tears of remorse clogged her throat as she bit her lip and thought, Good-bye, Matthew. I never meant to cause you such trouble. I only wanted to protect my child.

A streak of lightning illuminated the night sky, and her head snapped up, her eyes going round with astonishment as she suddenly realized that her child was at last safe. Thor had solved the dilemma facing her by misconstruing the identity of the babe's sire. A wobbly smile touched her lips as she shook her head and thought, That is another secret I will keep.

In seven years she would leave Misty Rose, but she would have a small part of Thor to take with her, his child. Life would not be easy for her, but she had learned it seldom was. She had survived the trials of the past and knew she would do so in the future as well.

The knowledge that she would not lose her child when it was born lifted her spirits and made her feel like herself again instead of the hollow shell she had been a few minutes earlier. She smiled at her reflection in the dark panes of glass and raised her chin in the air. The storm still raged without, but Storm Kingsley had found a small degree of peace within.

Chapter 15

Storm sat pensively staring out through the droplet-splattered window. For two weeks rain had battered the land. The sandy loam could not hold any more water, and the excess now flooded the fields, ruining them as it swept away the topsoil and returned much of the hard-won land back to the marshes from which it had been claimed. The Ashley swelled dangerously high, its waters muddy with the precious commodity that had made the plantations along its banks rich.

Worried and longing to see Thor come in from the fields, Storm scanned the gray landscape before her. Since Matthew's departure, Thor had spent long hours each day fighting the elements to save Misty Rose from the disaster that threatened. Though he had avoided her company since the night he had ordered Matthew off his plantation, she had seen him from her office window as he trudged across what had once been manicured lawns but were now only mire. His face had held the haggard look of one placed under great stress and she knew it stemmed from the strain of having to battle nature's forces without Matthew's help.

With his friend gone, Thor had to oversee his men all through the eighteen-to-twenty-hour days as they worked to fill bags with sand to make dykes against the encroaching waters. His shoulders drooped with fatigue, reflecting the exhaustion he suffered. When he finally managed to grab a few hours of sleep, he usually found it in the chair by the fire in his study.

He was unaware that it had been she who covered him with a blanket during his short naps. Nor did he know how her heart went out to him as he battled to save his treasured Misty Rose. She understood the desperation he felt, because she too had come to love his home.

In the moments when he dozed by the fire, she had often stood quietly in the shadows, watching the firelight as it played over his handsome face, her heart crying out with the need to go to him and soothe away the lines of worry that were present even as he slept. She wanted to cradle his tired head to her breast and murmur her love to him, but she never gave way to such feelings. He would not appreciate them, and his rejection would mean only more pain for her.

Not wanting to cause more trouble than she had already done by involving Matthew in her schemes to leave Misty Rose, she kept her worry to herself.

Now she scanned the gray foreboding sky. Seeing no break in the weather, she knew it would mean only more work for Thor. Guilt settled about her like a soggy cape. Had it not been for her, he would have Matthew at his side. If anything happened to him or Misty Rose, she knew it would be her fault for driving the wedge between the two friends. If there were any way she could change things, she would do so. Knitting her brow, she pondered what she could do to help but could find no solution.

She knew it was best for her own peace of mind to try to quell her love for Thor. She should forget about his problems and think only of her own, but that was far easier said than done. Too much lay between herself and him. The child she carried beneath her heart was proof of that. Storm knew she could no more turn her back on him than she could cut out her own heart.

Lowering her eyes to her tightly clasped hands, she whispered to the still room, "Mama, is this the way you felt about Father? Did you ever try to rid yourself of the love you had for him? Did you know all along that he would never return to you but feel you could not give up your belief in him because of your love?"

A melancholy little sigh escaped her as she placed one hand on her rounded belly. Time was passing swiftly, and each day her babe grew stronger. Fate had already begun to manipulate the life of her child as it had done her own. Like Lyle, Thor would never know he had a child, and Storm would again assume Alisa's role by keeping the painful past a secret in order to protect her offspring. Reflecting on the similarity of their lives, Storm felt as if some evil hand had taken Alisa's destiny within its brutal palm and would mold all those who carried her blood into the same wretched form.

Turning her back on the dismal view, Storm swept her gaze over the elegant appointments of the drawing room. Thor had built a magnificent heritage for his child, and she could not stop herself from wondering if by keeping her secret she was doing the right thing. Was it selfish of her to deny her child all Thor could give him? If Thor came to believe that he was the father, then her babe would be the heir to Misty Rose and all the wealth it represented.

Storm did not like to think of the advantages Thor could give her child that she could not. By considering such an idea, she knew she would be sealing her own fate and did not think she could survive the outcome. Her expression clearly showed the turmoil in her mind as she pondered her child's future.

Life would not be easy for them after her indenture was

up, but no matter what Thor could give her babe, she could not give him up. Her child was a part of her; her body nurtured him and was giving him life. It would be easier to forfeit her own life than to relinquish her babe.

A loud peal of thunder rumbled across the land, startling her out of her gloomy thoughts. She looked back out of the window, a tingle of apprehension creeping up her spine as she peered through the rain-drenched panes of glass. The cascading rivulets hindered her vision, but she managed to make out a lone rider approaching the manor. She recognized Thor immediately. Even with his shoulders hunched and his head lowered against the driving force of the rain, she knew his beloved figure well. Her eyes were glued to his soaked form as he rode up the drive and passed before the house to take his horse to the stable. Watching him, Storm tried to reassure herself that all was well. He was home safe, and her worry had been for nothing; however, she could not rid herself of the uneasy feeling that something was amiss.

By the time she heard his heavy steps on the veranda, her nerves were stretched taut. She strained to listen as he entered the foyer and spoke with Mamie. It took all her willpower to suppress the urge to go to him as she heard the weary note of exhaustion in his voice.

Mamie's high squeal of fright brought Storm to her feet, and she was already hurrying toward the foyer as the cook said, "Lawd, he done died from weariness. Master Thor done worked hisself to death. Lawd, do help us."

Storm knew she would never forget the sight of finding Thor sprawled upon the polished pine floor, his face a deathly white, his dark lashes ghostly shadows upon his ashen cheeks. She barely remembered giving orders for Mamie to get help a moment after she had done so. All her thoughts centered on the man she loved as she sank to her knees at his side. She could not stay the trembling that beset her hand as she laid it against his chest, nor was she aware of the moisture that brimmed in her eyes as she found his heartbeat. He was not dead.

Relief mingled with anxiety within her as Mamie came hurrying back into the foyer, huffing and puffing and followed by two large men. The cook was drenched to the skin, and her black gown was molded to her obese frame. In her rush to get help, she had taken no time to don a cape against the inclement weather, nor did she pay any heed to her condition as she ordered the men to lift Thor and carry him to his chamber.

Storm waited anxiously near the foot of the bed as she watched Mamie undress Thor and examine him. The cook's dark fingers contrasted starkly with his pale features as she held them to his brow to see if he had come down with a fever.

Finding him cool, Mamie clicked her tongue and looked at Storm. "Master Thor done took some years off my life today, but it seems he ain't fevered. I feared he had come down with an inflammation in his chest after being out in all this bad weather. That would have been serious."

Looking back at her patient, she shook her turbaned head. "I can't find nothin' wrong with him. I suspect he's just worked hisself into the ground. I tried to warn him, but he'd not listen. That there boy would kill hisself if he thought it would help save 'dis land of his. I told him 'tain't goin' to do him no good if he's dead."

Concern for Thor was etched across her heavy features as she pulled a patchwork quilt over him. "I jest don't know what been goin' on around here. I can't understand what ruffled Matthew's feathers so much that he took off the way he did. Right now Master Thor needs him more than he ever did." Mamie straightened up and wiped her hands on her apron. "I's goin' to let you sit with him for now, Missy," she said. "I'm goin' to fix some hot chicken broth to give him strength and take away the chill from all that rain. He looks like a drowned rat." With that the cook left Storm to ponder what she had said.

"What have I done to you?" she whispered as she settled herself in the chair at his bedside, her eyes never wavering from his ashen face.

Mamie paused in the doorway a few moments later, her dark eyes quickly taking note of the dejected droop of Storm's shoulders and the desolate expression on her face as she kept her vigil at Thor's side. Mamie knew how Thor and Storm felt about each other, but until they admitted it themselves, there was little that could be done for them. It was a sad state of affairs, but Mamie was helpless to change it. All she could do was to stay in the background and give her love and support when they needed it. Her double chin quivered, and she gave a slight rueful shake of her head as she entered the room with her tray. "We need to light the lamp," she said as she set the silver tray on the table at Thor's bedside. "A person can't see to think in here."

Striking the flint to the tender, Mamie lifted the glass globe and touched the flame to the wick. Instantly the room was filled with light. Turning her shrewd gaze upon Storm, she said, "From the look on your face, Missy, I'd say you need this jest as bad as Master Thor." Taking the silver teapot, she poured a steaming cup of the golden liquid and handed it to Storm. "For that matter, I'd say you need it worse than he does. You're nearly as white as the sheet he's laying on, and that ain't good for you nor that young'un you're carryin'."

Mamie then turned her attention to ladling out a bowl of the rich broth laced with finely minced bits of chicken before she said, "I think the best thing for him is a good night's rest. You eat this and let him sleep. He'll be as keen as a razorback hog by the time he wakes up. Take my word on it. Have some soup and then go get some rest."

"Mamie, I appreciate your concern, but I'm staying

with Thor. You have too many other duties to attend, and as his housekeeper it's my responsibility," Storm said and watched as Mamie eyed her dubiously. Holding up her hand to stay the cook's arguments, she promised, "I will eat and won't overtire myself, but I'm staying here no matter what you say."

Seeing the look of determination on her face, Mamie squelched the protest that rose to her lips and nodded her assent. Storm loved Master Thor, though few would think it if they ever heard the two of 'em tearing into each other. But that was neither here nor there. She would not budge from his side, and Mamie knew it was useless even to try to persuade her to do otherwise.

"All right, Missy, but you sees to it you don't get exhausted, or I'm goin' to take a keen hickory stick to your behind. Jest you remember that," Mamie said as she dusted her hands together.

"I'll remember, Mamie," Storm said, and could not stop herself from smiling at the way the cook expressed her affection for those she loved.

Glancing down at Thor, Mamie was pleased to see that his cheeks had regained some of their color. Giving Storm a reassuring nod, she said, "Yes, Master Thor's goin' to be jest fine." She waddled toward the door, then paused momentarily, glancing over her shoulder at the girl. "Now, you remember what I said. I ain't goin' to let anything happen to you or Master Thor's babe," she warned before closing the door behind her.

Storm looked down at the bowl of broth. She felt little like eating but forced herself to do as Mamie had ordered. She knew she would need her strength when Thor woke up. She also knew that if the cook came back and found the food untouched, she would receive a scolding that would make her ears burn.

Her meal finished, Storm leaned back in the chair, her gaze resting once more upon Thor's still features. The rain continued its relentless tattoo upon the dark window as she reflected once more upon the past strange, turbulent months.

Opening the dark passage in her mind where she had stored away the memories of her moments with Thor, Storm realized that no matter how hard she had fought it, she had found happiness at Misty Rose. Finally accepting that fact, she found that the events of the day had taught her a valuable lesson, one she would not soon forget. Thor's collapse had proven to her that it was best to let her heart rule her mind. A person could not wait until everything was perfect, because in an instant it might be too late. Time halted for no one, and once the moment was past, you could not retrace your steps, but had to look toward the future. Storm decided in that moment to tell Thor of her feelings when he awoke. If he rejected her, she knew she would have to accept it, but she would not let the moment pass as she had done the night he had come to tell her of Matthew's leaving.

Leaning forward, she took Thor's hand in her own and raised it to her cheek, whispering, "I love you. I have tried to keep alive the bitterness that has dwelled within me over the years, but I no longer can. You've shown me that you have a kind heart. You try to keep it hidden, but I have seen it even when your temper is kindled by me. We've said harsh words to each other in the heat of anger or jealousy, but you've taught me that men can be gentle, and by doing so have helped me rid myself of hatred. Even if you don't return my love, I owe you more than I can repay for making me realize that I can love."

Still holding his hand, she laid her cheek on the side of the bed and squeezed her eyes tightly closed as tears seeped from beneath her dark lashes to wash a damp path to the white sheet. "Thor, I pray for my sake as well as yours that the land you love will not be ruined because of me. I only wish I could help in some way. I would do so eagerly in an effort to make retribution for all the trouble I have caused you.''

The tension and worry took its toll on her as she lay clutching his hand, and she slowly drifted off to sleep.

A knock on the door brought Storm awake with a start, and she jerked upright. The muscles in her neck and back screamed in agony from the uncomfortable position in which she had slept. Worried that the sound had also awakened Thor, she was relieved to find that he still slept soundly.

Wiping the sleep from her eyes, she pushed herself to her feet. Stifling a wide yawn, she hurried to the door to find Mamie there, the cook's black face etched with deep lines of worry as she glanced past Storm to Thor and said, "Missy, I got to wake Master Thor. He's needed back in the fields. The men are hard workers, but they don't know anythin' about them new floodgates. Only Master Thor and Matthew know how to work 'em.''

Storm cast a quick glance at Thor before she stepped into the hall and closed the door firmly behind her. ''Mamie, you know Thor's condition. He's completely exhausted, and I fear if we wake him now he will have a total collapse. Can't the men see to things until he has at least a few hours' more rest?''

"That I don't know, Missy," Mamie said as she fidgeted with her apron worriedly. "If Master Matthew was here or we could get some help from one of the other plantations, it would be different. But everyone is jest like us except them at AshGlen. Every man and boy is workin' to fill sandbags. We can't even spare a man to go and try to get help.''

Before Mamie had finished speaking, Storm had already made her decision and had started for her chamber. Her hand was already on the latch to her door before Mamie's rotund figure caught up with her.

"What you goin' to do? I don't like the look in your eyes, not one bit. Now, you tell Mamie. What scheme is brewin' in that head of yours?" the cook demanded.

"I'm going to get help," Storm said as she opened the door and strode into her room. "Thor is in no condition to save Misty Rose, and I'll not stand by and let him lose everything he's worked so hard to gain." Crossing to the armoire, she pulled out a heavy cape and tossed it about her shoulders.

When she turned back to the door, she found her path blocked by Mamie, who stood in the doorway with her hands braced on her wide hips. The cook cocked her head to one side, her double chin set at a stubborn angle as she said, "Oh, no you don't. I ain't lettin' you take off in this weather and chance havin' an accident. You ain't goin' to be that foolish."

Storm's chin jutted out at a pugnacious angle as she faced Mamie. "I'm going, and there's nothing you can do to stop me. I'm the reason for Thor's trouble. Had it not been for me, Matthew would still be here to help him. Mamie, can't you see it's something that I have to do? I love Thor, but I'm not fighting for him alone; it's for his child. The heritage Thor worked to build is being destroyed, and I'll not stand by like some helpless female and do nothing to try to prevent it."

"It ain't right," Mamie said as her face screwed up with uncertainty. After a moment she gave a resigned sigh and stepped out of Storm's path. "But I understand why you have to do it. I jest know Master Thor done goin' to have my hide for sure this time. I only wish Matthew was here so none of this would be happenin'."

Storm had already started past Mamie when she came to an abrupt halt and looked sharply at the cook. "Do you know where Matthew is?"

Mamie worried her lower lip thoughtfully for a few

moments before her ebony eyes lit. "He's got a sister who works over at Hollings' Pride several miles down the road from AshGlen. He might be there, but if he ain't, she might know where he is."

The name Hollings tugged at some distant memory in Storm's mind, but she had no time to reflect upon it. Giving Mamie a swift hug of gratitude, she said, "Thank you. I'll go to AshGlen first and see if they'll send help to Misty Rose. Then I'll ride on and try to locate Matthew. If there's a way, I'll bring him back. We need his help, and I can't let this quarrel go on between Thor and Matthew any longer. Since I caused the rift between them, I'm bound and determined to mend it. Their friendship meant too much to both of them."

The cape swirled out about Storm as she hurried down the stairs and crossed the foyer to the front door. Mamie tried to keep up with her but had reached only the foot of the stairs when the girl paused to raise the hood of the cape. The cook's ample breast rose and fell rapidly as she gasped for breath and said, "Missy, what'll I tell Master Thor if he should awake before you get back? He's goin' to be powerful mad when he learns what you're up to."

"Tell Thor I've gone after Matthew, and I'll be back as soon as I can," Storm said as she opened the door and stepped out into the rain-drenched dawn.

Mamie didn't like it, but she would keep her word not to awake Thor unless it became absolutely urgent for him to return to the fields. She doubted her own judgment in the matter as she closed the door and stood for a moment in the foyer, her gaze going up to the door of Thor's chamber. Mumbling to herself, she said, "Master Thor done goin' to skin me alive when he learns what I let Missy go and do, but there was no stoppin' her. I should go up there right now and wake him so he can go after her, but I done promised. Lawd, this is a mess if I ever did see one.''

Grumbling to herself under her breath, she waddled in the direction of the kitchen, hoping that by the time she had a hot breakfast ready Thor would have awakened, and she would be spared having to break her vow to Storm. Glancing upstairs once more she said, ''Hurry and wake up, Master Thor.''

The wind rose and moaned its torment through the tall live oaks. The force of it swayed and bent the trees and sent the gray-green spanish moss sailing like ghostly specters through the rainy morning air. It buffeted the carriage relentlessly, blowing the sharp needlelike drops of water into Storm's face as she tried to control the mare. The flying leaves and moss frightened the animal, causing its eyes to roll wildly as it strained at the reins.

The few miles between the two plantations seemed nearly endless, and Storm breathed a sigh of relief when the arched entrance to AshGlen finally came into view. The tarpaulin had done little to protect her from the elements, and she was drenched right through her heavy cape to the skin as she managed to maneuver the chaise out of the mire that had once been the hard-packed roadway.

A strong gust of wind snapped several large limbs directly behind her as she drove through the entrance, the sound reverberating like the report of a pistol and startling the mare into a frantic gallop. Storm strained on the reins with all her strength as she tried to bring the animal once more under control. She could feel blisters rise on her hands beneath her gloves as she fought with the frightened mare. Even under normal conditions it would be dangerous for the horse to bolt, but with the drive rutted out by the constant deluge of water, she knew it would surely mean her death if the chaise overturned under such abuse.

Though she was chilled to the bone, sweat broke out across her brow as she pulled on the reins, bracing her boots against the footboard to give herself leverage. Just when she thought she could endure no more, the mare slowed to a trot, flinging her head nervously back and forth.

The breath Storm had been holding escaped her in an audible sigh as she sank back against the seat and maintained a tight hold upon the reins, guiding the chaise the last short distance to the Georgian manor. Her hands trembled violently as she drew the mare to a halt and tied the reins to the brake. She had to take several long breaths to try to steady her quaking limbs before she could step down. As her feet touched the flagstones, she felt her knees threaten to give way, but she jutted out her chin and forced her legs to move.

In the past she had been unable to help those she loved because of other people or circumstances that had stood in her way. However, now she was resolved she would not let her own physical weakness deter her. If necessary she would crawl on her hands and knees to see that Thor would receive the help he so desperately needed to save Misty Rose.

Storm rapped sharply on the brass knocker and waited for Zachery to answer the door. As it swung wide, the look of surprise on her face was mirrored on Miranda's.

"What on earth are you doing here?" the woman asked as her pale eyes took in Storm's soaked form, but she did not step back to invite her in out of the weather.

"Miranda, I hope you don't mind if I come in," Storm said as she walked right past her into the foyer.

"Since you take it upon yourself to do so without invitation, I suppose not," Miranda said as she moved away from Storm distastefully.

"I need to see Lyle," Storm said as she slipped the soggy hood from her head and glanced toward the stairs.

A gust of wind sprayed Miranda with mist, and she quickly closed the door. "I'm sorry, Storm. You can't see him today," Miranda said as she collected her wits and hurried to stop her from ascending the stairs. "He hasn't felt well the last few days, and I've had to give him a sleeping draught to help him rest. I'm afraid you ventured out in such bad weather for nothing."

Already annoyed by Miranda's rudeness, the idea of having to ask her for help galled Storm, but she swallowed her jealousy and pride. "Miranda, I didn't come here for a social visit. If it wasn't imperative, I would not be here, but Thor needs help. He has collapsed from exhaustion, and there is no one to oversee the workers since Matthew left."

"I'm sorry, Storm. I didn't understand," Miranda said as a cunning light began to glow in the depths of her eyes. "Please forgive my rudeness. Come into the drawing room by the fire. You look chilled to the bone."

"I can't; I don't have time.. If you can spare some of your workers to send to Misty Rose, I'll go on to Hollings' Pride to see if Matthew is there. Thor needs him, and I've got to try to make Matthew see it."

Taking a firm hold of Storm's arm, Miranda said, "I'm not going to let you say no. Thor and Lyle would never forgive me if I let you go back out in such terrible weather. My brother, Geoffry, has been staying here for a few days, and I'll have him send over some of our men. He can then ride on to Hollings' Pride and bring Matthew back here for you. In your condition, you don't need to be traveling on such bad roads. You could easily have an accident, and I could never forgive myself if you did."

Taken in by Miranda's feigned sincerity, Storm let her

convince her to stay at AshGlen. She was somewhat bewildered by the abrupt change in Miranda's personality, but at the moment she was too exhausted from her battle with the mare and nature to be suspicious.

As she slipped the wet cape from her shoulders and settled herself near the fire, Storm felt only gratitude toward Lyle's wife. Thor would have the help he needed, and if Miranda's brother could find Matthew, then all would be well.

Miranda smiled to herself at how easy it had been to manipulate Storm. Now all that was left was to see that Lyle and Zachary both had a cup of tea laced liberally with the white powder to make them sleep while she and her brother saw to Storm. "I'll go find Geoffry. You rest, and I'll order tea. You look as if you could use a hot drink to warm you right now."

"Thank you, Miranda. That does sound nice," Storm said as she rubbed her chilled arms to bring back the circulation. The words rose to the tip of her tongue to apologize for her own rudeness of moments before, but before she could say them her hostess had already swept out of the room.

Miranda's red mouth curved into a satisfied smile as she closed the door behind her and sped up the stairs to Geoffry's room. Her eyes glittered with malice as she banged on the door and heard his mumbled reply. Finding her brother still abed annoyed her. "Blast you, Geoffry, get out of bed. Everything we have schemed for has fallen into our laps without our having to so much as lift a finger."

Geoffry yawned widely as he sat up and threw back the covers. Scratching the golden mat of hair on his chest, he squinted at her. "It's too damn early for riddles, dear Sister. Will you please tell me in a few simple words what on earth you are babbling about?"

Folding her arms over her chest, her foot tapping a rapid tattoo of irritation on the carpeted floor, Miranda said, "Sometimes I believe you don't have a brain in that handsome head of yours. I'm talking about Storm Kingsley, damn you. She's downstairs now, waiting for you to send men to Misty Rose to help Thor, and then you are to ride to Hollings' Pride to bring Matthew back."

Perplexed, Geoffry knit his blond brows as he eyed his sister as if she had gone mad. "Perhaps I am slightly addle-pated this morning, because for the life of me I don't understand a word you've said."

Exasperated, Miranda rolled her eyes heavenward as if seeking divine help. "Geoffry, don't you see that now is our chance to be rid of her? Are you so truly dimwitted that you can't see that we could not have asked for better timing? Thor has collapsed, and once he is well enough to search for her, we will say she never came here. That way he will think she only used the excuse to get help for Misty Rose as a way to run away with Matthew while he was unable to stop her."

"I see your point," Geoffry said as his face lit with understanding.

"It's about time," Miranda told him, bracing her hands on her hips and eyeing her brother's naked form. "Now, get dressed. We've much to do to ensure nothing goes wrong. I'm going to order all of the servants to the quarters and see that Lyle and Zachery know nothing of what is transpiring. I'm also fixing Storm a cup of the same tea my dear husband and our butler will be served. That should warm her well enough and keep her from causing us any undue problems."

Leaving Geoffry with her orders still ringing in the air, Miranda strode to her own chamber, where she unlocked the small cabinet by her bed. Withdrawing a small glass vial of white powder, she held it up and smiled. This would ensure all went well. Pocketing the vial, she patted it lovingly as she turned and made her way back downstairs to prepare the tea.

Chapter 16

A drumming sound drew Thor back from the depths of his exhausted slumber. As it roused him to consciousness, he opened his eyes and stared up at the ceiling in confusion, the cobwebs of sleep clinging tenaciously to his mind. When the sound came again, even more urgently, he managed to collect his thoughts enough to realize that he lay abed while Misty Rose was in jeopardy. The knock came again at the door.

"Damn it to hell," he cursed under his breath as he pushed himself upright and flexed his muscles in an effort to relieve some of their soreness. Running a hand over his face, wiping the sleep from his eyes with his thumb and forefinger, he shook his head to clear it and reached for his britches. Jerking them on, he strode to the door and thrust it open, his abrupt action reflecting his annoyance at himself. Seeing the cook paused with her hand upraised to bang again on the door, he grumbled, "Mamie, why in the devil did you let me sleep? I'm needed in the fields." As he spoke, he was already making his way back across the room to where his shirt lay.

"The rain done stopped, and Dom says the river has reached its peak. The only damage the water done was to the eastern section, where the dyke gave way," Mamie said as she tried to put Thor's mind at ease before bringing up the subject she dreaded. Following him into the room, she muttered beneath her breath, "I wanted to do as you asked, Missy, but I got to think of you and your babe now."

Not hearing Mamie's last words, his mind still on Misty Rose, Thor looked at the cook, his face grim, his fingers lacing his shirt. "I feared that would be the first to go. But it won't be much of a loss if that section is the only one to sustain heavy flooding."

Pulling on his boots, his thoughts centered on saving the rest of the rice fields, Thor did not see the look of worry on his cook's face. Without glancing at her, he strode past her and down the stairs. He had already thrown his cape about his shoulders, and was ready to stride through the front door, before Mamie managed to catch up with him.

"Master Thor," Mamie breathed heavily, "all is taken care of in the fields."

Hearing the note of worry in her tone, Thor paused and turned to look at his cook. He knew the woman well enough to know that something had upset her. "Mamie, what's wrong?"

"It's Miss Storm. She done left here at the crack of dawn to get help from AshGlen, but she ain't returned yet. I'm worried about her, Master Thor. She said to tell you she'd gone after Matthew, but she should have been back by now. It's past noon."

"Damn, why did you let her leave?" Thor demanded as his face clouded with anger.

Mamie's dark hands played havoc with her white apron as she crushed it nervously. Her dark eyes were large and glassy as she looked at him. "I tried to stop her, Master Thor, but she would have none of it. She said she wanted to get help for Misty Rose, and I was not to wake you unless you was needed in the fields. She was goin' to AshGlen first and then on over to the Hollings' plantation to see if Master Matthew was there with his sister."

Thor's face hardened as he pressed his lips firmly together, anger swirling through him as all his suspicions burst in upon him. "The bitch didn't wait long to take flight once I could not keep an eye on her, did she? But she won't get away with it. Storm Kingsley will rue the day she tried to take advantage of me."

"Now, Master Thor," Mamie said as she sought to correct him, "you done got it wrong. Missy went to get help. She was afraid you was goin' to lose Misty Rose. You don't understand her, Master Thor. She ain't run off like you wants to believe."

"Mamie, I appreciate your loyalty to Storm, but I think I know her better than you do. She has no reason to want to help me or Misty Rose. She only used that as an excuse to get away while I could not stop her."

Bracing her hands on her wide hips, Mamie eyed Thor, her annoyance sparkling in her eyes. "Master Thor, I never did take you to be no fool until now. You can't seem to see the goodness in that child no better than a mule wearing blinders. You're as stubborn as that dumb beast and won't try to see it when it's as plain as the nose on your face. And why, I'll never know."

"You should ask Storm and Matthew that question, Mamie," Thor answered coldly, his tone indicating that the subject was closed.

Mamie regarded him thoughtfully for a few long seconds before she smiled and said, "You're jealous. That green-eyed monster is eatin' away your insides and makin' you act this away. You even more blind than I thought you was, Master Thor. For a man who acts like he knows all about women, you shore don't. That child went out in the storm to help you. She said it was her fault you and Master

Matthew was squabblin' and she intended to see it set to rights.''

The look Thor gave Mamie held the frost of a winter's morn as he said, ''Mamie, remember your place.''

Unintimidated, she clicked her tongue in disgust. ''I knows my place, but it seems you don't know yours. Storm is carryin' your young'un in her belly, and you treats her worse than you'd treat any of the people on your plantation.''

''Mamie, you don't understand,'' Thor said, no longer able to remain aloof under the cook's censure.

''I may not know every'thin' that's happened, but I do know that girl loves you despite all that's been said and done. She was willin' to risk her own life and that of her babe to try to help you. In her condition she shouldn't even be out in this kind of weather,'' Mamie said, her chins quivering as her irritation at Thor's lack of understanding mounted.

A shadow of worry passed over his features. ''Mamie, I wish to God I could believe what you're saying, but Storm has never given me any indication that she feels anything for me beyond hatred.''

Cocking her head to one side, the cook eyed him critically. ''Have you ever given her a chance? Have you ever told her how you feel?''

Seeing his negative response, Mamie pursed her lips and crossed her arms over her melon-size breasts. ''I thought not. For two people who love each other, you two is the stubbornest, pigheadedest couple I've ever seen in my life. Let me tell you somethin', Master Thor; that pride of yours will make a cold bedfeller through the winter months. If you've got any sense a'tall in that head of yours, you'll get on your horse and go after Missy before somethin' happens to her that you'll regret.''

Thor regarded Mamie thoughtfully for a few long moments as he considered all she had said. Perhaps it was true, but even if it wasn't, Storm could be in danger. She had little knowledge of the area, and in such bad weather it would be easy to have an accident with the rains making the roads into a quagmire of mud.

"I'll go after her, Mamie," Thor said as he wrapped his arms affectionately about the cook's rotund figure and hugged her close.

The day grew cooler, and the moisture-laden air formed into dense banks of fog that hindered Thor's vision as he rode up the winding drive to AshGlen. He could see no more than a few feet ahead of him as he reined in his mount and tied it to the hitching post in front of the Georgian mansion. A tight fist of worry gripped his insides as he scanned the eerie landscape before he strode up the walkway to the door. If Storm were out in this, she could easily become disoriented and lose her way. Even knowing the area as well as he did, at times like this he had to concentrate to recognize familiar landmarks.

At his knock, Geoffry answered the door, welcoming him congenially inside as he said, "Thor, it's good to see you." Extending his hand in greeting, he continued, "But from the look on your face, this is not a social visit."

The two men shook hands. "You're right, Geoffry. I was told my housekeeper had come to AshGlen earlier today to seek help for Misty Rose. Have you seen her?"

The hair at the nape of Geoffry's neck rose as he grew tense with apprehension, but he managed to look suitably perplexed as he said, "Thor, I'm sorry to say that we have not. I'm sure Miranda would have mentioned it to me if your housekeeper had come here in such weather. Is something wrong? I would think most women would be curled up by a blazing fire on a day like this."

Thor nodded ruefully. "Yes, most women would; however, I'm finding that Mistress Kingsley is not like most women I have met in the past. Would you mind asking

Miranda if by chance Storm did come here and she failed to mention it to you?''

''Not at all. She's with Lyle right now. He's been under the weather again, and she went up to see if he was sleeping a few moments before you arrived. I'll go up and tell her you're here,'' Geoffry said as he opened the door to the study for Thor. ''There's brandy and a fire in here to take away the chill.'' Ushering Thor through the door, he quickly closed it after him and sprinted up the stairs to warn Miranda of his presence and his reason for coming to AshGlen.

Geoffry had been right about Thor needing the warmth of the fire. A deathly coldness had settled about his heart when Miranda's brother had told him Storm had not come to AshGlen. Taking off his hat, Thor strode across the chamber to stand before the blazing logs. His shoulders drooped as he ran his hand through his hair and said to the jumping flames, ''You were wrong, Mamie. Storm did not come here for help.''

Hearing the door open, Thor glanced up as Miranda entered the study, a look of concern playing across her lovely features as she came forward and said, ''Thor, is something amiss? Geoffry said you came here looking for Storm.''

''Yes, I was led to believe she had come to AshGlen. You have not seen her today?'' he asked, his muscles tensing with hope that Geoffry had been mistaken.

Miranda's golden curls bounced as she gave a negative shake of her head. ''I'm afraid not, Thor. We haven't had a visit from Storm for several weeks. I assumed the bad weather had hindered her visits to Lyle. The roads are so rutted and muddy that it's dangerous to venture out on them. I can't imagine what possessed Storm to undertake such a thing in her condition.''

''I'm afraid I know the reason behind it: Matthew

Boone,'' Thor said as his blood began to boil once more at Storm's duplicity.

"Surely you can't think she has run away with Matthew Boone?'' Miranda asked innocently. She smiled to herself as she watched Thor's face suffuse with rage.

Thor heard his own teeth clash together as he clenched his jaw and strove to contain the fury seething in a hot volatile current through every vein in his body. He ground out, "That is exactly what I think, but I vow they will wish they had never attempted to cross me before I'm through with them.''

Miranda realized her mistake too late. She had goaded Thor with the hope of making him see what a fool he had been for ever caring for the little witch. She had not meant to make him want to find Storm to punish her. Placing her hand on his arm, Miranda urged, "Let them go, Thor. Don't do this thing. She has caused you nothing but trouble since you brought her to Misty Rose. She has hurt you in the past, and you will only suffer more in the future if you bring her back, only to watch her grow large with Matthew's babe. Forget Storm Kingsley, Thor. I beg of you. Someday you will find a woman who deserves your love where that little tart never did.''

Miranda's face was soft, her eyes pleading as Thor looked down at her. Releasing a long breath, he said, "This is something I have to do, Miranda. Don't ask me why. Perhaps I'm a glutton for punishment, but I will bring Storm back to Misty Rose if it's the last thing I ever do. She thinks she has outwitted me, but she will soon learn differently. What is mine, I keep.''

Miranda let her hand fall to her side as she watched Thor clamp his hat onto his head. She remained silent as he strode purposely to the door and left without a backward glance. She could have tried to argue further, but it might have only made Thor more determined to find Storm, and that she did not want.

At present she and Geoffry would be forced to complete their plans immediately. They had to get rid of Storm before Thor was able to reach Hollings' Pride and find out that she had never been there. Hopefully Matthew Boone would also not be there, so Thor would have to ride into Charleston to search him out before he found that Storm had not run away with the man. By the time he returned and had a chance to search the area, Storm Kingsley would no longer be a problem. She would have suffered a fatal accident.

Miranda's eyes narrowed, and a malicious light gleamed in their depths as she said aloud, "Thor, you will learn that I feel the same as you do in certain matters. What is mine, I keep, and that includes you."

Matthew Boone paused in his backbreaking labor, his calloused hand automatically going to the ache in his weary neck as he looked up at the gray sky. He rubbed at the dull pain absently as he scanned the clouds and was relieved to see a small break in them. That was a good sign. Hopefully most of the bad weather had ended. The rain had ceased that morning, but he had been afraid to hope that the storm had passed altogether.

Looking back at the laborers who trudged through the mud with bags filled with sand to add to the dykes, Matthew felt a strong sense of pride swell in his chest. He had managed to save Jenny's plantation, Hollings' Pride. It had taken every able-bodied man and boy from the field hands to the house servants to accomplish the feat, but they had done it working night and day.

He scanned the wet landscape as he thought of Jennifer Hollings, Thadius Hollings's widow. Until Matthew had come to visit his sister after his argument with Thor, her employer, Jenny, had overseen the plantation herself. When she had learned he no longer worked for Thor, she had eagerly hired him to take over the burden that had been placed on her by her husband's death. It had been fortunate for her that Matthew had accepted the position, because had he not been there when the flooding came, she might well have lost Hollings' Pride to the hungry river. As it turned out, the plantation had suffered only minor damage and would do well in the future if no other disaster occurred.

Matthew had worked long and hard to save Hollings' Pride. He had done his job well, but it was not just because he was the overseer; he had done it for Jenny. Feeling a slight tug on his sleeve, he looked down to see the woman of his thoughts standing in ankle-deep water with a pot of coffee. She gave him a shy smile as she handed him a cup and said, "I thought you might need something hot. I've also ordered the cooks to bring some down for the men. They must be chilled to the bone."

"Aye, we all could use something warm in us," Matthew said as he held the cup in one hand while he grasped her elbow with the other. "But I'll not have you standing here catching your death just to see me warm." He led the young woman out of the field to higher ground.

They paused beneath a huge live oak draped with spanish moss. He smiled fondly down into Jenny's lovely face, his feelings for her reflected in his brown eyes. She was not as striking as Storm Kingsley, but with her pert features and tiny turned-up nose, which was liberally sprinkled with freckles, Matthew thought her beautiful.

Over the past weeks at Hollings' Pride he had grown to know Thadius's widow and had found her to be the direct opposite of the fat, self-serving man who had been her husband. She was a warm, loving, and kindhearted woman who had lived a life of misery with Thadius.

Matthew had also learned that though she was shy, Jennifer Hollings possessed more courage in her tiny body than many a man he had known. It had been hard on her to take on the responsibilities of running the plantation, but she had fought bravely to keep it going. That in itself had drawn him to her, and as the days passed, he had found himself falling in love with her.

As his feelings deepened for Jenny, Matthew did not forget Storm but was wise enough to know that he could never replace Thor in her affections. He knew she would always have a small place in his heart, but that did not stop his love for Jenny from growing. The two women differed like night and day, like a vibrant rose and a dainty violet. Both were lovely and both could give much, but Matthew knew now that he preferred the violet to the exquisite rose. Its delicate blossom did not outshine the other, much brighter flower, but it needed more care and protection; something that Jenny had never received from Thadius and that Matthew longed to give her.

The thick fog surrounded them in a soft white cocoon as he tipped up her chin and gazed down into her wide brown eyes. "Jenny," he murmured, his voice growing husky with emotion, "I know I'm just your overseer, and I'll understand if you feel I'm overstepping my bounds. I had meant to wait until the proper time and place, but I find I cannot. Seeing you with the hem of your gown wet and muddy from trudging through the fields to give me comfort forces me to speak. I love you, Jenny. I know my working for you puts us into an awkward situation, but I'd be honored if you would consider becoming my wife." He gave her a sheepish, slightly fearful grin as he said, "Will you marry me, Jennifer Hollings?"

Jenny's soft eyes brimmed with tears, and a tremulous smile tugged at the corners of her delicate lips as she nodded. Her words did not even stir the air as she breathed softly, "Yes, Matthew, I'll marry you."

Matthew started to wrap his arms about her but found to his dismay that he still held the cup of coffee. Chuckling, his spirits soaring, he set it on the ground and then swung her off her feet as he said, "You've made me the happiest man on earth."

Jenny's girlish laughter filled the air as she threw her arms about his neck and rained kisses down on his brow, cheeks, and mouth. "Matthew, Matthew," she said, "I never dreamed I could feel the way I do. I love you."

Wrapped in their love, they failed to hear the approach of Thor's horse, nor did they know of his presence behind them until he abruptly jerked Jenny out of Matthew's embrace. "I thought I would find you in his arms. Did you think me such a fool as not to guess where you had gone?"

Thor's angry tirade came to an abrupt halt as he swung her about and realized the woman he had thought to be Storm was Jennifer Hollings. His eyes widened in shock as he stared at her, dumbfounded by his mistake.

"What in the hell do you think you're doing?" Matthew growled low and deadly as he took a step forward, but paused as he saw the look of stupefaction on Thor's face.

Thor gaped at Jenny and then at Matthew as he tried to make sense out of the scene. As he had ridden up, the fog had hindered his vision, making him think the dark-haired woman in Matthew's arms was Storm. Blinded by fury, he had not stopped to consider his actions and now found himself facing an outraged Matthew and a frightened Jennifer Hollings. "Jenny, I'm sorry. I thought you were someone else."

Unappeased by his apology, Matthew stepped protectively in front of Jenny, his fists balled at his side, ready to do battle. "You didn't answer my question, Thor. What are you doing here?"

"I came here to get Storm. I know she's here, so there is no use in lying, Matthew," Thor said as he managed to regain some measure of his composure and anger.

"Thor, have you been drinking, or have you just lost your wits? Storm is not here, nor have I seen her since before I left Misty Rose," Matthew said, eyeing his former friend warily.

"I don't believe you. She told Mamie she was coming here to get you to come back to Misty Rose, but that was only an excuse so the two of you could be together. I intend to take her back with me one way or the other, so you'd better not try to stand in my way," Thor said as he regarded Matthew hostilely, his muscles tensing, preparing for the other man's attack.

Jenny stepped between the two of them before Matthew could reply. She looked from one to the other. Like a tiny kitten with its claws bared, she said, "Thor, Matthew is telling you the truth. We have not seen your housekeeper. Had you been listening instead of acting like a bull enraged by a waving red flag, you would have heard Matthew ask me to marry him. Does that sound to you like a man who is hiding another woman? I can assure you I would not stand for it even if you think differently. Matthew and I love each other and have kept no secrets between us."

"Jenny, this is none of your affair. It's between Matthew and me," Thor said as he looked over her head at Matthew.

Jenny was not so easily put off. As Matthew had learned, she had spunk, and she faced Thor squarely with her hands on her hips. "I'm making it my affair. If it concerns the man I love, then it concerns me. I know of your quarrel as well as the way you feel about Storm Kingsley. If you weren't such a jealous nitwit and had the sense that God gave a billygoat, you would be worrying about her now instead of challenging Matthew over something he is innocent of doing, now or in the past."

The small woman's reprimand stung, and Thor had the grace to blush as he said, "That's the reason I'm here, Jenny. Storm is not at Misty Rose. She said she was going to AshGlen for help and then would come here. What am I to believe, since she was not at AshGlen, nor had she been there?"

"We haven't seen her," Matthew said as he stepped

forward and placed his hands on Jenny's shoulders. Looking over her head at Thor, he asked, "Are you sure she didn't go to AshGlen?"

Lines of worry traced a path across Thor's brow as he shook his head. "No. Miranda and Geoffry both said she hadn't been there." His gray eyes were haunted as he looked at Matthew. "If she isn't here, where is she?"

Jenny glanced up at Matthew, her eyes urging him to help his friend as her hand came up to rest on his. Nodding, she gave it a reassuring squeeze.

Understanding her silent message, Matthew gave her a quick kiss before he stepped forward. "Thor, we'll find her."

His solemn cinnamon eyes met the haunted silver ones, and in that moment all the past hostility vanished into the fog-shrouded afternoon. Thor had believed the worst of Matthew but knew as he looked into his friend's eyes that he had been wrong. Matthew had never betrayed him; it had been in his jealousy-ridden imagination where the treachery lay. Suddenly his throat constricted with emotion as he realized that neither had Storm ever deceived him about her relationship with Matthew. Both had denied his accusations, but the years of distrust he held toward all women had made him believe otherwise, and in doing so he now perhaps had lost the woman he loved.

Feeling the hot sting of tears in his eyes, he turned away, unable to say more than "I'll ride in the direction of Misty Rose, and you go toward Charleston. She may have had an accident."

He mounted and was preparing to retrace his path to Misty Rose, searching every inch of the way, when he felt a hand on his leg. Looking down, he saw Jenny Hollings. She gave him a reassuring smile as she said, "You and Matthew will find her, Thor. I'm sure of that."

He nodded as he gathered the reins in his hand, but Jenny did not move. "Don't let her slip away from you again. I learned from harsh experience that love does not come often into your life, and when it does it must be cherished. Tell her how you feel before it is too late.''

Swallowing hard, Thor spoke in a husky voice as he said, ''I pray that I am not already too late.''

Chapter 17

Groggily, Storm opened her eyes to a room completely unfamiliar to her. She stared at it in bewilderment. For several minutes she lay still and tried to collect her thoughts from the hazy maze that her mind had become, but no matter how hard she sought to remember, nothing beyond having tea in the drawing room at AshGlen with Miranda came back to her.

Squinting at the strange room, she pushed herself upright and winced at the dull ache the movement aroused in her head. Sliding her feet gingerly to the floor, she eased from the bed to keep from causing herself further pain by making an abrupt move. She swayed dizzily for a moment and had to brace herself against the side of the bed. When the room stopped spinning, she made her way cautiously across it to the door. Trying the latch, she found it would not give beneath her hand. For a few moments she stared at the locked portal, her brows knitting over the bridge of her slender nose. She tried the latch again, the misty veils that shadowed her drugged mind beginning to fall away, and she realized with a start of fear that she was locked in.

Unable to stave off the tingle of fright that made a chilling path up her spine, she glanced uneasily about the room for some clue to her whereabouts. Spying the velvet-covered window, she sped across the room and drew back the drapes.

Recognizing the leaden landscape of AshGlen, she felt annoyance replace her momentary fright. Turning purposefully back to the door, she banged loudly on it and shouted, "Miranda, unlock this door. Let me out of here!" She paused and listened. Hearing no response, she again pounded on the panel. "Miranda, I demand you unlock this door!"

After a few more moments, Storm heard the click of the latch and stepped back from the door, ready to do battle with Miranda if necessary to gain her freedom. As it swung wide, she froze, her eyes widening in shock and disbelief as she stared at Geoffry Chatham. In that moment it was as if the past months had never existed. Storm was carried back to the last time she had seen him in the courtroom in London. It had been his testimony that had sentenced her mother to death. Her heart began to thump in her breast as wildfire shot through her veins, but the only word to pass her lips was "You!"

Geoffry sauntered into the room and closed the door behind him. Leaning negligently against it, he eyed her, a semblance of a smile on his shapely lips as he asked, "So you remember me?"

Storm fought the urge to fly at the vile creature who smiled so smugly at her. She clenched her hands at her sides as she spat, "I could never forget the man who caused my mother's death with his lies."

Geoffry arched one blond brow at her as he casually rearranged the lace on his cuffs and said, "Ah, yes, that small matter. I can well understand why I stand out in your memory."

Fury exploded in Storm in a shower of blazing fireworks. "Small matter," she spat, her every word laced with venom. "Your lies sentenced my mother to the stake and me to Newgate. I do not call that a small matter."

"I can assure you, mistress, it was all necessary," Geoffry said as he strolled across the chamber to stand before her.

Suddenly sensing the air of menace about him that she had failed to recognize until that moment, Storm saw her own danger. Backing away from him, she said, "Sir, I suggest you leave this room instantly before I call for help."

A sense of power swept over Geoffry as he saw the flicker of fear in her sapphire eyes. He chuckled as he closed the space between them once more; moving his hand so swiftly that she was unable to avoid it, he captured the back of her head and drew her near. He gazed down into her wide eyes, one corner of his mouth curling up sardonically as he spoke. "My dear, you can call for help all you want. There is no one to come to your aid."

Storm strained against him as she braced her hands on his chest, saying, "I'll scream for Madame Ashfort. I doubt she would approve of the way you're treating her guest."

"My dear Mistress Kingsley, you are still innocent of my identity, aren't you?" Geoffry said as the humor of the situation hit him. His laughter filled the room, chilling Storm to the bone.

"What do you mean?" she asked as she gazed at his features, trying to deny the resemblance she saw there.

"Let me introduce myself properly. I am Geoffry Chatham, Miranda's brother."

Storm froze, her mouth going dry with apprehension, every nerve in her body tensing as she sensed that she would soon know the reason behind her mother's death. "Miranda's brother?" Storm whispered as she frantically tried to piece all the intricate parts of the puzzle together.

"Why?" she asked, her voice so soft that Geoffry had to strain to hear her.

Still holding her with one hand, he raised the other and traced the line of her cheek with one finger as he said, "Storm, you amaze me. Surely you know why by now? I would not have considered you so dimwitted."

She moved her head slowly from side to side.

"AshGlen, my dear, AshGlen and all the wealth that goes with it."

She frowned up at him, her brows knitting as she tried to see the connection between her father's plantation in the colonies and her mother's death in England. Moistening her dry lips, she said, "You lied to have AshGlen? I don't understand. My mother never knew anything of my father's plantation. She could not have harmed you in any way."

"Ah, there you are wrong, my dear," Geoffry said as a pleased expression crossed his face. "You see, your mother was Lyle's wife and legal heir while she lived. That made Miranda—ah, how should I put it—nothing more than his glorified mistress.

"You see, we had no other choice," he continued. "As long as your mother was alive, then Miranda stood to lose everything. I do regret that I had to be the one to make you an orphan, and if my first scheme had worked, then you and your mother would still be living happily in England, totally unaware of what you had lost. However, Lyle's accident did not prove fatal, as I had planned, and so I had to change my method of securing AshGlen for my sister."

Seeing comprehension and fear settle across her lovely face, he smiled. "So, my dear Storm, you now understand why your mother's death was necessary. You can also see why I have to finish what I started in England. As Lyle's daughter, you are now the legal heir to AshGlen. It would have been much better if you had died in Newgate. It would have saved me a lot of trouble; however, I intend to rectify that now."

Fear gave Storm strength, and she jerked away from him. Moving slowly back, she said, "No, you can't get away with it. People know where I am and will come looking for me."

"I'm afraid you're mistaken, Storm," Geoffry said as a mad light entered his eyes. "We've already seen to that minor problem. Thor came only a short while ago searching for you, and Miranda convinced him that you had not come here. He has now gone looking for Matthew, and by the time he returns, your body will be floating in the Ashley."

Glancing out at the foggy afternoon, Geoffry chuckled. "You see, you will have a terrible accident. You will have lost your way in the fog and, by doing so, made the wrong turn on the road. No one will ever suspect differently when your chaise is found overturned in the river."

Paling as he described his plans, Storm moved warily away from him, wanting to keep as much distance between them as possible. Her movements were halted as she came into contact with the bed. Seeking desperately for some means to put a stop to his scheme, she said, "If you come near me, I'll scream. Lyle and Zachery will hear me."

A predatory look changed his boyishly handsome face into a mask of a demon from hell as he began to move toward her as if stalking his prey. "Lyle and Zachery will never know you've been to AshGlen. You see, they were both served the same tea that you drank. There's no use fighting me, Storm. It's all been arranged, and there is nothing you can do about it."

Storm's fear threatened to engulf her, but she fought to keep it in check. She would receive no help except from her own resources. Her life lay solely in her own hands, and if she succumbed to the panic sweeping over her, all would be lost. Nevertheless, she could not stop the slight quaver in her voice as she said, "Stay away from me."

Storm's fear brought out Geoffry's craving for power that his sister's dominance had stifled through the years. It surged through him, making him aware of all his senses as well as Storm's vulnerability. Before him was a woman equal in beauty to Miranda but whom he could dominate. A cruel smile came to his lips as his eyes swept over her from head to toe and then came to rest on her full breasts. Feeling himself swell with the need to prove his supremacy over this beautiful female, he said, "It seems you're going to make this more interesting than I had thought."

Seeing the heat of lust sparkle in his eyes, Storm understood his intentions. Before he murdered her, he planned to rape her. "No," she cried. "Lay a hand on me and I'll tear your eyes out."

Before she could avoid it, Geoffry launched himself at her, knocking her back onto the bed. His weight crushed her into the down mattress, and he stifled her startled scream with his mouth as his hands came up to fondle her breasts through her gown.

Storm squirmed and struggled, but her efforts were hindered by his body pressing her into the confines of the soft mattress. She could find no way to free her hands until Geoffry became annoyed that he could not touch her flesh. Leaning back to rip away the offending garment, he gave Storm her chance. Her hands came up, curved into claws, and she raked several red trails down the side of his face.

Never a man who could stand pain, Geoffry recoiled from the tigress beneath him and growled, "Bitch, you'll pay for that," as he clamped a hand to his stinging cheek.

Storm took advantage of the moment and rolled away from him before he had time to collect his wits. Scrambling from the bed, she grabbed a vase from the bedside table and threw it at his head. He managed to avoid the full impact by dodging to the side and only received a minor blow to his temple as the vase sailed past his head.

It crashed loudly to the floor, sending sharp fragments scattering in every direction as Storm sped by the stunned man on the bed. She was already to the door and flinging it open before he recovered enough to follow her. She dashed out into the hallway, but her flight came to a momentary halt when she saw Miranda blocking her path. Hearing Geoffry close behind her, she did not stop to think but shoved the other woman out of her way and sprinted down the stairs, taking them two at a time.

"Catch her, Geoffry," Miranda screeched as she, too, joined in the chase.

The lead Storm had gained by her surprise attack was soon shortened by Geoffry's long strides, and his pursuit came to a halt as he recaptured her at the front door. She squealed in protest and kicked at her captor as he lifted her easily off her feet. She failed to make contact with any vulnerable spot as she struggled against his hold and was held fast, his arms cutting off her breath as he tightened his grip on her.

Miranda paused at the foot of the stairs, eyeing Storm through narrowed eyes. Her voice was laced with venom as she then came forward, patting a stray golden strand of hair back into place. "Storm, you are a fool. Did you honestly think you could come here and take AshGlen and Thor away from me?"

Looking down at the swelling abdomen beneath Geoffry's arms, she placed her hand on Storm's belly and chuckled maliciously. "You thought you could make Thor yours by conceiving his brat, but I ensured that he wouldn't believe he was the father. Now all that's left for me to do is be rid of you and Lyle. Then Thor will be mine as I have planned since I first met him."

Storm shrank back from Miranda's touch as she looked into the woman's crazed eyes. In their depths she saw the light of madness, and a tingling apprehension for her father's safety began to take root in her mind as she asked, "What do you mean?"

"You know exactly what I mean. You've suspected it from the first," Miranda sneered.

"You're mad, Miranda. I have no idea what you're talking about," Storm said, though her memory served her well enough to recall the suspicions that had come to her about Miranda at the onset of Lyle's strange illness.

"You're a convincing liar, Storm, but I know you've suspected the truth from the first," Miranda said as she reached into her pocket and withdrew a thick velvet drapery cord. She tossed it to her brother and watched as he bound Storm's hands behind her back. "Your fate was sealed even before I found out you were Lyle's daughter. I couldn't let you go to Thor and tell him you suspected me of poisoning Lyle. When Geoffry recognized you that day hugging Matthew, it gave me the weapon I needed to erode Thor's faith in you."

Standing back, Miranda smiled smugly at Storm. "Your death will serve two purposes. First Thor will be free, and then poor Lyle will have another attack. But I'm afraid my dear husband will not survive it. His heart won't be able to stand the strain of losing his dear little English wren." Miranda's laughter filled the foyer. "Then Thor, AshGlen, and Misty Rose will all belong to me."

The sound of her evil mirth made Storm tremble. The wicked pair had planned their vile deeds well. No one would suspect them of murder when her body was found, nor would any suspicions be roused when Lyle succumbed to his lingering illness. She alone knew of Miranda and Geoffry's villainy, and that knowledge would die with her. With a growing sense of horror, she realized there was nothing she could do to thwart their diabolical scheme.

"Get her out of my sight," Miranda ordered. "I've seen enough of Storm Kingsley to last me a lifetime and beyond." Tossing Storm's cape to her brother, she hissed, "Put this around her. I want no reminders left here of her existence once this day is done."

"Don't worry, Miranda." Geoffry chuckled as he draped the cape over Storm's shoulders. "After today it will all be over, and you can have the pleasure of comforting Thor in his grief while in turn you let him console you over the death of your husband. I'm sure you'll find no hardship in that."

Miranda's smile mocked Storm as she said, "I doubt that Thor will suffer much grief after losing this little tart. She's been nothing but trouble to him. But I can assure you that I will not object to any comforting he tries to give me." Wanting to hurt Storm even further, she said, "I'm sure the thrusts of his hard, lean body will appease any grief I might suffer."

The vision brought forth by Miranda's taunting made Geoffry's face tighten with jealousy. The thought of Thor's muscular, tanned body covering his sister's pale form infuriated him, and he jerked Storm roughly across the foyer as he mumbled beneath his breath, "I'll see to that problem later."

Without further comment he dragged her toward the rear entrance of the house and paused upon the threshold as he scanned the gardens beyond to make sure that his actions went undetected. Seeing no one in view, he strode quickly through the damp garden with Storm in tow, keeping close to the tall boxed hedge.

He had hidden her chaise soon after her arrival in the copse of trees beyond the garden. Now with little consideration for her condition, he pulled her through the underbrush to it and tossed her up onto the seat like a sack of grain. Climbing in beside her, he cast one last furtive glance toward the mansion, and then snapped the reins sharply against the mare's back.

Storm sat mutely at Geoffry's side as he maneuvered the

chaise along the drive and onto the road. She strained against the velvet bonds about her wrist as her mind worked furiously, seeking a means of escape. She knew if she could free her hands, it might be possible to take her captor by surprise and jump from the vehicle before he could stop her. Visibility was limited by the dense fog, and that would work to her advantage. If she managed to get away from him, the fog would help her to hide.

Chewing thoughtfully on her lower lip, she glanced at the man at her side as he turned the chaise off the main thoroughfare, onto the muddy side road that led to the river. Even in this, he and Miranda had planned well. It would be easy for anyone to make a wrong turn here in such weather.

At the same moment that Geoffry reined in his horse, Storm felt the cord give slightly. However, to her regret she realized it was not enough to give her the freedom she sought. Fear clogged her throat, and her heart began to pound violently against her ribs as he stepped down and turned to her.

"We're here, mistress," he said as he reached up to pull her from the carriage.

She struggled against the hands that clamped down onto her arms, but her meager efforts did little good as he lifted her from the chaise and set her on her feet. "It's no use fighting me," he murmured as he turned to look at the rolling river, one hand still firmly grasping her arm.

Expecting him to try to throw her into the muddy water at any moment, Storm dug her heels into the soggy ground but could find no leverage to withstand him. Her only hope lay in getting her hands free so that she could at least try to fight him. Suddenly an idea flickered into her mind, and she looked up at Geoffry, saying, "This will never work."

"I'm afraid you're mistaken. Miranda's plans always work. Isn't this proof of that?" He chuckled as he jerked her forward, dragging her even closer to the edge of the bank above the rapidly flowing water.

"No, you're wrong to believe in her this time, Geoffry. You'll be the one to feel the noose about your neck," Storm said, trying desperately to gain time.

He paused, cocking one blond brow questioningly as he said, "Since you seem to doubt that your death lies only a few feet away, I'll ask you why you believe otherwise."

"I don't doubt that you can kill me. But no one will believe it was an accident when they find my body with my hands tied behind my back. It seems neither you nor your sister remembered that small flaw in your plans." Storm sent a silent prayer heavenward that he would be foolish enough to rectify their mistake and give her the opportunity she sought.

A cruel smile curled Geoffry's lips as he looked down at her. "Mistress, it's a shame that I have to put an end to your life. You are one of the few women I've met that can equal my sister in her intelligence. I have looked for a woman with beauty and a mind like Miranda's, but until you came along, I had found none. It will not save you, however, but I do appreciate your warning me of the small item we overlooked. This mistake could have been serious."

Jerking her about, he tossed her cape into the chaise and untied the cord from around her wrists. Storm tensed as she felt the velvet begin to give, readying herself to take advantage of the moment while he was unprepared for her escape.

As her bonds fell away, she brought her elbow up and hit him in the stomach with all the strength she could muster. She heard him groan but did not waste the precious moment by looking back. Jerking up her skirts, she sprinted toward the thick underbrush.

"Bitch," Geoffry howled as he lunged after her. "Your death will be long and slow because of this."

Hearing his heavy breathing behind her, Storm did not

slow her pace. She had nearly gained her destination when she felt his hands close about her waist as he launched himself at her. A scream of terror tore from her throat as they tumbled to the wet ground.

Knowing her death would be at hand once he subdued her, she turned on him and fought like a wildcat, biting and clawing. He struggled to pin her to the ground but could not avoid her nails as she dug them into his face like talons, trying to reach his eyes. Blood dripped from the furrows she made to join her earlier marks.

"You little bitch," he growled as he straddled her and brought his hand back. Another scream ripped through the fog-laden air as he slapped her across the face.

Geoffry silenced her by locking his fingers about her throat to choke off her air. She fought against his death grip until shadows began to dance before her eyes. At last, knowing she no longer had the strength or air to fight, she let her hands fall away.

Dabbing at his bloody face with the back of his sleeve, he got to his feet and stood over her, breathing raggedly from the battle. "I should kill you now, but I'd rather watch you sink below the muddy water of the Ashley. I'll enjoy every moment you fight for your life."

Dragging her roughly to her feet, he pushed her forward. She staggered and nearly fell, but he kept her upright with a firm grip on her hair. Her throat was swollen from his brutal hold, but she fought to gain enough air to resist until the last. She would not go meekly to her death.

As they inched ever closer to the edge of the embankment, she strained against him. She felt the roots of her hair give way in his hand but paid no heed to the pain. Fear gave her strength, but not enough to thwart his efforts. Geoffry lifted her easily above the rushing water, then chuckled as he released her.

Storm screamed as she felt herself begin to fall and flailed the air with her arms in a desperate attempt to find

some meager hold to save her from a watery death. As the
river enclosed her, the tips of her fingers came in contact
with a low-hanging limb. The rough bark tore at her skin
as she grasped it tenaciously, clinging to it as the current
sought to drag her away from her last hold upon life.

Chapter 18

Thor jerked his mount to a halt as a terrified scream pierced the fog-shrouded air, overriding the roar of the river nearby. He listened intently, trying to discover from which direction it came. Only silence greeted him for several long, agonizing minutes as he sat straining to hear. Apprehension raised the hair at the nape of his neck and prickled along his taut body as the next scream rent the gloomy afternoon.

Giving his horse a hard kick in the side, Thor urged him in the direction of the Ashley, praying desperately that he would not be too late. Though the fog hindered his vision as he entered the small clearing, he saw the struggle between Geoffry and Storm, but he was unable to reach them before Geoffry dropped her over the embankment into the river.

A cry of rage and pain erupted from Thor as he launched himself toward the riverbank, his mind centered totally on saving Storm.

Surprised by his abrupt appearance, Geoffry was slow to

collect his wits and to realize his own danger. This unexpected discovery of his deed made it imperative for him to rid the world of Thor Wakefield much sooner than he had planned. Seeing his chance as Thor lay prone, his arm outstretched in his effort to reach Storm, Geoffry drew back his foot and aimed it at Thor's head. The direction of the blow was offset, however, as Geoffry slipped slightly in the mud, making the toe of his boot land in Thor's ribs instead.

The blow knocked the breath from Thor, and he rolled to one side, gasping for air as he came to his knees. Daggers of pain laced his chest as he rose to his feet before Geoffry had time to land another blow.

Seeing the blood lust in Thor's eyes, Geoffry felt his courage desert him. He turned to flee Thor's wrath, knowing his own life was now at stake. At the same moment, Thor launched himself at Geoffry, knocking him to the ground. They battled viciously for survival. Though smaller in size than his opponent, Geoffry fought with the strength of a much larger man. Like a rat cornered by a cat, he received his power from his fear.

The two men rolled on the muddy earth, raining bone-shattering blows upon each other, but Thor's size and strength soon decided the outcome. Geoffry sensed his defeat was at hand and struggled free of Thor to gain his feet. But he was not fleet enough to escape as Thor also rose, his fists balled and bloody. As he stalked Geoffry, a deadly gleam sparkled in his silver eyes.

Geoffry retreated. Blood dripped from his broken nose and split lip as he warily watched Thor move toward him. Trying to determine how best to evade his attacker, he began to back away, unaware of the peril that lay behind him. His pale eyes widened in shock and then terror as he felt the water-soaked earth begin to give way beneath his feet. The bank crumbled under his weight and he tumbled backward into the muddy water. A strangled cry escaped Geoffry's lips as he landed upon the jagged point of a broken limb thrust from a submerged log. It pierced him through, and the already-reddish water grew crimson with his blood as his life drained away and he floated out toward the sea.

Thor did not take the time to consider Geoffry's death but instead rushed toward the part of the riverbank that was still intact, his heart in his throat, fearing Storm had been swept away by the rapid water. Relief rushed over him as he saw her clinging to a branch, but it was short-lived. With her weight and the pull of the river, the roots of the small tree were beginning to give up their meager hold in the soft earth. Thinking of nothing beyond saving Storm, heedless of his own danger, he slipped down the embankment into the water at her side. The river sucked at him as he reached for her, trying to capture him as well in its deathly grip. As his hand came into contact with hers, the tree uprooted, leaving him to battle for them both against the swirling current. His fingers dug into the muddy bank, but he could find no hold. The river fought him, seeking to pull Storm out of his grasp, her heavy skirts aiding its efforts as they weighed her down.

Thor's lips were white with strain as he sought to maintain his hold upon her. Each second seemed an eternity as he felt her begin to slip away from him. When he thought he could hold on to her no longer, he heard Matthew's shout over the sound of the water. Looking up, he saw his friend lying on the edge of the crumbling bank, extending his hand to him.

Focusing all his remaining strength on hanging on to Storm, Thor reached for Matthew's hand and felt his friend grip it tightly with his own. Together they fought the river and won.

*   *   *

With his hands in his pockets and his shoulders slightly hunched, Matthew stood silently in the doorway to Storm's room. He felt the same anxiety he saw etched across Thor's face as his friend continued his vigil at the side of the still, pale figure on the bed. Thor had not ventured away from Storm since they had brought her back to Misty Rose. Giving a rueful shake of his head, Matthew asked, "Has she regained consciousness?"

Drawing his eyes away from Storm's ashen features, Thor looked up as his friend entered the room. He shook his head and said, "No. Mamie seems to think she collapsed from exhaustion, but I fear she may lose the babe."

A bright sheen of tears glimmered in his eyes, and he leaned forward, covering his face with his hands to hide them. "My God, Matthew, I've been sitting here for the past two hours trying to understand everything that has taken place today, but for the life of me, I don't have a clue to the reason behind Geoffry Chatham's actions."

Placing a comforting hand on Thor's shoulder, Matthew said, "I've never liked Geoffry, and neither has Lyle, but that doesn't answer your questions. Storm is the only one who can do that."

Thor pressed his lips tightly together and swallowed several times before he could voice his fears. "But what if she doesn't recover? I'll never forgive myself, Matthew. During the past months I've put her through hell."

Turning to give his friend a view of his haggard face, Thor said, "Did you know that I intended to ask Storm to marry me the day Miranda told me that Geoffry had seen the two of you together? After talking with her, I was so consumed with jealousy that I could not think straight."

Glancing back at Storm, he continued, "And look what it has done to her."

Matthew squeezed Thor's shoulder, trying to convey his understanding. "Thor, when a man's heart is involved, it makes him do many foolish things. Storm will recover. You've got to believe that."

"I'm trying my best, Matthew. If God will grant me that one wish, I'll do everything within my power to right the wrongs I have committed. I love her, and it makes me tremble to think how close I came to losing her. My only regret is that Geoffry got off so easily. It would have given me great pleasure to make him pay with my own hands for even attempting to harm her," Thor said vehemently.

"I can understand your feelings, Thor. I feel the same way about Jenny. When I learned of the years of abuse she endured with Thadius Hollings, I wished I had been the one to put the bullet through his fat gut." Matthew gave Thor a wry grin. "But that was taken out of my hands also. So we both have to look to the future. We can't do anything about the past."

Thor nodded. "You're right, and I intend to do just that once Storm recovers. I'll never let anyone else harm her."

Matthew smiled warmly down at his friend. "Good. That's all I ever wanted to hear. I've known from the beginning that you loved her, but you were too stubborn to admit it. You let people like Miranda Ashfort convince you otherwise. Now that you've come to your senses, I feel I can leave Storm in your care and get back to Hollings' Pride, where I belong. I need to reassure Jenny. By now she'll be frantic with worry."

"I guess that means you'll not be coming back to Misty Rose as my overseer," Thor said as he stood and extended his hand to Matthew. His face reflected all the love he held for the man as their hands clasped. Smiling, he continued. "I well understand. Take care of your lady, Matthew, as I will mine."

His friend nodded, and the two men embraced. "I'll do that, Thor," Matthew said before leaving him to his vigil.

Thor leaned forward in the chair, his brow furrowing as he propped his elbows on his knees and rested his bowed head against his hands. Something Matthew had said troubled his mind, but he could not pin it down.

Deep in thought, he failed to note the slight flicker of Storm's lashes as she began to emerge from the dark void into which she had fallen after Thor and Matthew had dragged her from the river. Thor was startled as she sat bolt upright in the bed and began to flail the air, mentally reliving her fall into the rushing water. Going quickly to her side, he took her in his arms, stilling her frantic movements as he murmured tenderly, "You're safe, Storm. You're safe."

She stared up at him, her eyes wide and terrified as the mists of her nightmare slowly faded from her mind. As she became aware of her surroundings, tears of relief burned her eyes and she threw her arms about him, holding him tightly and sobbing against his chest as she murmured over and over, "He tried to kill me. He tried to kill me."

Thor cradled her gently in his arms until her sobs began to abate. When there was nothing left but sniffles, he eased her slightly away from him and tipped up her chin. Wiping the moisture from her damp cheeks, his eyes spoke clearly of his feelings as he said, "I thought I had lost you, Tempest. And part of me died at the thought of never holding you again or being able to tell you how much I love you."

His voice caught in his throat as he looked down into her wide, glistening eyes. They were filled with an expression he could not read, causing his heart to tremble with fear. Swallowing back the sudden tightness, he forced himself to continue. "Storm, I know you despise me for all I have done to you, and I'll understand if you want to leave me. I only pray that someday you will find it in your heart to forgive me."

Stunned by the words she had so longed to hear, Storm was unable to move or speak. She feared she was dreaming and if she made a sound she would awaken to find she had been imagining Thor's avowal of love. She bit her lower lip as he moved away from her and rose from the bed, thinking her fears were being realized.

Instead of vanishing as in all her other dreams of him, he crossed to the dressing table and picked up the small book that lay upon it. A timid smile played over his lips as he came back to the bed and settled himself once more at her side. Laying Alisa's Bible between them, he looked at Storm as he said, "Today has made me realize how foolish I have been from the beginning. I believe I began to love you when you faced me, so brave and defiant, over this small worn volume. I admired your courage, but I tried to deny any other feelings you aroused within me. I told myself that I wanted to solve the mystery I sensed about you and used your mother's Bible to hold you until I did. But it was all a lie. I wanted you and nothing more. I was selfish and thought I could force you to love me. But this day has taught me a hard lesson. Love cannot be forced but must be earned."

A look of distress came into Thor's eyes as he cupped her chin in his hands and gazed at her as if to imprint her image on his memory to serve him when she was no longer there. Letting out a long breath as if dreading his next words but knowing they had to be said, he continued, "You are free, Tempest. I release you as my bond servant."

Storm's eyes brimmed with new tears, and a tremulous smile came to her lips as she placed one hand against his cheek and caressed it gently. Her voice was soft and filled with all the love for him that she had hidden over the past months. "I thank you for my freedom, but I'm afraid my bondage to you goes much deeper. I will never be free of the love I feel for you, Thor. If I am your Tempest, then you are my God of Thunder who makes my heart pound with passion and who has taken his great hammer and crushed the cold hard surface I had built about my heart, making me realize I can love. My love for you is more binding than any paper of indenture, because it makes me yours, body and soul."

Thor's lean, muscular body seemed to tremble with his relief as he drew her into his arms. Her sweet feminine odor aroused his passion, and his voice was husky as he said, "Storm, I love you."

"And I love you," she breathed, throwing her arms about his neck, her fingers curling in the silken strands of his hair as he drew his head down to hers. Sparks seemed to shimmer in the air about them as their lips met and clung, each savoring their small piece of paradise.

Thor felt his body respond immediately to the touch of her soft mouth, but he forced himself to gently pull her arms away from his neck. His breathing was labored from the effort it took to keep from making love to her, but he was afraid he might hurt her after such a harrowing ordeal as she had endured that afternoon. Seeing the hurt look that entered her eyes, he said hoarsely, "Storm, I love you, and I want nothing more in this world than to make love to you, but I fear I might harm you or the babe."

Storm's heart swelled with love. His unselfish act proved his love to her more than anything he had said. A mischievous twinkle entered her eyes as she moved one finger along his cheek with calm deliberation and teasingly traced the outline of his lips. Seeing the muscle in his cheek work as he fought his desire, she whispered in his ear, "I can think of no better way for you to help me recover. Being in your arms is all the medicine I need." She paused and touched his ear with the tip of her tongue enticingly before murmuring huskily, "Love me now, Thor."

Thor needed no further encouragement. He disrobed quickly and lay down beside her. Taking her into his arms, he whispered, "I love you, my Tempest," before his lips captured hers.

The heat of their passion rose, scorching away the past, the present, and the future as his mouth devoured hers. Their tongues met, tasted, and savored the sweet essence of the other before Thor's need to rediscover her body outweighed all else. His lips traveled across the smooth planes of her cheek as she arched her throat to give him access to its sensitive flesh. His hot breath and mouth against her skin made her tremble with desire as she wrapped her arms about his wide shoulders and thrust out her breasts to offer the taut peaks to his caress.

He greedily accepted. His lips closed over a rose-colored nipple, his tongue teasing the hard orb as his hand moved over its twin, his thumb grazing it, making her firm breast swell under his touch. Storm's breathing became labored as she ran her hands through his dark hair, pressing his head closer to her breast.

The junction of her thighs seemed to smolder with need for his caress and was soon rewarded as he moved his hand sensuously along her rounded abdomen and down to the shadowy valley. Her thighs opened to let him find the moist warmth of her. She gasped with pleasure as his fingers discovered the tiny, sensitive part of her that beckoned for his touch. Her hips arched upward as he stroked her soft flesh, and she trembled with the sensation it aroused in the very core of her being.

The shaft of Thor's manhood answered the quiver of passion he felt within her as he explored the dark passage of love. He felt the nectar of her body moisten his hand, and trailed his lips along her satiny flesh to the curling silk between her thighs. Craving the taste of her, he lowered his mouth to his desire, his tongue eliciting a moan from her as he touched and probed the secrets known only to him. She cried out as she moved against his mouth, yearning for the fulfillment that only he could give her. Her nails dug into his shoulders, urging, pleading for him to come to her.

When he knew that neither Storm nor he could wait any longer, his sinewy body covered hers, his mouth recapturing her lips as he moved between her eager thighs and thrust deeply within her, a moan of pleasure escaping his own lips. He savored the heat of her body united with his as he began to transport them to the heights of ecstasy.

Her legs wrapped about his waist, Storm moved with him into the fiery realm where only the Tempest and the God of Thunder existed. Ecstasy's lightning seared their heated bodies, branding and forging their hearts and souls as one. The splendor of their rapture was so intense it seemed to split the heavens asunder as their bodies exploded with passionate fulfillment.

Trembling and breathless they lay with limbs entwined, each savoring the precious moments of bliss when nothing existed beyond the love they shared. As their heartbeats slowed to normal, Thor moved to Storm's side. Propping himself up on one elbow, he rested his cheek against his hand and gazed down into her flushed, sated face. Dropping a light kiss on the tip of her nose, he said, "Had I lost you today, my life would have also ended."

Laying her head on his shoulder, Storm cuddled against him as she clung to the warm afterglow of their lovemaking. Dreamily she gazed up at him and said, "I felt the same about you when you collapsed. I knew then I could never leave you."

Thor lay back and pulled her into his arms, at peace at last. He had the woman he loved, and she carried his child. He had been a fool ever to doubt Storm, and because of it he had come close to losing her. Matthew had been right. He had let Miranda feed his jealousy and raise suspicions in him against the two people who meant the most to him. Absently he twirled a silken strand of Storm's hair about his finger as he gazed up at the ceiling and mused aloud, "I should never have listened to Miranda."

The last veils of lassitude fled Storm's mind at the mention of Miranda. She sat up abruptly, her eyes growing wide with horror, her face paling as she realized she had let her joy in Thor's love make her forget everything else. "Miranda! My God, Thor, we've got to stop her," she said, already sliding her feet to the floor.

Puzzled, Thor sat up. "Stop Miranda? Storm, what are you talking about?"

"She intends to kill Lyle." Storm searched for her gown and found it laying near the foot of the bed. Slipping it on, she fastened it as she turned back to Thor, her urgency making her fingers fumble over the tiny buttons. "She's been poisoning Lyle and was also the one to plan my murder. Geoffry was only doing Miranda's bidding."

Thor leaped from the bed, pulling on his britches and boots as she briefly explained what had transpired at AshGlen before he rescued her. Shrugging into his shirt, his chiseled features granite-hard, he turned toward the door. "You stay here. I'll take care of Miranda.'' He paused in the doorway to say something more to Storm but found her at his heels as he glanced back.

"I'm coming with you," she said.

Drawing in a resigned breath, he nodded. He knew by the determined light in her eyes and the pugnacious set of her chin that there was no use arguing with her. It would only waste the precious time they would need to reach AshGlen before it was too late.

Chapter 19

Tiny lines of worry etched an unflattering path across Miranda's brow and fanned her pale eyes as she paused before the drawing room window. During the past hours a gnawing, uneasy feeling had settled in the pit of her stomach as the night opened its arms and the foggy day slipped gently into them. Her anxious eyes swept over the gloomy landscape for some sign of her brother's return.

She gave a nervous start as a log sizzled and popped in the fireplace, sending a shower of sparks up the chimney. Turning back to the window, she looked at the face reflected in the darkened panes and for a moment did not recognize the tight pinched features as her own. Her mounting apprehension that something had gone amiss with her plans had worn away the tight control she maintained over herself, and her feelings showed clearly on her face.

Catching her lower lip between her teeth, she looked once more in the direction of the river. She knew it would take Geoffry longer to make his way back to AshGlen on foot, but there had been no other choice if their plan was to succeed. When she had decided how to rid them of

Storm Kingsley, she had tried to see every flaw to her
scheme and had feared it might arouse questions if her
brother were seen taking a ride in such dismal weather.
Everyone who knew Geoffry would know he would never
venture out except in the fairest weather. He deplored the
thought of ruining his fine hats with a few drops of moisture. She had also considered it best for all to believe he
had remained at her side all afternoon. Then she and
Geoffry would be beyond suspicion should anyone question
Storm's accidental death. She had planned every detail
well and could not understand why it was taking her
brother so long to carry out his part.

"Geoffry," Miranda said aloud as she tried to calm her
jittery nerves, "if you've decided to have a little fun with
the wench before you get rid of her and are worrying me
for nothing, I'll take a coach whip to you when you get
back."

Miranda heard the crunch of wheels on the crushed-shell
drive before she saw the shiny black carriage pull to a halt
before the mansion. As she peered at the dark figure that
alit and recognized it as Thor, her heart began to pound
furiously in her breast. The breath caught in her throat,
and the blood slowly receded from her face as she watched
him step down and turn to help the other passenger from
the vehicle.

Miranda gasped and backed away from the window, her
eyes darting about the drawing room as if to find a place to
hide. She could hear the blood drumming in her temples as
her mind cried out, Storm Kinglsey, Storm Kingsley. Somehow her plans had gone awry, and from the expression she
had glimpsed on Thor's face, he was set upon vengeance.
Her usually quick wits deserted her, and she was still
frozen by the window as Thor and Storm entered the
drawing room.

Though her knees threatened to buckle beneath her at
any moment, Miranda scraped her reserves for a boldness

she was far from feeling as she turned to face them. Her nostrils flared as she drew in a breath and raised her chin arrogantly in the air. "Thor, you startled me. Have you begun to make it a habit of entering a person's home without first having the courtesy to knock so they may invite you to enter?" she asked, seeking to brazen her way through the precarious situation until she could find a means to flee.

Undaunted by her haughty attitude, Thor cast a brief glance at Storm, nodding in the direction of the stairs as he said, "See about Lyle and Zachery. I'll stay here with Miranda."

Storm obeyed without question. When they were once more alone, Thor turned his cold gaze back to Miranda's pale face. His own features were grimly set as he said, "My etiquette is not what I've come to speak to you about, as you well know, Miranda."

Hoping the charm she had always used successfully on him would work again, she said innocently, "Thor, I don't know what you're talking about."

"Then let me refresh your memory. It seems I have been led down a road of deceit where you are concerned, Miranda," he said.

"Surely you don't believe the lies that little wretch has concocted against me?" Miranda asked as she feigned an air of disinterest and patted a few stray strands of hair back into place.

The iciness left Thor's eyes, and they began to smolder instead as an acrid smile curled the corners of his mouth. "Lies, Miranda? I have heard no lies from Storm about you."

"Then I suggest you take your little housekeeper and leave AshGlen immediately. I don't appreciate your rudeness or your insults. Furthermore, I don't want my husband disturbed. He has not been feeling well today and is sleeping," Miranda said calmly, though a tingle of fear crept up her spine at the hostility she heard in Thor's tone.

"Considering your plans for your husband, I feel it's in his best interests to see that he *is* disturbed," Thor said, and watched as Miranda's already-pale features turned a deathly white.

It took every ounce of willpower she possessed to remain calm under his insinuations. "For the life of me, Thor, I have no idea what you're talking about. Now, if you will excuse me, I will see to my husband. You can show yourself to the door." She made to walk past Thor, but his hand stayed her.

"Good God, Miranda. Are you so coldhearted that you are not even going to ask about your brother?" Thor's voice was glacial with contempt.

Beneath his hand he felt the tremor that shook her before she could manage to suppress it. He watched the muscles in her slender throat work convulsively before she shakily replied, "Geoffry has gone back to Charleston."

"I thought you would say as much. If you said anything else, it would implicate you even deeper, would it not? Looking at you now, it is hard for me to believe that you could have planned to have Geoffry murder Storm while you saw to Lyle's demise." Giving a rueful shake of his dark head, Thor continued. "Miranda, I was gullible enough to believe you were the only woman I had ever met beyond reproach. I fell for your innocent, unselfish act all along. Had Storm not come into my life, I would have probably asked you to be my wife. I would never have known that you killed your husband to get your hands on AshGlen and me."

Seeing everything she had ever dreamed for slipping from her, Miranda lied desperately. "Thor—I—Geoffry made me do it. He wanted AshGlen, and Storm recognized him as the man in London—" Thor's hand tightened painfully about her arm, cutting off her words.

"No more lies, Miranda. I know everything. You made your mistake in thinking yourself the victor before the battle had been won. You never considered the idea that your scheme would not succeed, and you had to gloat over your cleverness to Storm. You can't lay the blame on the dead, Miranda. I will not believe you, nor will the authorities in Charleston."

"Dead?" Miranda gasped as the full impact of his words assaulted her.

Thor nodded grimly as he fought to suppress the flicker of sympathy that rose in him at the grief-stricken look on her face. "Yes, Geoffry died in his attempt to carry out your plan. Had I not arrived when I did, your brother would have succeeded, and no one would have been the wiser."

Miranda swayed, covering her face with her hands and shaking her head back and forth as she wailed incoherently into them. Her weeping did not cease as Thor led her up the stairs to her chamber. "It's late; and I'll give you time to grieve. Tomorrow morning will be soon enough to contact the sheriff," he said as he closed the door and locked it to ensure that she did not escape during the night.

Storm was unaware of Thor's presence until his hand came to rest upon her shoulder. Turning her pinched face up to him, her eyes large and luminous with unshed tears, she said, "Thor, I can't wake him." Casting a brief glance in the direction of the lounge near the window, she added, "Nor can I wake Zachery."

Thor gave her shoulder a gentle, reassuring squeeze. "Miranda said he was sleeping. I don't think she would attempt to murder Lyle on the same day she ridded herself of you. That would rouse too many questions that she would be unable to answer. I feel she only drugged them so they wouldn't know what she and Geoffry were doing."

"I pray you're right," Storm said as her hand crept up to his, seeking his strength and comfort.

Casting a worried look at the still figure on the bed, she whispered, "What will it do to him when he learns about Miranda?"

Kneeling beside Storm's chair, Thor took her hand in his, interlacing their fingers as his gaze followed where hers had led. "I don't know. We can only pray that he has the strength to take such news. It would be hard on a healthy man to learn his wife planned his death, much less one in Lyle's condition. All we can do is wait and hope."

"He can't die," she murmured, her voice and eyes full of tears.

Thor stood and pulled her into his arms, cradling her tenderly against the length of him as he laid his cheek against her fine raven curls. "If it is in our power, he will not."

Feeling her tremble, he placed her at arm's length and, with his thumb and forefinger, tipped up her chin. His silver eyes reflected his concern as he gazed down into her glistening ones. "I want you to get some rest. Lyle will need you when he wakes." Seeing a flicker of defiance enter her eyes, Thor shook his head. "No; I'll not hear any arguments. You've been through too much today already. I know Lyle means as much to you as he does to me, but I cannot let you jeopardize your own safety or that of our child for the sake of friendship."

The words rose to the tip of her tongue to tell him that Lyle was much more to her than a friend, but she bit them back before they could be spoken. Now was not the time or place to tell Thor of the secret she had carried for so long.

He cupped her face in his palms as his lips touched hers softly, caressingly, conveying all his love. "Rest well, Tempest. All will work out for the best."

Storm wrapped her arms about his waist and pressed her cheek against his wide chest as she whispered, "I know it will as long as we have each other."

Storm tossed restlessly upon the bed, all the terrible events of the past months merging into one nightmare that haunted her slumber. In it she saw the mocking face of the fat-jowled judge as he loomed over her, a sneering grin on his thick lips as he slammed the gavel down on the high desk and pronounced her sentence. Then the image blurred, to become Geoffry Chatham smiling down at her before he dropped her into the roaring waters of the Ashley. She trembled with the terror the vision aroused. Sweat beaded her brow and drenched her body as the sound of the dream blended with the frantic beat of her own heart.

No longer able to endure the horror, she came abruptly awake, bolting upright in the bed. Her breathing was ragged, her breasts rising and falling rapidly as she gripped the white sheet to them and tried to dispell the vivid images from her mind, telling herself that the past was done. Geoffry was dead, and Miranda would be punished for her part in the evil scheme.

"But is it all over?" she murmured aloud to the quiet room. "Will it ever be behind us as long as there are secrets still locked away?"

Only silence greeted her, and it seemed as if the room held its breath, waiting for her to answer her own question.

"But how can I tell Lyle I'm his daughter without proof to support my claim? He has no reason to believe me, and it would only bring him more suffering to know that Alisa had been killed because of him." Storm drew up her knees and laid her head upon them as she pondered the dilemma.

"But is it right to spare him that pain, never letting him know the babe I carry is his grandchild?" she mused aloud as she tried to find the answer. However, before she could, a sharp rap sounded on the door. Pushing her unresolved problem to the back of her mind, she slid her feet to the floor and crossed the room. Swinging the portal open, she found Miranda's personal maid, Phoebe, paused with her hand upraised to knock again. The girl's ebony eyes were bright with unshed tears and her voice quavered as she said, "It's Madame Ashfort. You'd best come."

Without thought to her bare feet on the chilled floor, Storm hurried to Miranda's bedchamber. She paused at the threshold as she saw Thor standing by the bed. Looking from him to the still white form on the bed dressed in an elaborate ball gown made of gold satin, Storm knew that Miranda would never again have need of such finery.

Hearing her entrance, Thor looked up from the glass vial he held in his hand and shook his dark head. "It's too late. Miranda's dead."

"How?" was all Storm could say as she crossed to his side, her own face pale.

He glanced at the beautiful woman on the bed, holding out the small bottle to Storm. "It seems she took her own life. Damn! I shouldn't have left her alone last night. But I never dreamed she would commit suicide. I knew she was distraught about Geoffry, but I did not think she would react in such a way."

"You couldn't have known, Thor," Storm said as she placed a comforting hand on his arm. "Miranda was a troubled woman, or she could never have done the things she did. There is no one to blame."

Thor's arm came about her shoulders, drawing her close as he looked down at her. "You can say that after everything that has happened?"

Storm looked away from him to Miranda, whose face in death held a look of peace that had never been present while she lived. "Yes, Thor. I've learned that bitterness does no one any good. You have to be able to forgive before you can love. Miranda has paid for her crimes with her life, and it will only harm us if we don't put what has happened behind us. It's over, and now we have to think of the living.''

''You mean Lyle,'' Thor said as his arm tightened about her and his heart swelled with love for her.

Storm nodded, glancing up at him, her lovely face reflecting a wisdom far beyond her years. ''Yes. As I said, it's over, and there is no need to add to his pain by telling him of what Miranda had intended for him. Let him believe she took her own life because she was so over-wrought after her brother's accidental death.''

Thor brushed his lips lightly against Storm's temple before he turned her to face him and said, ''Has anyone ever told you how wise you are?''

She nodded as she recalled the day Lyle had said as much to her. However, at the present time she did not feel wise at all. Her earlier thoughts haunted her as Thor led her from Miranda's chamber.

The stark white rays of the winter sun filtered through the window, warming Storm as she sat with her feet curled beneath her and her hand resting on Alisa's Bible. It lay unopened as she laid her cheek against the side of the wingbacked chair and stared unseeingly out across the lawns of Misty Rose.

Her features were shadowed with worry as her thoughts lingered on the man that rested only a few doors away from her own chamber. At her insistence, Lyle had come to stay at Misty Rose after his wife's funeral. It had been over a month since they had stood by Miranda'a grave and watched as the minister sprinkled the dark loam over the top of her coffin, saying, ''Ashes to ashes, dust to dust,'' but Lyle had not recovered, and with each day he seemed to sink further into a state of depression. She and Thor had tried to bring him out of his morose state, but he had remained impervious to their efforts, refusing to return from the distant plane where his mind dwelled.

From day to day Storm was able to see the deterioration in his health and found to her frustration that she was helpless to stop it. Her father was dying, slowly fading away before her eyes as if willing himself to release his hold upon life. It seemed with Miranda's death he had given up his own will to live, and no matter how Storm struggled to make him well again, he would thwart her.

Unaware that Thor had entered her room, she mumbled, "Damn, I just can't stand by and let Lyle will himself to die. There must be something I can do."

"Storm, you've got to stop this. You're worrying yourself sick," Thor said as he came to her side, his hand reaching out to caress her dark hair, feeling its silken texture between his fingers. "It's not good for you or our babe."

Instinctively, Storm reached out to him for comfort. "I'm afraid we're going to lose him, Thor," she whispered.

"I know. But there isn't anything else we can do. I've seen this happen before; unless a man has some reason to live, then he will die."

As he spoke, Thor recalled another who had been like Lyle Ashfort. He, too, had lost his will to go on when he lost his wife, but it had taken Raymond Wakefield years to accomplish the task of dying after Angelina left. When he had finally come down with the inflammation in his lungs, he did not fight to live but seemed to welcome the release it would bring.

As the memories of his childhood came back to haunt him, a need grew within Thor to hold Storm to his heart, to reassure himself that he would never lose her. Unmindful of the book in her lap, he drew her from the chair and wrapped his arms about her as he said, "Storm, I love you."

Alisa's Bible fell to the floor at Storm's feet, but she paid no heed as she savored his arms about her. She, too, needed the comfort of hearing him speak of his love. It eased some of the ache that Lyle's state aroused in her heart. Wrapping her arms about Thor's waist, she laid her cheek against his chest, saying, "And I love you, Thor. My world would be complete if we could only show Lyle that he has a reason to live."

Resting his own cheek against her raven head, Thor said, "When Miranda died, it left Lyle alone. He's old and sick and feels that he now has no family to work AshGlen for. There was little love left by the end of their marriage, but at least Miranda was his family. Storm, Lyle is much more like me than I ever realized. To both of us, the land means nothing if you have no heirs to inherit it.

"Lyle knows that at his death, the Ashfort line will come to an end. He feels he has failed all the past generations of Ashforts because he was unable to continue the family. To him Miranda's suicide signaled the death of all his hopes for his future."

As Thor spoke, guilt rose in Storm's throat and threatened to choke her. She knew she was the weapon to slay the dragon that sought to take her father. But like an unloaded pistol she was useless. The evidence to prove her identity would be her ball and powder to save Lyle's life. However, it did not exist.

Feeling the tremor that shook her and wanting to bring a bit of happiness to her day, Thor dropped a light kiss on the crown of her dark head before he held her at arm's length and said, "Storm, I love you and want you to be my wife. I've hesitated to speak of it over the past weeks because of Lyle, but time is growing short. If we don't set a date soon, we'll have an extra guest at our wedding." Thor cast a wry look at Storm's protruding belly.

Joy mingled with pain as she moved away from him and stared out the window. "Thor, are you sure you want to marry me?"

Bewildered by her question, he said, "Of course I'm certain. I love you, and you are carrying my child."

Unable to look at him, Storm kept her back to him as she said, "I love you also, but sometimes love is not enough. You know nothing of my past. Can you be sure that you will not someday regret marrying a woman convicted of prostitution?"

No longer able to control his annoyance, he said, "Blast it, Storm. I don't give a damn about your past. All I know is that I want my child to have my name before he enters the world. I see no reason for us to wait any longer."

Feeling suddenly as if he were standing on quicksand, he said, "Why, Storm? Why are you asking me all these questions? You should know by now that I care nothing about your past, no matter what you think."

Drawing in a ragged breath, she turned to look at him, her eyes brimming with tears. "Thor, I love you so much, but I'm afraid."

In two short strides, he was beside her, taking her into his arms. "What is it you fear, my love?" he asked as her arms came about him and she pressed her face against his chest.

"It frightens me to think that someday your love for me will turn to dust because of the lies scribbled on some paper by a judge," she said as she looked up into his chiseled features.

Cupping her chin in his palms, Thor studied her lovely face for a few moments before he said, "They *were* lies, Tempest. I've known that from the first time you came to my bed, but I was too stubborn and foolish to admit it to myself. I feared my feelings for you, but now I've learned my lesson. I know the person you are. You have a kind and loving heart, my darling, and that is all that matters to me." Tenderly he caressed her lips with his own before moving them slowly across her cheek to the sensitive spot beneath her ear. "Tempest, I love you. Are you strong enough to deny that love?" he murmured huskily against her satiny skin.

A moan escaped Storm's lips as her head fell back to give him free access to the slender column of her throat. "No, Thor, I can't deny your love or mine."

"Then marry me, Tempest," he whispered as he nuzzled her neck.

"I'll marry you, Thor, but first I need to tell you . . ." Her words were cut off by his lips. As he finally released them and began a leisurely assault upon her susceptible senses, he murmured, "Later, my love, much later."

Storm had no strength to argue as his hands moved over her. She stood savoring his touch, her passion mounting by the moment as his fingers worked swiftly to unfasten the tiny pearl buttons at the front of her gown, exposing the ivory mounds to his heated gaze.

Thor captured her swollen breasts in the palms of his hands and slowly caressed them until their rose-colored peaks stood taut and pleading for his kisses. Slipping the soft woolen gown from her shoulders, baring her down to her round belly, he stood mesmerized by her beauty.

The afternoon sun caressed the two lovers, making Storm's fair skin glow translucent as it played over it, highlighting the tiny blue veins that her pregnancy had caused to be visible as her body prepared itself to give life to their child.

She was no longer the slender nymph he had first met, but to Thor she had never looked more beautiful than at that moment. Her loveliness filled him with awe as he slipped the remainder of her clothing from her, leaving her standing naked in the splendor of her approaching motherhood.

His knees trembled with the force of his love as he slowly laid his hand on her belly and traced its outline, reveling in the sensation. Something akin to reverence swept over him as he felt his child stir beneath his palm. Needing to touch and taste all of her, he gathered her up in his arms and carried her to the bed. Everything was forgotten as he laid her tenderly upon the down mattress and spread her tresses about her on the satin pillow.

After disrobing, his eyes never leaving her, he joined her on the bed, kneeling at her side as his hands began their exploration along her body, learning anew the places that roused her to the peak of passion. He could feel her response, the quiver in her thighs, as he caressed her and knew she felt the same burning desire that ran in a torrid current through his own sinewy frame.

Capturing her lips, he devoured the sweetness of her mouth before he began a slow descent to her shoulder, letting his tongue play an enticing game over her collarbone down to the silken mounds that seemed to swell even fuller at his touch. He taunted the rose peaks with his tongue and teeth and felt her shudder with the sensation it aroused in her.

Thor lingered there, teasing her sensitive flesh before moving into the valley between her breasts and down to her round belly. There he paused, laying his head upon it, listening to the life he had sired before letting his lips travel over the smooth, taut surface and through the meadow of silk to the honeyed glen of her womanhood.

A ripple of pleasure swept over him at Storm's moan of desire. He tantalized her thighs with his tongue until they opened to reveal the end of his quest. The heady, sweet feminine odor and the taste of her excited him until his own body felt on fire, an inferno that only she could quench.

"Love me, Thor." The words seemed torn from her throat as she arched her back to his caress.

Her cry did not go long unanswered; his hard body eagerly covered hers. He ached for immediate release but restrained his own passion to ensure that his lovemaking did no harm to her or their child. He came to her gently, stemming the violent, greedy urge that possessed him and made him tremble.

The last rays of the evening sun set the sky on fire as they came together. The day's final burst of beauty flamed across the heavens but paled in comparison to the shimmering explosion of ecstasy Thor and Storm shared as they received that rare and cherished gift given to lovers.

Fulfilled, they lay side by side with limbs entwined as both savored the moment of bliss. Thor's eyes were soft with contentment as he propped himself up on one elbow and gazed down at her love-flushed features. His voice reflected the depth of his emotion as he said, "I love you, Tempest."

Storm's lips curled up as she snuggled against his lean body and laid her cheek against the dark mat of hair on his chest, whispering, "And I love you, Thor."

Holding her to him, he slowly drifted off to sleep, satisfied that at last he had everything in the world he had ever wanted.

Storm lay quietly in his arms, listening to his even breathing and the steady beat of his heart. She loved this man, and their future would hold only happiness if it were not over-shadowed by the secret she carried.

Suddenly she came to a decision. She owed it to those she loved and who loved her in return to lay the past to rest once and for all. Easing from Thor's arms, she slipped quietly from the bed, unaware that her movements had roused him from sleep.

Finding her gown still lying on the floor near Alisa's Bible, she dressed before picking up the book. Gazing down at the only legacy her mother had been able to leave her, Storm murmured softly, "Am I doing the right thing?"

Thor's voice came from the bed where he lay watching her. "What troubles you, Tempest?" he asked as he rose and came to stand behind her, his arms drawing her back against his muscular body.

Drawing in a tremulous breath, she turned in his arms and looked up at him, her eyes filled with uncertainty. At that moment she needed his strength and love to help her follow through with her decision. "Thor, I need you to come with me to speak with Lyle."

Thor seemed to feel the tension that radiated from her as he gazed down into her pensive face. Sensing that some mystery was about to be revealed, he nodded. Her mood aroused his curiosity, but he refrained from voicing the questions that rose to his lips. He dressed in silence and then, with his arm about her, went with her to the chamber where Lyle lay, pale and dejected.

The servants had already lit the lamps, and they cast a warm glow over the still figure in the bed. He stared up at the ceiling as if unaware of their presence in the room until Storm spoke. "Lyle, how are you feeling?"

A semblance of a smile touched the older man's lips as he turned his head on the pillow to look at her. "I'm as well as can be expected."

Settling herself on the bed, she glanced up at Thor, who stood close to her side, his hand resting comfortingly on her shoulder. She held Alisa's Bible tightly, trying to gain enough courage to speak. Swallowing back the constriction in her throat, she said, "Lyle, I've come to tell you . . ." Her voice caught in her throat, silencing her words. Glancing up at Thor for reassurance and feeling the slight pressure of his hand, she moistened her dry lips and tried again. "Lyle, I have something to . . ." But before she could finish the sentence, Lyle's eyes widened and his already-pale features blanched to the color of the sheet.

"Where did you get that?" he gasped, his hand trembling as he reached toward the book in Storm's hand.

She froze at the look on his face and did not try to stop him as his fingers closed about the frayed leather binding and pulled it from her.

"It's Alisa's," he murmured as he pushed himself higher on the pillows, holding the book to his chest. Eyeing

Storm suspiciously, he asked, "How did you come by this? What devious method did you use to gain this book?"

Bewildered by the sudden hostility she saw in his eyes, Storm opened her mouth to speak, but no words would come.

Seeing her reaction and mistaking it for guilt, Lyle said, "You've had this all along, haven't you? You knew about me before we ever met. What did you plan to do with this Bible? Did you think to sell it to me at a high price once you found how much I loved Alisa?"

Seeing all her own misgivings come to light and knowing that now she could never tell him that she was his daughter and make him believe it, Storm only shook her head as her eyes brimmed with tears. She managed to say, "No. I only wanted to—" before her throat clogged with misery, halting her words.

Wanting to flee Lyle's angry accusations, she tried to rise from the bed, but Thor's hand stayed her. Looking up, she saw his face, set and angry as he glared at the man on the bed.

"That's enough, Lyle," Thor said as he felt Storm tremble beneath his hand. All the missing pieces to the puzzle had fallen into place as Lyle spoke. He had solved the mystery Thor had sensed about Storm from the very beginning. And he now understood why she had never seemed like a girl from the gutters, though her papers had indicated otherwise. The subtle refinement that had intrigued him all along had been his first clue that she was not from the streets, and the proof of her virginity on his sheets had reaffirmed it. However, until that moment he had not been able to unravel the rest of the riddle about her.

Glancing down at her pale face, he suddenly recalled Miranda's words: "Storm recognized him as the man in London." If Storm was Lyle's daughter as he suspected, Thor knew from what Miranda had said that there was much more to Storm's conviction and Geoffry's attempt to murder her than had been revealed thus far.

"Enough, you say." Lyle's face suffused with color for the first time in months. "How dare you say that to me when this girl has the Bible I gave to my first wife on our wedding day."

Lyle's fingers fumbled with the frayed binding as he began to leaf through the book. "I'd know it anywhere, because it has been in my family for years. It was given to my mother by my father." Holding up the book for Thor's inspection, Lyle continued. "See, here on the spine are her initials, A. A. And if that is not proof enough . . ." Lyle paused as he flipped to the last page. There beneath the curling yellow lining lay the edge of a piece of paper. Pulling it from its hiding place, he unfolded it and held it up as he said, "Here is our marriage license."

Storm swayed and thought she would faint. The proof she had needed had been with her all along, but now Lyle would never believe it had been her mother who had given her the book. He still thought Alisa had died with her stillborn child many years before. Dark shadows began to float before her eyes as she looked at Lyle's angry face and realized the futility of even trying to explain how she had come to have Alisa's Bible.

Thor caught Storm as she collapsed. Lifting her into his arms, his own face pale with worry, he eyed Lyle Ashfort. "My God, Lyle, don't you even realize the girl you've been accusing of stealing that blasted book is your own daughter?"

Lyle could only gape at him as he laid Storm upon the lounge and bent to rub her wrists to try to revive her.

"Storm's my daughter?" Lyle said as his gaze came to rest on the marriage license still in his hand. Scanning the fading ink, he saw at the bottom of the paper scribbled in Alisa's own untrained hand the date of Storm's birth and her name.

Lyle's features crumpled with the overwhelming emotions that swept through him. His eyes brimmed with tears, and his lips trembled as he said, "Storm is my daughter. Mine and Alisa's." Overcome, he wept into his hands until he felt Storm's arms about him. He looked up into her lovely face and said, "Can you forgive an old man his foolishness?"

She nodded and smiled timidly down at her father as she said, "Can you ever forgive me for not telling you sooner?"

Lyle returned the gesture as his hand came up to gently trace her features as if seeing them for the first time. He marveled at the resemblance he had noted but had failed to recognize until that moment. He spoke as if he were talking to himself. "I should have known without having any proof. I felt the bond between us from the beginning, and now I know why." His sapphire eyes met Storm's as he said, "You are much like your mother, though you have my coloring. You have the same loving and gentle nature as Alisa." His voice cracked, and new tears shimmered in his eyes. "Tell me about Alisa, Storm."

Thor stood at the foot of the bed and watched father and daughter as she told Lyle of Alisa. He knew she left out much and only told her father of the happy moments they had shared and the love her mother still held for Lyle until her death. She never mentioned Geoffry or Miranda or her own suffering at their hands. Her valiant attempt to protect Lyle made Thor's heart swell with pride and love. And he remembered what she had said the day Miranda died. The past was over, and they now had to think of the living.

As Storm finished her story, she looked up at Thor and saw in his eyes that he understood what she had done. He knew that later when they were alone, she would tell him all, but for now she only wanted to touch him. Holding out her hand to him, she had her wish. He came around the bed and took her small hand into his larger one, pressing a kiss into her palm before he pulled her into his arms and brushed her temple with his lips. Looking down at Lyle, he said, "Sir, would you do me the honor of giving your daughter to me in marriage?"

The first twinkle that Storm had seen in many weeks entered Lyle's eyes as he looked up and feigned a frown. "Sir, would you take her from me so soon after I have just found her? I had thought to see her beauty grace AshGlen."

Wrapping his arms about her, Thor placed his hands against Storm's swollen belly and chuckled. "That I would, sir, or your grandchild will lack one name."

Lyle regarded Thor and Storm thoughtfully for a few minutes before he said, "It seems we have a small problem here." Seeing them exchange puzzled looks, he continued, "Since you want to be married, I will have to give Storm a dowry. And seeing that my first grandchild is already on the way, that means a birth gift also."

"There is no need, Lyle. All I want is to marry Storm," Thor said quickly.

"No need?" Lyle said as if offended. "Of course there is a need. It seems that fate has granted me what I have wanted all along, and so as a wedding gift and to ensure my grandchild's birthright, I'm giving you AshGlen." Lyle chuckled and held up his hand to stay Thor's denial. "But I do have one stipulation, and that is that you let me live here to watch my grandchildren grow."

Seeing them nod in unison, Lyle chuckled again as he settled back against his pillows. "Now I will have a daughter and a son. And from the love I see glowing in both your eyes, I will have many grandchildren to keep me company in my old age."

Thor winked at Lyle over Storm's shoulder as he said, "I will not abscond from my duties as your son-in-law. If it is your wish to have many grandchildren, then it's my desire to please. I can assure you it will be no hardship on me."

Joining the banter, Storm looked archly up at Thor. "Sir, it is not my father you must please but me."

"Tempest, I am at your service at any time." Thor chuckled as he dropped a light kiss upon her mouth. "I am your humble servant, madame."

"As humble as I was as yours?" she quipped, causing him to give her a mischievous smile.

"More so, Tempest. I can promise never to put up a fight when you try to take me to your bed," he murmured against her ear.

Storm blushed and glanced at her father, to see him smiling his approval. It was hard to believe that only a short while before, he had been only a shell of a man waiting for death. Now his face glowed with life, and he looked forward to the future nearly as much as she did. Savoring the feel of Thor's arms about her, she knew the echoes from the past had now faded and all their futures would ring with love and laughter.

ABOUT THE AUTHOR

Cordia Byers was born in the small north Georgia community of Jasper and lives there still, with her husband, James, and their two children, Michelle and Michael. Cordia likes to think of her husband as being like one of the heroes in her novels. James swept her off her feet after their first meeting, and they were married three weeks later. After nineteen happy years together, Cordia is looking forward to at least another fifty.

From the age of six, Cordia's creative talents had been directed toward painting. It was not until late 1975, when the ending of a book displeased her, that she considered writing. That led to her first novel, HEATHER, which was followed by CALLISTA, NICOLE LA BELLE, and SILK AND STEEL, which has been nominated for a Reviewer's Choice Award from *Romantic Times*. Cordia is at work on her sixth book. Finding more satisfaction in the world of her romantic novels, she has given up painting and now devotes herself to writing, researching her material at the local library, and then doing the major part of her work from 11:30 P.M. to 3:00 A.M.

Cordia enjoys hearing from her readers. Her address is Route 1, Box 63E, Jasper, GA 30143.

A touch of romance... from Cordia Byers

14